Protector of the Grey House

Also by Cat Stark

Novels
The Elven Prince
The Grey House
Inside the Grey House

Collections
Enter the Maze

Protector of the Grey House
A World of Contagion Trilogy Book Three

Cat Stark

www.catstark.com

ISBN: 978-1-7333985-2-7

DEDICATION

This trilogy is dedicated to Travis Legge for allowing me to use his world as a setting for this trilogy.

This book is dedicated to all artists who have encountered issues with getting their art out to the world.

ACKNOWLEDGMENTS

This trilogy has been years in the making. This journey started out as a short story written in 2005. That short story turned into what I thought was a novel, as the formatting was not done correctly. It also woke my muse and helped me to write more than I thought possible. It wasn't until years later that I decided to publish the trilogy. It took a lot longer to get the entire trilogy out than I thought. Part procrastination, part not knowing what I was doing, part covid. I did not get covid, but the pandemic halted a lot of things in life.

I have learned a lot from this trilogy though, and I hope to take those lessons and use them for the next books I release. What those will be, I'm not certain, but I will be releasing more. I hope you continue following along with my works and enjoy them as much as I do.

Thank you to everyone who has helped in this process and who continue to help in my writing adventures. Love you all.

Cast of Characters

These are the characters that appeared in the previous two books, in case a refresher is needed. They are in alphabetical order, not in order of appearance.

Angela (Angie): Human Vincent uses for food.

Anthony: Vincent's trusted friend, who does not trust Natalia

Ben: Vampire medic who works for Vincent

Bethany: Natalia's human best friend

Charlie: Werewolf who works for Vincent, and Rebecca's husband

Christopher: Edwin's sire and Captain of San Francisco (missing)

Dean: Human who helps Slayers

Donald: Vampire who killed Natalia's mother

Doug: Werewolf who works for Vincent.

Dr Elving: Doctor/vampire who works for Vincent

Edwin: Acting Captain of San Francisco

Jeffery: Slayer Natalia kills after he gives her a lot of information on herself.

Joseph: Vincent's trusted friend, and Mierka's lover

Julia: Vampire who works for Anthony. She is his girlfriend.

Kari: Edwin's lackey

Kimberly (Kim): Vampire who works for Vincent

Lilly: Natalia's healer.

Lorraine: Vincent's Sire

Markus: Human who works for Vincent

Marnia: Natalia's mother

Mierka: Vincent's trusted friend, and Joseph's lover

Morgan: Edwin's lackey

Natalia: The female lead

Orlando: Werewolf who works for Vincent

Owen: Vampire who works for Vincent and is Kim's boyfriend.

Rebecca: Vincent's Alpha werewolf and Charlie's wife

Rowland: Vampire who works for Lorraine. Lorraine is his sire.

Theodore: Slayer Natalia kills in The Grey House.

Torin: Incubus who is in Vincent's debt.

Vincent: The male lead

Wayne: Vampire who works for Anthony and spies on Natalia.

Zechariah: Slayer who kidnapped Natalia

1

Vincent stared out the window of his study, and tried to peer into the darkness beyond the limits of his sight. Natalia was gone. She had been missing for three days now, and he was worried. His men had started to notice, as he yelled more and was short even with the delicate humans who ran his house.

Two years ago, after she killed Dean, she started hunting for confirmation of the information he gave her. In order to find any information, she came into contact with more and more Slayers. Consequently, she fought them and came home with bruises. She also came home with names, locations and sometimes, items that would otherwise be used against him and his people. He didn't want to tell her to stop. Her actions protected his house, but she found herself in more and more dangerous situations.

Natalia told him that she often had to infiltrate groups of Slayers. Before, it was one at a time. Now she often spoke with three or four at a time. She told Vincent she took care of the Slayers cautiously and avoided going against Slayers in groups all at once. Still, she started training for the inevitable. She fought his vampires two or three at a time. Vincent didn't care for these sessions but allowed it, as she needed the practice. It didn't help that Joseph and Mierka both thought she was doing a worthy job and helped to push the human to her limit and beyond. Joseph fought her often and Mierka gave her pointers on stealth tactics.

Joseph and Mierka believed she had a right to fight and train as if she were her own army. She fought Slayers and had to watch her back for Edwin's men, too. Edwin finally had his coronation, without the presence of Vincent and his men. He ignored them for the better part of a year, then had taken an interest in Vincent's businesses again. It was all part of the plan. If Edwin was interested in the human aspect of Vincent's world, he would not be interested in what Vincent's vampires were doing.

"No word from your spies?" He aimed the question at Anthony's reflection.

"No sir." Anthony told him about having her followed when she did not return after the second day. Vincent was angry, but not surprised. He took the information in stride and asked for any information. Unfortunately, Wayne had not reported for four days.

"Still don't understand why you had her followed." Mierka was aggravated, which was rare for her. It showed the men in the room how angry and worried she really was about the situation.

"Calm yourself Mierka, he was only doing his job." Vincent turned from the window, and regarded the only silent one in the room. As always, Joseph kept his opinions to himself, until he had Vincent's ear only. Since he wondered at his loyal friend's thoughts, he caught Mierka and Anthony's gazes. "Leave us. Go and train. We'll join you shortly."

The two left without a word; this was not a new situation. Joseph stepped out of the corner he almost hid in and poured himself a glass of brandy from the mini bar.

"You never ask my permission." Vincent accepted the glass Joseph handed him.

"I gave you a case of this." His voice grew soft. "Though only you know where it is."

Vincent was silent for a moment, still annoyed. "What do you think of Anthony's actions?"

"I think it's time you told him the truth of his first meeting with Natalia. It might be better if he knew why he didn't trust her."

"Do you think he would trust her if he knew?" Vincent set the untouched glass on the windowsill next to him.

"Possibly." Joseph slowly spun his glass, to allow the brandy to breathe.

"Then I will keep my secret."

"Why? After seven years with her, why have one of your top men be suspicious of her?"

"Keeps me from having to." Vincent strolled to his desk, but left his glass on the windowsill.

"Emily was human for far less time than that, and you had more reason to distrust her, yet no one followed her."

Vincent smiled at the name, and pulled his key ring out of his pocket as a vision of the lovely lady came to him. She was blond with green eyes, of average height and very shapely. Emily was as beautiful as Natalia, almost as smart, but had no desire to fight. "None of the women I've loved have been like Natalia. Natalia is smart, beautiful, and dangerous. Perhaps I want to make sure I know what I'm getting myself into."

"Even after seven years?"

"She's hunting a vampire and is still human. She will one day catch the vampire, but what happens when she does? Will she stay with us, ask to be turned, or will she leave and turn Slayer? None of us know and we won't know until her quest is finished."

"Is that why you haven't shown her your actual bedroom?"

"Among other reasons, as you know." He gave Joseph a pointed look.

Joseph raised his eyebrows. "You could remove those items."

"They would cause more trouble elsewhere."

Joseph said nothing as Vincent turned his attention back to the desk. He pulled open the drawer he had unlocked and pulled out a flat red velvet box. He looked down at the box, then presented it to Joseph.

"I suppose this won't make any sense to you or Mierka." His stoic expression was broken by a glint of trepidation in his eyes.

Joseph saw the odd look and wondered about it and the statement. Though the head vampire asked for Joseph's opinion on a regular basis, he never acted as if it mattered. Curiosity filled him as he placed his glass on the desk, took the jewelry case, and opened it slowly. Inside lay a silver necklace with a crimson stone pendant. There was a delicate silver inlay of a sword pointed down. The hilt was a fleur-de-lis and two lilies wound their way up the sword. "You mean to give her rank."

"She deserves it. She's been protecting us all for a lot of years and has given us more Slayer weapons than I thought existed. She may be doing all this to find the one she wants to kill, but it has been to our benefit."

A smile came to Joseph's face as he understood Vincent's nervousness. "And you're happy to have her in your life."

Vincent gave him a sardonic look as Joseph closed the box and handed it back. "That was not a factor in my decision, and you know it."

A twitch of a smile came to his lips. "Of course not. But if she has rank and knows how important she is to you, perhaps she'll stay after she kills Donald."

Vincent was silent as he locked the box back in his drawer. He looked to Joseph. "One can hope."

Joseph nodded. "When do you plan on presenting this to her?"

"Next time I see her."

Joseph nodded, picked up his glass, fetched Vincent's off the windowsill and presented the untouched liquor to his master. The two toasted to Natalia, and hoped for her quick return. They finished off the liquid, exited the study, and joined the others in the training room.

附 附

It was three hours later, and the training session was at an end. Joseph and Mierka spent the better part of that time battling Vincent to help him work out his frustrations. He fought Mierka last, which proved to be a mistake. She had riled him up plenty. With Natalia still missing, he considered taking the lady to his bed. He had approached Mierka to ask her when the double doors of the front entrance slammed open.

Angry steps announced her approach. Vincent waited in anticipation for Natalia to walk through the doors and into his arms. She stepped through the door, gave everyone a dirty look, then stood still, as vehemence rolled off her in waves. She was dressed in hospital scrubs and wore men's shoes on her feet. She locked eyes with someone, Vincent couldn't tell who, and snarled. With a bellow of rage, she ran at Anthony with all her speed.

Anthony was too stunned to move and simply let her hit him. He allowed her to knock him to the ground. She straddled him, balled her hands into fists and hit him, over and over. Mierka pulled her off and held her back as Vincent pulled Anthony to his feet, none the worse for wear. Natalia tried hard to pull away from Mierka, despite the vampire's strength.

Vincent turned to her after he dusted Anthony off. "Mind explaining what that was about?"

"Did you know?" Her voice shook with unbridled wrath. "DID YOU KNOW?"

Upon seeing her, Vincent had wanted nothing more than to take her in his arms. Now he understood that would have to wait. "Know what Natalia?"

"That he sent a spy after me?" She managed to calm her voice, but only a little.

"I was informed two days ago, when it became apparent you and Wayne were missing." He stood in front of her and Mierka, and indicated Mierka should let Natalia go. He reached out and held on to Natalia's arms, to restrain some of her agitation. She calmed noticeably after he spoke. "What happened to you?"

Natalia sagged against him; she believed his words. He was known to lie to his people, but she didn't see any indication of that in his eyes. She pulled away, still upset with the events of the past three days. She looked Vincent in the eye and started her tale. "I found a group of Slayers four months ago who seemed to know a great deal about the other Slayers in the Bay Area. They'd been around and for some reason or another decided to catalogue their brethren. It helped them to decide who was best for what job or some nonsense. There was a core group of four Slayers, all of whom lived in the city and shared an apartment. It took me three months of meetings for them to trust me."

Natalia pushed away from Vincent and started to pace back and forth. She stared at Anthony with loathing the whole time. "The Slayers knew who I was, or rather, what I was. They had heard of the dark-haired human who slept with the powerful vampire. Some even knew me as Jeffery Tathers' did: The One Walking the Edge. Lucky for me, these Slayers wanted to know why I was with you and why some of their own couldn't see me as Hellspawn. What kind of twisted human would sleep with a vampire who allowed his followers to torture and kill innocent children? I told them the truth.

"I told them about Edwin, and all his friends. They didn't believe me, so I went back to Theodore's on a hunch. His house hadn't been touched in years, but his trophies were still there. I took the Slayers there and showed them the wall and the pictures. In some of those pictures stood Edwin, performing atrocities on the young humans."

She paused as the words sunk in. Anthony was glad that Julia, for a change, was not present. She didn't need to be reminded of what Theodore, and possibly Edwin, had done to her young niece. His thoughts were brought back to the present as Natalia started to talk again.

"They believed me. They still didn't understand why a human hunting a vampire would sleep with a vampire. I told them I was lying to you and biding my time until Edwin could be killed. My plan was to wait until the worst of your kind was dead then kill you and yours when it was safe to. They loved the plan; wanted to help eliminate Edwin's group. I pointed them toward his lot, telling them where to find his people and their holdings.

"They passed along the information to those willing to do the dirty work and continued to talk to me. They finally allowed me to look at their information. I didn't tell them what I was really looking for. I told them one of their Slayers had information I needed to find Donald, but that I only had a description. Three days ago, I was supposed to meet with them to read the names of those they cataloged."

She paused again. Vincent went to stand behind her and placed a restraining hand on her shoulder. She looked as if she wanted to pounce on Anthony. "I went. I had no desire to hurt the Slayers; they gathered knowledge, not bodies. I arrived at their apartment and Wayne was there, tied to the wall. There were six Slayers there I had never met, along with the four that I had been talking to. The six new ones were dressed in tight comfortable clothing, like we do when we spar here. I figured them for warriors, rather than information gatherers. Apparently, Wayne didn't know not to look through Slayer's windows. The four I knew had seen him and called reinforcements. When I arrived, two of the warriors grabbed my arms. I let them, as I wanted to understand what was going on. I recognized Wayne but wasn't sure why he was there."

She ground her teeth and her hands formed into fists. "They spent the next few hours cutting his skin off in thin strips. When he wouldn't talk, they fed him my blood." Vincent's hand tightened on her shoulder. Anthony glanced away from her to watch Vincent's reaction. The lead vampire revealed no emotions, therefore Anthony once again captured

Natalia's gaze. He listened to her story, to try and find any lies.

"He healed himself and they pulled his skin off again. Halfway through, he broke. Told them I was sleeping with Vincent but that his own boss didn't trust me. He had been sent to spy on me to reveal my betrayal so that I could be exposed. At this point, they stopped interrogating him. His words helped my story, and I felt we would both be able to escape with our lives."

Natalia closed her eyes and shook her head. "I hoped we would both escape with our lives." She took another breath and glared at Anthony. "After a few minutes of silence, Wayne started to speak again. They weren't doing anything to him. They hadn't fed him again, but they were leaving him alone. He told them what I had done to try and convince Vincent of my loyalty. The Slayers weren't pleased to learn that I killed their kind. They had stopped interrogating him at that point. There was no reason for Wayne to keep talking. So why did he? Did you tell him to sell me out? Do you want to get rid of me that badly? Or is it just that your man was poorly trained?"

She moved away from Vincent to pace again. When she looked his way, he saw the pure hate in her eyes. He saw also that she told the truth. Wayne continued to speak when there was no need. He looked to Joseph for confirmation, and saw his expression mirrored on his friend's face. Vincent's hands formed into fists as Natalia continued to speak.

"When he finished talking, they opened the black curtain blocking out the sun. They let him fry in the horrid beauty that is the Morning Star. One of them threw some ash in my face and it took four Slayers to throw me in a closet. They had to knock me unconscious to do so." She stopped to calm herself down. She wanted badly to take out her frustrations, but knew she could not. She needed to finish the story so that Vincent knew everything and could judge whether or not she could beat the shit out of his trusted vampire.

"Sometime later, one of the Slayers I had been communicating with threw some water on me to wake me. She led me into the basement at gunpoint. The original four were there to question me. They wanted to know where the vampire's truth started and where my truth ended. Instead, I asked them if it mattered. I told them they could believe what they wanted to about me, as long as they took care of Edwin and his clan. One understood and sided with me, one said I wasn't to be trusted no matter what and the other two wanted to gather more information. I asked what they planned on doing with me. They told me I would be kept in the basement until they had come to an agreement. They brought me water and chained me to the wall with a manacle around my neck."

Her hand went to her neck, where the marks were still evident. Her silver necklace had been pressed into her skin hard enough to pierce the flesh in a few areas. She was grateful her necklace had not broken.

"How did you escape?" Mierka's voice was almost too quiet to hear.

Natalia turned her head to look at the lady. She sighed heavily and continued. "The one who believed me gave me back my cell phone in secret. When I was sure they had all left the house, I used my cell phone to call the police." She paused, an odd look in her eye. The youngest Slayer, Ashley, gave her back her cell and confirmed she believed Natalia. She shook her head and continued her story.

"I reset my phone to clear all the information off it. When the police showed up, there was no one in the house. I pleaded amnesia and the police took me to the hospital, where I found out I had been missing for less than two days. I was weak and needed nourishment. The police questioned me, but I told them I didn't know how I had gotten there. They asked if my cell phone had any information about me. I told them it didn't. One officer took it, looked quickly at the empty contact list, and gave it back. They left, telling me to contact them if I should remember anything."

She took a breath to calm herself. "The thing that bothers me is that after the police left, two men dressed in black suits claiming to be with the police asked to see me. I was in a private room and a nurse told me they wanted to talk to me. I saw them through the open door. They worried me, so I told the nurse that I was tired and didn't want any more visitors. After she left, I was hit with paranoia and destroyed my phone. I flushed the pieces down the toilet, then laid down for a nap.

"I woke at sunset this evening. I slept for more than 24 hours. Someone took my clothing. All I had was the gown the hospital gave me. I called the nurse, but she had no idea what happened to my stuff. She left, and said she would try and find out. As I didn't want to stick around, I left the room. I stole my clothing from a doctor I met on the stairs. My luck his clothing fit."

"Why didn't you call? We could have sent the werewolves if it was dangerous for us." Vincent's voice was tight with palpable emotion.

Natalia turned to him, gave him a look of defiance. "I didn't know if I could still trust you."

"But you came back here." He moved closer.

"I had to know the truth. I found out that he," she nodded toward Anthony, "was here and figured I could confront you both."

Vincent stood before her, and looked down into her eyes. "And what do you plan on doing now?"

"With your permission, I would like to take my frustrations out on Anthony. The Slayers trusted me and were about to let me find the information I needed. Now, all that's gone. I don't even know if I'll be able to approach a Slayer after this. He destroyed all that I've built for the past two years. I want his blood."

Vincent took her face in his hands, stepped close to her, and leaned in. He whispered into her ear to make sure that only she heard. "You would destroy a man for doing what we created him to do?"

Natalia's eyes grew wide. She pulled back from her lover, balled her hands into fists and pounded him on the chest. "NO!"

The word reverberated in the high ceiling room. Several of Vincent's men stepped away from the pair. Vincent grabbed her to him, and let her bellow into his shoulder and neck. She calmed, but only because she had no other choice. He was right. Had either of them decided to tell Anthony the truth about their first meeting, he might not mistrust her so completely. It was their fault he sent someone after her. She sagged into her lover, and felt the solid weight of him. To contain her anger at herself, she bit down on his neck, not aware she did it.

Vincent felt the bite and his body reacted. He crushed her to him, and curled his fingers into her back. His eyes closed, and hid the passion that swan there. To control himself, Vincent pulled away from her gently. The situation with Anthony had not reached its conclusion. He spoke softly to Natalia. "Go upstairs, shower, change, relax and forget the past three days."

"I'm angry and riled up. I want release." The fires of her furious passion burned beneath the surface of her calm exterior. Heat radiated from her skin and the scent of her blood invaded Vincent's nostrils. He ground his teeth, closed his eyes, and dipped his head down to her neck. He growled softly near her jugular. His hunger grew as she whimpered and dug her fingernails into his arms.

"Go upstairs. I'll be up shortly, and you can release your anger on me." He still spoke quietly, and tried to control his own cravings.

She backed away from him. She wanted the seduction to continue, but knew it could not. She wanted Vincent to follow her upstairs, but there was unfinished business. If it were anyone other than Anthony, she would demand Vincent follow her. She stood still for a moment and gave him a look that swam with passion, anger, frustration, and determination. His jaw twitched, but he turned away from her. She turned as well, her head high as she walked out the door.

The head vampire turned to the room at large, and breathed slowly to stop himself from running after his lover. He had wanted to give Natalia her rank as soon as he saw her again, but knew the ceremony had to be postponed. He sighed heavily and decided. "You are dismissed. You have duties to attend to. Go to it."

Vincent turned to Anthony, who stood and waited for a closure to the Natalia situation.

2

V incent started to pace, as he waited for his people to clear the room. Once he was alone with Anthony, he stopped and stood in front of his Information Gatherer. "I can't punish you for having Natalia followed. It's your job to spy or send spies after those you don't trust." He gave Anthony a hard stare. "You didn't tell me until two of our people were missing. That is the issue."

"Had I told you, you would have told her." There was venom in the last word.

"Yes, I would have, and perhaps Wayne wouldn't be dead. From now on, tell me if you're having Natalia followed." Vincent started to pace again, as thoughts ran through his head. Anthony knew better than to interrupt. "I'm impressed that someone was finally able to track her. Where was he trained?"

"He was Special Ops in the armed forces before he was changed."

Vincent shook his head. "It took a vampire with human training to track my human. Interesting. Any more like him?"

"Wayne had pointed me toward a friend of his."

"Take care of it if you see fit." He waved the subject away. Vincent asked his people to check with him before they changed a human. He did the same when he wanted to change someone. He knew Wayne, and knew the vampire had been trustworthy, despite his last act. If Wayne thought someone a worthy candidate, and Anthony concurred, all was well.

Anthony spoke up, as he felt dismissed. "Sir, if I may, why should I tell you if I have someone tracking Natalia?"

"Because she'll stop the spy from following her without killing them. If she had known Wayne was there, she may have been able to throw him off her scent and save his life. She isn't stupid, and her goal isn't to kill those under my protection. You know what she has done for us; you've seen the Slayer items she's brought us. Why do you continue to think she's trying to betray us?"

Agitated, Anthony started to pace and gesture grandly. Vincent stood still to watch Anthony's actions. "Because she stays human and hunts a vampire. What happens when she kills him? What will she do to us?"

"I'm hoping she'll stay and ask to be changed. I have every reason to believe she will. She has told me of her desire to be changed, eventually. And soon, I may give her one more reason to consider it."

Anthony stilled his movements. His voice showed his anticipated terror. "How?"

"Calm yourself Anthony. It doesn't concern you directly."

"With all due respect sir, will you allow her the blood she demands?" Anthony wondered how far Vincent would go to keep the human here. She had demanded his blood earlier.

Vincent went to Anthony and placed his hands on the man's tight shoulders. "You fret too much over her, Anthony. As I said earlier, you were doing your job. I'm upset about the way things turned out, but you did nothing against your nature or position. Natalia can't take your blood. I don't enjoy taking blood from my people when all they've done is the job I've assigned them to do. As for not telling me, I believe Wayne's death is punishment enough. Calm yourself, have a drink. We're done."

Vincent stepped back from Anthony and crossed his arms. This time he truly was done with the subject. As Anthony still doubted somewhat that his neck wasn't on the chopping block, he stood still for a few seconds. When Vincent raised an eyebrow, Anthony nodded and left. He exited through the front door, where his limo and driver waited. Though Vincent had offered him a drink, Anthony felt it best to leave without one, to prove a point. He didn't feel the situation was resolved.

Vincent watched him leave from the ballroom door, and knew he needed to discuss the situation with Natalia. She had to release the man and they had to tell him the truth. It was too dangerous to keep Anthony in such a state. He caught movement to his left and turned to regard Joseph.

"No words. I know what must be done with him."

"And with Natalia?"

"Tomorrow. Tonight would be inappropriate."

"He would agree with you."

"Is there anything else that needs my attention?" He turned fully to face Joseph.

"No, sir."

"Call those in my service here tomorrow. I wish them to bear witness to the ceremony."

Joseph stepped away from the wall. "Of course."

Vincent stepped away from his side of the wall and started toward the stairs. Only Natalia needed his attention now. His speed increased as he walked to and up the stairs. He heard Joseph snicker but ignored his friend, as he wondered what stage of undress he would find Natalia. He crossed his sitting room in less than a second, noticed her absence in the bedroom and went into the bathroom. She stood by the mirror, drying her hair. She was in her silk robe, which was untied and open. Every part of his body wanted to grab her and possess her quickly. Except there was something they needed to take care of. He went to her slowly, pressed himself against her, and pulled the hair dryer out of her hand. He turned it off as he placed it on the counter.

Natalia leaned into him, and let her thoughts drift from her mind. His hands wandered up and down her torso, and massaged her skin through the silk.

"We have something to discuss." He whispered into her ear, but his voice held a business tone.

"We need to release Anthony." She tried to calm her speech, tried to match his tone, but it had been a long three days and all she wanted was relief.

"Correction. You need to release him, and I need to calm him down." His hands slipped under her silk robe to caress her soft skin unhindered. His eyes closed as his need intensified.

Natalia closed her eyes as memories unfolded and flooded her with grief. When she was fourteen, she used her necklace to hypnotize her mother's abusive boyfriend into leaving them alone. Natalia slept with the man to weaken his defenses. When Marnia learned of this, she hid the memories from Natalia as she didn't want her daughter to suffer. When Marnia died, Natalia regained those memories. It threw her mind into chaos until she understood what was done.

Natalia pulled away and turned to face Vincent. She leaned against the counter and crossed her arms. Her voice had achieved the seriousness she desired a moment before and now despised.

"If I were to release Anthony..." She shook her head. "From my own experience I've learned that simply releasing someone is dangerous for their mind. Simply releasing him would only aggravate his suspicion for me. He would remember all that I asked him."

"You never did tell me what you asked." He caressed her cheek with the back of his hand. He wished the act would wipe away the pain in her eyes.

She sighed and pushed away the unpleasant memories, then gave him an impish smile. Natalia uncrossed her arms and placed her hands on the counter. Her movement caused her robe to slip open. "I asked about the club, at first. Then I asked about you. My main concern was what kind of woman you were attracted to."

"What did he tell you?" Vincent let business go for a moment, and closed the slight distance between them.

"That your women were usually strong in some way. Most could stand up for themselves with either words or weapons. It didn't sound like any of them were as stubborn as I am."

Vincent placed his hands on her waist, lifted her slightly and sat her on the counter. It was marble and well built. They had used it before. He nuzzled her neck, and wondered if he could take her blood, or if she had lost too much to Wayne. "None of the women I've loved have ever been as stubborn as you. Or as incredibly frustrating."

Natalia's thoughts stopped as his words seeped into her mind. It was the closest he had come to saying he loved her. She had never expected to hear it. Since her declaration two years ago, she hadn't repeated her words. It wasn't necessary. She closed her eyes. "Have any of the women you've loved been like me?"

"You remind me of Lorraine, and Mierka. You are more dominating than Mierka, and far more adventurous than Lorraine. And you never back down." He listened to her heart, to try and to hear her heartbeats, as he wanted to assess her blood loss. Her heartbeats were quick though, as always when he touched her. Aggravated, he bared his fangs, and pressed the points into her flesh. He dented but did not break her skin. She would let him know if he couldn't feed off her.

Natalia placed her hands on his chest, and pushed him away lightly. They had to finish their business. "What do we do with Anthony?"

He pulled away from her neck, but left his fangs visible. "Options?"

Natalia, breathless with longing, wrapped her legs around his waist and squeezed him close. Her hands dove into his soft blond hair, and gripped tightly. "Let me speak with him. I think I can release him without hurting him."

"You mean to hypnotize him again?"

"Only to ask him some questions and allow him his mind." Her hands slid out his hair, down his neck, chest, and hard stomach to the waistband of his pants. She pulled out his shirt and pulled it over his head. "Are we done with business?" Her voice indicated she wanted to be.

A thought tried to assert itself into his mind, but thoughts became impossible as she kissed and nibbled his chest. "Yes." His hands found her silky hair. "If you think we can do this, yes, we're done." He growled, and showed her his fangs. "Have you been fed off lately?"

She smiled, as they both knew the answer. Natalia gave him an innocent smile. She knew he wouldn't take her blood until she told him he could. A feeling of power overcame her, and she wondered just how far she could push him.

Vincent saw her expression change from one of innocence to one of dominance and understood her mood. He knew he could easily take control from her, but instead he relinquished control, and let her lead him however she pleased. She led him to the bedroom, and teased him all the way to the bed. He begged for many hours before she allowed him to drink from her.

3

Natalia woke in stages, and realized slowly that Vincent was not in bed. She sighed as she rolled to the edge of the bed. The curtains and windows were open, which revealed the night sky and city to the south. She felt the cool breeze on her warm skin and sighed again as she sat up then stood. Images of last night kept wafting through her mind. Vincent only allowed his hunger to show in his voice; every other part of his body had shown a tenderness they rarely used with one another. When he fed, he took more than usual. Then, he took over and made her feel as if nothing else in the world mattered but her pleasure.

She sighed again as she took her robe and went to shower. There was business she had to attend to. After she showered, she dressed in a long flowing red dress and ate the simple breakfast someone brought up for her. She then went downstairs to find Vincent. From the loud voices, she judged that Vincent and Anthony were in the study. She knocked on the door quietly, and waited for permission before entering.

Anthony stood fuming. Vincent sat behind his desk, a slight smile on his face. She didn't know what they argued about, but she guessed it was her. She smiled, closed the door, and walked to the desk under Anthony's hard scrutiny.

"Gentlemen."

"Natalia. Good of you to join us. We were just speaking of you." Vincent's voice betrayed his thoughts. He thought about last night as well.

Anthony barely nodded and turned back to Vincent. "I thought the situation was done."

"I asked her to come to me when she woke, as I desire her close." His voice challenged Anthony. The man did not take the bait.

Vincent motioned Natalia over, as he knew Anthony had to be in her line of sight. Natalia went to stand behind Vincent. She leaned against the wall and started to twirl her necklace. Anthony continued to argue with Vincent for a few moments longer, but Natalia didn't hear their words. She found as time passed, that Anthony's will had grown stronger. She concentrated on catching and trapping his will. Natalia broke into the conversation with a soothing voice when she felt she could. Her voice soft and agreeable, she slowly wove her will into his until, finally, she felt his will give way. He stood immobile, his face slack, his eyes glazed over. Natalia instructed him to sit, and he did.

Natalia turned to Vincent, the strain evident on her face. "We should do this quickly. I may not be able to hold him much longer."

"His will is comparable to yours now?"

"He doesn't trust me, so it makes it harder." She walked from behind the desk and went to sit beside Anthony. "Anthony? Nod if you can hear me." He nodded slowly. She could feel his will fight hers. "Do you remember when we first met?"

"At The Red Thread…beautiful…lily."

"Do you remember what I asked you?"

"…yes…"

She sighed, wrestled with his will, and captured it again. "Is that why you don't trust me?"

"…can't trust Slayer…"

"I'm not a Slayer. You know that. I've been with Vincent for seven years. I would never kill any of his men. Why do you think I'm a Slayer?"

"Hunting a vampire." His voice sounded too confident. Natalia knew she should keep this short, but she needed to know how deep his suspicion ran.

"Even though I fight to protect Vincent's men, I'm a Slayer?"

"…yes…"

Vincent tapped her on her shoulder. She stood and took him away from Anthony. "Can you change his mind?"

"I'm loath to. It may damage his psyche if I try to make him trust me. But I think I have an idea." Her face was awash with strain. Vincent started to worry.

"Do it quickly." He went back to his desk, sat down, and waited for the end.

Natalia went back to Anthony's side, and devised a plan. She felt she knew how to help him change his mind. "Anthony. You must do as you think best with Natalia. If you feel that she can't be trusted, then you must act on it. But you must also be willing to change your opinion of her. She may not be as bad as you think. You must make your own decision regarding Natalia but listen to those around you and the things they say about her. She may not be as untrustworthy as you think." Natalia paused, took a deep breath. "When you awake you will be able to give yourself permission to change your opinion regarding Vincent's human. It will take a while for the thought to formulate, but it will come. When it does, you should allow it grow."

Natalia rose and went to stand behind Vincent again. She stood in roughly the same spot, her hand at her necklace, and twirled it. She took another deep breath to compose herself, asked Anthony to stand and said the word that would wake him. His will snapped back into control and she sagged, grateful the wall behind her was as solid as it was. She pushed herself against it, and tried hard not to look as tired and overwrought as she felt.

Anthony continued his previous rant then stopped, as he felt as if he had missed something. Vincent still had his sardonic smile, but Natalia looked beaten. He stared at her for a moment, and wondered if he had ever seen that look on her face. He didn't think it had to do with his conversation with Vincent.

"What happened?" His voice reflected his distraught will.

"Why do you think something happened?" Vincent took over. Anthony indicated Natalia with his head. Vincent turned and saw the expression of defeat on her lovely features. He turned back to Anthony and thought to get the man out. "Ease your mind, Anthony. What she is thinking probably has nothing to do with either of us. Now, have you finished yelling at me about my woman?"

Anthony looked at Vincent, and felt as if the situation were not truly done. He stared at Vincent for a moment and realized anything else he had to say would fall on deaf ears. Therefore, he nodded, turned, and left the room to stew in his own frustrations.

As the door slammed shut, Vincent turned and caught Natalia as she collapsed. He took her carefully in his arms, sat her on his lap, and cradled her close. "You won't be doing that again."

She nuzzled close to him, and slipped her arms around his neck. "I don't think I could if I wanted to. His will is too strong."

"This is done, then?" He massaged the back of her neck.

"It has to be." She sighed with pleasure as she melted against him. She had a raging headache, and her stomach was upset. She felt as if her brain had been fried. It was hard to keep control of Anthony; even harder to look as if everything were fine. She had failed, as he saw her pain, but it didn't matter. The situation was taken care of. Other than releasing him completely, she could do nothing more to change his mind. He would have to decide whether or not he wanted to trust her on his own. She moaned as Vincent applied more pressure to her aching shoulders.

Vincent nibbled on her neck. He wanted to take her blood, but knew he shouldn't. She felt good in his arms, felt like she belonged. He turned her head to his, kissed her, and gave her a long, deep kiss. One hand massaged her neck, the other massaged her thigh. Though they were expected in the training room, he nevertheless continued his slow seduction, and wondered if she were up for a quickie. Except they almost never did anything quickly. Even if they started quick, want would take over and they would continue long past satisfaction. He pulled away from her, and growled low.

"Are you well?" The question was still a growl.

"My head aches, as do my shoulders and stomach." Her breath sounded ragged due to her pain and her desire. She wanted to sleep, to get rid of her pain, but she also wanted to screw her lover. She got off him, stood then stretched her neck and upper body to relieve the tension. It worked well enough, but Vincent's touch worked better. "If there's nothing else you need from me, I'm going back to bed."

He caught her hand as he stood. "You're needed in the training room. Rebecca is back and wishes to speak with you. Also, Kim expects a rematch."

Natalia nodded. "I'll go, but don't expect me to do any fighting, especially in this dress. You took a lot out of me last night and I'm having trouble focusing my thoughts."

Vincent shrugged to indicate it was her choice. She leaned into him and gave him a lingering kiss. She pulled away and left the room, as she continued to stretch her muscles. Vincent took a deep breath, let it out slowly, and tried to control his utter need for her body and blood. He bared his teeth and fangs in an imitation of a bite. His control had started to slip recently. Almost every time he touched his human, he had to fight to gain control of his more primal urges. He often felt like digging his teeth deep into her neck to suck all the blood out of her prime, supple, willing body.

Last night's encounter had left him wanting. She controlled him well and reminded him of Lorraine's abilities. When she relinquished control, he had to remind himself that he could not do to her what he could do to his sire. Natalia was much too fragile to take the brunt of the more animal aspects of his nature. He held back, contained his primeval appetites, and reassured himself with the knowledge that he could have her whenever he needed her. Last night, it was enough. Tonight, it barely pacified his hunger, and skimmed just the barest need off a mountain of want. He would have to do something about this soon, or risk killing and changing Natalia against her will. An image of her bathed in her own blood flowed into his consciousness and overtook his mind.

He could see her on his bed in the tower room, olive skin marked with streaks of glorious crimson. She appeared dead, but he knew better. In his vision, she turned to look at him and opened her mouth. Though she lay on her back, the blood in her mouth poured out as if she were on the ceiling. It surrounded him, soaked him, and aroused him beyond his original state.

Vincent grunted in pain as the vision continued to wrap its hideous claws into his psyche, dug its nails of delusion deep within his mind until he couldn't distinguish between reality and fantasy.

The large vampire clutched the edge of his wooden desk in an attempt to funnel his appetite away from himself, as he knew he couldn't release it on his woman. She wouldn't be able to take it. As he felt the wood dent, he knew he had to leave for a day or two. He had to be with a woman who could take him on and feed his aggressive tendencies. After this evening's affairs he would visit Lorraine. It would be easier to sleep with Mierka, but that was dangerous. The idea of releasing his hunger on one woman when Natalia would be accessible down the hall terrified him. Should he take another with the knowledge that his true lover was within reach, he would go to the human and conceivably harm her.

Vincent took deep breaths and finally calmed himself. Once calm, he took out his keys, unlocked the top drawer and removed the jewelry case which held Natalia's necklace. He opened the case and caressed the stone. She was the first human to receive such a privilege. He hoped she would understand the significance. Vincent closed the box with a snap and left the room. He headed for the training room, where the others waited.

At the doors to the training room, Vincent regarded the creatures present. Most of the assembled were vampires loyal to him. There were more in the area than Edwin knew of. He had brought in vampires from all over the world that wanted to see the monster dead and out of power. There were about twenty vampires present, all of whom knew about the strange attraction between Vincent and the human. Vincent sought out his human, not surprised to see her with the werewolves. She stood at the back of the room against the wall and spoke with Rebecca. Both women looked happy to see each other. Charlie, to the other side of Rebecca, looked even happier. He had his arm around his wife and grinned from ear to ear. Vincent stepped into the room, and went right to Joseph, who stood near Anthony. Vincent whispered to Joseph, then pulled away, and went to the front wall to wait.

Natalia watched her lover come into the room and wondered at the look on his face. It was a surprise to see all the people present. Natalia went straight to Rebecca, as she knew she could ignore the rest of the room if she spoke with her friend. As Vincent caught her eye, she felt the peace that had crept over her while she talked to Rebecca try and slip away. She held onto it. If the feeling left, her stress and headache would return. She took a deep breath and continued her conversation with Rebecca. The Alpha wolf was explaining how the dynamics of her family worked. Due to the pact they made with Vincent, it was easier for Rebecca's parents to raise the twins. Rebecca's grandfather raised her and her brother. They continued the conversation as Natalia tried to ignore the look on her man's face.

Vincent stood silently and allowed the tension in the room grow. He watched patiently while Anthony nodded to Joseph then went to join Julia, who stood with the other vampires. Vincent stepped forward, crossed his arms behind his back and waited for silence. It didn't take long. The room was thick with anticipation. All under his protection were present. The only creature that didn't know something was amiss was Natalia.

Vincent turned his attention to her and caught her eye. "Natalia, front and center."

Natalia gave him a quizzical expression. Even with her headache a memory, she didn't want to fight, and had already informed him of such. She crossed her arms and shook her head. "I'm not fighting today, Vincent."

He stared her down with a stern look, as if disciplining a disobedient servant. "Natalia, do as I ask."

Rebecca nudged her into movement, and hid a smile when Natalia turned to give her the same look of wonder. Unsure of what was going on, Natalia started forward.

Vincent watched her approach, and loved the look of confusion on her strong features. It was a rare expression to see on her face. He relished the fact that he had caused it. When she stood before him, their sides to the crowd, he placed his empty hand on her shoulder, and pushed her down slightly. "Kneel, Natalia."

Behind him, he heard Anthony's negative utterance as it finally sunk in what his leader was about to do. He heard Julia ask what was wrong, but she was ignored. Natalia, even more confused, knelt in front of her lover, and waited in nervous expectation. She had never seen, read, or heard about what was happening. Once on one knee she raised her eyes to her lover, her features clear of worry. Whatever was to happen, she would accept and meet the situation with no doubt in her mind.

Vincent fell into the look, as pride and lust swelled in his head. He stepped back from her, as her mouth was currently level with his waist. It was too suggestive a position. It was one of the reasons he had his people kneel when he gave them rank. It was meant to be a subservient position. It had never been so arousing. He took two deep breaths before speaking, and tried to keep his voice calm and level.

"Natalia, you have been in my house for seven years. To this day, you have requested to stay human to continue the hunt for the monster that killed your mother. During this time, you have done nothing but better your fighting skills to be able to face him when the time presents itself. You have also used your skills to reduce the Slayer problem in the area and on more than one occasion, protected those that call me leader. You have brought us several Slayer artifacts and books, freeing us from their danger, and you have declared yourself our protector. It is with these reasons that tonight I,

Vincent LeGris grant you, Natalia Mirela Liliana Dveski the rank of Protector of House LeGris."

Vincent stood behind her now, therefore she couldn't see him; couldn't see the expression on his face. She didn't believe his words, wanted to be able to confirm what he said with the look in his eyes. She was human, he only granted rank to vampires and one werewolf. A silver pendent appeared in her line of sight, and she knew it wasn't a joke. She couldn't see the front but knew the size. It was identical to the pendants that Joseph, Mierka, Rebecca, Anthony and several others wore. She felt the weight of the pendant against her hair and neck, closed her eyes as her lover and now master, slipped his hands under her hair and allowed the necklace chain to rest against her skin. It slipped below her hypnosis necklace, and fitted nicely against it.

He walked back around her and told her to rise. She obeyed as her thoughts swam with disbelief. Her hand reached up and covered the stone; it didn't belong there. "I can't."

Vincent cocked his head, and wondered at her two little words. "Natalia?"

She looked into his clear blue eyes, and saw his unspoken words. She was quite adept at reading her lover. "I can't accept this, Vincent. I don't deserve this. I'm not like you. I'm not a vampire. This shouldn't be mine."

Undeterred, Vincent stepped forward and caressed her cheek softly. "Are any of the words I uttered a lie?"

She shook her head, and tried to quell the feelings. "No, but-"

"Do not deny what I do Natalia. You deserve it. Take everything I offer you."

There was so much more in his words than just the rank he offered. She could hear it in his voice and see it in his eyes. She fell to her knees again, and bowed her head low enough for her hair to brush the ground. "My blood and life are yours, vampire. Do with me as you see fit."

There was a murmur as the others in the room processed her words. For a vampire to pledge life and blood was one thing. For a human, it meant death. She spoke a pledge of loyalty, one that could only be broken by Vincent. The large vampire stared down at the head of the beautiful creature that knelt before him. A great part of him wanted to take her words to its fullest extent, wanted to change her then and there. She had pledged her blood and life and he saw fit to change it. He took a step toward her, his intent clear on his face, for those who knew how to read it. He noticed Joseph and Mierka change posture as he reached out, touched the top of Natalia's head, and caressed her soft hair.

"Rise, Natalia." She did as he obeyed. He suppressed his idea to change her, as he knew it wasn't the right time. He stepped forward again, placed his hands on her shoulders and kissed each cheek. As he did so, he whispered softly in her ears. "This ceremony calls for me to drink your blood and for you to drink mine. If you wish, we can skip the second part."

He faced her again, and fought the beast that raged against his control. She looked at him calmly as he expressed his desire.

Natalia had no problem with him drinking her blood. He usually drank at least a swallow each time they had sex. She was unsure about drinking his blood. She had never done it before, mostly because she knew she had to drink his blood to be changed into a vampire. Intellectually she knew he had to drain her first and then give her his blood to change her, but knowledge did not stop emotion. To consider his proposition, she pushed aside her fright. She had never backed down from any challenge. She didn't want to start when he was giving her rank.

"Don't skip anything on my account, sir." She spoke as quietly as he had.

Vincent smiled. "Turn around."

Natalia turned, sighed as his arms encircled her. She laid her head against his shoulder, and pulled her dress away from her shoulder. She tensed as he growled softly into her neck and then traced her vein to her shoulder. She dug her fingers into his thigh as she became aroused. She moaned when his teeth sank into her flesh, and succumbed to his lustful sucking. He took three swallows, pulled away, and placed his handkerchief to her shoulder to stop the flow of blood. She reached up to hold the kerchief in place as he brought his arms in front of her. He tried hard not to contemplate the taste in his mouth as he used his nail to cut into his wrist and instructed her.

"Take three swallows."

Crimson spilled from his open wound. Natalia's hands went to his arm; one near the elbow and the other gripped his fingers. She brought the bleeding wrist to her mouth, and breathed deep to calm her doubt. She closed her eyes as her lips closed around the wound. Vincent's sigh of pleasure whispered past her ear. She sucked at his wound carefully, as she did not want to have a mouth full of blood.

His salty, coppery blood spilled over her tongue and down her throat. It wasn't pleasant, but it wasn't awful either. She took her three swallows, pulled back, and tired not to react badly. She was able to contain her distaste long enough for him to turn her around; by then the taste was mostly gone. There was a small tremor in his face; his jaw seemed clenched. Natalia wondered at his barely suppressed emotions. Then, her head swam, and her vision blurred, and she waited for him to tell her what to do next.

She had a drop of his blood at the corner of her mouth. His gaze returned to it over and over, a lure in the darkness of his overwrought mind. He started to breathe to try and calm himself but stopped when his nostrils picked up the scent of fresh blood. His hands shook as his control slipped, and Vincent brought his woman closer. She could feel the tension in his strong hands as he pressed her closer and gave her a crushing kiss. He could taste his blood on her lips, gums, teeth, and tongue. The flavor mixed with the one in his mouth and his control snapped.

Vincent pulled away from the kiss, his eyes unseeing. He bared his fangs, drew his head back, and grabbed her by her hair to pull her head to one side. He howled as his head came forward to plunge his fangs into her tender neck. He was halfway to her neck, and incapable of stopping when he was slammed against the nearby wall. The howl of want turned to a howl of anger as his prize was denied. Vincent, uncontrollable in his lust, fought against the restraint that held him to the wall.

Mierka and Joseph recognized the look on their leader's face and knew they had to act. Should he kill her now, she would never forgive him. He would never forgive himself, though he would tell himself he did. Natalia had given Vincent leave to do with her life and blood as he wished. Mierka and Joseph knew she did not mean she wanted to be a vampire. When Vincent lost control, both rushed forward to stop the inevitable carnage. Joseph pressed Vincent against the wall with one hand, and Mierka stood in front of Natalia to protect her.

Anthony watched the scene in front of him with trepidation. He understood what it meant that Mierka and Joseph protected the human from their master. Anthony started to shake. Should he step out of line too much regarding Natalia, he would have Vincent's most powerful allies against him. His discomfort eased though, as he realized the inverse was true as well. If she were to betray Vincent or any one of his top people, her pain would be infinite. She had integrated herself well into this household. Should she step out of line, her punishment would be glorious. Anthony settled into his skin and his place and waited to see if he were needed.

Rebecca assessed the situation quickly, and knew she had to get her pack out. She could hear them murmuring behind her. It was close to the full moon, and they were unsure of how to proceed. Should they attack the vampire holding Vincent back, or let them have their business? What the others seemed to miss was that if Vincent were released, Natalia would be killed. Her mind made up, she barked her order.

"Dismissed." She threw the order over her shoulder. When her pack didn't move, she turned around, stared down her people, growled and repeated her simple order. "Dismissed!"

Orlando and Doug left the room. As Natalia's guardian, Charlie stayed. Rebecca nodded at his decision then turned to the vampires. She wanted to get as many people out as she could. Most did not need to see this spectacle. Mierka and Joseph were unavailable to give orders, therefore she looked to the only other authority figure in the room. She caught Anthony's eye, indicated the rest of the room, and looked toward the door. She didn't want to be vocal about it, as it was not her place. She silently thanked him when he understood quickly and ordered the others out. There was no hesitation with the vampires. They knew what could happen if they didn't listen to orders. Most respected Anthony and followed his orders as if Vincent gave them.

Once the room was clear, Anthony joined Rebecca. "I'll take over the security room. No one sees any of this."

Rebecca nodded as he left, glad to have the man on her side. His only flaw was his distrust of Natalia. She pushed thoughts of Anthony aside and joined Charlie, who stood behind and to the left of Natalia.

"Remember to check with me if you don't know what to do."

"Yes, ma'am."

Rebecca smiled tersely to her husband, ready for whatever was to come. There might be bloodshed, but she hoped there would be no death.

4

Mierka and Joseph stood between the snarling Vincent and the entranced Natalia. Mierka did not like the look on either of their faces. She understood Vincent's expression; had seen it many times before and knew how to cure it. Natalia's expression worried her. The longing on the human's face was evident, but out of place. Mierka didn't know why, but Natalia wanted to take Vincent on. If Vincent had his way with her tonight, she would be changed or killed outright.

"Let her go."

Mierka was amazed Vincent was still capable of speech.

"If we let her go, you'll kill her." Mierka turned to Vincent; she expected a fight. Joseph held him back, so it would be a fight of words, not fists. She was ready.

"Why would I do that?" His words revealed the depth of his hunger. Mierka shuddered with anticipation. She was the only woman in the household who could take him in this state.

"You're not in control of yourself Vincent. Let me take you to bed. You'll be better tomorrow evening." Her voice was soft and soothing. Vincent shot her a look of disgust, and turned the full power of his gaze on the lovely Natalia. She tried to step toward him but was hindered by Mierka and the two wolves behind her. All present seemed to understand what was at stake, except for the two that mattered.

"She seems willing to be in my bed." He struggled against the solid object that held him from his fresh meal. His vision was still clouded, but he could smell the blood that came off the human in waves. He would have her blood, even if he had to rip through his restraints.

"She doesn't know what she's doing. I do. Come with me and I'll do as you please." Mierka's voice became seductive.

Natalia stood silently and stared into her lover's eyes. She wanted nothing but him. She heard the conversation between Vincent and Mierka but didn't comprehend it. All she understood was that he wanted her, but four people kept her from him. She tried to step forward but was once again stopped. She felt a hand at her lower back, which held her in place by a handful of her cotton dress.

Vincent closed his eyes as he took a deep breath and inadvertently inhaled the human's scent. He opened his eyes and revealed to Natalia the depth of his desire. He heard her sigh in response, and grinned. "Ask her what she wants."

Mierka shook her head, turned to Natalia, and saw how much of a problem the situation could be. She stepped directly in front of Natalia, to try and block her line of sight to Vincent. "Natalia? What do you want?"

Natalia glanced down at Mierka then back up into Vincent's eyes as she licked her lips. "Vincent."

Vincent growled behind them and Mierka's jaw tightened.

"Let her…To me…" He spoke through clenched teeth; his voice was frantic. He no longer made any sense.

Natalia started to walk forward but was once again stopped. This time, Charlie simply wrapped his arms around her and held on. She struggled against him and tried to get loose. The struggle became more pronounced as she tried to obey her lover. All she wanted was to do as he said, and he wanted her to go to him.

Charlie, afraid of what the vampire would do to her, finally tripped Natalia and held her to the ground. Whatever had happened to her it was clear she was in a heightened state of out of her mind. He held on to her, and crushed her to the floor as she screamed her frustration. Why the vampires weren't getting one or both out of the room was beyond his comprehension. He thought of taking Natalia out of the room himself, but knew he couldn't handle her on his own.

Joseph tried to understand what was going on with Natalia. She enjoyed being with Vincent and would often indulge him in his baser tastes. To try and take him on when he was in this state was beyond reasoning. All in attendance knew she didn't want to be changed; yet she would risk her life to please him. Joseph thought back on the evening, to the point when she had taken Vincent's blood.

Anthony had researched Edwin's ritual of giving his people his blood. Edwin fed humans and vampires his blood every night. With humans, it almost always seemed to negate their will power. With vampires, it depended on their age. Anthony and Joseph seemed to think it had more to do with the person who drank, but were unsure how it worked. Some who drank Edwin's blood were affected in a similar manner as Natalia. The mayor of San Francisco drank Edwin's blood and was under the Captain's control. Joseph nodded to himself. Natalia would do anything Vincent wanted because she was under his control. He continued to assess the situation. Charlie struggled on the ground with Natalia. Vincent strained against Joseph's hold.

"Mierka." There was only one thing to do. Mierka had to take Vincent to bed. Mierka turned to Joseph. "Take him. There's no reasoning with them."

Mierka knew it would come to this. She walked the few steps to Vincent, pressed herself against him, which allowed Joseph to let him go. Vincent growled. He wanted the human beyond his reach, not the vampire who confronted him. Mierka leaned her head to one side, raised her hand to her neck and sliced open her jugular with her nail. Blood flowed freely down her neck, crimson on cream. Vincent breathed deep, and eyes rolled back as the scent took over his nostrils. The blood was not as fresh, but the donor was willing.

Vincent snarled. The meal he wanted struggled with the beast on the floor. She continued to try and come to him, and he wanted her. The woman in front of him offered her body and blood, and no one stopped her. With a bellow of rage, he grabbed the willing woman, sank his teeth into her neck and drank deep of the blood that flowed in the old veins. She fell against him, gripped him tightly and dug her fingers into his flesh. He pulled away, and let her close the wounds on her neck.

"Take me away from this room, Vincent." Her voice was pure seduction; it was easy to obey. Vincent picked Mierka up, gave Natalia a final look, then ignored her for the creature in his arms. She was not Natalia, but now that his mind was more under his control, he knew the one he held was the right choice. His vision still murky, he swept past his men, but barely saw them.

With Vincent gone from the room, Charlie let Natalia up. She howled her lover's name, and tried to run after him. Joseph caught her and held her lightly, like a rag doll. She didn't have the strength to battle against him and quieted quickly.

"He left me." Those present cringed at the tone of her voice. It was petulant and whiny. She sounded like a spoiled child not given her way. Joseph, finally fed up with her attitude, spun her around and slapped her. The slap was harder than intended. Her head rocked back, and her body followed. She spilled to the ground, and a cry of pain escaped her lips. Rebecca held Charlie back. She thought that if anyone were on the spoiled brat's side, Natalia would not return.

Joseph stood over the weeping child, as hatred grew inside him. He had learned something useful about vampire blood tonight, but at what cost? What would it take to separate Natalia from Vincent's hold? He could try his own blood but didn't want the strong woman under his control. He reached down to pick her up off the floor. There had to be a way to break Vincent's hold. He tried to stand her on her feet, but she wouldn't have it. Annoyed, he slung her over his shoulder, dismissed the wolves with a wave and walked out of the room toward the library.

He didn't know where else to take her. All the bedrooms, although currently empty, belonged to someone. Even the guest bedrooms were being used. He couldn't place her in her bedroom, as Vincent might smell her. Joseph was pretty sure Mierka, and Vincent had ended up in the tower room and wanted to keep Natalia far away from there. His only other options were the library or the room he shared with Mierka. Under other circumstances, he wouldn't hesitate to take Natalia to his bed, but now was not the time for that. If he were to sleep with her, he wanted the woman, not the brainless child that sat and pouted angrily at him.

"I was supposed to go to him. He wanted to be with me."

"Does it matter that he would have killed you?" His tone was harsh.

She barely reacted. "He would never harm me."

"Did you see what he did to Mierka?"

"He only did that to Mierka because he couldn't do it to me." She stood and faced him with her stubbornness. He usually enjoyed matching wits with her. Now, she had no wits to match.

"Had he done that to you, you would be dead."

"I already told you, he wouldn't kill me."

She said it with such conviction; he wanted to wipe the smirk off her face. He didn't know how. It was possible it would just take time for Vincent's hold on her to loosen. He suddenly pitied her. He raised a hand to her cheek and touched her tenderly. He would have to lock her in the dungeon until she was herself again. He couldn't risk locking her in a room upstairs, since she knew Vincent's code and could pick a regular lock. She couldn't pick a lock if she were chained to the wall.

Natalia closed her eyes briefly at Joseph's compassionate touch. She leaned into it for a second, then pulled away as she was wanted elsewhere. As if to leave the room, she turned from him and started to walk towards the door.

Joseph caught the look and understood. His thoughts changed and evolved into a new plan. Perhaps he could seduce her out of Vincent's control. He was behind her in a second, and captured her in his arms. She stiffened as he plunged one hand into her hair and slid the other around her waist. Joseph growled into her neck, and allowed his hand to slip down her side to gather her skirt in his fist. She tried to pull away, but he held her in place. She whimpered, and it egged him on. It was her true voice, not the one under another's control. His cool fingers touched her willing flesh, and she whimpered again.

"Take me to him!" Her words were breathless. He couldn't tell who commanded him. Her overwrought mind still battled Vincent's control.

"You wish your master?" He whispered into her ear, as he understood how to help her.

"Yes! Take me to Vincent." She tried to pull away.

He captured her again, ran his hand up and down her thigh. "But I can do so much more than he can. Give me leave and I will please you, Natalia. Give me permission to touch you the way you wish me to touch you."

He unbuttoned her dress at her neckline. The buttons ran down the length of the dress. Most had conveniently been left undone, probably to entice Vincent. Her hands found his and tried to still his actions.

"Vincent-"

"Is sleeping with another tonight. Why let him have all the fun Natalia? Do you really want to sleep alone tonight? There is no reason to." His words were whispered in her ear, as his hand breezed over her skin. He wondered how far he would have to go to break Vincent's control. He enjoyed toying with her but wanted her willing. His fingers brushed her breast, which caused another whimper. There was a different tone to her next words.

"But I don't belong to you. I belong to him!" Her will strained to make sense of the situation. Somewhere in her mind her true personality was trapped by her lover's blood, and the vampire behind her made sense.

"You belong to yourself, child. Your blood and body belong to you, despite the words you spoke earlier. Let yourself feel what you truly want to feel. Come to my bed Natalia. Say yes." His seductive words whispered past her ear as his arms pulled her closer.

Natalia's mind finally snapped. She cried out, pulled away from Joseph, and collapsed to the ground as she reinstated control over her own mind. She wept as the headache from earlier came back tenfold. She covered her head with her hands and tried to soothe the pain. She felt Joseph's hands on her shoulders as he knelt next to her. She leaned against him, and enjoyed the solidness of him. She quieted as her headache slowly eased.

"What happened?" Her voice was back to normal, if still strained.

"Other than my attempt to seduce you?" His voice showed his humor. "You drank Vincent's blood and came under his control."

"I can't be controlled." Her voice revealed her conviction in her belief.

"Perhaps if you tell me of your evening before you came to the training room, we can decipher the situation."

"Are we in a secure location?" She had a vague idea Anthony might be in the security room.

Joseph stood and picked her up as he did so. "I will take you somewhere we can speak freely."

He carried her out of the library and up the stairs to his bedroom. Once inside, he set her on the bed, locked the door and pulled out his remote to secure the room. He turned back to Natalia as she buttoned her dress. He smiled slightly then went to sit in a chair opposite the bed. She looked around the room as she had never been in here before. It was as big as Vincent's sitting room, contained a king-sized bed, several dressers, a desk, and several chairs. There were also two wardrobes. She turned her attention back to Joseph.

"You released Anthony tonight?" It was almost a statement.

She nodded. "It was hard. It took a lot out of me."

"Your will was already weakened." He leaned forward.

She nodded again. "But I can't be controlled. My mother assured me of that a long time ago."

Joseph let the comment pass, as there was more to puzzle out. "What about this morning Natalia? Were you tired when you woke up?"

"I suppose I was. What are you thinking?"

"I believe your will was susceptible to control due to the circumstances of this evening. You were exhausted after your three days as a captive. You lost blood to Wayne and then before you were completely healed, Vincent took more and most probably kept you up long after sunrise, correct?"

Natalia nodded. They had been up until past noon making love.

"Then when you woke, you had a battle of wills with Anthony. He must have been hard to control. I saw you when you entered the training room. You looked exhausted."

She nodded again, as her hands went to her head to massage her temples.

Joseph stood and went to the bed he shared with Mierka. He sat behind Natalia to massage her shoulders, neck, and temples. She sighed, and relaxed as his fingers loosened her muscles. "This is how I see the events of the evening. You were tired, your will was battered and the vampire you love, and trust fed you his blood. We have learned that a vampire's blood can be used to control other vampires, but it seems to work better on humans. I believe that had he fed you his blood on any other night, you may not have been affected. It is also possible that he may be the only one who would be able to."

Joseph leaned in to whisper in her ear. "You have been with him for seven years. When was the last time you denied him anything Natalia? You trust that he will keep you well and operate on the knowledge that he will not harm you unless you harm him. He is your love, Natalia. We all know this. He can control you because you allow it."

Joseph turned his head slightly and bit her earlobe. Her breath caught, and she pulled away from him, a look of wonder on her face. "Why are you trying to seduce me?"

"I started to seduce you to break Vincent's hold. Now that I've had a small taste of you, I want more. Can you give me more?"

She tensed, unsure of what to do. She wanted Vincent but had a vague idea that he was uncontrollable and with Mierka. "You're not my lover and I'm not yours."

"But you could be, for the night. Mierka and Vincent aren't thinking of us. They're enjoying each other's bodies, tearing into each other, and screaming their pleasure. Do you want to be alone tonight, Natalia?"

She relaxed into his hands, and leaned into him. Joseph was thinner than Vincent, not as broad, but he still had the strength. He made sense, but she didn't feel it was right to sleep with another. Her voice was low, reluctantly seductive. "No, but this isn't what I want."

"Then why do you sound willing?" His hands found their way under her dress.

"Because he's not sleeping with me tonight." She arched into him as his hand found her breast and squeezed. His touch tempted her, and Vincent slept with another tonight. Anger suddenly consumed her as thoughts of what he was doing to the lovely Mierka flooded her mind. Why not be with Joseph tonight? He wanted her. "I would be screwing you to get even with Vincent."

"And I would be screwing you to get even with Vincent as well. He has my woman; I want his tonight. Give yourself to me, Natalia."

Reason left as his hand slipped under her skirt and found its way up her thigh. His hand brushed against her underwear. He could feel her wet heat through the thin fabric. She cried out, more than ready for a lover. As he kissed her and stilled her cry, she gave herself over fully to Joseph's more than capable hands. She wondered briefly if Vincent would consider this a betrayal and realized how little she cared.

5

Natalia woke as she inhaled sharply. Her dreams scattered but left her with a vague feeling of being watched. She pulled her limbs close to her torso, as confusion graced her features. She looked around and memories replaced the dreams and ill feelings as she sat up. This was not her bedroom. Her gaze went to the body sleeping dead next to her. That was not her lover. As she stared at him she frowned. Though she enjoyed Joseph's skills, he had not satisfied her fully. After seven years with an aggressive lover who never seemed to stop, a calm lover who took his time with everything had been too much of a disappointing contrast.

She stole out of bed unnoticed, found her dress and slipped it on. The key for the lock was still in the door. It was an old-fashioned skeleton key, which meant she could have easily picked it if Joseph had removed it. Natalia left the room and closed the door softly behind her. Unsure of what she would find, she sighed and went to her bedroom.

The door to the sitting room was ajar, which was unusual. Natalia crinkled her nose as she pushed the door open. The door to her bedroom was open wide. She stopped halfway through the sitting room, and wondered at her plans. Vincent and Mierka were in the bedroom, probably asleep. She didn't need to go in there. A frown creased her brow. She wanted a shower and clean clothing. There were other showers in this house she could use, but her clothes were in that room. She needed to proceed.

Natalia nodded to herself and moved forward. She would have to be quiet, to not wake the pair, but she would still go to her bedroom. At the door to the bedroom, Natalia stopped dead in shock. There was no one in their bed. Confused, she walked inside and stared at the bed for a few moments, unsure of how to proceed. She shook her head and grabbed new underwear, t-shirt, and jeans from her closets.

As she gathered clean clothes and headed to the bathroom, the thought of where the pair might be slipped into her mind. If they weren't in the bedroom, where were they? Natalia pushed the thought aside time and time again, but it returned. The thought overrode other desires and instead of showering as planned, she stripped and pulled on her clean clothes. She paused several times as the thought overpowered her, but she was able to breathe deeply and control her actions.

Once dressed, she allowed the thought to return carefully as she headed slowly to the security room. Due to the number of people in the training room last night, she guessed that all the bedrooms were occupied. The couple weren't in the sitting room, library, or ballroom. That left Vincent's study, the large meeting room, or the dungeon. She could look in the remaining rooms and would if the guard in the security room didn't want to help her. At the door to the security room, she took a deep breath then opened the door. Charlie grinned at her as she entered.

"Hi! What's up?"

As it was Charlie, she tossed aside her carefully thought-out speech. "Where's Vincent?"

"Don't know." He looked at her for a long time with a slight frown on his face before he turned back to the screens.

"Bullshit." She slammed the door behind her, leaned against it, and crossed her arms.

"No, really, Nat. I don't know. He's not on the screens." He turned and gave her a sincere look. It slowly turned concerned as he noticed how fidgety she was. It was out of character for her, but it had been a rather odd few days.

She gave him a look of disbelief as she brushed hair out of her eyes. "I don't believe you."

"I'm not lying, Nat."

"Prove it." She came forward. She rubbed her arms to stop the sudden nervous feeling in her gut.

He turned around and pulled up all the views he could from all the rooms in the house. As there were more rooms than screens, he scrolled through each one on the main monitor. "See? No Vincent." He frowned and typed a command into the keyboard. "I guess I didn't see Joseph's room either."

"He turned off the screen last night. We didn't want anyone listening to our conversation. And I didn't see my siting room, bedroom or bathroom on the monitors."

Charlie typed in a few codes to try to pull up those rooms and couldn't. "Huh. That hasn't happened in a long time."

"What?" She leaned over the side of his chair to get a better look at the monitors.

He pulled back a little as she hoped from foot to foot and wondered if he had ever known her to be this agitated. "His rooms were never on screen during the day before you came. Whenever I was on duty, his rooms would black out one at a time as he went into them at sunrise and would come back on after he was awake."

"You saw the sitting room but not the bathroom or bedroom?" She pulled back, crossed her arms, and tried to decipher the odd news.

Charlie thought about if for a moment then shook his head. "No, didn't usually see any of them. Didn't think much of it since it's his house."

A thoughtful look took over her features and Charlie wondered if he should have said as much. Natalia simply stared at the floor, as she chewed on her lip. She understood why he would turn off the cameras in his bedroom, but why in that bathroom? On further thought it seemed strange he would turn any off at all. He liked to let people think he was paranoid and kept the cameras on as a matter of protection. So why would he turn any off...unless it was to hide the fact that he was never in that bedroom at all. Without a word, she turned and left the room.

Charlie sighed heavily and reached for the cell to call Rebecca. He wasn't sure he'd need her, but he thought he might. He watched Natalia walk back upstairs as he requested Rebecca's presence in the security room. Moments later, she walked in, as on the screen Natalia walked into her sitting room and look around slowly.

"What's going on?"

"Natalia's looking for Vincent. I didn't know where he was. She didn't believe me, and I showed her the screens. She said her rooms were missing and they are."

Rebecca frowned, then a memory clicked in. "Oh, he's..."

When she didn't finish, Charlie turned around to look at his wife. "What?"

Rebecca shook her head.

Charlie's mouth dropped open. "He has a secret room?"

"No, and you don't know anything. Get out of the chair and let me take over."

Charlie moved but watched his wife closely. He wanted to know more, but shook his head and turned back to look at the monitors. As the Alpha, Vincent often gave her information she couldn't share. Charlie was used to it and therefore would not ask for any further information. Rebecca typed quickly and brought up Natalia's rooms on all the screens. The human could be seen finally walking through her sitting room and into her bedroom.

"There was something off about Nat."

Rebecca turned to glance at Charlie. "Tell me quickly. I'm still trying to decide if we need a human. We may need to wake Joseph."

He glanced sharply at his wife. "Why?"

"Tell me about Natalia." Her voice was an order.

He shook his head. "She was real fidgety. Seemed agitated."

"Ok?"

He placed his hand on Rebecca's shoulder until she turned and looked at him. "Have you ever known her to fidget? When she's agitated or angry, she shows it with anger. I don't have a memory of her ever acting nervous," pain flashed across his features, "not even toward me after I bit her."

Rebecca's mouth and eyes popped open wide as she thought for a moment. She took a deep breath. "Get a human. Joseph might be better in this situation. We take down with force. He can subdue her better."

Charlie nodded and headed out of the room. On the screens, Natalia walked through each of her rooms, but locked the doors as she passed through them. The wolf frowned. Natalia never locked the doors. As Rebecca watched she realized Natalia did seem off. Her movements weren't as decisive as they usually were. She seemed to hesitate a lot, as if dazed. Rebecca narrowed her eyes as Natalia went into the bathroom, lit a few candles, then turned off the overheads.

Rebecca slammed her hands on the counter. "Charlie!"

"Right here."

She turned and saw Charlie and Angie. Rebecca nodded, turned back to the monitors, and typed in a few commands. Though Natalia's sitting room came into view, the other rooms remained black. "If she comes back into the sitting room, you come get me. Angie, we need to wake Joseph up. Are you well?"

"Yes."

Rebecca nodded, and turned to the lockbox on the wall. She pulled out her own key, opened the lockbox and grabbed the master key to Vincent's rooms. She then left the security room and headed quickly to Joseph's room with Angie in tow. Rebecca didn't waste any time but raced up the steps. At the top she turned quickly to Joseph's room and rushed in without knocking. He was asleep on the bed. Rebecca went to his side, but waited until Angie was beside her. She then shook Joseph's shoulder. His eyes fluttered, but quickly stopped.

Rebecca frowned, turned to the nightstand, and pulled open the top drawer. She grabbed the knife and unsheathed it. The wolf very carefully cut her palm, stuck her hand between the vampire's lips, and placed the knife on the nightstand. She then shook Joseph's shoulder. When his eyes fluttered this time, they stayed open as he sucked down a bit of her blood. He frowned then woke completely as he pushed her hand away.

"That is not what I like to wake to." He did not like to wake to the taste of werewolf blood in his mouth.

"Angie's here for your meal. I knew you would wake up quicker with my blood though." Rebecca moved out of the way as she grabbed cloth from the nightstand.

As Angie positioned herself to feed Joseph, he looked to Rebecca for information.

"Remember when you told me about Vincent's last human valet?"

He locked eyes with the wolf as he took a few sips of Angie's blood. He nodded.

"Our master's favorite human is acting out of sorts. From what you described, it's the way the valet acted before he was taken over." She looked to Angie, then back to Joseph. "And I suspect the master's favorite human may know there is a secret to find."

Joseph's eyes went wide. He looked to Angie. "How much may I take?"

"I haven't been fed off of in three weeks."

He nodded, turned back to her arm, and drank what he needed. Once full, Angie moved out of the way, and Joseph stood. He grabbed his pants off the floor and turned to Rebecca, who held out a key. He took it then slipped on his pants.

"Thank you, Angie."

The woman nodded as she wrapped her bite. She left to tend to it elsewhere. Joseph looked to Rebecca.

"Are we sure?"

"No, but when's the last time she seemed agitated or nervous? Not angry, mind you, but nervous?"

Joseph reviewed the events of the past few days in his mind and nodded. "Go back to the security room. No one witnesses this but you."

"Yes, sir."

They parted ways and hoped for a good outcome.

6

Natalia sat on the edge of the tub, and watched as the light danced off the mirrors and reflected off the tiles. Her hand tapped on the tile next to her, unnoticed. She thought the low light would confuse the cameras enough. She wanted a little bit of privacy and time to examine the room. In the security room, she deduced Vincent must have a secret room. The entrance was probably in the bathroom, which is why he turned off the security cameras in here. All the doors that led to the bathroom were locked, and the keys were in her pocket. The werewolves and vampires could break down any locked door, which only gained her a minute or two per door. She would have this puzzle figured out before anyone came in, anyway.

Natalia continued to stare at the wall next to the shower, as her fingers tapped out a nervous tune. There was a space of about five feet long next to the shower stall. Most of the walls had something on or against them: shower stall, toilet, sink, shelves, or mirrors. That spot was oddly empty. She wondered why she had never thought about it or the large empty area of the second floor beyond Vincent's room. She realized it didn't matter. She pushed off the tub and went to the wall, as she wondered what the trick was. There was a door here; she would find it.

Natalia thought it out in her head and bounced on her heels as she measured out the possible door. It had to be about this far away from the shower and about this wide for the wiring, if it was an electronic door, and she knew it was. She started to search the wall beside the shower, to find a catch or release that would trigger the door. She took her time, as she knew Vincent would have hidden it well. This was a secret room; the door would be even more of a secret. A tile at about the height of Vincent's shoulder moved slightly when she pressed against it. She pressed harder and heard a click. The tile slid up into the wall and revealed a keypad.

She didn't hesitate. Either it would open with Vincent's code, or it wouldn't. She stepped back when she heard a second soft click and watched as the wall slid back two inches and then to the left, away from the shower stall. Natalia gazed into the darkened room and took a candle off the bathroom counter. There was no light in the room. Once through the entry way she understood why she had missed the empty space. The brass towel rack that normally stood in front of the space lay on the floor just inside the room. Natalia grasped it, placed it back in the bathroom, and wondered at the hard fabric her hand brushed against. She carefully brought the candle to the towel and saw that the hard fabric was darker than the rest of the towel. Natalia figured it was blood.

Surprised the door did not close on its own, she looked around the entrance of the room and saw the lit keypad. The numbers were lit from underneath. The keypad was on the same side of the wall as the one in the bathroom. She entered the code again and the door slid shut. The room brightened but only a little. It was unnatural light, but she couldn't see the source. She put out the candle, and placed it on the floor. She bounced in place as she waited for her eyes to adjusted. When she could see, she looked around and saw the boxes piled high. The boxes started at the wall next to the door and headed straight for a few steps then ended at a t-intersection. She rubbed her hand against her forehead and glanced down in frustration. Damn him for his paranoia.

The spot on the floor stared back up at her when she opened her eyes. She frowned, knelt, and touched the spot. Dried blood. She glanced further up the walkway and realized the irregular blood trail would lead the way. Natalia chewed her lip and wondered whose blood it was as she started down the hall. She heard her name being called through the wall as she followed the trail. She ignored it and jogged through the maze, sure the voice was Joseph's. Natalia knew he would be able to follow her through here. Probably created it with Vincent or for Vincent. To not lose her way, Natalia took a deep breath, and followed the blood trail.

It led to a door with another lit keypad. She entered Vincent's code as Joseph bellowed her name in the room from the other entrance. The door slid open, and she took two steps in. She entered Vincent's code into the next keypad and waited for the door to close as she bounced from foot to foot. She took a chance and entered a random set of numbers. The keypad blinked red. She waited for thc light to return to normal, then entered in another random sequence. The keypad flashed red, then went back to its normal hue. She waited another second, then entered another set of numbers. This time the keypad flashed and went dark. Natalia closed her eyes, turned, and ran up the stairs. That ought to buy her a little time.

She reached the top of the steps, and stepped into the room. The room opened to either side of her. There were doors all along the wall to each side. She stared at the closets to her left for a long moment before her eyes went to the bed. The canopy bed, crimson curtains hiding its occupants, was centered on the far wall. She closed her eyes and turned her head away as an old dream came back to her. She took another look at the wall to the right of her and saw the difference in the wall. Two of the doors were windows. She walked to the windows slowly, entranced by what lay beyond.

Natalia reached the doors, placed her hand on the doorknob and paused. She closed her eyes as something seemed to call to her from behind. She shook her head then opened the left door. The doors opened in and allowed the sun to spill light onto the floor and wall but not toward the bed. She gasped when she saw the deck and the view beyond. It stopped all thoughts.

This was the room; this was the view. This was where her dream took place. This was where Joseph would give her her first drink of blood as her sire. She stepped onto the deck and gazed in wonder at the ocean beyond. It was a beautiful, awful view. She held back a sob, as she understood that one day, she would no longer be able to see the ocean during the day. She wondered at the deck, but figured the glass had to be protected. Vincent told her that even with the protected glass, it was dangerous for vampires to be in direct sunlight. Vincent probably didn't usually use the deck during the day.

"Natalia," a soft, stern voice called.

When she turned to the door, Joseph's hand was held out to her. His skin became pink as she watched. As she had suspected, even with the protective glass, full daylight was dangerous to vampires. With a sigh, she stepped back to the door and took his offered hand. He pulled her through and closed the glass door behind her.

"This is it. This is where my dream takes place." She paused to look toward the bed.

Joseph stayed silent as her eyes went first to the closets on the far wall, then found his gaze.

"Why didn't he tell me about this room?" She raised her hand to still his words and shook her head. "Never mind. I know."

"We must leave, Natalia." He thought quickly. He couldn't tell her the real reason for his trepidation. "There's no telling what state he'll be in when he wakes."

He spoke quietly, as if afraid to wake the sleeping pair. Natalia walked with him to the stairs and down to the storage room. Joseph entered his pass code and led the way back to his and Mierka's room. They had things to discuss privately. Natalia let him lead her, as she reflected on Vincent's secret room. She felt drawn to the room.

Joseph kept silent until they were back in his room and the door was locked. He pulled out his remote, entered the code to reset the cameras and microphones, then entered the code to secure the room. He didn't know if Rebecca had overridden the security devices but wanted to make sure he and Natalia had privacy. Resetting the devices ensured the off code would work.

Joseph faced Natalia and stared into her eyes. He didn't want to bring attention to what might have been calling to her, but needed to know if she were under its spell. "Why did you look for something you should not have gone looking for?"

She frowned. "He hid this from me for seven years. I wanted information and I didn't want to wait until you were all awake and able to distract or stop me."

When she held his gaze, Joseph was confident she was in control of her own mind. He switched tactics and spoke of the room only. "It's not always smart to wake Vincent after a night like he had. We need to make sure he is under his own control before he sees you again. Had he woken, he may have killed you. Even if he's satiated, he'll be ravenous when he wakes." He pulled her to him, grabbed her by her hair, bared his fangs, and looked at her longingly. "You'd be a tasty bite for a hungry vampire."

His actions didn't faze her. When she spoke, there was a bit of sadness to her voice. She heard it and hated it. "Why didn't he tell me? Does he still not trust me after all these years?"

The hand not in her hair touched the pendant around her neck. "You wear his symbol. You were made part of his household. This isn't about trust Natalia. It's about safety."

She pushed away from him, aggravated. "It's a room. It's the room in my dream. He knows about the dream, yet he stayed silent. It made me wonder if I was with the right man. It's one of the reasons I've refused to be turned. Why didn't he tell me?"

"No human is allowed in that room." Joseph shook his head. "You would need to ask him for an explanation. He is the master of this house; his word is my law."

"Only when it pleases you." Her arms were crossed, and she looked angry.

His only answer was to shrug. She stared him down. Natalia wanted an argument. She felt a bit off and didn't like how these past few days had gone. If Joseph knew anything, he would never tell. She let her sadness go, let the anger take over. It was unfortunate she didn't have anyone to pit that anger against. She needed release and from what she learned of Joseph, he wouldn't be any help there. He never showed anger even when fighting. And his lovemaking was too gentle for her tastes.

"Will Vincent tell me the truth?" She watched as a slow smile spread across his features as he heard the bite in her words.

A look flashed in his eyes, and mirrored the criminal smile on his lips. He stepped to her, and slid his fingers back into her supple hair. One hand caressed its way to the small of her back, while one stayed in her hair. "He will tell you all you wish to know. You have to ask him in the correct manner. You seem angry Natalia. Do you wish to challenge me again?"

"You're not worth my time." Her words were harsh as she tried to remove his hands, but he held on, which reminded her of his strength.

He leaned in to whisper in her ear. "Do you really believe Mierka would return to me after sleeping with Vincent, if all I did was caress her softly? Give me more credit, human. You don't know my triggers. You might be able to change Vincent's attitude by pleading, but I want more."

Joseph pulled back a little to brush his lips against hers. The light kisses were pleasant but were far from the deep crushing kisses she craved. She tried to kiss him harder, but when he wouldn't oblige, she tried to pull away. He continued to hold her in place with the hand at her back, while his other hand lightly caressed her skin, like a cool feather against her neck. She whimpered and half-heartedly pulled her head away from his touch. She yearned for so much more than he gave. Her hands went to his chest, and she pushed with all her might away from him. He simply grinned and grabbed her wrists.

"Do really wish me to stop?" The devil was in that smile. It promised Natalia all she desired.

She yelled with frustration. "I want more!"

"Does that mean I can continue?"

"Will I get more?"

"If you ask correctly."

She bared her teeth and he laughed as he continued his slow seduction. He removed her cloths, but did not allow her to remove his when she tried. He drove her insane with the lightness of his touch. Eventually, she begged and pleaded, but he still touched her with an aching weightlessness.

"God damn you, Joseph! Please give me what I want!" She pleaded as he slowly sucked at her breast.

He grinned around her nipple. "God can't help you in this household, woman. And I've already been damned by worse than He."

Natalia cried out in frustration, as he continued his soft touch. Finally, fed up with his aggravating strokes, she grabbed his shirt and spat her words into his face through clenched teeth. "Give me what I want, you pitiful excuse for a man!"

The devil showed in his smile again. "The insult was not necessary."

Joseph bared his teeth, plunged his fangs into her tender breast and drank two swallows. He wanted more but knew she had already lost too much. She cried out in surprise and gripped his bald head. He spent the next few hours showing her why Mierka returned to him time after time.

7

A kiss woke her that evening. Her lover pulled her into the cool circle of his arms and gave her a deep lingering kiss. When he pulled away, she realized it was not the vampire she wanted.

"Good morning, Natalia. Did you sleep well?" Joseph had a slight smile on his lips and caressed her back softly.

Natalia pulled away gently, as she wanted to shower and return to her own bed before Vincent woke. She saw that Joseph was already dressed and knew his next stop would be the tower room to wake his woman and his master. Natalia found her clothing and dressed while Joseph watched and smirked. He watched her movements to see if there were signs the nervous ticks had returned. When he saw nothing, he moved to stand right behind her.

"Have you no words for me?" He brushed her hair away from her neck, pulled the strands slightly, and reminded her of his hidden abilities. "I don't expect you to run to my bed each night Natalia, but an acknowledgment would be pleasant."

"I'm…sorry. I'm not sure…Will he consider this a betrayal?" She stepped away from Joseph's touch, as she did not want to accept her body's reaction to his caress. She knew how to unleash the devil. And the devil was a fine lover. Both Vincent and Joseph used pain to enhance pleasure, but Vincent carefully pushed her limits and stopped when she asked him to. With Joseph, safe words were necessary, and he only stopped when she used them. Her body tingled with slight pain in various areas, but it only reminded her of the pleasure she felt.

Joseph observed her reactions and almost laughed. She desired him, but obviously didn't want to admit it. It thrilled him to see her pull away but try and draw him to her. She spoke over her shoulder, with half closed eyes, as if to share a secret.

He stopped his snicker with his response. "Considering he spent the night with another, he would have a hard time convincing anyone this was a betrayal."

Natalia nodded briefly, closed her eyes, straightened, and composed herself. "Is there time for me to shower before you wake him?"

"Not really. I'm on my way now. I suggest you stay in the sitting room until I find out his attitude."

Natalia nodded again, turned, and caught his eye. There was no hesitation in her attitude, just confidence. Whatever she might think about spending the night with another man was hidden by her stubborn determination. She had apparently decided not to be upset about the situation. Joseph searched her eyes for a moment, saw nothing out of out of place, then returned the look to mock it. She frowned, then grinned when he mocked that look too. He stepped to her, gave her one last kiss then led her out the room.

In the sitting room, Joseph left Natalia and headed through the other rooms to the master bedroom. He opened the curtain on the end of the bed, saw Mierka on the left side and Vincent on the right. Joseph tied the curtain open and went to the left side first. She lay on her side, facing Vincent. Joseph pulled gently on her shoulder until she lay on her back. He leaned in and kissed her to wake her. Mierka opened her eyes and pushed her lover away carefully.

"Hello."

"Stay quiet for a moment." He nearly whispered.

Mierka frowned but kept her voice low as well. "He's fine."

"Natalia may not be. There was an incident this morning."

"Wake him and tell him."

"Were you able to help him?"

"He'll be under control. He usually is after a night with me." She did not speak in a boastful manner.

Joseph nodded and went to the other side of the bed. "Vincent."

Mierka rolled her eyes, then reached over and shook Vincent's shoulder.

He woke and glared at her. "There are better ways of waking me."

"You've had enough of me. Wake and find your own woman." Her voice dripped with seduction.

He glared at her as she left the bed then turned and saw Joseph. The look in Vincent's eyes was not kind. "You didn't bring blood?"

"I wanted to speak with you privately."

"I'm hungry."

"This is also not the place for humans, or have you forgotten that?"

Vincent glared at Joseph again. "I'm hungry."

"Sir, there was an issue today with Natalia."

Vincent threw back the covers and stood. He looked around and found his cloths. As he dressed, he glared again at Joseph. "When is there not an issue with that woman?"

"Sir…" There was an odd tone to his voice, to indicate he needed to continue.

"I want blood and I want my woman. Once I am fed and have seen to her, I will listen to you. For now, get out."

Mierka and Joseph exchanged glances. Mierka shook her head and as she was dressed, started to leave the room. Joseph followed her. Once dressed, Vincent left the room as well.

❧ ❧

Natalia stood by the window in the sitting room and stared out at the land around her. She tried to peer into the darkness, and wondered where the wolves were. The sky was clouded over and hid the nearly full moon. Time spun away as she stared into the gloom and a small voice in her mind called to her and urge her to return to the secret room. Worn out from the past few days, she stood at the window and pushed all thoughts aside. She didn't hear when Mierka and Joseph passed her. They moved silently which allowed Vincent to sneak up behind his woman. Her first indication of his presence was when he placed his hands to either side of her on the window and pressed himself against her. The action trapped her between the windowpane and the large vampire. She leaned into him fully and waited for his next move.

"Did he do anything to you that I haven't?" He nuzzled her neck as his hunger grew.

"He told you?" The glass was warmer than he and she could feel his desire in his strength.

"He didn't have to. You smell like him. If you didn't reek of his scent, I'd have thrown you on the floor and taken what's mine."

"Am I still yours then?" She sounded slightly bored.

"Did you think last night changed anything?" He bit her neck gently.

His actions threatened to drive her thoughts from her mind, but the thought of the room came back easily. "Why didn't you tell me about your room?"

Vincent tensed at her words and stopped his seduction. "How did you find out?"

"I woke up around noon and went looking for you in our bedroom. When I didn't find you, I found out you used to disappear each day. It didn't take long to figure out where the room had to be. I can understand that you don't trust me enough to take me to a room with no cameras, but why not tell me? I will eventually sleep there."

"It's not a matter of trust Natalia." He reached up and pressed his hand against her new necklace. "This should be proof of that. There are objects

43

in that room I don't want to reach out to you."

"What do you mean?" She turned around to face him, and placed her back against the warm window.

Vincent stepped away from her, as he needed some space. His thoughts went to what Joseph tried to tell him upon waking, but hunger gnawed at him. He told her the truth to bring a quick end to the conversation.

"You're not the only one who's given me enchanted items, Natalia. Some of them are dangerous to humans. I used to have a human valet. Each night, he would bring me blood, his or someone else's and tell me of the day's events. He was with me for a long time; he was very loyal. Then one day I woke to find Joseph fighting my valet. It seems one of the items in my room had taken over his mind, and turned him into a Slayer, of sorts. It gave him a strength and agility he had never possessed. It took Joseph and myself to stop him." He grew quiet. "We had to kill him to stop the item from possessing him." He gave Natalia a hard look. "That's why I don't allow any humans into that room, especially you."

"How do you know it will affect me? I've been in this house for years."

"I'm not willing to take that chance. You are a formidable human without additional help. Were you to be possessed by the same item, I'm not sure I would be able to stop you."

"I can't-" she shook her head and started over. "It's hard for me to be possessed, Vincent."

He crossed his arms, determined to end the conversation. "You're not allowed in that room."

"I know how to get in." She crossed her arms, and her right hand absentmindedly rubbed the side of her left breast.

Vincent's eyes strayed to her hand. He knew there was a scar there, from a wound he inflicted the last time she disobeyed his rules. He did not bring attention to what she was doing. It intrigued him that she touched the scar while she thought to disobey him again. "Why would you want to?"

She thought for a moment. "Curiosity."

"Natalia, love," He stepped to her and caressed her cheek softly. "There is no reason for you to be in that room while you are human. If I find that you've been in it, the punishment I will bring upon your pretty head will only be stopped short by the fact that you are human and fragile. But remember, I know your limitations."

His voice and touch were tender, but the look in his eyes betrayed the deadly seriousness. Natalia felt compelled to argue, but knew she had no reason to, therefore changed tactics. "When I told you of my dream, why didn't you tell me the room existed?"

"I want you to ask me to change you into a vampire because you wish it to be me, not because I have a room that was in your dreams." Irritated with the conversation, he turned and started for the door. "This discussion is over. Shower while I feed."

She watched his retreating back, but kept her words to herself. She trounced off to their bedroom, grabbed her robe and headed for the bathroom, as she fumed about his attitude. A tiny thought in the far reaches of her mind tried to speak up about her own attitude, but it was stomped into oblivion before it had a voice. She angrily ripped off her clothes, threw them aside and stepped into the shower.

Natalia rubbed a small ache on her left breast, to try and make an old scar stop hurting. It didn't help. Instead, she used hot, hot water, but the heat did nothing to dissipate her anger or the ache. She showered quickly, stepped out and toweled off. Still pissed at his attitude, she roughly pulled on her clothes. She tried to calm herself, and found that she couldn't. It angered her that he would think she was weak enough to have her mind taken over by a mere item. The more she thought about it, the more furious she became. Finally, her rage overtook her like a thunderous wave breaking on a tiny grain of sand.

The glass shower door shattered when she slammed it. She entered the code in the secret entrance without thought. Natalia was through it and into the maze before Vincent could be alerted to her actions. She followed the same trail of blood, and nearly ran to the next door. She was through it and up the stairs with more speed than a human could normally attempt. At the top of the steps, she paused. Calm descended as she went to the closets on the left wall.

8

Joseph tried to talk to Vincent when his master entered the kitchen. There were plenty of humans to feed from as all three vampires needed sustenance. Anger and hunger overrode all other emotions and Vincent cut Joseph off. Mierka tried to talk to him as well, but the glare in his eyes silenced her. She glared back but waited for Vincent to finish feeding. Once he was done, Mierka stepped into his way.

"Move." He said as he stared her down.

"No. You need to listen to us." She glanced at the humans. "Leave the room."

They did as told as Joseph walked to behind Mierka. "Vincent, something may be wrong with Natalia."

He growled. "If something is wrong with her, then I need to return to her."

"There are items that need to be removed from this house."

Vincent continued to glare. "It hasn't affected her thus far."

"She hasn't been in her right mind for a few days. She's overwrought and that is a dangerous situation."

"Then let me return to her and keep her safe."

Mierka shook her head. "I'm not convinced you're in your right mind either."

Vincent took a breath and sighed. "I've had blood. I want my woman. After that, I will examine what I need to do. For now, I want her."

"How badly?" Joseph's voice was soft to help Vincent calm down and hopefully think of the situation.

He sighed again. "I have been on edge. She was missing and now she is back. There is nothing more that needs to be said."

"Sir…"

Vincent bared his teeth, but the other two were spared any more talk as Joseph's phone went off. It was the ringtone for the security room. Instead of answering, the three went to the room. Rebecca turned to the three as they entered.

"She's headed to the room again."

Vincent, Joseph and Mierka turned and ran for the stairs. In their haste and urgency, they used their vampiric speed and were in the secret room in seconds. The scene made all three open their eyes wide. All the closets were open, either by a crack, or thrown wide open. No items had been taken out, but there was broken glass at Natalia's feet. She had broken the fifth case in. Vincent knew what was there and was ready to thrash Natalia for her insolence. She had gone too far. He started toward her, but Mierka moved quickly and stepped in his way.

"Stop. Look at the situation better." Mierka held him back as he appraised the room. Natalia stood in front of the case, hand out. She stared at her outstretched hand, which shook noticeably. Her face showed strain and deep concentration, and her teeth were clenched. The look on her face indicated she fought with herself.

"Natalia." He was able to control his voice enough to sound pleasant.

Her head turned minutely as her hand reached forward. She turned back to her hand, and it came back. She strained a little more and managed to talk, but each word was broken into its own sentence as she struggled with her will.

"Get." Her hand went forward with the word, came back as she concentrated. "Me." Forward and back. "Out." Forward and back. "Of." Forward and back. "Here." Forward and back.

Vincent took a step, as did Joseph, but Mierka stopped them both. "I risk my life for my master, he does not risk it for me."

"I'm not your master." There was a tinge of humor in Joseph's voice.

"But you are his protector. Stand ready." Mierka positioned herself and pounced. Natalia saw her coming and relaxed her hold on herself. If she were tense when Mierka hit, she would get hurt. With her will released, she almost touched the ring. Mierka knocked her to the floor before she could do so.

As soon as Mierka landed, Vincent and Joseph came forward. Mierka tried to hold on to the human, who gave her a hell of a fight. Vincent wasn't sure if the human fought Mierka or herself. Once Joseph and Vincent stood close to Mierka, she stood and held Natalia to her. Once up, Natalia tensed, closed her eyes, and tried not to touch any of the closets. Her whole body shook. Joseph closed the closets and stood in front of the one housing the ring.

"Let her walk on her own." Vincent's voice was unreadable.

Mierka looked to Joseph. A look passed between them, and Joseph nodded minutely. Mierka released Natalia then quickly walked to Vincent's side. Unseen, she withdrew something from a secret pocket, and waited for the inevitable.

As her body shook, Natalia started forward, and refused to look anywhere but the floor. She took one step then another, and allowed herself to relax as she drew closer to Joseph. She couldn't get through him; she was safe. She was a step away from him when she felt the presence in her mind again. It urged her to place the small insignificant metal band on her finger. As the ring called again, her body trembled, and she lunged toward Joseph.

Joseph watched Vincent as Natalia walked to him. He was more worried about what Vincent would do, than what Natalia would try and do. He could see Natalia's progress in the look on Vincent's face and knew the instant the human attacked. When Natalia attacked, Vincent's face contorted into hatred, and Joseph knew his master wanted blood. Joseph saved Natalia in the only way he knew how. With one hand, he grabbed Natalia to him. With the other hand, he reached into his pocket and withdrew a tranquilizer dart. He jabbed Natalia in the neck and her struggles quickly ceased.

Once she was down, he looked to his right and saw what he expected. Vincent was in Mierka's arms and there was a stake in his heart. Joseph and Mierka nodded to each other as they assessed their charges. Mierka moved to place Vincent on his bed.

"And where did you get the dart?" She said with admiration.

"Same place you got the stake." He gave her a smirk.

Mierka's look sobered. "What do we do?"

"I don't think either of them were in their right minds, but we need to keep them apart until they wake."

"Can you break the ring's hold on her?"

"I hope to. It needs to be removed from this house."

"And where do you suggest we take it?" Mierka didn't sound convinced. "It calls to those it can use."

"Can it be destroyed?" Joseph asked in a contemplative voice.

"It can be, I think."

Joseph nodded, went to Natalia, and picked her up. "I'll take care of this one and then talk to Anthony about the ring."

She nodded as Joseph left the room to Mierka. He took Natalia to the only place in the house that was probably safe for her. If Natalia were left in one of the regular bedrooms, it would be sinfully easy for Vincent to get to her. If he placed Natalia in the dungeon, it meant Vincent had to think about what he was doing and where he was going. The dungeon would ensure Vincent thought with his mind instead of his emotions.

As he went, Joseph also thought about the objects in Vincent's secret room. The ring was not the only object with a dubious reputation. Those items needed to be removed, and the closets needed to be secured. He thought perhaps all the cases should be replaced with shatterproof or possibly bulletproof glass. The closets also needed alarms.

By the time he reached the dungeon, he knew which items needed to be removed and had all the specifics for the alarms worked out in his head. Joseph placed Natalia in one of the cells, then went to the storage room and gathered the items he needed to teach Natalia her lesson. Vincent's bite was not enough. It was time for true fear.

Items in hand, he stepped back into the hallway. To his surprise, Natalia sat up against the wall. She looked confused and groggy, but looked to be trying to stand. He thought he used enough tranquilizer to keep her asleep for at least a half an hour, but he must have underestimated the dose in the dart. Joseph dropped his items back in the storage room as another strategy came to mind. He went to her and smiled a rather cold smile. She looked up at him, took a breath and gagged but continued to try and stand. The smile on his face dropped a touch.

Natalia gagged again, doubled over, and tried hard not to throw up. Though this was not her first time in the dungeon, the smell was worse this time, and her company was not as pleasant. The stench of meat rotting in the hot sun was so strong it was hard to concentrate. Natalia did not know why they were down here but did not really want to find out. Under those thoughts was the desire to leave; there was something she needed to find.

Joseph watched briefly as the human struggled with her environment. When she started to crawl toward the exit, he frowned softly and wondered at her game. He grabbed her around the waist and pulled her back gently. She looked to him and grimaced.

"Where are you going?"

"Out. I need…" but her thoughts stopped her. She clamped her mouth shut and refused to speak.

He stared at her with curiosity and wondered again if her adventures into Vincent's secret bedroom had been of her own doing – either time. It would not be the first time that ring took over the mind of a human. Natalia, usually strong willed, had been through more in the past few days than she had in a long time. Also, Vincent's blood had hypnotized her. Perhaps it had made her more susceptible to the ring's call.

"Natalia. Where are you going?"

Natalia glared at Joseph. "I'll tell you nothing, Hell-"

He watched as she clamped her mouth shut tightly, and seemed to struggle with her words. The look in her eyes was not the same as usual. Usually when she glared at anyone, there was a certain defiance, to show she would have her way. This look was defiant as well, but not in the same way. It was more…predatory. Joseph narrowed his eyes as he decided. He needed to ensure he was talking to her. Not a mind taken over by the ancient soul of a monk trapped in an otherwise insignificant steel band. Joseph grabbed her arm and herded her to the last door in the hallway. He paused and pushed her against the nearby wall.

The stench grew worse, but she found if she breathed through her mouth, it was not as bad. "I demand you release me."

He raised an eyebrow. His hand pressed against her chest and kept her held to the wall. He didn't say anything and opened the door to the last cell in the dungeon. Natalia looked horrified as the stench was released from the room.

She gagged and finally it was too much. Natalia turned her head and vomited as Joseph released his hold on her. Since she had not eaten recently, it was mostly bile. Finished, she wiped her mouth with her sleeve and started to move away from the cell and Joseph. He watched her for a moment, then looked to the other end of the hallway. The door was closed and locked, but she did know the code. He stood patiently as she moved away. When she was halfway down the hall, he moved quickly and caught up with her. He grabbed her upper arm.

"Where are you going?"

She struggled against his hold and tried to pull her arm free. "Let me go!"

"Not until you answer my question. Where are you going?"

With her free hand she slapped him hard on his cheek. He barely felt it and did not turn his head. "I said let me go! You have no reason to have me down here!"

He moved fast and her head spun. She was up against the wall, his hand around her neck. There was a glint of fear in her eyes, that quickly turned to anger.

"You wish me to let you go? Tell me where you are going."

She bared her teeth. "Away from you!"

"And then where?" His voice stayed mild.

Natalia kicked at his legs, but Joseph barely felt it. With his hand still around her neck, he moved toward the last cell in the dungeon. She threatened to kill him, but her voice turned raspy as he restricted her air flow slightly. Once inside the room, he stopped moving and looked at her coldly.

"Look down, Natalia."

She bared her teeth. "I said let me go, you miserable Hellspawn!"

He gazed at her dispassionately as he understood her mind was once again not her own. "If I were to let you go, you would fall. You are over a twenty-foot drop. If you struggle and cause me to let you go, you will drop to your death. The fall may not kill you, but the ghul in the oubliette will. As there is no way out, you will die. Do you wish to die today, human?"

Still, she snarled. "You think this will make me fear you? If you kill me today, another will come to take my place!"

Joseph held her over the oubliette for a long, long moment. He did not fear that she would fall, as he would not let her go. She tried to fight him, but could not. As he stared into her eyes, he came to an unfortunate realization. She was no longer fighting the monk's ring. He needed it gone from this house. Joseph nodded and reached into his pocket for his phone. As he dialed a number, he took Natalia to one of the other cells in the dungeon and shackled her to the wall. She screamed at him the entire time. By the time Anthony answered his phone, Natalia was locked up and Joseph was headed out of the dungeon.

"Joseph, how can I help you?"

"Do you remember the monk's ring?"

There was silence for a moment. "I think so."

"It needs to be removed from this house tonight."

"Why isn't Vincent asking about this?"

"There are things that transpired that I do not wish to speak of over the phone. I need it gone tonight."

There was a moment of silence again, then, "I'll be over as soon as I can. There is much to discuss if you want that gone."

"Thank you. I'll see you soon." Joseph hung up and went about securing the dungeon before exiting.

9

When Anthony arrived about two hours later, Vincent and Mierka were still occupied in Vincent's room. Joseph hoped they would stay there a while. He took Anthony to Vincent's study and turned off the recording devices as Anthony took a seat.

"I still don't understand why Vincent isn't present."

"Vincent is in the grips of his emotions and is more animal than thinking creature."

Anthony frowned and looked about to speak.

Joseph held up a hand to still the man's words. "Mierka is handling the situation. You know she's capable of it."

Anthony appraised Joseph for a moment then nodded. This was not the first time Mierka needed to help Vincent with his emotions. As he felt confident Vincent was in good hands, he let that part of the conversation go. "The problem isn't in removing the ring. It's what to do with it. I can't take it to my place. I have humans living on both sides of me."

Joseph looked frustrated. "I forgot about that. Can we throw it in the ocean?"

"It'll come back, being worn by a human. A diver or someone will hear it. It's how Vincent acquired it in the first place."

"I can't remember all the lore surrounding it. Can it be melted down?"

Anthony shifted in his seat as he remembered the lore. "It's steel, therefore in theory we can. The information I found on it did not indicate if melting it would truly destroy it."

"You didn't find passages stating it had spells on it?"

"The monk's soul was not bound to the ring by a spell, but by zeal and prayer. I've talked to a few mages. None were able to find spells."

"There are foundries in San Francisco." Joseph sounded as if expected

Anthony to remember this.

"It's about getting into the foundry, Joseph."

"We have many, many ways of taking care of this situation without humans knowing and interfering. You seem to forget this at times."

Anthony looked away and seemed annoyed. "There are many times I must forget my abilities to find the information I need." He took a slow deep breath to calm himself. "I will do as I must, but there are limits. If things become volatile, I will need Vincent's word to continue."

"Let's hope he's in control of his emotions before that happens." He paused as he hated to speak the next words to this man, but then did. "There is another issue. The ring calls to Natalia. She is not fighting it."

Anthony's eyes grew wider still, then narrowed. "I knew-"

"Stop. You don't know all, and I will not tell you all. She does not want this, despite her current actions."

He frowned. "I don't like being left in the dark."

"I am not authorized to offer you all the details."

Anthony narrowed his eyes and stared at Joseph with anger in his eyes. He felt he needed more information, but Joseph wasn't prone to offering more when he didn't feel like it. The issue at hand was whether or not he should take care of the ring, as it was affecting someone in the house. As he realized this, he let the anger go. "All right. I'll take care of it."

"I'll fetch the ring. Did a human drive you here?"

"Yes."

"I'll fetch Rebecca as well. Make sure your human driver is not near the car when I arrive."

Anthony nodded, but gave Joseph a quizzical look. "Where is Vincent?"

"In his room with Mierka."

He gave a short laugh. "I will never understand why you allow her to sleep with him, even if she does help him."

"Mierka does as she feels is best, and she returns to me every time." The smirk on his face stilled further questions and Joseph left the room.

He took the stairs at a leisurely pace, but his mind thought of the possible confrontation in the bedroom. If Vincent were awake, he might have to explain things. He pulled out his phone to text Mierka, but knew there was a chance she would not respond. In the sitting room, he paused for a moment to allow her to respond. When none came, he continued on his way, his phone in hand. It did not go off, but by the time he reached the tower bedroom, he knew what to say if the master were awake.

Joseph opened the door and looked surprised to see his woman sitting with her back against the headboard and Vincent stiff on the bed, the stake still in his heart.

"I thought you would have woken him by now."

"I woke him. He was beside himself with anger. I offered my blood, but he wanted my head."

"And staking him again will assuage that anger?"

"No, but if you allow me to feed off you, I may be able to calm him down with more blood."

"You play a risky game."

She smirked and shrugged. The conversation thus far had been calm as if the two lovers were discussing a trivial matter and not their boss staked and incapacitated. "I have played this game before. I know the risks." She looked Joseph up and down. "And you? What are you up to?"

"Anthony has agreed to take the ring and destroy it."

Her eyes opened wide. She looked to Vincent, then back to Joseph. "He doesn't want that."

"Natalia is under its spell. Our benefactor is currently not in his right mind. He doesn't have a say in this."

She gave a short laugh. "You play a dangerous game as well, love.

Joseph shrugged, went to the cabinets, and took the ring. "I refuse to allow this dangerous item to continue to try and entice that woman. She will not be the cause of our deaths." With the ring in hand, Joseph turned to look at Mierka. She had an odd look in her eyes. "Yes?"

She held his gaze. "Her death should be in our hands."

"It will be in his hands if all goes as they want."

There was a bit of silence, but the serious look did not leave Mierka's face, therefore Joseph stayed where he was and did not speak. Mierka licked her lips and looked away.

"And if something should happen to our fearless leader, would you allow her death to be in my hands?"

"That question can mean two things."

"I will kill her if she harms him, Joseph." She looked at Vincent as she caressed his cheek. "You know I love him almost as much as I love you. If she takes him away from us, nothing will stop my wrath." She looked back to Joseph. "But, if what I believe is true, and she does not harm him and we lose him to another force, I want to change her. Will you allow that?"

"I second both thoughts, Jacqueline."

They looked at each other for a moment before Mierka nodded. He only used her birth name on rare occasions and generally only for matters of import. She licked her lips.

"Some time ago, I told her she could come to me if he died before changing her."

He gave her an interesting smile. It was a smile she knew well.

She rolled her eyes. "Oh hush."

He smirked. "Be careful if you decide to pursue your thoughts."

She laughed. "He would love to see me with her."

"Perhaps."

It was her turn to smirk. "You would."

He licked his lips in answer.

Mierka laughed, then pointed to the deadly ring in his hand. "I have a few ring boxes in our room if you want to put that in something. Might be easier."

Joseph nodded. "Thank you. When Anthony has left, I will return to give you blood."

"Thank you." She continued to caress Vincent's cheek. "We will both need to tell him about Natalia's actions."

"Yes. We can do so upon my return."

She nodded and he turned and left. Within moments, he had retrieved the ring box from his room. He then headed to Anthony's car and handed the man the box.

Anthony stared at the box for a moment before he took it. He nodded to Joseph and headed to his car. Rebecca started it up and headed out. Soon enough, the lights from the car had faded into the night. Joseph nodded and headed back inside as he made a mental list of all the things he needed to do. First, he would feed, then he would give Mierka blood, then they would take care of Vincent. He did not look forward to waking his longtime friend.

Ω Ȣ

He woke with a roar, his teeth bared. "Twice in one night? Tell me now why I shouldn't take your life."

Vincent stood tall at the end of his bed, his hands at his side in fists. His voice was deadly calm, but his eyes flashed with anger. Mierka sat on the bed, and looked rather relaxed. The stake was still in her hand. Joseph stood to the side of the bed, and waited to see if he were needed.

Mierka brought the stake to her mouth and licked the blood that coated it. Vincent growled at her actions. She gave him a smirk. "You usually like when I lick the stake."

He growled. "Twice."

She handed the stake off to Joseph and looked at Vincent. "The first time was to stop you from killing Natalia. The second was to stop you from killing me. I will take my usual punishment."

"You do not dictate my actions." He spoke through clenched teeth.

"No, I don't. But you have set the precedence on this." She still spoke mildly and didn't look at all worried about her actions or his.

He bared his fangs and turned his anger on Joseph. "She skates on thin ice."

"She speaks the truth." Joseph's voice was also calm. Both had been around Vincent enough to understand if they stayed calm, he would as well. Or relatively so.

Both watched Vincent as he thought his thoughts. Finally, he calmed.

55

"Fine. But why did you do this?"

"Vincent, you're not yourself and neither is she. We're trying to understand what is going on with you."

Vincent turned from his long-time friends and presented them his back. His hands still formed fists. "It would perhaps be prudent for me to visit Lorraine."

Mierka moved off the bed and went to Vincent. She stood to his side and touched his arm gently. "Because?"

He turned and gazed intently at Mierka. "Because you are not enough. She may have a different type of treat that will help me."

Joseph and Mierka both relaxed. He sounded like he was in his right mind. This was phrase he used previously with them. Mierka nodded and turned to Joseph. He nodded as well and left the room. Vincent turned to Mierka fully.

"I have blood for you. After you feast upon me, there is more we need to discuss."

"I want release first." His hand went to her neck and squeezed lightly. "Distract me."

She gave him a wide grin and led him to the bed.

捲 捳

Natalia greeted Joseph with a glare. "Let me go."

"Where would you go if I did?"

When she looked away, he knew her mind was not her own.

"Fine. This ends now." He turned and headed out of the room as she started to scream at him.

"You bastard! Once I get out of here, you will see what I can do to you!"

She continued in this manner as he went to the airlock and partially left the dungeon. A human stood in the stairwell, a key in hand. The man handed the key off to Joseph and left after the vampire took the key. Joseph went to Natalia and unlocked the shackles. She immediately tried to fight him. He grabbed her around her neck and gave a slight squeeze as he slipped the key into his pocket. He lifted her about a foot off the ground and stared at her as her hands went around his wrist.

She bared her teeth. "Let me go."

"I told you once, that I listen to and protect Vincent. You betrayed him when you went off to kill Theodore, and we gave you a small lesson to remind you not to betray us again." Joseph reached out with his other hand and pinched her scar.

Natalia howled but didn't seem to understand what he was doing. Joseph continued his tirade.

"This time, you placed this house and the people in it in grave danger. Though you are not a Slayer, you are well trained. You have been trained by vampires and, though you may not realize it yet, are skilled enough to kill us all. You know our habits, you know our lives, you know our strengths and weaknesses." He reached out and placed his hand around her new pendant with a gentle hand.

Natalia's breath hitched and something changed in her look. Internally, Joseph felt relief. Externally, he showed no reaction. "He gave you rank, human. Rank. I saw your thoughts when he placed this around your neck. You did not think you deserved this. After your actions today, I have to concur."

During his speech, Joseph carried the human into the newly opened cell. He held her out over the oubliette, his arm outstretched. He stood still and gave her a cold, hard look.

"Do not struggle, Natalia. You are over a twenty-foot drop. If you struggle and cause me to let you go, you will drop to your death. The fall may not kill you, but the ghul in the oubliette will. As there is no way out, you will die. Do you wish to die today, human?"

He could see as she struggled with her own will. As he spoke, she stopped trying to claw his hand off her neck. Her hands held his wrist again, as if she didn't want to fall, as if she trusted that he would not let go. He watched as she continued to struggle.

Finally, Natalia shook her head carefully. "What do you want?"

"If I were to place you on the ground and let you walk away, where would you go?"

His voice was calm and stern. Her eyes closed tight, and her mouth opened and closed as she continued to struggle against her will. "I… I don't know!"

This time, her voice was loud and full of doubt. When she looked at him again, there were tears in her eyes. Joseph saw this as a good start, but it wasn't enough. He continued to treat her as if she were an enemy.

"Vincent believes you to be an asset to this house: our strength. He believes you do well by us and wished to show you what he thinks of you by giving you rank." He finally took his hand away from the pendant. "Though I believe your actions were not entirely your own doing, it is still the most foolish thing you could possibly have done. The ring that called to you was made by the same monks that you believe created the sword. They call to each other. The ring knows the sword exists. It wants a master that is able and willing to wield them both. If your will was any weaker, this house would be dead, and you would be standing victoriously over our ashes." He paused to watch the emotions in her eyes. "Do you wish to stand victoriously over our ashes, Natalia Mirela Liliana Dveski, Protector of House LeGris?"

Tears streaming down her face, Natalia violently shook her head.

"I didn't think so, but, as you did betray Vincent," he shrugged and let

Natalia go.

Eyes wide, Natalia clawed Joseph's arm, and tried to keep from falling. Joseph twisted his arm, and she no longer held on to him. A scream ripped through her throat as she fell. The scream cut short when her back hit the wall. Natalia looked around, and realized she was not in the oubliette. She sat against the wall as Joseph towered over her.

"Where were you trying to go?"

Her entire body sagged, and a sob escaped her throat. "I was…" her body sagged again, but with relief, "I was trying to get to the ring." She pulled her legs closer to her body and tried to make herself tiny. "Oh God, I was trying to get to the ring."

He closed his eyes in relief, walked to Natalia, and picked her up in his arms. She didn't struggle, but wrapped her arms around his neck. He carried her to the main room in the dungeon. He placed her on her feet and made sure she continued to stand.

"Will you stay right here until I lock the other room?"

Natalia nodded. Her body showed she felt defeated. Joseph nodded as well, then went to close the door to the oubliette. He also closed the door to the private cell and to the equipment room. He returned to the main room and saw Natalia had not moved an inch. He nodded and went to stand before her.

When she met his gaze, he gave her more to think about. "You are greatly valued in this house Natalia and are often allowed to disobey Vincent. I am sure that he enjoys some things that occur when you disobey him, but that ring on your finger would have been our death. Had you somehow been able to get through me, Vincent would have killed you."

She nodded carefully as tears still streamed down her face.

"Is your mind fully your own?"

"I believe so. I need sleep and food."

"Vincent isn't himself. It may be best to have you stay down here."

"Is that really the best idea?"

"You can't stay in your room. He needs time, as do you."

She frowned softly and thought her thoughts for a moment. "Why keep us apart?"

"He is dangerous right now."

"To me or to humans in general?"

"To you."

"How do you know this?"

"This isn't the first time he's been like this, Natalia."

"Then let me leave the house. Let me go to a hotel room. I'll find one myself, use an alias."

His eyes narrowed. "Why?"

"I need rest and food. This is not a place for rest. Not for a human."

Joseph opened his mouth to speak, then closed it with a snap. She was right. The dungeon was not a place to heal and rest. "Are you certain you are under your own control?"

She nodded sadly. "I can remember all I said and did. I remember calling you Hellspawn. At the time, I wanted you dead." She gave him a familiar look as she licked her lips. "I don't want to kill you; I know how you are in bed."

He grinned as her words echoed her true self. He gave a small bow. "I will allow you to leave. Do you wish an escort?"

"I can't take Charlie, can I?"

"It's too close to the full moon."

She almost asked for Charlie or Rebecca anyway, but shook her head. "Another vampire or a human, then?"

Joseph shook his head. "It may be best not to take a vampire or anyone from this household."

"Because you don't want Vincent to think someone else betrayed him."

"True."

"Then why ask if I want an escort?"

"I would assign someone if you felt it was better."

Something clicked in her mind. "And the longer we take, the more you can assess me."

"Yes."

She sighed. "Are you satisfied?"

"Yes."

"I'll go alone. I have to get my keys and money from the bedroom."

"I will go with you."

"Thank you. I'm going to take my phone, but buy a prepaid one along the way. Once I get the prepaid one, I'll send you a text with its number and turn off my phone so I can't be tracked."

"Good plan."

She nodded, gave Joseph another defeated look, and closed her eyes. She took a few deep breaths, then stood tall and gave him a determined look. "All right. I'm ready."

Joseph nodded and led the way out of the dungeon.

10

Vincent opened his eyes and listened to the sounds of the room. When silence greeted him, he turned his head left then right. Mierka still slept to his right, her back to him. His eyes narrowed. Though she woke him earlier to talk, he was still angry that she staked him. His eyes narrowed further: twice. He elongated his fangs and growled. She heard the growl, stretched, then took her time to turn to him. The lazy smile on her face spoke volumes.

Mierka reached out and placed her hand on his chest. "And how are you this evening?"

He batted her hand away. She smirked and he growled again.

"Are you angry with me?"

"Twice."

She rolled her eyes then moved onto her back. "We went over this. There is precedence."

He growled and moved on top of her in the blink of an eye. His legs straddled her waist and his hands rested next to her shoulders. His face hovered no more than an inch or two above hers. He bared his fangs again growled his utter displeasure at the situation and her detachment.

Mierka smirked. "What will you do? Do you wish to fight me? Will that make you feel better?" She ran her hand down his bare chest. "Fighting you is always such a pleasure."

He bellowed and threw himself off the bed. Though Mierka was smaller and not as strong as he, when they fought, she won. As a small woman, she had learned to fight dirty. When she fought Vincent, she seduced him to distract him and get close. She then would often kick or grab his genitals. She also learned a few grappling techniques to be able to grab onto the person she fought, and sucked their blood. It weakened her opponent and strengthened her. He wanted to fight but he wanted a fair fight. He growled.

"Get out. Get me blood and get me Natalia. I wish to," he gnashed his teeth, "speak with her."

Mierka smirked, stretched leisurely, then left the bed. She grabbed her clothes and dressed slowly as she crossed the room and left. Vincent growled at her. After a moment, he decided to leave as well. He didn't feel like waiting for anyone in this room. On his way through his bedroom, he grabbed a robe and tied it tightly around his midsection. Angry, hungry, and spoiling for a fight, he went to his sitting room and waited for a human to show up. A few minutes later, Joseph entered with two humans.

Vincent nodded and looked beyond the humans to the closed door. "Where is Natalia?"

"I'll answer after you feed. Do you need to drink from me?"

"That would probably be best."

Joseph nodded, rolled up his sleeve and bared his arm to Vincent, who immediately bit into his arm. Vincent drank until Joseph indicated he needed to stop. When the bite wound was closed, Joseph looked to Vincent. His master had taken a good deal of blood, but it was nothing he couldn't replenish.

"Do you need more?"

Vincent felt a hunger worming its way through his mind, but he knew he had enough blood. Anger continued to consume him. His animal instincts had not been satiated by Mierka's presence in his bed. "I need Natalia."

"Allow me to feed and then we will talk."

"No. Fetch me my woman."

Joseph stared at Vincent and wondered if his friend had taken more blood than usual for a reason. No matter, he could still handle the younger vampire. He turned to the humans. "Leave us. You won't be needed for the moment."

The men nodded, turned, and left the room.

Joseph looked to Vincent. "She left."

Fear clouded his eyes for a brief moment, then left. He hid his emotions as he started to pace the room. "What do you mean, 'left'?"

"I felt it best if she wasn't here when you woke. I wasn't sure what state you would be in."

Vincent stopped pacing, stared at Joseph, and felt the anger blossom again. He gnashed his teeth but kept his mouth closed to hide the action. "I want her here. She betrayed me and needs to be punished."

"Oh? How did she betray you?"

"She found the room and went into it against my will."

"Her mind was not her own."

He stilled his movements, his hand at his side. His hands were balled tightly into fists. His voice was deadly calm. "That woman has told me time and time again she cannot be controlled. Anything that happened is her fault. Get her back here now."

"You need time to think. I will leave you to it." Joseph started to walk to the door.

"If you leave here without telling me where she is…"

Joseph stopped and turned to look at Vincent. "You'll what? You stopped that sentence as you know your anger is unfounded. There is more here than you understand and a part of you knows that. Allow yourself time to calm. If you need time to visit Lorraine, then do so. You'll talk to Natalia when you are calmed."

With that, Joseph walked out of the room. Vincent bellowed his displeasure, but did not follow. A part of him knew he was in fact, not fully in control. He did not want to harm Natalia irrevocably. He growled then went to his master bedroom to look for his phone. With any luck, Lorraine would be able to help him.

❧ ❧

Vincent waited impatiently for the prey to come closer. The man jogged along the path oblivious of any dangers. He wore headphones and looked to be lost in the motion of running. During the day, this path was well used by joggers, bicyclists, and walkers. As it was two in the morning, it was empty of people. The large vampire was surprised there was anyone here. Lorraine informed him this path was rarely used this early in the morning, and generally only by one or two people. Vincent kept himself hidden as he thought of his next steps.

They were in a Nature Preserve. Technically, the park was closed. Technically, neither he nor the man should be here. Lorraine looked for these types of things, to find humans they could use for sport, if it were needed. His sire assured him it was safe. The man lived nearby and snuck into the park every night after work. He was a supervisor at a nearby call center. If he went missing, humans would look for him; Slayers would not.

All this information ran through the large vampire's head as the man came closer. Satisfied with the situation, Vincent used his full speed and ran at the human. The man didn't even notice. When Vincent slammed into him hard, the man screamed, but it was cut short. Vincent banged the human against a nearby tree which knocked the air out his lungs. As the man gulped for breath, Vincent laid his hand over the man's mouth. The man tried to scream again, but Vincent grinned, elongated his fangs, and hissed.

The man screamed through Vincent's hand, but the sound didn't carry. In seconds, Vincent had his mouth wrapped around the man's neck, his teeth buried deep in the human's flesh. He ripped open the jugular and

62

drank the coppery liquid that bled free. The man didn't have time to struggle before all his blood was gone. Vincent pulled back from the corpse and dropped it to the ground.

"Did that satisfy you?" Lorraine's voice called softly from the shadows.

Vincent turned and watched as she slipped out of the trees. She was dressed in a white see through negligée. He growled and was on her before she could say another word. Lorraine caught him in her arms and held on tight as he thrust her up against a tree. He growled and showed off bloody teeth.

"I have people here to clean up, but we must return to my home."

Vincent licked his lips and pulled away. "Will you satisfy me further there?"

"Of course."

"Then let's return."

He started to walk away as Lorraine turned to the people nearby. When she nodded, they went for the human's body. It and all traces of their presence would be erased from the park.

⊗ ⊗

Vincent lay in Lorraine's bed, on top of the covers, a euphoric smile on his face. After the nearly unsatisfying hunt, Lorraine had spent the better part of the day pleasuring him. She had also allowed him to let his anger and hunger show. She was able to take his appetites. Mierka was as well, but Lorraine knew how to control him better. She had him wrapped around her finger. He grinned. He liked when women controlled him.

The bed shifted slightly, and Lorraine came into his view. "Good evening. Feeling better?"

He gave a pleased growl and reached up to take her in his arms.

"Really?" She pulled away. "You call, demand my assistance, take advantage of me in more ways than one and offer no explanation?"

His arms fell to his side. "Haven't I?"

"No, you haven't. Once you were on your way, I received a call from Joseph. He said you needed release. Care to inform me as to what happened?"

He growled low, but decided to sum up the issues with one sentence. "Sometimes a human lover is not enough."

She hid her smile badly. "Really? Could have fooled me."

Vincent threw back the covers and sat up. Lorraine was fully dressed. He decided to change the subject. "I'm surprised to find myself well satisfied. You haven't taken my blood yet."

She glared at him as he tried to avoid the subject at hand. "I didn't think it was a good idea. Are you in your own mind? Is your hunger under control?"

Without pausing, he answered, "Yes."

63

She watched as he looked for his clothing and started to dress. "Are you certain? Perhaps take a moment to think about your answer and how you feel?"

He growled again. "I'm fine."

"Are you simply angry with me for asking?"

"Yes."

She watched as he pulled on his clothing and knew he wasn't completely fine. "Vincent!"

He stopped at the sound of his name. There was anger and authority there. He turned to regard his sire. "Yes, mistress?"

"Where are you going?"

"As I feel better, I am returning home to be with Natalia."

"If you lie to yourself and leave without being fully satiated, you will harm her."

He stared his sire down for a good minute. When she did not look away, he did instead. "I'm fine."

"And if I don't let you leave?"

"Why do you care, anyway? You don't seem to want me to be with her." He pulled on his suit jacket but stopped when he felt her hand on his arm. He turned and regarded the small woman. "What is it?"

"I care as I know how you would react if you killed her. We've known each other a long time, Vincent. Stop for a moment and make certain you're fine."

Annoyed, Vincent nevertheless stopped and took a breath. He felt as his lungs took in air, then released it. When he did not immediately feel anger or any residual animal hunger, he turned to Lorraine. "I'm fine."

She believed him, to a degree. When he was in this state, he often overlooked how he felt until it was too late. He had release some of his frustrations though, therefore she nodded. "Fine, but do you really want to leave yet?"

"I have things to take care of at home."

She nodded. "Would you like to take a few minutes to freshen up before your flight?"

"I wish to leave."

Lorraine didn't like the short answers, but knew she could do nothing about it. She nodded. "Let me know if there is anything more you need."

Vincent nodded, gathered the rest of his clothes, and left the room. Lorraine shook her head, then went to her office to call Joseph. She felt it best to inform the man of Vincent's state of mind.

11

"Hello?" Natalia paced the small room as she answered the prepaid phone.

"He's returning tonight and would like to see you." Joseph's stoic voice revealed nothing.

"How is he?"

"He isn't listening to either Mierka or myself. He still thinks you betrayed him by going into his room."

She stopped and looked out the window. There was a motel parking lot beyond the glass and not much else. "Didn't I?"

"Think of this carefully: is this really something you would have done on any other occasion? Has there been an occasion where you wondered if there was a hidden room?"

"Joseph, I don't know. It's never come up."

"Why hasn't it?"

She paused. "What?"

"In all the years you've lived in this house, why have you never wondered about a hidden room? You've seen that hallway thousands of times. Why did you never, until this instance, feel the need to question its lack of doors?"

Natalia turned and went to the bed. She sat down in silence for a moment. The moment grew longer, and Joseph's voice came through.

"Are you still thinking?"

"Yes."

"Continue to think on it. Come home when you have an answer. He'll be here before sunup."

The phone went dead in her hand. Natalia stared at the phone for a moment, then allowed the screen to go black. She sighed in contemplation then shook her head and began to get ready for the night. She would think on it on her way home. The motel was near Redding, California. She had plenty of time to drive home, but as she had a lot of thinking to do, she needed to give herself extra time. Though Joseph suggested she find an answer first, she wanted to be home when Vincent arrived. Despite all that had transpired, and all that might transpire, she wanted to be with the vampire. She could only hope he would still want her there as well.

CB &D

Mierka greeted her in the garage. "Hello."

"For some reason, I almost expected Joseph." She gave Mierka a weary smile as she closed the car door.

"Am I a good stand in?" There was a smirk on the woman's face.

Natalia laughed nervously as she rounded the car. "Yes, but he was keeping me up to date during all this."

"I was taking care of Vincent. As he is not here yet, I choose to be where you are."

"Thank you." She stood next to Mierka now. "When will he be back?"

"Couple more hours. Did you find an answer to Joseph's question?"

"No, but this is home."

Mierka nodded and pointed the way to the stairs. "You still sound off."

"I left here to find a safe place to sleep. Though I did sleep, it was fitful."

They were in front of the door to the stairs. Mierka placed her hand on Natalia's arm. "Are you sure you should be here? You'll need your wits about you with Vincent."

Natalia looked down as she folded her arms close to her torso. She rubbed her upper arms as if nervous. "This entire situation has me feeling out of sorts. Why did I go into that room, Mierka? Why did I look for it? I was always told I couldn't be possessed, but Vincent was able to control me, as was that ring."

"You feel as if your entire existence hangs by a thread?"

Natalia nodded.

"I've felt that way many times in my life, until I was turned. After I was turned, I threw all my doubt away and did as I pleased."

Natalia laughed. "Of course, you did."

Mierka grinned. "Come. Let's find a place where we can talk until Vincent arrives. Perhaps I can help you find the answers?"

"Thank you, Mierka."

Mierka nodded and led the way upstairs to the library.

CB &D

Joseph met Vincent at the front door when he arrived home. He even opened the limousine door for his boss. Vincent's first words were stated briskly.

66

"Is Natalia here?"

"Yes, but I wish to talk to you first."

"That isn't necessary. Did you call Anthony like I asked?" He pushed past Joseph and headed to the house.

"Yes." Joseph slammed the car door and moved at his full speed to beat Vincent to the door. He placed himself in Vincent's way in front of the entrance.

"Good." Vincent stared Joseph down.

"Sir, there is a lot you are missing from the past few days." Joseph spoke with a calm voice.

"He's here to determine if that is true. Natalia betrayed me. He wants to prove her a betrayer. He now has the opportunity. Step aside."

As he moved out of the way and into the house, Joseph tried again. "Sir, there may be details you don't want him to know."

"I am done with secrets. Fetch Natalia, now."

"Really? Fetch? As if I'm a plaything? Or a bone?"

Her voice stopped him dead in his tracks. She stood to the left of the staircase, her hand on the railing. She wore a flowing blue top, with slacks and sensible shoes. He narrowed his eyes. He wanted her out of those clothes and in his bed. Vincent growled and turned his attention to Joseph. "Where is Anthony?"

"Here, Vincent." His voice came from the right, near Vincent's study. The man looked troubled but relaxed.

Vincent looked back and forth between the two, then growled at Natalia again. "You betrayed me." His anger, which he thought satiated, came back ten-fold. "Tell me why I shouldn't strip you of your rank and toss you into the oubliette."

Mierka appeared in front of Natalia out of nowhere. "You do and you'll have to deal with more than you bargained for. Her actions were not her own."

Vincent bared his teeth and growled at Mierka as his hands formed fists. Joseph moved to stand between Mierka and Vincent. Vincent growled louder and elongated his fangs.

"I will fight both of you! Step aside and let her speak!"

"You wouldn't listen to us, which leads me to believe you would not listen to her either."

Anthony watched from the sidelines as Mierka, and Joseph protected Natalia. He did not like this in the least. He had seen it before a few days ago. It didn't sit well then and it didn't sit well now. But, as Vincent's entire demeanor changed to one of deadly calm, Anthony became terrified for the human. Vincent's anger showed itself in different stages. The first was calm, then demonstrative, then back to calm. The second calm was deadly. In those moments of calm, he pretended to himself that he thought of his actions. He did not. He merely acted, and killed indiscriminately.

All this happened in a second. Anthony knew Vincent well. As Vincent's jaw twitched to reveal he was about to move, Anthony shouted.

"Enough!" Those in the foyer looked to Anthony. Anthony looked to Vincent. "I was asked here to reveal a betrayer. I mean to complete my task." He looked at Natalia. "I will start with your story. Please come with me. I believe Vincent's study will do for an interrogation room."

"Natalia!" Vincent's voice echoed throughout the house, his anger palpable.

Natalia stopped her forward motion toward Anthony, and she looked at Vincent. "Yes?"

"No more secrets. Tell him all."

Her mouth dropped open. "All?"

Anthony felt chills run down his spine. He did not like this conversation, but wasn't sure why.

Vincent looked to Anthony, then to Natalia. "All."

She nodded, stood taller, and walked with confidence into Vincent's study. Anthony spared Vincent one last look before he followed Natalia into the study and closed the door. Sequestered in the comfortable room, the two looked each other up and down. Anthony placed his back against the door and watched as Natalia moved to the window. She moved the curtain out of the way and stared into the darkness.

"I'm here to listen." He said after a few moments of silence.

"Do you remember how we met?"

He frowned. "Not particularly."

"We met at The Red Thread. I was there as a distraction as Slayers cased the club."

"I feel as if you're trying to distract me."

She shook her head. "No, this is part of the last few days." She turned to regard him as she leaned against the wall by the window. She crossed her arms. "I found my way into the private area. I wanted information on Vincent and knew he spent his time there while in the club. I spoke to many people, including you."

As she spoke as he shook his head. "You weren't that memorable."

She gave a short, almost inaudible laugh. "I hypnotized you."

He stared at her as the news sank into his thoughts. He shook his head once, and tried to continue the conversation. "What does that have to do with anything?"

"Do you believe me?"

"I'm not sure I do."

Natalia nodded and stood taller as she continued her tale. "I did it a few times after coming here. Vincent knew about it each time. It wouldn't surprise me to find out he sent you to me that night to see if I could hypnotize you."

Anthony revealed nothing as he stared at her.

She stared at him intently. "You're taking this well."

"I'm leaving that alone for later consideration. There's more here than this story."

Natalia nodded then sighed. "After Wayne betrayed me, and I expressed my desire to have your blood, Vincent told me I couldn't, as we had created your distrust of me."

Anthony stopped himself from nodding in agreement. That sounded like something Vincent would say, if any of this were true.

When he still didn't say anything, Natalia continued. "I didn't sleep well that night, if at all. Vincent kept me up all night. We also discussed you, and knew I had to release you of any lingering hypnosis. We both think it's coloring your judgement of me."

He gave a short, harsh laugh. She could tell he didn't believe any of what she said, but as the story wasn't done, she continued.

"That morning, the morning he gave me rank," her hand went to her pendant, "I hypnotized you. Your will is much stronger now and I had a hard time with it."

His eyes went wide. That morning now made sense.

"Do you believe me now?"

"That has yet to be determined. Also, I'm still not certain this has anything to do with why you were in his room."

"My mind was already in shambles when I drank his blood. He controlled me with his blood, Anthony. You saw how we were that day."

"Fine. Go on."

She paused for a bit longer. "There is a way I can prove to you I hypnotized you."

"Oh?"

"I can release all your memories."

"Why haven't you done that yet?"

She looked away. "When I was young my mother hid some memories she didn't want me to have. When she died, the memories came back." Natalia looked up. Her eyes showed her sheer pain. "They came when I was trying to escape from the vampire who killed my mother. They interfered with that escape, and later, I had to slowly work through the double memories until I understood what really happened. It's not pleasant if you're not prepared for it."

He crossed his arms and looked at her. "Do it."

Natalia looked him up and down, saw his posture and understood he didn't believe her in the least. A smug little smile came to her features as she spoke the release word she programmed into his mind all those years ago.

12

Anthony grunted and fell to his knees as she spoke in Romanian. He shook and took deep breaths as memories he didn't remember slammed through his mind. He felt a hand on his shoulder and looked up. Natalia no longer had the smug look on her face. She looked remorseful. He drew back in surprise.

"I'm sorry. Think of each memory in turn. It helps. The newest one first. The one from a few days ago."

With gritted teeth, he closed his eyes and thought of the night she gained rank. He remembered talking with Vincent, remembered when Natalia came into the study and went to stand behind the desk. The memory seemed to split in two at that point. One memory was of him and Vincent speaking, the other was of Natalia twirling her necklace and then talking as if he were her puppet.

His eyes grew wide as he continued to see the different memories. There weren't that many, but there were enough. Antony growled as anger consumed him, but dissipated just as quickly. Anger would do him no good. He pushed all the memories aside, calmed himself and stood. He regarded Natalia with mild annoyance.

"Fine. You controlled me. Then what?"

She stood, surprise on her face. "You're not angry?"

"My feelings on this matter little. We're here to find out if you betrayed Vincent or not."

Natalia frowned. "What did you do when you were human?"

He gave a short harsh laugh. "That matters little, as I haven't been human in a long time."

"I suppose you're right." Natalia took a deep breath and continued her tale. "My will was destroyed by everything that happened. Then I drank his blood." She closed her eyes. "I was his to control. Joseph removed Vincent's control of me by seducing me. Once my mind was my own again, we slept together. He took some of my blood as well and I, again, didn't sleep much. When I did wake, I went looking for Vincent and Mierka. That's when I understood there had to be a secret room. I eventually found it."

His eyes narrowed. Joseph recounted most of the events of the past few days. Though Anthony knew Natalia found the secret room, it now struck him as odd that she didn't think of the secret room until now. "That's when you realized there was a secret room?"

"Yes."

"I knew there had to be something off when I first saw the hallway upstairs and went into rooms for the first time. How did you not know there was something going on?"

"I didn't think about it."

He gave her a quizzical look and pursued the line of questioning. "How could you not? The hallway is rather long. There are no doors, even though everywhere else upstairs, there are doors at regular intervals. Most people wonder about it."

"I don't know."

Anthony moved a bit closer when he saw herself questioning her actions. "But how could you not wonder? You're an inquisitive human, bent on knowing every detail of the man you sleep with. How did you not see?"

"I don't know!" She screamed. Her hands hid her face for a minute. She lowered her hands and walked to the nearest chair and collapsed in it. "I didn't think about it, all right? I don't even know how many rooms there are upstairs. Unless Vincent and I have slept in a room, I don't think about it."

"That's a bit shallow."

Natalia gave him a piercing look. "And?"

He looked at her for a moment in silence and then laughed. It was not pleasant, and did not endear him to her. As he shook his head, he went to the liquor cabinet and poured two glasses of brandy. He brought one to Natalia and sat in the chair near her.

Anthony raised his glass. She did as well, with a frown on her face. He clicked his glass to hers. "If nothing else, I was able to wipe that dammed high and mighty look off your face. Cheers."

She gave him an incredulous look then laughed humorlessly. When she calmed, she took a slow sip of the fine liquor. It felt good in her stomach. "You're an asshole."

"Oh yes, because you're a saint."

Natalia glared at Anthony as she took another sip.

"Why did you go looking for the room? Joseph told me he asked you to think about it."

She opened her mouth to say she didn't know, but stopped and thought about it carefully. She sighed as she finally admitted the truth to herself. She spoke softly. "I felt something pulling at my mind. When I found the room, when I stepped into it, I realized it was the room I had dreamt of. The room where I become a vampire. That distracted me, and I went to the deck to see the view. Joseph showed up and coaxed me out." She gazed into her glass. "When Joseph woke me the next night, it was still there, but I was able to ignore it until Vincent and I argued. That's when I went looking for the ring."

"What happened when you found the ring?" He took a sip of brandy as he stared at her.

Natalia looked at the wall. "I saw it and wanted nothing more than to put that thing on my finger. As I reached for it, something inside me screamed. I did everything I could to stop myself from taking it." She looked to Anthony. "The rest is fuzzy, but I woke in the dungeon. Joseph was holding me over the oubliette."

Anthony gazed at her dispassionately. "How fuzzy?"

"Flashes. I called Joseph a miserable Hellspawn." She rolled her eyes. "Which I'm sure feeds into your thoughts that I'm here to kill you all."

"Well, aren't you?"

"To what end? And if I wanted everyone dead, don't you think I would have tried that by now?"

He opened his mouth to argue, but stopped and thought about her statement. After a moment, he placed the glass on the desk in front of him, stood, and started to pace.

"You never thought of that did you?" Her voice was decidedly smug.

He glared at her, but then let his emotions go and shook his head. "No, I didn't."

Natalia shook her head. "Good. Now that you have more to think about, perhaps you'll change your mind about me."

"That remains to be seen. What else do you remember?"

"Does it really matter? You have the information you need to decide, don't you? I wasn't in my right mind. That ring took me over. Do you really believe I betrayed Vincent?"

He stopped pacing and stood quietly for a moment, then looked her way. "I will only tell Vincent my decision."

"As if he's not watching from the security room."

Anthony shook his head. "I will only tell Vincent."

Understanding descended upon her and she nodded. Natalia finished the brandy, stood, and placed the glass on the desk. "That sounds like I can leave then."

"Yes."

"Good."

Without another word, she left the room. He went to the door and watched as she walked upstairs. A moment later, Vincent appeared from around the corner, from the direction of the security room. The men nodded to each other as Vincent went to sit behind his desk. Anthony closed the door then took his seat again. He picked up his glass of brandy and took a sip.

"Well?"

"You're a bastard." He looked Vincent in the eyes as he stated the fact.

"You knew that already."

"You let..." his voice trailed off as a memory consumed him. His eyes opened wide, and his mouth dropped open. "She hypnotized Edwin."

"Perhaps." The look in his eyes indicated he would say no more on the subject. "Why are you more affected by that than the fact that she was able to hypnotize you?"

Anthony regarded Vincent, a slight frown on his face. Vincent's stoic expression now revealed nothing. "What good does anger ever do me? It clouds my judgement and makes it impossible for me to do my job. Also, I've known you a long time, Vincent. It doesn't really surprise me that you allowed this to happen."

"You allowed her to hypnotize you."

Anthony regarded Vincent mildly and kept his voice calm. "And you sat by and let it happen. She gave me my memories back. I heard you laughing in most of those memories. In the end, you were more concerned about her safety than mine. As I stated, you are a bastard."

Vincent stared intently at Anthony for a moment. "What is your verdict on Natalia? Did she betray me?"

"You heard the same thing I did, Vincent. I find the information and you pass judgement. It's been this way since we first met."

Vincent took a deep breath and let it out slowly. It was done so quietly, Anthony heard nothing, but saw the action. "What did you do with the ring?"

"As it was calling to her, I took it to a foundry and threw it into a furnace."

Vincent raised an eyebrow. "That explanation sounds far simpler than I would imagine it would be."

"Not really. Rebecca drove me home, held onto the ring as I went inside the house. I drank more than I needed, and Rebecca drove me close to the foundry. She kept it in the car as I used my abilities run reconnaissance. Once I knew where to throw the ring, I ran back to the car for the ring. I then used my abilities again to throw the box and ring into an open furnace."

Vincent stared at Anthony for a long time before he spoke again. "Did the ring call to anyone as it melted?"

"There has been no news of anyone throwing themselves into the furnace."

"How do you know it didn't spread the monk's will to all the metal in the furnace?"

"That will be fairly easy to find out, Vincent." He stated this as if he spoke to an infant.

Vincent narrowed his eyes. "I don't appreciate your attitude."

"It was not a good question, and you know it. We know that destroying artifacts breaks them and does not spread their magic."

Vincent continued to glare at Anthony.

Anthony glanced to his side as both men heard the buzz of an alarm. He looked back to his boss. "I have a meeting soon."

"Someone more important?"

"The one who waits to return."

"Is he well?" Vincent nearly whispered.

"He doesn't like what he has to do but knows following Edwin's word is important."

"Perhaps it's time to start leaking information through him."

Anthony nodded. "I'll see what I can do." He looked to Vincent for a long time. Finally, Anthony asked, "What have you decided about Natalia?"

Vincent took another deep breath and let out a sigh. He then reached into his pocket and pulled out his remote. He turned off the cameras and looked to Anthony. "I need you to continue being suspicious of her."

His face exploded in confusion. "Why?"

"I don't want to worry about her motivations."

Anthony frowned but slowly, realization dawned on his face. Before he could speak, Vincent raised a hand to silence him.

"Keep your thoughts to yourself. Continue to monitor her actions."

Anthony nodded. "Are we done then?"

"Yes."

Vincent stood, as did Anthony. They shook hands, then Anthony left the room and the house. Vincent sat back down in his chair and stared towards the window as he thought of Natalia and the past few days. He replayed all the information Anthony found out a few times before he reached for the intercom. He buzzed the security room.

"Yes?"

"Send Joseph in here." He clicked off the intercom and settled back in his chair.

A moment later, Joseph walked in. He closed the door and went to stand behind the chairs.

"Tell me."

A slight smirk graced his lips. "You wish me to tell you all that I tried to tell you previously?"

Vincent glared at his longtime friend. Joseph nodded and proceeded to tell Vincent all that transpired in the past few days. At the end, Vincent still sat back in his chair, a pensive look on his face.

"She did not set out to betray you. She was controlled by a powerful item. One we have seen take over others previously. It took the ring a long time to find her. To avoid future issues, I removed certain other items and placed them into Anthony's holdings."

Vincent nodded. His hand was near his mouth which helped to hide his reactions.

"Are you satisfied?"

Before he could answer, the intercom buzzed. He narrowed his eyes and reached for the answer button. "This is not good timing."

"Lilly is back with her new apprentice."

Vincent looked to Joseph. "Send her to me."

When the intercom clicked off, Joseph went to the door and opened it. Once the ladies were in the room, Joseph closed the door and stood out of the way.

"Lilly."

"Good evening, Vincent. This is Diana. Diana, this is Vincent LeGris. He's our benefactor."

Vincent looked the new healer up and down then let his eyes move back to Lilly. "She's young."

Lilly nodded. "Though she is young, she knows the arts well. She comes from a family of healers and has been studying the arts from birth. She is worthy of Natalia. Is she awake? I would like the ladies to meet."

"She's in our bedroom. You may leave."

Lilly nodded and left with Diana. Once they were gone, Joseph poured two glasses of brandy and handed Vincent one. He placed his on the other side of the desk, then picked up the two glasses left behind by Natalia and Anthony and set them in the minibar. Someone else would clean those later.

Once all was set, he sat in a chair and regarded his boss. "Well?"

"I need more time to think."

"Do you need blood?"

Vincent nodded. Joseph took a sip of brandy, then got up and left the room.

13

Vincent sat at his desk; chair turned to the side. A human stood near him with their arm held out. Vincent finished his drink, pulled away from the human's arm and nodded. The human placed gauze on her arm and walked out of the room. The vampire turned to Joseph, who leaned against the window, his glass of brandy in his hand.

"Did you make a decision yet, sir?"

"I was thinking of something else."

"Oh?"

"I controlled her with my blood."

"Yes."

"Do you think she could be controlled by anyone else's blood?"

"Mine or Mierka's, possibly. Anthony's? Probably not. Edwin's, never. Yours? Possibly all the time."

"What is it that would determine her susceptibility?"

"Whether or not she trusts the vampire. Perhaps we should test the theory if she is willing?"

"If she is willing."

Joseph held back the smile. He understood by Vincent's answer that the head vampire had made a decision concerning Natalia. "Who?"

"You, Mierka, Anthony, myself. When she's up to it. Maybe two or three weeks from now."

"Do you think it's wise to use Anthony?"

"We need to use someone we trust whom she wouldn't want to possess her."

"As you wish."

Vincent stared at his bodyguard, another subject rising to the surface. "I hear the smirk in your voice."

"You've decided in Natalia's favor for all this."

Vincent leaned back in chair and thought about Joseph's statement for a moment or two before nodding. "I suppose I have."

"It's the right course of action, sir. She wasn't to blame. She sits in the bedroom, on the bed she shares with you, a pensive, almost lost look in her eyes. She feels remorse for her actions."

Vincent stayed silent for a moment. The look in his eyes changed and he gave Joseph a dark look. "Did she give you permission?"

Joseph nodded slowly. It amused him that Vincent changed the subject, but the smile on his lips was there for different reasons.

Vincent did not like that smile. "Share the joke."

"It was not my intention to sleep with her, but while trying to break your hold, I saw that my touch might work. I used it, freed her and she responded in kind. I did nothing she didn't ask for."

Vincent drummed his fingers on his desk and narrowed his eyes at the look on his friend's face. "It's obvious you enjoyed yourself with Natalia last night. Don't let it happen again while she's mine."

"You enjoy Mierka when you will." Joseph's voice was pleasant, with just a tinge of irony.

Vincent's fingers drummed quicker, annoyed at the truth in Joseph's simple words, and at his own jealousy. His thoughts stopped as he understood he had come to a conclusion regarding Natalia. He looked away from Joseph, toward the door, then looked back. He stood.

"We're done."

Vincent left the room as Joseph nodded. The vampire headed up the stairs quickly but stopped at the sitting room door. He composed himself and walked in slowly. He continued on to his bedroom and found Natalia. She stood at the window, her back to the door. Vincent leaned against the doorframe and wondered at his woman's thoughts. She hadn't heard him and therefore stayed at the window, the curtain slightly open.

"Natalia."

She drew in a deep breath and turned at the sound of his voice. He frowned slightly at the look on her face. She did, in fact, look remorseful. "Hello."

He moved a few steps into the room, closed the door and continued closer to her. Natalia watched his movements, and tried to read his expression. Her own thoughts crowded in, and she decided to wait for his words rather than try and decipher his mood.

Vincent's movements took him to the bed, to lean against a post. "I have made a decision regarding all this. Have you?"

"I have options?" She sounded off and he did not like it.

"There are always options. Tell me, in your words, what happened."

"I thought that was for Anthony to decipher?"

"He did. But I want to hear it in your words, with your voice."

She shook her head and looked away as her entire body seemed to sag from exhaustion. Natalia leaned against the wall and crossed her arms. "I've lived through this enough. I don't want to relive it again."

She gasped as he was suddenly before her. His hand was on her chin, guiding her face to look into her eyes. "Tell me."

"If you hadn't stopped me in time…"

He inhaled sharply at the devastated look in her eyes. His eyes narrowed a touch as he caressed her cheek. He had never seen her this distraught. Vincent's own expression grew soft as he drew her into his arms. He kissed his woman and held her tightly to him. She wrapped her arms around his neck and returned the kiss. After a moment he pulled away and whispered into her ear.

"Tell me you're still mine."

"Yes."

He shifted a bit, then, "Tell… tell me I'm still yours."

There was hesitancy in his words, in his tone. He had never asked her that before. Vincent often referred to her as being 'his', but never questioned that she wanted him. Natalia wanted to draw back to look into his eyes, but he wouldn't let her. His arms tightened around her and held her still. Natalia moved closer still and spoke softly. "Yes, you're still mine."

His grip tightened, then loosened and shifted to pick her up. Vincent carried Natalia to their bed, laid her down and pulled away to look into her eyes. He licked his lips when he saw her confidence was back. Vincent let go of his unstated fears, leaned in and kissed Natalia softly.

When he pulled back, she clutched at his shirt. "Is this done?"

"Yes."

"Make love to me."

Vincent grinned, and pulled back to undress. Natalia hastily pulled off her clothing as well. Once her clothes were off, she threw back the covers and laid herself down on the bed. Vincent slipped into bed and encircled her in his arms. As he drew her closer, he understood he still had some residual animal hunger toward Natalia. Since he hadn't been able to appease his hunger with his human, it had been growing. Now, he fought against his nature and tried to take things slowly. As usual, she took control and made him forget what she had been through the past week. She almost passed out from exhaustion twice, but held on to her consciousness, to prove her worth.

In the end, when she lay enfolded in his arms, he felt the raging beast within rise closer to the surface than he was willing to admit. Her actions fed his hunger and made it blossom and grow into every part of his being. She stirred and rubbed herself against him in her sleep. He growled low at the inferno her touch set on his chilled skin. He growled again and admitted to himself the depth of his hunger. He knew he needed to visit Lorraine and ask his sire for help again, until another solution came to his famished mind.

No, not Lorraine. Though Lorraine knew where prey could be found, it would be years before she would allow him to hunt again. Most cities did not have a ruling vampire of any kind. It was rare to see such a thing. It meant he could go to any city and hunt. He would not stay close though, to keep the Slayers away. Vincent smiled as a plan took shape in his mind. He would finalize plans tonight. For the moment, he turned back to Natalia and growled into her neck. Soon, he calmed enough to slip into unconsciousness.

14

Vincent stared at Natalia as she and Anthony stared each other down. His emotions were under his control again, after some hunting in Reno, Nevada. He'd done things carefully, and had not drawn Slayers to the area. It helped calm his hunger better than Lorraine's runner in the forest preserve. Now, he waited for the blood experiments to start. They were in Anthony's living room. Four weeks had passed since Vincent found he could control Natalia with his blood. She wanted to test Joseph's theory of whose blood could possess her and whose could not. They decided to start with the most unlikely candidate.

Natalia stood with arms crossed, her eyes narrowed. Anthony looked annoyed and bored. Julia stood behind him, a slight smirk hidden in her eyes. Vincent was beside them, and waited to see if the two would put aside their differences long enough to run the experiment. A smile came to Natalia's face as she decided to goad Anthony.

"Do you fear me? Is that why you don't want to do this?

He frowned and his arms were crossed. "This has to be done?"

"No real harm to you, vampire. I'm the only one at risk."

Though he had his memories of all the times Natalia hypnotized him, he still didn't trust her. Joseph theorized Anthony didn't trust her due to being hypnotized. As she continued to stare him down, he uncrossed his arms and rolled up the sleeves of his sweater. He motioned for Natalia to step into his embrace. She moved closer and turned to place her back against his chest. He stiffened, as he did not want her that close, but placed his wrist in front of her face. Anthony reached up and split his wrist open with a small dagger Julia handed him. Natalia gripped the vampire's hand and arm and brought the bleeding wound to her mouth. She inadvertently closed her eyes and placed her lips around the wound. She took three swallows, pulled his wrist away and turned to face him. She shook her head at the taste.

"Well?"

"I don't feel any different."

"Order her to do something." Vincent's voice held no emotion.

Anthony rolled down his sleeve over the already healed wound as he regarded the perplexingly beautiful human who stood before him. "Tell me why you're with Vincent."

Natalia's eyes glazed over, she leaned closer to Anthony and whispered, "Sex." Natalia shook her head and waved Anthony away. "Next."

Anthony gave her an annoyed look. "This was pointless, Vincent. We knew this wouldn't work."

Vincent glared at Anthony. "She was the control group. I would like you to try this on various humans, known and unknown to you. See if it works."

Anthony nodded curtly. Vincent gave Natalia his arm and the couple left, as Anthony plotted out his new assignment.

ଓ ଞ

The next day, in Vincent's sitting room, security devices turned off, Natalia stood in Joseph's arms. She felt the man's now familiar form press against her back. As he opened his wrist with a dagger, he leaned into her ear and whispered to her. "Do I get as much blood as you take?"

Her nails dug into his flesh as she considered his proposition. Vincent had refrained from drinking her blood for the past month, to allow her to be at full strength for the experiments. She grudgingly accepted his explanation, as she knew it was probably for the best. But now, as Joseph scraped his fangs against her tender skin, she wondered if it had been a mistake. Her nails dug in deeper as he bit her ever so gently on her neck. He retracted his fangs as he bit, as he knew better than to draw blood without permission. Instead, he pulled his wrist to her mouth and beckoned her to drink the salty liquid that poured from his wound. She drank more than she meant to as he whispered dark ideas into her ear.

Vincent watched the spectacle, hands forming into fists. Mierka sat at his desk, fascinated by the look on Natalia's face. Her expression kept changing from a pained expression to one of desire. Mierka guessed the human did not want to enjoy being in Joseph's arms. When Joseph let the human go, Natalia staggered, and tried to catch her balance. She looked around nervously, as if unsure of those around her. Vincent reached forward and lifted her chin to look in her eyes. The glazed look she had faked with Anthony threatened to come into her eyes.

"Natalia." Both were surprised by Joseph's quiet voice. "Come to me. Your blood is mine tonight."

She turned to him, and shook her head to clear it. She took one step forward, then another, but stopped herself. Natalia pressed her palms into her eyes, took an enormous breath and let out a silent bellow.

"Natalia. Lovely Natalia." He stepped to her, touched her cheek, and raised her chin in an imitation of Vincent to be able to look into those beautiful dark eyes. He watched as she fought for control, won, then lost briefly. "Your body and blood belong to me this night. Come with me."

It was such an inviting thought. Natalia struggled with her mind, and fought against the blood she could still taste in her mouth. She pulled away from his touch and reeled back from the soft words he threatened her with. Joseph stepped toward her to try again. Toying with the strong, gorgeous woman was a pleasure. She thought herself immune to possession. It was a joy to watch her struggle with herself, knowing he had caused it. Vincent wanted to stop Joseph but knew he couldn't. They needed to see if Natalia could snap out of the vampire's control.

Joseph ran his fingers along the side of her neck to her shoulder and along the line of her t-shirt to her exposed cleavage. Her breath caught as his fingertips brushed lightly against her breasts. Her eyes flew open as her breath came faster. Joseph saw the look in her eye and knew he had her. He leaned in, kissed her ever so lightly on her lips, and bit her bottom lip carefully as he pulled away.

"Come with me tonight, Natalia. You will not regret the way I make you feel." He whispered the words, so only she could hear. Natalia's mind pulled against the control and started looking for a way out. She looked to Vincent and felt her mind. She continued to stare at her vampire, and allowed him to stare deep into her. Joseph's control slipped completely, and it was done.

Natalia pushed Joseph away and went to Vincent. She kissed him deeply, felt his arms trap her to him and knew who was in control. Vincent pulled away, growled at Joseph. "Mine."

Joseph bowed his consent. "We have learned much."

"We have learned nothing." All three turned to regard the still seated Mierka. "This is a safe environment, with Vincent close at hand. It's too controlled a situation."

"What would you suggest?" Natalia's voice showed intrigue.

Mierka extracted herself from the comfortable leather chair and vaulted over the desk in one smooth motion. She stood in front of Natalia and spoke to her only. "Let me try to seduce you, but not here. I'll feed you my blood, then see what you allow." She gave a small bow, then looked back into Natalia's eyes. "With your permission, of course."

Natalia blushed a bit as she regarded the petite woman in front of her. She wasn't opposed to the suggestion, but Mierka had never made any indication there was an attraction. The human thought about it for a moment, then decided. She gave Mierka a smirk.

"All right. Sounds fun. Let's see what you can do."

Mierka mirrored the smirk, then slipped one hand behind Natalia's neck.

She drew the woman down for a kiss. Natalia returned it and slipped one arm around Mierka's waist. Natalia reached out to Vincent with her other hand as the kiss grew aggressive. He took her hand and watched as the women kissed. Joseph made a pleasured noise as Mierka finally broke away from Natalia.

"I will have you." She breathed quietly to Natalia.

"We'll see." Natalia stated with a smirk.

The woman laughed and Mierka let Natalia go completely.

Vincent looked to the two women and pushed his lustful thoughts aside. "As long as Natalia agrees, do as you see fit. Now leave, this evening is mine."

Vincent picked Natalia up in his arms, turned and carried her into their bedroom. Since his time in Reno, had felt completely under control. Today was the first time he felt he needed to prove anything. Joseph's attitude was too smug. He slammed the door to block out his bodyguard's laughter.

ભ છ

Lava was packed, and Natalia didn't want to be sitting in the booth. She hadn't been back to the club since a week before she was kidnapped by Zechariah. Bethany had convinced her to come out to listen to a local band. The band that night was good, if she remembered correctly. She and Bethany had a great night. Natalia brought her thoughts back to the present and looked around. Tonight, there was a DJ and people were dancing. She played good music, and Natalia wanted to join the crowd. She didn't see Bethany, or anyone else she knew, but that was a good thing. She didn't need the complication of old friends to disturb her outing with her new friends. Natalia suspected Mierka would try and hypnotize her tonight. It wouldn't do to be interrupted.

Natalia glanced at Rebecca and Mierka and rolled her eyes. They were engaged in a heated discussion about something; Natalia didn't know what. She didn't want to pay attention. It had been a long time since she had been to a club. Finally fed up, she pushed past Rebecca, sauntered onto the dance floor, and immediately moved in sync with the music.

Natalia was dressed in a short tight white skirt and tight striped burgundy and white top. Her burgundy sandals snaked up her legs, to tie just under her knee. She danced with whoever wanted her, and let the people touch her but not possess her. Rebecca and Mierka stopped their discussion to watch her interact with the other humans, then started to discuss their plans for the evening. When the drinks came to the table, Rebecca went to grab Natalia. She came willingly as she was rather thirsty.

Natalia sat at the table and smiled to the two women. "The two of you should be dancing."

"Maybe in a bit." Rebecca raised her glass. "A toast. To friendship in unexpected places."

Natalia smiled warmly, raised her glass as did Mierka. The three laughed as they toasted and took a drink. Natalia set her glass down and turned to Mierka as the woman tapped her on the shoulder. Once Natalia faced her, Mierka reached out, took the human's head in her hands, and brought her lips closer. Mierka kissed Natalia deeply and slid her tongue against Natalia's.

There was blood on Mierka's tongue. Natalia could taste it. She almost pulled away, then drank deeply of the elixir Mierka offered. The woman's blood spilled down Natalia's throat, and she fought against the control she knew would come. Her head swam as she continued to swallow Mierka's blood. Natalia pushed the vampire away. Mierka pulled away and stared into Natalia's eyes. The human's eyes were closed, but Mierka waited for the inevitable.

Natalia took deep breaths to try and stop the feelings coursing through her head. It was as if she could hear Mierka's thoughts in her mind. She breathed deep; her eyes stayed closed as she pushed away some of the thoughts. The kiss was nice, but Mierka was not her partner. She opened her eyes and looked right at Mierka, who smiled her secret smile. At the look, everything seemed to coalesce and calm itself into the pretty pattern of the vampire's smile.

Mierka watched the human's posture change from one of dominance to one of subservience. Before the blood laced kiss, Natalia sat up straight, and had a look on her face as if she could control the world. Now, she leaned forward expectantly, and looked just at Mierka, as if the vampire knew everything there was to know. Mierka smiled triumphantly.

"I'm thirsty. Natalia? May I drink from you?"

"Yes." Her quick response surprised Rebecca, who honestly thought Natalia would be immune.

"Can I take a drink here? Is it safe?"

Natalia nodded her head, ready to do as she was bid, then stopped. "No, wait. What was your question?" She shook her head, rubbed her eyes, and locked gazes with Mierka. Something caressed her mind and she smiled as her tension melted away. "You asked me something?"

Mierka leaned forward and caressed Natalia's cheek. "You were telling me if it's safe for me to drink your blood in public. Is it?"

The glazed look was back in her eye. Something fought in her mind. "Yes?" She shook her head, took a breath, and looked to Mierka with a glint in her eye. "No. Upstairs would be safer."

The women stared each other down, neither looking to concede. Rebecca leaned back in her seat and watched the women. The blood control had slipped, but Natalia appeared to want things to continue. Rebecca had come along at Vincent's and Joseph's instance, to make sure both women came home safe. She wasn't sure what the men were afraid of but as she watched the human and vampire stare each other down, she wondered if <u>she</u> were safe.

Mierka laughed and broke the tension. "That was rather quick."

Natalia bit her lip as she thought her own thoughts. She took a deep breath and looked back into Mierka's eyes. "Part of me wanted that to last longer. To see how far you would go."

Mierka leaned in a little. "Because you're curious?"

Natalia nodded. "Yes, but also because I want to tell Vincent all that you do to me. I have a feeling he would enjoy it greatly."

The women stared at each other again and Mierka held her hand out to Natalia. Natalia placed her hand in Mierka's. The vampire licked her lips.

"Let's go upstairs. Allow me to drink your blood. Then drink more of mine. Allow me to control you. I will not harm you. I will not do anything to get us arrested. I will stop if you feel uncomfortable."

Natalia blushed and she turned away. "Give me a moment. Go upstairs if you want but give me a moment."

Mierka nodded and watched as Natalia left the booth. The vampire turned to Rebecca. "Follow her. Make sure she wants this."

Rebecca frowned. "Do you think she's still partially under your control?"

Mierka shook her head. "I have no idea. Make sure she isn't."

Rebecca nodded, grabbed her beer, and followed Natalia out the back door to the fenced-in deck. Mierka smirked and went upstairs to find a good spot.

 C3   80

"Hey." Rebecca walked to Natalia, who sat at a table outside by the fence.

Natalia nodded but didn't say anything. The werewolf sat down across from her and sipped at her beer.

"How are you feeling?"

"I don't know. I think that's what I'm trying to figure out." She rubbed her temples with her hand, as if to prevent a headache.

"Ok, so you can totally bow out. We can go upstairs, find Mierka, tell her to hell with it and leave. Isn't this your decision?"

"Yes, but…" She frowned. "You reminded me a lot of Charlie right there."

Rebecca smiled. "Happens when you're in a long relationship. You sometimes look like Vincent. Or rather, you get a look in your eye like he does."

Natalia smiled a little but didn't know what to say.

"So, want to leave or what?"

"You think I should, don't you?"

"I think you should do what you want, which is what you always do."

Natalia laughed, but sobered quickly. "When I was a child, my mother told me that I could not be controlled. It's odd knowing I can be."

"Why did your mom think you couldn't be?"

Natalia reached up to touch her necklace. "She never explained it, but I always thought it had to do with the fact that I can hypnotize others."

"That's pretty powerful stuff, but if someone has a stronger will, then they might be able to." She shrugged. "I mean, who has controlled you so far?"

"Vincent, Joseph and Mierka."

"Do you trust them?"

Natalia opened her mouth to speak, then stopped and thought about it. After a moment she nodded. "I was going to answer yes rather quickly but wanted to think about the answer."

"It's still yes, isn't it?"

Natalia nodded.

"You trust them. Maybe that's why it worked."

Natalia nodded slowly.

Rebecca sipped more of her beer and finally spoke again after a few moments of silence. "Look, I'm not trying to tell you what you should do, but Mierka is waiting for you, and she wants to control and seduce you."

"I know. Mind if I talk this out a little?"

Rebecca chuckled. "I think that's why I'm here tonight. To make sure nothing goes awry."

Natalia nodded. "I want to know what she'll do to me. I want to know what Vincent will do to me once I tell him of this night."

"Sounds like you have your answer. Why the hesitation?"

Natalia pursed her lips, sighed, and finally answered. "I didn't know I liked women."

Rebecca laughed, and raised her beer in a salute. "Here's to learning about yourself even late in life."

She gave her friend a cold look. "You're not helping."

"As I've said, you are your own woman. You're going to do what you want anyway."

Natalia shook her head. "And where will you be throughout this encounter?"

"Close enough to make sure no one hurts you, not close enough to intrude."

Natalia smiled. Then, a gleam came to her eyes as she finally made her decision. "All right, Rebecca. Let's go find out where Mierka is hiding."

Rebecca, feeling much better about the situation, nodded, and followed Natalia upstairs.

15

Natalia found Mierka upstairs, in the darkest corner of the bar. She sat on the couch, her arms spread out on the back, waiting. Mierka smiled as Natalia approached and licked her lips slowly. Natalia sat down on the couch close to the vampire and sighed. Mierka leaned in and whispered into her ear.

"Why the hesitation?"

Her voice eased Natalia's nerves; she placed her hand on Mierka's thigh, almost grateful the woman wore jeans and not a skirt. She sighed and pulled away to look into Mierka's eyes. When Natalia felt nothing but her own thoughts, she knew she was no longer under the vampire's control.

"I didn't realize I was bi-sexual until you suggested we try this. Tonight has brought out a lot of odd feelings."

Mierka looked deep into Natalia's eyes, and carefully brushed her fingers under the human's chin. "Say no and we leave."

She closed her eyes and licked her lips. "I don't want to."

Mierka smiled, leaned in, and gave Natalia a soft kiss. Natalia returned the kiss and allowed it to become more intense as the vampire pulled her closer. Natalia pulled away to breathe a shaky breath.

"I won't try to control you yet." Mierka whispered.

"This is a little intense for me."

"I know. My first time with a woman was far more intriguing than my first time with a man."

Natalia pulled back a little. "How so?"

"The first man I slept with used me in every way he could. He thought I was younger than I was and kept me until he tired of me. I allowed it to happen as I had nowhere else to go. The first woman…" Mierka turned her head away and sighed. "I think Cara loved me."

Natalia leaned back on the couch and took Mierka's hand. "Was she your sire?"

Mierka shook her head. "No, I was hers. She died to Slayers three years later."

Pain crossed Natalia's features. She reached out to Mierka and placed her hand on her cheek. "I'm so sorry."

"Life is not easy for those of us who live a long time. My life is full of stories of loss."

Natalia stared the woman down. "As is mine, and I've lived a lot less years. Life is pain." The last sentence was almost a whisper. She looked Mierka in the eye as she said the next words. "But there is love in that pain, and beauty. That's what makes us hold on."

Mierka sighed. "You are correct."

Natalia brought Mierka closer and kissed her softly. Mierka let go of her memories and slipped her arms around Natalia. They held onto each other and kissed for a few moments. Mierka's hands started to roam Natalia's body. Natalia moaned into the kiss and Mierka smiled. The vampire withdrew from the kiss, smiled to Natalia as she bit her own tongue and brought Natalia closer for more kisses.

Natalia knew the moment Mierka leaned in she would taste blood. When Mierka slipped her tongue into Natalia's mouth, the human tasted the copper and drank it down readily. She took as much as Mierka gave her and allowed the taste to carry her senses. Mierka pulled away, looked at Natalia, and cradled her head in her hands. The vampire watched and waited for Natalia to once again look into her eyes. Mierka held Natalia up with one hand and allowed her other hand to roam Natalia's torso. She cupped Natalia's breast and pinched the nipple. Mierka looked around, noticed no one was watching, but still brought the human closer to hide her actions.

Natalia felt the hand on her breast. She moaned and shuddered. She looked at Mierka as the vampire drew her closer and let all her thoughts go. She wanted to be with Mierka tonight; wanted to see what would happen.

So be it, was the last thought that Natalia had before Mierka caught her glance.

"Natalia." Mierka breathed the name.

Natalia had a glazed look in her eyes and did not respond.

The smile fell from Mierka's lips as she stared at her slave. "Will you do anything I want you to do?"

Natalia smiled an odd smile. "Ask me whatever you want."

Mierka placed her hand on Natalia's thigh, and let her hand stray under the human's skirt. "Will you let me play with you? Allow me to slip my hand under your skirt and pleasure you?"

Natalia spread her legs as she continued to stare into Mierka's eyes. "I would like that."

Mierka pulled her hand away and stood. "Not here. Come my dear."

Natalia hopped up from the couch and waited. She watched Mierka as the vampire looked around. Mierka found Rebecca with her eyes and beckoned to her. The werewolf came quickly.

"What's going on?" The werewolf finished her beer.

"We're leaving. I want privacy."

"Where are we going?" Rebecca noticed the human was not herself.

"To the limo. You'll ride in front. I want to be with Natalia in the back."

Rebecca shrugged and led the way outside. They found the limo quickly and got in. Rebecca went to the front with the driver, and Mierka ordered Natalia into the back. Once the ladies were situated, Mierka informed the driver to head back to the estates, the long way. The entire time, Natalia did not move, as if she waited for instructions.

Mierka looked at Natalia as the car started to move. "Sit back and relax."

Natalia did as told. Mierka also sat back in the seat but turned to look at Natalia.

"If any part of you can hear me, I don't want you like this. If we are to sleep together at some point, it will not be while you are under my control." Mierka reached out and caressed Natalia's cheek. "I too, prefer strong, willing women. Can you hear me, Natalia? Can you break my hold on you?"

Natalia stared at Mierka while the vampire talked but didn't seem to understand.

Mierka sighed. "Merde." As she stared at the human, she decided. "I wonder if pain will do it?"

Mierka reached out and pinched Natalia on her left breast, about where the scar from Vincent's bite would be. Natalia cried out but pouted and looked confused. Mierka then slapped Natalia on the cheek, hard. Natalia's head rocked back, but not hard enough to hurt her further.

Mierka reached out for another slap, and Natalia's mind snapped back into control. It wasn't so much the pain as the utter and complete annoyance on Mierka's face that did it.

"Stop it!" Natalia sounded rather perturbed. "What are you doing?"

Mierka sighed and smiled a real smile, not her usual smirk. "I didn't want to be in control."

"Oh." She rubbed her cheek and her left breast which hurt her for some reason. She looked to Mierka. "Did you pinch me?"

"I thought it might do the trick." There was an odd look in her eyes.

"You want me willing?"

The vampire nodded.

"So does Vincent."

"Joseph wants you willing as well but enjoys toying with Vincent's women."

Natalia settled against the seat. "Why is that?"

Her smirk was back. "I sleep with Vincent when he needs me, regardless of Joseph's desires. He seeks revenge in the only way he can."

Natalia shook her head. "You two are trouble."

Mierka reached out and caressed Natalia's thigh. Natalia closed her eyes as the chill touch set her mind racing. "Can I cause trouble with you?"

Natalia looked to Mierka then looked out the window. They were in the city; she didn't know where. "How long before we get back to the estates?"

"I don't know, nor do I care." She slipped closer to Natalia and allowed her hand to slip further under the human's skirt. Natalia's breath caught as Mierka's fingers brushed lightly against her underwear. "May I cause trouble with you, mistress?"

Natalia spread her legs, allowing Mierka better access. "Yes."

Mierka grinned as permission was granted.

೭   ೮

Natalia and Mierka lay on the longest limo seat, whispering to each other. Neither were dressed and they were pressed close together, chest to chest. Natalia's back was to the seat back. They kissed occasionally and caressed each other as they talked. Mierka paused as the car stopped. She listened to the sounds of a gate opening for a moment then sighed.

"We're home."

"You sound disappointed."

"I wanted the evening to last longer." Mierka moved to sit on the edge of the seat. She grabbed her clothing.

"I enjoyed being with you, but I want to drive Vincent crazy." Now that Mierka was out of the way, Natalia was able to sit up as well. She grabbed her clothing and started to dress.

Mierka stopped. "We still can. If you drink my blood, allow me to control you…"

Natalia looked to Mierka. "Tell me your plan first, then I'll decide."

The lady vampire smirked and told Natalia her plan.

Natalia smiled and finished dressing. She grinned playfully. "I can do that without being under your control."

Mierka smirked then laughed. "Do you really think you can keep a straight face?"

Natali licked her lips. "To annoy Vincent? Yes."

Mierka leaned closer and gave Natalia a kiss. When she pulled back, she glanced toward the driver. "You may need to act as if you're in my control for Rebecca's sake and for the camera's sake. Make it seem more real."

Natalia nodded. "I will."

Smiles on their faces, the ladies finished dressing. Once fully dressed, Mierka, moved to the seat nearest the door. She indicated the floor in front of her. "Sit here. It'll help the ploy."

Natalia sat where Mierka indicated and leaned back against the vampire's legs. She closed her eyes, thought of what they were about to do and breathed slowly. Mierka caressed her hair and Natalia relaxed into the woman's touch.

Mierka's eyes caressed the human's face, almost surprised by the look she saw there. She ran her hand through Natalia's thick black hair, and brushed the strands away to see her face. There was so much trust there. Natalia often had that look. It was odd for a human to show that much trust in a vampire. The look warmed Mierka. Before she could say anything on it, the car slowed. She leaned back in the seat and concentrated on the task at hand. The evening was not yet done.

16

The car stopped shortly after, but Mierka didn't move. When Rebecca opened the door, Mierka left the car then turned to Natalia and held her hand out.

"Come my dear. It's time to have fun."

Natalia looked up at Mierka with an expectant smile and climbed out of the car. She slipped her hand around the vampire's waist. The ladies headed toward the door, with Rebecca in the lead. The werewolf didn't like seeing Natalia like this, but knew it was no longer her place to say anything.

The car was parked in the drive, right by the front door. Once they left the car, the driver closed up and took the limo to the garage. Rebecca felt it was easier to go in through the front door. As Natalia stumbled up the few steps, the wolf knew she made the right decision. Rebecca looked at Mierka with a quizzical expression on her face. Mierka answered with an equally confused look and shrugged. Mierka helped Natalia up the rest of the short flight of steps. Natalia leaned into her and giggled.

To make sure nothing unforeseen happened, Rebecca went with Mierka up the steps to Vincent's sitting room. Mierka helped Natalia, who seemed more drunk than anything else. They sat Natalia on the couch at one end and let her rest against the armrest and back. She sat there and stared at Mierka, as if waiting for the lady vampire to pull her strings. Mierka asked Rebecca to fetch the men. Rebecca nodded and left the room.

Mierka sat near Natalia and whispered in her ear. "You convinced Rebecca. Well done."

In answer, Natalia leaned her head closer to Mierka's ear and nibbled on the woman's neck. The vampire closed her eyes in pleasure but pushed the human away when she heard Vincent and Joseph enter the room. She looked to the men and smirked. She reached out and caressed Natalia's cheek. She then gave her man a private look and he mirrored it. Mierka stood, went to Joseph, and whispered to him the events of the evening. Vincent stood feeling uncomfortable, and wondered why Natalia did not greet him. She still sat on the couch, and gave Mierka an odd look.

Vincent frowned. "Mierka? What did you do to her?"

Mierka extracted herself from Joseph and went to stand behind Natalia's perch. The human sat taller on the couch, and craned her neck to look at her mistress.

"I'm thirsty, Natalia. Let me drink from you."

Natalia turned and smiled at Mierka. She moved her whole body to place her legs on the couch. One arm she positioned on the back of the couch with the other held up and out toward Mierka's side. Mierka caressed Natalia's arm as she came around the couch to sit with her. Natalia readjusted her body to allow Mierka to sit beside her, her arm still presented to the vampire. Mierka smiled at her, gently took her arm, and sank her fangs into the yielding flesh.

Natalia did everything she could to stay in character. As far as she was concerned, reacting mildly to Mierka's bite would be the hardest part of the act. As Mierka sucked on her blood, Natalia had to stop herself from moving closer to the vampire. She turned her head a little and licked her lips as she looked into Mierka's eyes.

Vincent tensed as pain crossed his woman's features then gazed in wonder as her expression changed to one of pleasure. She turned her head away and he could no longer see her expression. He frowned as Mierka stopped feeding. The lady vampire then placed a hand on Natalia's knee and slid it slowly up her thigh. The touch implied too much to Vincent. As he watched, Natalia pulled Mierka to her by her hair, and gave the vampire a long kiss.

Vincent, aroused and angered, looked sharply to his left when he heard a low growl. Joseph wasn't hiding his emotions. He snapped his attention back to the women when he heard them whispering.

"Release her."

"Make it happen." Mierka didn't even bother to turn toward him.

Vincent stared hard at Mierka, and clenched his jaw in aggravation. He released the frustration, went to the couch, and threw Mierka away from his human. He knelt in front of Natalia. He placed one hand on her knee and the other went to her cheek. He tried to draw her attention to him. Her eyes found his, briefly, then looked over his shoulder.

Vincent turned his head to look behind him. Mierka had moved quickly. She stood a few feet behind him, and kept Natalia's gaze. Vincent growled at her then turned back to Natalia. He sat on the couch next to her, grabbed her head in both his hands and turned her face to make her look at him. Except she wouldn't look at him; she still stared at Mierka. Vincent growled again then brought Natalia's lips to his and kissed her hard.

His lips were on hers and she could feel his desire and frustrations. Natalia understood this was the hardest part: to deny the man she wanted to be with. Natalia looked at Mierka as she continued to kiss Vincent, then closed her eyes and slipped her arms around his neck. His grip became firmer, his kisses more passionate as she continued to kiss him. A few minutes passed and he pulled away.

"Are you mine then?"

"I wasn't under her control. We thought it might be more fun to pretend."

His eyes narrowed a bit. "Was she able to control you at all?"

"Yes. But I didn't want to sleep with your human while she was under my control." Mierka interjected from behind Vincent.

He let go of Natalia completely, stood, and faced Mierka. The smaller vampire smirked. "What happened?"

Natalia stood and placed her hand on Vincent's shoulder. "Perhaps we can speak privately?"

He looked to Natalia. "Why?"

Mierka snorted, walked close to Vincent, and pulled his head down for a kiss. He drew back in surprise when he tasted Natalia on Mierka's lips. It wasn't just blood he tasted. Mierka smirked as she let him go. She turned to Joseph and went to him. "I'm sure you'll enjoy her report far more in private." She stopped in front of Joseph, licked her lips, and continued toward the door. "Come love, I want to tell you what happened in private as well."

When they were alone in the room, Vincent turned to Natalia. "What did she do to you?"

Natalia gave him a sly smile. "As stated, Mierka refused to do anything to me while I was under her control."

"You smell like her. When I kissed you earlier, you tasted of her blood, but there was another taste as well. What happened?" He was speaking quickly, intrigued, and turned on.

Natalia looked her lover in the eyes. "We talked, I admitted to being curious to be with her. We left the bar and went to the car. We had sex in the limo."

He hissed in air. "Will you tell me all the details?"

"Yes, but something occurred to me earlier." She pushed him away and started to walk to the bedroom. She gave Vincent a come hither look over her shoulder when she reached the bedroom door. "And we really should speak in the bedroom."

He watched as she turned and walked into the bedroom. He licked his lips and followed her. Vincent watched from the doorway as she started to remove her clothes. He wanted to hear all the details, but watching her strip always distracted him.

"If you wish me to listen, perhaps you should stay dressed."

Natalia grinned and pulled her shirt back on. "Noted." She took a deep breath as she took a seat on the bed on the side close to the door. "This entire evening, I wanted Mierka to control me, to do things to me. I gave into her control easily. With Joseph and with Anthony, I fought the control from the start. It made me wonder if the mayor is allowing himself to be controlled. As far as I know, a person under any sort of hypnosis still won't do anything against their moral beliefs. Won't kill when ordered to unless they wanted to in the first place, that sort of thing."

He nodded and started to pace as she continued.

"According to Anthony, the mayor's been attending Edwin's Red Tie Affairs; letting it happen, watching and even joining in. He wants to do what Edwin orders him to do, Vincent. He's as bad as the rest of them."

Vincent paused and thought about it for a moment. He then sat close to Natalia and gave her an incredibly soft, slow kiss. "None of us ever thought about that. This evening proved to be rather informative."

Natalia smiled. "For me as well."

He stared into her eyes. "What else did you learn?"

"I'm bi-sexual. I enjoyed sleeping with Mierka."

His eyes narrowed a touch. "While we are together, I would prefer that I am the only man you sleep with."

She smiled maliciously. "Oh? And other women?"

He gave a soft growl. "Do not sleep with other people while we are together."

"Was that a demand?" Her eyes mocked him as she ran her hands up his chest.

Vincent invaded her space and pushed her back onto the bed. He growled on her neck. Natalia turned her head and allowed him better access. "If I demand you stay away from all other people, is that really a problem?"

She laughed. It made him pull back to look into her eyes. Once he was staring down at her she grinned. "If I demand you stay away from all other women, will you listen?"

He growled. She could hear his anger. The smile on her face made him bare his teeth. She laughed again. Before he could say anything, she caressed his cheek and spoke.

"I don't want to place restrictions on you, Vincent. I understand sometimes you need someone else, for my own safety. But don't order me to do anything. It gives me reason to rebel."

He growled again but could think of nothing to say.

She kissed him softly on the lips. "Would you like to know what we did to each other?"

"Every detail."

"Because it excites you or because you need to know if Mierka did anything you haven't thought of?"

"Both." He pulled back and started to undress. Natalia followed suit. Once they were undressed and laying comfortably in the bed, Vincent took her in his arms and started to suck on her breasts.

Her hands found his hair and pulled painfully as he bit into her breast and suckled her blood. He sucked slowly, causing her to moan. He pulled away, and used her discarded shirt to help stop the blood flow.

"What did Mierka do? Please tell me."

She shuddered. "You make me think it's other men you don't want me to sleep with, not other people."

He growled on her skin. "Tell me."

Natalia licked her lips as Vincent kissed his way down her torso and slipped his tongue between her legs. Grinning and laughing, she described in absolute detail what Mierka did to her in the car.

؃ ؄

When Natalia drank his blood one week later, Vincent couldn't tell if he had her under his control or not. She was generally willing to try anything he suggested; this time was no different. Or so he thought. Half an hour after giving her his blood he pulled away frustrated, seething with annoyance. He was downstairs in the security room confronting Joseph in seconds.

"Break my hold on her." His annoyance showed in his voice. Joseph was not worried; Vincent was annoyed with the situation.

"You wish me to break your control on your woman? And why would that be?" Joseph smiled and watched as Vincent's hands formed into fists.

"I want a willing, experienced woman with a mind of her own. Not a child who needs to be told what to do with every movement." He paused, took a breath, and calmed his raging emotions. "Go break my hold."

Joseph's smile grew wider. "Does this order supersede the order that I'm not to touch her while she's yours?"

Vincent grabbed Joseph by his shirt, pulled his friend into a standing position, and stared him down. "I could locate Mierka and have both women for the night. Would you prefer that?"

Joseph pulled his master's hands off his shirt, and smoothed out the wrinkles. He indicated that Vincent should lead the way and followed his master up the stairs to the bedroom. Vincent's hold on Natalia was easily broken, as she wanted her usual lover and not a stand in.

17
Eighteen Months Later

Edwin's house was packed. He had invited all the people he controlled, both vampires and humans. The mayor was there, as well as three of his top men and their dates, the police commissioner, and the police chief. It was still early in the evening, and Edwin's treats had yet to be revealed. The silly twit had enough sense to hide the children until after most of the humans left. Vincent could at least be grateful for that. Vincent's people were scattered throughout the room, mingling to gather information. Ten human children were hidden somewhere in the house, probably in this room, but the usual stage was missing. There was a wall where the edge of the stage should be, which made Vincent think that the wall was false. Only time would tell.

Vincent swirled his red wine slowly, and looked through the glass, which distorted the people around him. He disliked being here, but there was a reason for it. Tonight was the culmination of a year and a half of deception. Anthony found out easily that Morgan passed on information to Edwin about Vincent's household. Morgan spent time at Vincent's but stated he never gave anyone information. He told stories though which made it easy for Edwin's people to know what was going on with Vincent's people, notably Natalia. As Morgan also told stories about Edwin's people to Vincent, Vincent decided not to kill him.

When word reached Edwin that Natalia might mean more to Vincent than previously presented, the LeGris household did what they could to change Morgan's mind. They made Morgan believe that Natalia was under Vincent's control. Natalia played along nicely around Morgan. She did everything Vincent asked, even when he knew she normally wouldn't.

Vincent smiled slowly as a memory unwound in his mind. One day last week, Morgan showed up while Vincent sparred with Natalia in the training room. Vincent caught her in his arms and pretended to feed her his blood. They had practiced the act and were able to fool most people, but she acted as if she were under his control. They sparred a little bit more while he seduced her. When they were both aroused to the breaking point, he threw her against the wall and screwed her as everyone watched. That morning, alone and secure in their bedroom, she informed him that should he do something like that again, she would slice him in half.

He didn't doubt that she would. Her statement only made him want to try it again.

Vincent sipped the wine but wanted blood. He declined it though, as the blood in Edwin's house was suspect. Edwin didn't feed his guests his own blood; he fed them the blood of children. At times, Vincent took blood from the unwilling victims, but not from children. Missing and dead children brought too many police officers around. Dead children drained of their blood brought Slayers faster than adults drained of blood.

Vincent felt a presence beside him and turned to address the creature who smiled at him. "Good evening Torin. How can I help you?"

"I was wondering why Edwin's greatest rival would be at a Red Tie Affair? You normally stay away from these." Torin was dressed in his usual attire: jeans, red button-down shirt open over a black t-shirt and black and red wingtip shoes. He looked much like a male model. It was one of the ways he drew women to him.

"Actually, I usually destroy these parties." Vincent kept his voice low, as others were nearby. He turned his head to regard the demon. "Why are you here, Torin? I thought you stayed away from these parties."

"As you said, you usually destroy these parties, and word on the street is, you're planning something interesting."

Vincent stayed silent.

"I've come to offer my assistance."

"You never fight."

"You're right. I don't. I thought I might help to keep all your people here."

Vincent gave the Incubus a skeptical look. "I will not hand them over to another monster."

"I don't like children." A slow smile came across his features. "I like women who know how to please, like Natalia."

Vincent's features hardened, but he ignored the comment. "What do you want?"

"Many things. But this time, a chance to clear part of my debt."

"You drive away the cargo and I erase part of your debt?" He set down his wine glass on the large table behind him.

Torin gave a slight bow with his head. "If you agree."

"Two were going to drive the cargo. Now, I'll send you and one other."

"Who?"

"Owen."

"You will tell me when?"

"It'll be obvious." Vincent crossed his arms, to show he wanted Torin to leave. "Was there anything else?"

Torin paused, leaned against the hors d'oeuvres table, and gave Vincent a wide grin. "I was also wondering when your lovely lady would arrive for the festivities?"

"Why would an Incubus want to know about my human?" Vincent's voice was light.

Torin grinned wider. "I was wondering if she would dance with me."

"Touch her and I will kill you." His voice was still light.

"How does she feel about your possessiveness?"

"Ask her when you see her next."

"When will that be?" His voice showed his eagerness.

"When it's appropriate. Now leave. I find your presence distasteful."

"As you wish, sir."

Torin left to flirt with one of the human guests. Vincent stared after him, and shook his head. He wasn't sure why Torin was here but felt it had little to do with helping the children to safety. Torin had his own agenda and never helped unless profit was involved. Vincent didn't think Edwin had hired Torin, even though the Incubus' loyalty was suspect. The Incubus was not to be trusted. As the demon owed him a great deal, he would stand by Vincent's side until the debt was paid, mostly because his life depended on it.

Joseph interrupted his thoughts, and whispered that the humans had finally started to leave. "Our people are ready. But there's something out of place."

"Isn't there always?"

"It appears this is an initiation. The mayor, and two of his aids, will be staying to the end."

"He and his people left an hour ago."

"Three are coming back."

"This changes nothing. It will only show Gary the power I possess. Tell everyone to get ready. The children will be our sign."

Joseph gave him a slight bow and left to attend to the business at hand.

❧ ❧

Natalia shifted anxiously in her seat, wishing it were time. She sat in the largest of Vincent's limos, with the werewolves, and waited for the signal. She wore a white silk Asian style dress, with white high heels. Her hair was tied up, more to keep it out of her way than for style. The only color on her was her red stone necklace, which she wore over her high-necked dress.

Her other necklace was hidden by the dress. On her lap was her sword. It was currently in a leather scabbard, which had been covered in white lace. When strapped to her back, lengthwise, it would be slightly hidden, as it would almost fade into her dress.

It took nearly six months for Vincent to convince her to use the sword this evening. She wanted to hide the sword to keep House LeGris safe, but Vincent knew it was the quickest way to kill off Edwin's men. She relented, as she knew he was right. A large part of her couldn't wait to use the sword. Edwin's men didn't know what was coming.

Next to her, Rebecca took slow deep breaths. She laid a hand on Natalia's knee, to calm her. All were silent; all were tense. They could smell the battle adrenaline. The wolves wanted to be out of the car. Vincent wanted the element of surprise, which meant the wolves and Natalia had to stay put until they received the text. The other werewolves meditated, breathed deeply, and tried not to think about the fight, in order to stay calm. It wouldn't do to start a fight in the car. By contrast to Natalia's dress, the wolves were in older jeans and t-shirts. Their clothing would be ripped once they changed.

It was three a.m. before the text came. Natalia nearly jumped out of her skin. Orlando, who sat to her right, opened the door, and stepped out. He held the door open for Natalia then helped her on with the scabbard as the others left the car. Once the sword was strapped on, she stood a little taller. Orlando took a step back; a little disturbed by the way she looked. He still wasn't used to seeing that look on a human. It was an animal look. It was the look a cat had right before it pounced on an unsuspecting mouse; meaning to toy with it until the poor thing was dead of fright.

It was also the look that made her so damned attractive.

Orlando shut his eyes, took a deep breath, and closed the car door. All were ready. Orlando led the way. Rebecca and Doug walked behind him side by side. Natalia came next, with Charlie at the rear. Orlando made an impressive figure and easily intimidated the doorman, who simply got out of the way of the five approaching creatures. The group was through the door and in the house before any of Edwin's people noticed.

The crowd parted as the group approached the center of the room. Vincent's vampires moved with the group, to stand behind the crowd. Vincent continued to lean against the hors d'oeuvres table, Joseph by his side. The false wall had been removed ten minutes ago to reveal ten children who sat on wooden, high-backed chairs. Edwin, dressed in a dark blue suit, went to them to caress their hair, and pet them in various ways.

Vincent's men informed him that the only humans left in the room were the mayor, his date, two of his men and their dates. After speaking with the women, Mierka learned the mayor's aides' dates were call girls. The mayor's date though, was a little more trouble. She was human, an innocent. Her attitude showed how little she knew about the secret world hidden beneath the floorboards of her own existence. Vincent believed the mayor brought her back as a sacrifice for the Captain. Vincent made a note to get her out with the others but knew it would be a hard task as she did not stray from the mayor. Deep in thought, he almost missed his woman's entrance.

Natalia was a sight. The werewolves, who still guarded her rear and flanks, were in ripped, dirty clothing, adding to the effect. He had wanted her in white specifically to make her look angelic. He dressed all in black. Vincent could see the hilt of the sword over her right shoulder. The smile on her face made her look impish. He growled low as he caught her eye, wanting the fight over with. At the end of the night, he would take her home, throw her on the bed and screw that smile into an orgasmic scream. The growl grew louder, and Joseph elbowed him in the side to bring him back to the moment.

Natalia's hand went behind her back to caress the sword. Even sheathed she could feel its eagerness. She trembled to use it. The sword was her absolute power, her absolute authority. Every vampire it touched would die. She smiled a seductive smile over the crowd at her lover. The look he gave her back showed his trust, his pride, his respect, and his love. She quivered at the look, and desired his touch. First, the battle. She grasped the buckle of the sheath, and released it as she gripped the hilt of her sword. The sheath fell from her body as she swung the sword over her shoulder. Natalia brought the sword in front of her, the hilt now in both hands. She allowed the blade to half hide her face then swiveled it slightly, making the edge run down the center of her face. She took a deep breath and bellowed for the Captain.

"Edwin! Show yourself!"

The words reverberated in the large room, and creatures moved even further away from her, afraid to get near her. None but Vincent's men knew what the sword was. All feared it and wanted nothing to do with it or the woman who wielded it. The crowd parted, and revealed Edwin to the beautiful creature in white. The obtuse Captain stood with mouth agape and stared at her. He knew this one and couldn't believe she was in his home demanding anything. Reports stated this human, who seemed to have power at his aborted inauguration, was now just Vincent's whore.

Annoyed beyond reason, Edwin stormed over to Natalia. He stopped ten feet away from her, confusion evident on his face. "Who dares call me out, at my party, in my house?"

Natalia twisted the sword in her hand as he advanced. Light glinted off the steel and she smiled. It would be a pleasure to kill this one. Too bad she had to leave him for Vincent. "Natalia Mirela Liliana Dveski. Protector of House LeGris. I demand you leave this city and turn over control to your betters or face us and die."

Edwin stared at her, then started laughing. "On whose authority do you order the Captain of this city to do anything, human?"

"She's already told you who she speaks for. Weren't you listening, you malodorous twit?"

All turned to see Vincent leaning against the table. He looked rather relaxed and in control. His attitude seemed to suggest he was in his home dealing with a disobedient child.

"You use a human to challenge my rule? What absurdity is this?" Edwin tried to intimidate Vincent with his tone of voice. "If she kills me, it means nothing. You can't be Captain if a Slayer kills me. My first lieutenant would receive the honor."

"I'll kill you myself. She's just here to take care of all the others." His voice was nonchalant.

"What can a human do against all my people?"

"Send them against me and you'll see." Natalia was now barefoot. She had slipped off her shoes during the verbal battle. She held the sword at the ready, and waited to use the beautiful blade on Edwin's perverted men. A memory of long ago came to her mind and she gave the room a cold, evil smile. The first monster she ever met was a human named George. People like him and Edwin deserved nothing less than death. Natalia was happy to be their executioner.

Edwin looked back at the woman dressed in white who held the orange blade lightly in her hands. Vincent seemed to think much of this one. Her death would be worth the loss of his own men. He barked orders, told his most conniving to guard the exits, and ordered his oldest to surround and kill Vincent's human. He shrank back when the smile on the woman's face grew.

Natalia stood taller and waited. She watched as Vincent's men shrank back from the crowd and went for the guards. Natalia waited as the first of Edwin's men came forward and rushed at her. He was dust with one flick of her wrist. A second one followed. Edwin ordered them to rush her, and they did. Natalia took time to laugh then swung the sword. Dust flew all around her as the sword whispered through the air. The first group was dust at her feet within a minute of Edwin ordering them to face her. She faced him and grinned as ash settled around her. She started toward him.

"They can't stop me, Edwin. Would you like to try something different?"

"The one who kills her gets Vincent's estates!"

Vincent snorted as the crowd rushed her. She let them get near and swung the sword, acting as if she were untouchable. Even if one of Edwin's could grasp the sword to pull it away from her, they would burn themselves on the blade. A few did.

His people were being slaughtered. When she threw the challenge down to fight his people, Edwin thought no more than two or three would die by her blade. He heard she was adept with a sword, but this was a massacre. No human was this swift with a sword. She would have to decapitate his men in order to dust them. She didn't look to be moving that quickly. Afraid for his reign, Edwin hurried across the room. He thought to use one of the children as a hostage, but the stage was bare. The ropes were gathered at the foot of the chairs and on the empty seats. He looked toward Vincent, who was currently engaged in a fistfight. Joseph was headed toward a wall where weapons hung.

The dethroned Captain turned toward the exits and looked for a way out. Vincent's men had replaced all his guards. Vincent himself moved purposefully toward him with one of his people behind him. He had a smug victorious look on his face. Edwin's eyes darted about, to find a way out. The mayor and his date were nearby. The mayor stood still, as if watching a show on television. His date cowered next to him, unsure of what was happening. She tried to pull the mayor toward the door, but he didn't move. Edwin had instructed the mayor to stand still before this massacre began.

Edwin moved with all his speed, captured the woman, and placed his fingers at her neck as if about to rip her throat open. "Back away Vincent, or her death is on your hands!"

The woman tried to pry Edwin's hands off. Terrified for her life, she cried and screamed. Vincent caught her eye but took no pity. "She is no one to me, Edwin."

His nails dug in deeper, and the woman's screams stopped as he cut off her airflow. "Will your human feel the same way?"

Vincent was five feet from Edwin and his victim. He stopped and turned to glance at Natalia, who still killed off Edwin's men. When they ran, she chased them, glee bright on her face. The werewolves, in Blitzkrieg form, joined the fray, and ripped apart any vampire that came near them. Rebecca stayed human, to stop her wolves at Vincent's word. He turned back to Edwin.

"I don't think she'll notice. And if she does, I don't think she'll care."

Edwin's gaze darted around again, his terror evident. Vincent started to worry when Edwin's expression changed drastically to a toothy grin. His voice held victory. "She's good against vampires, Vincent. But how will she fare against Shattered Glass demons?"

Edwin yelled the three short lines of Latin he knew and watched as two pillars of smoke formed into hideous beasts in front of him. Christopher taught him the lines when he had placed him in charge, and told the younger vampire never to utter the words unless absolutely necessary. The demons the words called forth were unpredictable at best and would only perform one task for their temporary master before running off.

Edwin stared at the horrors that stood before him, pointed to one then to Vincent. "Kill him." He pointed at the second then at Natalia. "Kill her."

The first demon bellowed and advanced on Vincent, who watched in terror as the other went for his woman. He had never seen these demons before and had no idea how to banish them. They were taller than he by a head and twice as wide. They were formed by broken pieces of mirror, glass, razor blades and what looked to be hypodermic needles. Their hands were broken glass, with long bits acting as claws. Their mouths resembled sharks' mouths, with row after row of needles. Their eyes looked like bent spoons. Vincent could see no flesh. The thing before him bellowed and he backed off to assess the situation. Joseph stood by his side, handed him a short sword, and brandished an identical one.

"Help Natalia." He gave the order as he took the short sword. He had a better chance at fighting this thing than Natalia did.

Joseph shook his head. "The wolves are her protectors. I am yours. I stay by my master's side."

Vincent glanced in her direction and saw the wolves indeed surrounded Natalia. She seemed oblivious to the danger coming toward her, but the wolves were not. He nodded and turned his attention back to the demon before him.

18

N atalia heard the sound of glass scraping and crunching and turned to the monstrosity that was now not ten feet from her. Her eyes widened as she backed up, mind torn between panic and laughter. This thing coming toward her could not be real. She then remembered where she had heard of it and why it was hard to think of it as real. Slayers heard of these creatures from junkies, pushers, and dealers. It wasn't surprising they weren't believed.

Natalia continued to back up as she wracked her memory for the demon's weak spot. It was something obvious, but she couldn't remember. She slowed her breath to calm her nerves and give herself time to think. Its movements were unhurried. It bellowed and threatened but didn't attack as if assessing her strengths. Natalia backed up again. She danced out of its way as it swung and realized her mistake. She had forgotten where she left her shoes, stepped on one of them, and almost stumbled to the ground. Rebecca caught her and pulled her to the right as a dark brown form leapt from her left and hurled itself at the advancing demon.

Natalia yelled a warning too late. The Blitzkrieg howled in the same instant as it landed on the deadly creature. The Blitzkrieg's foot long claws broke in succession; ten dry twigs under the pressure of a heavy boot. The bits of glass and metal sank deep into the pads of his feet and flesh of his hands. The wolf still flung its mouth open and tried to sink its teeth into the demon's nonexistent flesh. The wolf gave a mangled howl as his snout, gums and tongue were ripped into ribbons. The demon brought its glass hands up almost leisurely as the wolf tried to pry his teeth off the demon. As the wolf continued to struggle, the demon wrapped its deadly hands around the Blitzkrieg's throat and started to squeeze.

Natalia pulled herself out of Rebecca's arms and stood. Her anger at the creature and fear for the wolf's life clashed in her head and clouded her mind. She watched helplessly as the wolf's head was ripped off by the sharp, jagged edges of the demon's hands. The Blitzkrieg's neck nearly exploded as the glass and metal creature sliced through the wolf's flesh and showered Rebecca and Natalia with blood. The human saw Rebecca start to change and, in that instant, understood the reality of the situation. The wolves gathered nearby, ready to try and take this monstrosity down. All of them would die if they did. Calm battle instinct gripped her mind and all thoughts stilled. She took two quick steps to Rebecca and knocked the woman to the floor.

Natalia Mirela Liliana Dveski Protector of House LeGris rushed the demon brought forth by her enemy. As she flew through the air with her sword held over her head, she knew exactly how to kill it. She landed with her knees tucked to her chest on the Blitzkrieg's body. The corpse sank into the demon a little bit more but protected her legs as she plunged the sword deep into the demon's eyes. It shrieked as the sword came out the other side of its head. Natalia gave a push with the sword and flung herself off the disintegrating demon.

She landed nearby feet first, turned quickly and watched as the demon fell to the ground in tiny pieces. She grabbed her sword and turned to face the other. It was looking in her direction. It had heard its comrade's death howl and was backing away from Joseph and Vincent. Neither vampire appeared hurt. Natalia advanced forward quickly. The thing howled, turned, and ran toward the exit. In order to reach the door, it had to run in Natalia's direction. As it ran near her, Natalia threw the sword, and knew she had exactly one chance. She could not take this demon down by jumping on it.

Her aim was true. The sword flew in between the demon's legs, and tripped it. She grabbed the sword off the floor where it landed and ran to the demon's head. It was on its face but turned over and roared at her. There was no emotion on her face as she brought the sword up and slammed the sword into its eyes. It gave the same shriek as the first and slid apart. Natalia pulled her sword from the debris and turned back to the wolves. Rebecca stared at her, her face a blank mask. Charlie and Doug gave her odd looks. She sighed as she walked to them, and knew now who had leapt to her rescue.

Charlie watched as the beautiful human walked toward his group. No one had moved since she pushed Rebecca out of the way and launched herself at the demon. They had been too stunned at her actions and at Orlando's death. Charlie stared at her face, and wondered at the transformation. She stood tall and looked sure of herself, but for the tears that streamed down her face. He caught the look in her eyes, closed his own, and looked away. There was no emotion in her eyes. Although the tears betrayed the humanity that lay in her heart, her eyes did not look human. She had come a long way from the scared 18-year-old that had been thrown into the room with a trapped werewolf.

Charlie looked back to the woman he used to call his lover and found her staring at him. The look in her eye grabbed him and threatened to hold him up as the world crumbled at her feet. Charlie shook at the look, and understood it completely. She was his leader. The others around her seemed to sense the same thing. Rebecca handed her the scabbard for her sword, with her head bowed. Natalia sheathed the sword and called to him. Charlie came forward and fell to his knees at her feet. She handed him the sword and whispered for him to take it to the car. He nodded and left, as he knew his place well. He was her sword bearer and protector; would carry out his duty until she couldn't wield the sword, and until he repaid his debt.

Vincent watched as his lady handed off the sword then walked to Orlando's body. She knelt beside the corpse and carefully tried to remove him from the demon's remnants. He watched also, as Rebecca came and helped to pick the headless body up and lay it carefully on the floor. Doug went for the head and laid it at the top of Orlando's severed neck. Vincent thought it strange that though the body was human, the head was still Blitzkrieg. The wolves didn't seem bothered by this and Natalia appeared not to notice as she picked the glass bits out of Orlando's human body. Vincent also saw how the others reacted to her and wondered why. He handed the short sword to Joseph and hurried to Natalia.

Vincent placed his hand on her shoulder and waited until she turned the full force of that look upon him. He understood what the others had seen. She stood and faced him as his equal. He wondered if she realized how she looked. Vincent wiped her tears away and knew that later, much later, she would lie in his arms and cry for the loss of life. But now, as she removed the traces of the demon from Orlando's skin, she would show nothing but her warrior's face. It was something a leader would do. The others had seen that and responded to it.

Vincent found himself responding to the look as well. All he wanted was to draw her to him and give her a deep kiss. There was carnage around them, though and they were not done. Orlando was dead and Edwin escaped during the attack after he killed the mayor's date. They had to get out of the house, as Edwin might have called the human authorities. He pulled away from Natalia, and gave orders. The others listened and did as they were told.

In minutes, his people were out the door, in the cars and headed back home. The sun had started to show itself in the east. Humans drove the limos and moved dividers up as soon as they could. Vincent and Natalia were in the back of the medium sized limo and the rest of his people had found their way into the large limo. He had not planned on this arrangement, but knew his people made it happen to give their leaders some privacy. Natalia leaned against him. She sighed as battle instinct left and his lover returned. He turned his head, kissed the top of her head, and inhaled her scent.

Natalia gave a weary sigh at his touch. She leaned a bit further onto his shoulder, to relax and sleep, but felt rest might be impossible. Orlando's sacrifice, and her inability to stop him, filled her thoughts. Had she remembered the demons' weakness a few seconds earlier, Orlando would be alive. His death was her fault. She wanted to talk to Rebecca about it, but the look on the wolves' faces confused her. Charlie was the only one who hadn't acted out of character, but that had thrown her too. Why he knelt to receive the sword, she didn't know. She felt it was in bad taste.

Natalia moved her head and winced as a bobby pin poked her in the head. The discomfort stilled her thoughts. She pulled her head away from Vincent and absentmindedly reached up to let down her hair. Vincent caught her hands as she reached into her hair.

"Leave it." He spoke quietly, but his voice was thick.

"It's uncomfortable." She pulled her hands away from his and reached for her hair again. Natalia glared at Vincent when he caught her hand again. She turned to look at him and her breath caught. Her weariness vanished, to be replaced with far more complex emotions.

His free hand went to her cheek, and drew her in for a deep lingering kiss. He pulled away, whispered into her ear, and tried to hide the emotions in his voice. "Leave it."

It was such a simple command, such a simple action. There was more there than she had previously assumed. She didn't understand why he wanted her to leave her hair alone, but it wasn't to control her. He did that at times, to test his dominance. If she felt like playing along, she would obey. If she didn't, she would laugh and tease him with her own dominance. They both enjoyed the game. The look in his eye and the tone of his voice did not suggest dominance; it suggested subservience, which intrigued her.

"What do you wish to do?" Her hands relaxed in her lap, and one of his hands rested over hers.

Vincent traced her jaw line with his forefinger. He closed his eyes, to hide his emotions again. He leaned in, whispered in her ear, as he wanted the words to stay between them. "If you were a vampire, I would make you my Captain."

He pulled back as she tensed considerably. Her eyes grew wide, and her mouth was hung agape. "That's not funny."

There was no humor in his expression. Natalia suddenly felt the need to leave the limo. It was too confining, too small of a space. She tried to back away, but he caught her and pulled her into his lap. He held her tightly, and stilled all her movements.

"Do you believe I would hurt you?"

"No."

"Then why struggle?"

"Why would you say such a thing to a human?"

"It doesn't matter what type of creature you are, love. If you are worthy of leadership, then you are worthy. I know you've had declarations of protection from other vampires in my House. Tonight, a werewolf threw himself at a demon to keep you safe. Do you understand how rare that is, Natalia? I demand that my people be willing to protect me at all costs, because I give them a home and I provide for them. You have earned the same respect in a far shorter amount of time. You are worthy of leadership, Natalia. You protect us and respect us and ask nothing in return. Why is it so odd that we would worship you?"

"Because I'm still working toward my own goals."

"But that goal has not hindered your dedication to me or my House."

She looked Vincent in the eye, a sharp edge to her thoughts. "If I found out where Donald was, I would leave this instant and go track him down."

"And then you would return." He paused. "I know the nature of a life led by revenge, Natalia and would be worried if all you had was revenge." His hand covered the stone hanging around her neck. "If you didn't have something greater holding you to my house, I would not have given you rank. You are loyal to your mother and wish to kill one monster, but you are still here in this limousine, allowing a vampire to hold you close enough to drain your blood..."

He pulled her arm to his mouth, bit into her wrist, and made her gasp. He drew three swallows of blood, pulled away, and staunched the flow of blood with his handkerchief. "...with no fear for your life. I have no doubt that if you left my house to find Donald, you would return to me. You are loyal to me and to my house. You will return when you leave to find him."

"You sound so sure that I'll win." A bit of doubt crept into her voice.

"You have the sword. And if you didn't have that you would have your intelligence, and your determination. Nothing will stop you from winning, Natalia."

"What will stop me from dying in the process?"

"Your will and determination, and the knowledge that you might come to me and live forever, should he try and kill you."

"You have no doubt, do you?"

"None."

She leaned into him and felt as his body stole her heat. She felt safe in his arms. She leaned back further and was once again reminded of her bobby pins. "So why can't I take my hair down?"

He turned his head to whisper into her ear. "I will take everything off you when we return home. I plan on worshipping every inch of your body and making you scream until sunset. Is that reason enough?"

She was breathing heavily, and her eyes were closed. "Will you have the strength?"

"I'll always have the strength to worship you."

She gave a short slightly embarrassed laugh then settled her head on his shoulder. Vincent wrapped his arms around her, and felt her warmth as it seeped through the thin silk. The dress still looked stunning on her, even with the crimson stains on it, or perhaps because of them. Vincent closed his eyes, leaned into her neck, to nuzzle and nip at her skin. She pulled away after a moment of squirming, to try and keep her thoughts about her.

"Vincent, stop. This isn't right. Orlando died. Show some respect." Her voice was hardly convincing.

Vincent grabbed her again and made her straddle him. "I know, Natalia. Orlando was a fine fighter and very loyal. I will miss him and mourn him in three days' time when we have the wake. But you are here with me in this small space and as I've told you before, it's very hard for me not to take your blood or body when I see you. You can try and convince me with words, but it won't work. You can struggle and fight against my hold, but that will only excite me. Or you can give in to the desire I see swimming in your eyes." He pulled her closer and kissed her hard on the lips. "Which is it, my lovely Natalia? Will you try and find the right words to convince me, struggle and excite me or give in?"

Natalia was lost in his soft touch. His hands ran over her body, to caress and tease her through her dress. She reached for the zipper to give him better access, but he prevented it, caught her wrists, and wrapped them behind her. His teeth found her neck and nibbled softly. Her breath caught, then whispered past her lips as his fangs pressed against her skin. He pulled back. She moved toward him and whimpered when he didn't bring the arousing kiss to its fruition.

Vincent released one of her wrists to wrap his fingers carefully in her bound hair. He brought her ear to his lips. "As you asked. Not yet, my love. Not yet."

"You're the one tempting me, vampire." She leaned into his neck, opened her mouth slightly, and scraped her teeth on his skin. He growled low in his throat as she gently, then not so gently pressed his skin between her teeth. His growl became louder as her bite came closer to breaking his skin. Natalia felt his hand around her neck, and she suddenly found herself on the floor of the limo, Vincent pressed down on top of her.

"Don't. Until you can sustain the damage I am capable of, do not bite my jugular." His words growled past her face, a chill wind threatening her cheeks.

"I thought to deter your passion until we arrived home." Her voice was too innocent as was her look.

"Tell me another, weaver of tales." He growled into her neck, to chill her jugular. She shivered in anticipation, and desired his bite. She cried out in frustration when he pulled away and sat back down on the seat. She glowered at him as she propped herself up on her arms.

"Which is it, Vincent? You act as if you're going to ravish me despite my predilections against it at this time, then warn me against enticing you."

He gave her a hyena smile from his seat. She shivered: prey caught in a predator's lair. "I plan on worshipping you, love, but I still would prefer waiting until we were in our bedroom, as there is more space."

She glared at him. "You're toying with me."

"Perhaps." He held his hand out to her and helped her up. She gave him an angry look as she sat next to him and crossed her arms. She had never seen him in such a mood. Generally, he was more predictable, and only changed his mind once per night. Currently his mood and mind seemed to be changing within seconds.

Natalia opened her mouth to let out some angry words, but the car slowed and came to a stop. The engine died as the driver side door opened. The driver slammed the door shut, ran around the car, and then opened the passenger door. Natalia closed her mouth with a snap, and decided to keep quiet until they were alone in their room. Vincent gave her another hyena smile before his face became stoic and he exited the car. Natalia took his offered hand and climbed out. She glared at him again then noticed that Rebecca stood nearby. Charlie was behind her, the boxed sword in his arms. The look on her friend's face drove all thoughts of Vincent out of Natalia's head.

Rebecca reached out a shaky hand and gently touched the crimson on Natalia's white dress. "We will mourn him in our way tonight. In three days, we remember his life." She caught Natalia's gaze and showed her own grief. "If for some reason you aren't there, I will take it as a personal insult. Stay here these next three days, warrior. You are needed."

Rebecca turned and left up the garage steps. Charlie stepped forward, handed her the box with her sword, bowed low then followed his mate up the steps. Doug nodded to her then followed the others up the stairs. Natalia turned to Vincent as the last of them disappeared. "Where's Orlando's body?"

"I believe some of the humans already took him out to the pyre. She was waiting for you and the others would not go to his body until she did."

"Why wait for me? Why not leave instructions?"

"More impact this way. You don't understand what's going on here, do you?" There was a small smile on his face, which was a vast difference from his hyena smile.

"He died saving my life, she wants me here to mourn."

Vincent continued to give her his slight smile, then placed his arm around her lower back and steered her toward the stairs. She held onto the box as if it held delicate roses. They walked silently to their sitting room. Once inside Vincent took out his remote and shut down the surveillance equipment. He let her lead the way through the bedroom and the bathroom, and turned off the recording equipment as they went. He opened the door for them but allowed her to travel through the maze and to his bedroom without him. All the dangerous items had been removed from the tower room. She was allowed in the room, but only to retrieve the sword or return it.

Vincent went back down to the kitchen where he knew there would be humans. He made sure to take enough blood to stay awake long enough to do as he pleased to his lovely Natalia. Done, he returned to Natalia, who he found leaning over the bathroom sink. She stared at herself angrily in the mirror. He came up behind her, caressed her arms as he wrapped himself around her and brought her to a standing position. He leaned in and kissed her neck softly.

Natalia tried to pull away, but he had her trapped. "Vincent, this isn't… I'm not…" She shook her head, as she tried to find the words. "This isn't right."

"What? My wanting to make love to you in the wake of a battle? One passion replaces another. Why is that wrong? Because someone died? We will mourn him in three days' time, Natalia. Tonight, I worship you."

She tried to turn around to face him, but once again he simply held her in place. She had to resort to looking at his face in the mirror. "Why do you wish to worship me? Why did Charlie kneel and bow when he took the sword and gave it back? Why did Rebecca specifically ask me to be there when she knew I would be?"

"He died to save your life."

Vincent shook his head, leaned into her neck, nuzzled her skin, and tried hard not to bite into her jugular. He knew how easy it would be to simply sink his teeth into her supple body and change her. When he took her blood earlier, he fought not to continue past the three swallows. It was why he flipped back and forth between possessing her immediately and waiting until he could take her slowly. He wanted her skin to burn from his touch. He knew the consequences of changing her before she desired it. He caught her eye in the mirror and closed his eyes quickly, to stop her from seeing his thoughts.

Natalia stood carefully in his hold. Though it was not always easy to read her lover, she saw in his eyes what he wanted. Vincent wanted to change her; she was not ready. Natalia knew she couldn't fight him without a weapon. The closest thing to a weapon within reach was the hairdryer, which sat on the counter, cord wrapped around the nozzle. It was hefty enough, but she knew she wouldn't be able to knock him out with it. Natalia groaned and leaned into her vampire as his hand ran down her side and he growled into her neck. Her breath caught as she realized she almost wanted him to do it.

Her hand found his hair, tangled in the short soft mane. "Vincent. Please."

Her voice was so torn by desire; neither knew what she asked. Vincent pulled away gently, as his desire gripped him to the breaking point. He turned her around and tipped her head up to look into her fiery eyes. Her lower lip quivered. With a shaky hand, he reached into her hair and started to pull out her bobby pins. Her hair fell softly over her shoulders. He moved very slowly, to tame the raging beast that threatened to tear out her jugular.

Once her hair was loose, he ran his hands through her tresses. His eyes closed as the warm strands threatened to wrap around his questing fingers. She stared at him, her eyes full of trust and determination. She had the same look as earlier: a leader's look. He fell into the look, pulled her close and kissed her deeply. She melted against him, and gripped his back with her curled fingers. She wanted him to move quicker, but Vincent pulled away and caressed her cheeks with a feather touch.

The evening had proved overwhelming for Natalia. She did not want to remember Orlando's sacrifice or how her lover and the wolves reacted toward her. One sure way of forgetting things, although temporarily, was when Vincent pounded into her like a rampant beast. Now, he moved slow and kissed the skin he exposed as he unzipped her dress. She plunged her hands into his golden mane, tugged fiercely, and tried to draw him back up to stare into his eyes.

"Vincent! Give me what I want!"

Her tone of voice made him growl. There was sheer determination: she would not be denied. His mind was made up; he would not be turned from his current actions. Vincent straightened himself. He then slid her dress off her body completely, and let it slide down and pool onto the floor. He growled at what he exposed. She wore a corset. He fell to his knees before her, grabbed her by her hips and bit her inner thigh. He bit her just to the right of the garter belt strap that held up her now ripped nylons. He used his teeth to undo the snaps as her hands continued to pull his hair.

Vincent stood to turn her around and played with the laces that held the corset together. It had been a long time since he had the pleasure of unlacing a lady. Natalia had no idea how much she enticed him with the corset. He pulled the laces free of the knots, then wrapped the laces around his hand and pulled the laces tighter. She inhaled sharply as the garment bit into her skin and squeezed her ribs closer together. He let go of the lace tips, grasped the lowest and highest lace crossing, and pulled until the laces were taunt. He worked his way to the middle of the corset slowly and watched his lover's face in the mirror. She moaned as the metal boning constricted her lungs and inhibited her breath.

"The next time you wear one of these, you'll have to let me help you." He pulled the middle-crossed lace, and leaned into her ear. "Breathe out, love. Let me tie this proper."

"Can't breathe."

Oh, the desire in her voice. He growled into her ear and pulled the lace hard. She cried out as the metal boning pressed further into her skin.

"Do you like how it feels? Do you like how it constricts, cutting off your air supply? This is another of the things I desire to do to you Natalia. Having you shackled to my wall? Just the start. If you let me, I'll tie you into all sorts of positions." He pulled the lace again, which made her cry out and exhale. "But that will have to wait. Tonight, I wish to worship you. Tell me Natalia, what will you let me do to you? How may I worship your body, mistress?"

"You seem to know how to do that without instruction, Vincent. Why is tonight any different?"

He fell to his knees again and turned her around. "I wish you to tell me what to do, mistress, because tonight it pleases me to please you in any way you want. Instruct me, my love; tell me how to make you scream."

She looked down into his eyes and saw the same look as earlier: a look of subservience. Whatever his motivation, it was now clear to her that he wanted her in control. Part of her mind showed her the image of Orlando's head being ripped off his body and all she wanted was to forget. Here was her escape. Vincent had always offered her shelter from the pain in her life.

Tonight was no different. She started breathing hard and fast as the implication of what he wanted set in. She had taken control before, many times, but this was the first time he asked for it. He wanted her to control him. It made her heart race. She could push him to his limit. She smiled a hyena smile as she realized he would be the one screaming tonight. She placed her hands on his shoulders and pushed him to the floor. She took one step then placed her foot on his chest.

"I still don't understand why you want this Vincent, but by the time you fall asleep, you will regret giving me control."

He saw the look in her eye and understood her smile. He wondered, as she stood above him and grinned, whether he had made the right decision. Until he realized, there was no decision in his actions, only desire. In the end, he didn't regret one single action. She did get him to scream many, many times. Somehow, he managed not to change her.

19

Six Months later

Vincent sat at his desk, and stared at his smartphone, an inscrutable expression on his face. He sighed then switched to staring out at the darkness beyond his study's window. Joseph moved from his corner to sit in the far chair in front of Vincent's desk. He made sure to cut in front of Vincent's line of sight to break his master's concentration.

"She needs you?"

"Yes."

"Is it serious?"

"She doesn't call unless it is. You're coming with me."

Joseph raised an eyebrow. "Where else would I be?"

Vincent gave his friend a bored look. "You didn't last time."

He crossed his arms and smiled. "Last time you needed your strongest to stay and look after your new mate. Now, your mate can take care of herself. Who else do you take?"

"Anthony and Ben."

"Should we call Owen and Kim back?"

He considered. The pair was on vacation. Occasionally, Vincent's loyal vampires needed to get away and do as they saw fit. If there were too many rules chaining his vampires to his side, it chafed against their nature and made them ornery. When they asked for a vacation, Vincent granted it, as long as nothing was linked back to him. He was loath to call them back, as he understood how much the time away was needed. Vincent tapped his fingers on the desk, and concentrated on the task at hand. He leaned forward in agitation. "This is really bad timing. Morgan's close to finding Edwin but there is still too much dissension in the ranks."

"But your sire needs you."

"Yes."

"And you will go to her."

"Yes."

"And you will help her."

"Yes."

"And you will sleep in her bed."

"Yes."

"And this bothers you because you're with Natalia."

"Yes." He leaned back, then stood to pace to release his anxiety.

"Why don't you talk to your human about this situation and find out how she feels? Or simply ask her to come along? We might need her and her sword."

"She won't accept that."

Joseph smiled. "Who won't accept what?"

Vincent stopped behind Joseph's chair and stared down hard at his friend's head. "Where is she?"

"She's in the house, I'm not sure where." He leaned forward and pressed a button on the intercom on Vincent's desk. "Mierka?"

"She's in your bathroom. Taking a bath." She clicked off.

Vincent took a moment to breathe deep and let it out slowly in a sigh. He tossed instructions over his shoulder as he left the room. "Gather the house in the training room. I'll fetch Natalia."

It was six months after Edwin's dethroning, and the spineless weasel had yet to be found. Vincent acted as if he oversaw the area. Most of the vampires still in the Bay Area were either loyal to him or saying they were in order not to be staked.

Morgan and Kari, who had come to him some years ago, pleading for help, were being watched. He didn't trust either of them, but would allow them their lives, as long as they did nothing rash. Morgan had pledged loyalty a week after Edwin's Red Tie disaster. Kari, who had not been present at the function, came to Vincent the day after Morgan and pledged her loyalty. As she seemed to be interested in information, she was given to Anthony for instruction.

Morgan too, expressed an interest in information gathering. He seemed to find enough information on Edwin's stragglers that Anthony quickly promoted him to Second Sergeant. Vincent, Joseph and Anthony kept their heads about them. Though Morgan had not been part of Edwin's inner sanctum, he had been on the fringes. It was possible the young vampire was trying to get Edwin back into power. As a result, they had him watched.

Another addition, or rather return, was Franklin. He had been spying in Edwin's home for House LeGris for eight years. He did not enjoy it. To prove his loyalty, he had to drink Edwin's blood and do everything the twisted Captain asked. He was happy to be home and did nothing more than reacquaint himself with his comrades. Vincent had been glad to see him return. He was a faithful and loyal friend, which he needed currently.

Lost in thought, Vincent found himself at his bathroom door and paused. He could hear soft conversation on the other side of the door. He frowned as he realized Mierka had not told him everything. Someone was with Natalia. When he realized the two voices were female, his thoughts calmed, and he opened the door.

Natalia sat in the large round tub, and faced the door. Behind her, washing her hair was Diana. There were candles for light instead of the overheads. Vincent closed the door and walked quietly to lean against the nearby counter. There was a touch of something in the air, which wove itself around and into his will. Diana was casting a spell of some sort. He wondered why. Natalia was not hurt and didn't appear to need any help. He waited for his woman to acknowledge him. She made him wait as she and Diana finished their conversation.

Diana helped her rinse her hair then helped her out of the tub. Vincent watched with jealousy as the healer dried his woman off with a large towel, steps away. He crossed his arms, and balled his hands into fists. Though he wanted to reach out and grab her, there was business to take care of first. Vincent stared at his woman instead, and ground his teeth with impatience as he waited for her to acknowledge him. Diana left before Natalia said a word.

"Did you need something?" She looked at him sidelong, barley turning toward him.

"I have to speak with you."

"About what?" She took the hair dryer and plugged it in. She turned it on low to continue talking undisturbed. She felt sleepy, and calm, and wanted nothing more than to lie on her bed and drift in her thoughts.

"I just finished a conversation with Lorraine." His eyes traced Natalia's body, as he wished he had time.

"Your sire?" She sighed and turned off the dryer. She finally faced him, her calm still fully intact. "What's going on?"

"I have to go. She needs my help."

"How long?" She stepped in front of him and let the towel drop from around her torso.

He ground his teeth, closed his eyes, and squeezed his fists tighter. It was becoming increasingly difficult not to throw her down on the floor and have his way with her. He just didn't have the time. "I leave tonight and stay no more than three nights."

Natalia reached out and caressed his closed fist. He opened his eyes when he heard her gasp. "What did you do?"

Surprised by her question, he looked down at his now open hand. There were four half circles of crimson on his palm. Blood pooled in the shallow of his palm, and ran down the sides of his hand. He hadn't even felt it. Vincent opened his other fist and saw a similar scene. He frowned into Natalia's eyes. Her eyes were clouded and dreamy, as if drugged. He almost asked what had transpired between her and Diana when Natalia brought his hand to her mouth and licked his hand clean. Once the tiny pool was gone, she sucked on his hand. Vincent growled, closed his wounds, and gave her his other palm to clean.

When his hands were clean, Vincent turned Natalia around and pressed her back into his chest. Reading his intent, she brushed her mostly wet hair away from her neck and tipped her head to the side. He growled into her skin and bit her shoulder as gently as he could. She tensed with the pain but relaxed into him when he sucked her blood.

Natalia felt the calm she felt pass to her lover through her blood. Rather than take it away, his feeding seemed to spread it and complete it. When he pulled away and turned her around to kiss her, she could see the same look on his face she felt on her own.

Vincent placed his hands on her cheeks and drew her lips closer. Every movement seemed to take a lifetime, but there was no longer any hurry to his thoughts or anxiety to his actions. The kiss was long and drawn out, unlike his usual frantic embraces when he tasted his blood on her tongue. The slow seduction continued, unhindered by the absence of time. Vincent knew that at any moment, someone, probably Joseph, would knock on the door and disturb this calm, slow dance. As time passed and no one knocked, his thoughts faded away and he became one with the touch of her.

Vincent placed her on the counter, caressed, and kissed her softly which caused her head to spin. Her smile of earlier continued to grow, until it was nearly a laugh. To laugh, she would have had to think, and the fog of her mind was too complete for something as complex as thought. She knew nothing but his touch and his stroke, as he had somehow found his way inside her. Euphoria set in slowly, climbed up their bodies and surrounded them in a hazy cocoon.

ℭ ℬ

It felt like hours later when the knock finally came. Joseph opened the door before anyone could answer. Vincent turned slowly toward the door. Natalia still caressed him gently to draw him back into her charms.

Joseph glanced around, felt something in the air, and frowned as Vincent turned his attention back to his woman. Both their movements were languid, as if they were swimming through water.

"Your men are waiting for you, sir. Perhaps you should join us?" His voice was stern, slightly louder than usual. Both turned to him, identical looks of serenity awash on their faces.

Vincent spoke reluctantly, as if through years of distance. "How…

long… waiting?"

Joseph stared at the couple and understood. He shook his head. He needed to get Vincent out. Diana must have woven a spell, and the pair was caught in its delicate web. Joseph stepped forward, and tried not to look amused. He extracted a half-witted Vincent and moved him toward the door of the bathroom. He threw Vincent into the bedroom and went back for Natalia. He wrapped her in a towel and picked her up. Once in the bedroom, he placed her on the bed, and ignored her light inviting touch. By the time he turned back to Vincent, his boss had regained his senses.

"How long?" He zipped himself up and tucked in his shirt.

"For what?"

"How long since I came up here?"

"Few minutes."

"What?" Nothing but shock.

Joseph shrugged, and enjoyed the confused look on his boss' face. It wasn't often Vincent didn't know what was going on. "Few minutes."

Vincent frowned and pulled out his cell. Barely twenty minutes had passed since he came to talk to Natalia. He frowned again, and wished the cobwebs would dissipate. "What…" He shook his head and started again. "Where are they?"

"I thought the meeting room more appropriate. I'll bring Natalia up to date. Go brief the men."

Vincent nodded and left, as time crunched in around him. Joseph turned his attention back to Natalia, who was leisurely stretched on the bed in imitation of a cat. Her towel had fallen away unnoticed. His eyes traced her nakedness, as she purred her contentment. He shook his head, walked to a closet, and pulled out clothing. By the time he returned to the bed, she seemed to be coming back to herself. She didn't hide her body, which boiled his generally frigid blood. He threw her clothing at her, leaned against the bedpost, and waited for her to speak.

Natalia pulled on the dress Joseph had launched at her, her mind still groggy. "Where's Vincent?"

"Giving the men instructions."

"You're going?"

"Yes." He stared at her upturned sleepy face, and caught her glance. "Would you prefer it if I didn't?"

She gave him a sly look. "I understand he has to go. I won't prevent him from going. But if you stayed, at least I'd have company."

"He is my master; I am his guard. I protect him." He hid the laughter in his voice.

Natalia sighed heavily. She wouldn't have slept with him anyway. She wanted to tease, but he wasn't taking the bait. "You said he was where?"

"Meeting room. I'll escort you." He held his arm out to her. Natalia stood, fully dressed in a red cotton dress. She took his arm and he led her out the rooms, down the stairs and into the meeting room. There was a long table with twelve wooden chairs around it. Vincent was at the head of the table, seated on the throne he had pulled out of storage one month after Edwin's party. Anthony was seated at the other end. Mierka was to Vincent's right, facing the door. Next to her was Ben, then Dr. Elving, then Franklin then Julia. To Anthony's right were Lilly, Diana, Angie, and Rebecca, with an empty seat to Vincent's left.

The talk stopped as the pair walked into the room. Joseph let Natalia's arm go and went to whisper with Diana before he sat in the empty chair. Vincent stood and greeted Natalia with a kiss. Then, to Anthony's chagrin, Vincent led his lady to his throne. The head vampire chose to stand behind her as he continued to talk.

"As I was saying, Mierka, you will be in charge. With Edwin still at large, I want everyone on guard, as we have been for the past six months. If Morgan finds Edwin, have him brought here and lock him in my dungeon. Ben, Anthony, and Joseph will be accompanying me. We leave in half an hour. Get ready. The rest of you know your posts; go to them. Lilly, Angie, Rebecca, a word with you."

The others left, dismissed. Natalia stayed where she was. Her place was with her man. She watched as he sat next to her, but waited for everyone else to leave before starting. She was surprised when he addressed her first.

"Natalia. Lilly is leaving us. She wishes to return to New York. I have granted her permission. She will be leaving with me. Diana is coming too. Her skills will be tested to see if she is worthy of being your healer."

Natalia looked at Lilly, a little hurt. "You didn't tell me."

"I was going to. This trip came up before I could tell you."

Natalia stood and went to Lilly, who stood when the human was by her side. Natalia embraced Lilly, as tears threatened behind her eyes. She had connected with Lilly on a deeper level than any other person, as Lilly had to get inside her head on many occasions to heal her. They also spent many mornings talking over breakfast. She sobbed and heard Lilly sob in return. The tears ran unchecked.

"I'll miss you."

"You will see me again."

"When?"

Their silence gave the answer. Lilly could come out here if she wanted, but family might keep her from doing so. And Natalia had no desire to leave the west coast before she found Donald. The hug became tighter, then the women let go; there was nothing else to do.

"We will see each other again. I won't have it any other way."

Lilly kissed Natalia's cheek, wiped away the tears and left the room, quickly. She had been caring for the human for almost nine years; it was hard to leave her.

Vincent stood and wrapped his arms around Natalia. He wanted nothing more than to comfort her. He had two more pieces of business, thought. He spoke to the other human without letting Natalia go.

"Angie. I want your people patrolling the grounds day and night. The wolves will not be out. Go with goodwill." She nodded and left. Vincent turned to Rebecca, as he released Natalia. "Keep your wolves away from the main house.

Rebecca gave him a look. "You don't trust someone."

Vincent nodded. "Mierka has separate instructions, should anything happen. Do not stay on the grounds at night. Come back each day that I'm gone and check on things."

Rebecca bowed low then left the room. Vincent turned back to his woman as she dried her tears.

"Did Lilly tell you earlier than today?"

"No. But I suspected." He went to Natalia, picked her up and carried her to his throne. He sat and cradled her to him, to comfort her. All he could do was caress her and kiss her neck and jawline. He would be without her for four days. Even with Lorraine at his beck and call, he would desire Natalia's warm touch.

"You didn't share your thoughts?"

"Didn't feel the need – I need you. Come with me."

He kissed her hard and made her straddle him; her legs hung over the dragon head armrests. Her breath was taken by his kiss.

"Come with me." He repeated, his voice thick with emotion.

She answered breathlessly. "Why?"

"I need you." He held her in place as his arms tightened around her.

"As your protector? Or as your woman?" She caressed his cheek softly, as she tried to read his intent.

"Both." He closed his eyes to hide what simmered there but showed off his fangs.

"And you wish me to bring my sword?"

His eyes opened, and he caught her gaze. She saw the hunger in his eyes but didn't allow herself to dive into his blue depths. He nodded, incapable of speech. She sat in a very provocative position, but he had no time to take care of his hunger. He wanted to have sex with her while he sat in his throne.

She took his head in her hands and forced him to pay attention. "That would be foolish. The sword must be kept secret. And if any of Lorraine's vampires touched the sword, they would be dead. I will not go as your protector."

"Then come as my lover."

"What about Lorraine?" She caressed his cheeks again, loving the feel of him against her fingers.

"What about my sire?" He was tired of talking. She was distracting him too much. He contemplated biting her neck to quiet her words but couldn't reach her neck from his lower position.

"Will she seduce you?"

"Yes." He didn't seem to want the questions to continue.

"Will you let her?"

He looked in her eyes, to ensure she saw he told the truth. "Yes."

"Even if I'm there?"

He was quiet as he stared into her trusting, loving eyes. He closed his eyes then stood and sat her on the table. He started to pace to avoid answering. He felt her hand on his arm and turn to look at her.

"Your answer, vampire."

"Yes. I will sleep with her, even if you're there."

"Why do you want me to accompany you?"

"Because I desire your body and blood every day that I'm with you."

She leaned in and gave him an intense kiss, then pulled away and slapped him. "Am I to wait for you at your sire's house while you fight and screw and then get the leftovers?" She crossed her arms and gave him her determined look. "Fat chance, vampire. I have no desire to watch your sire seduce you from my side. I'll stay here."

She started toward the door, but felt his hand on her arm a second later and stopped.

"Natalia."

She turned to him and slipped into his arms. "Be careful, Vincent."

"Yes." He bent and nuzzled her neck. "You won't reconsider?"

"I have appointments during the day I want to keep."

He sighed heavily. "All right." He pulled back slightly and lifted her chin to look into her eyes. "I will return to you in four nights. Will you be waiting for me?"

She smiled seductively. "Where do you want me to meet you and what do you want me to wear?"

Vincent grabbed his woman to him again and gave her a hard kiss. They left the room together a few moments later as it was time for him to leave. She waited at the door with Mierka, who didn't like to be left behind either. Her skills were geared more toward stealth, not brute force. There were young vampires indiscriminately killings humans in New York. Lorraine wanted a show of force, not stealthy killers to stop the gang.

When the limo left the drive, Natalia returned to bed. Her first meeting of the day was in the early morning. She needed to be alert as she was meeting one of the Slayers who had helped lock her in the basement some time ago. They were meeting in a public place, but it was a trap, and Natalia had to be on her toes.

20

Natalia watched through binoculars from across the street as yet another Slayer walked nonchalantly into the corner café. She sighed, hung her head, and wondered how many she would have to kill to get out. She currently sat on the roof of the apartment building kitty corner to the arranged meeting place. She told Ashley that she needed to get her some information, and to come alone. Ashley decided to disobey her wishes. Natalia sighed again and slung her backpack across her shoulders. She left the roof the way she came, by the back wooden steps that at one point had been a fire escape.

It took her two months to decide whom to tell about the demons Edwin summoned. It took three months to convince Ashley to meet her, and another month to plot the best place to meet. Natalia watched the place for the past two weeks, to find as many ways out as possible. There were two conventional ways: front entrance and back kitchen door. The two walls that faced the street were adorned with beautiful picture windows. She was sure the windows were regular glass and could be busted with a diner chair or Slayer if necessary. She also noticed who were regulars and who were not. Half of the people frequenting the small café today were not regulars. She was ready for the battle she hoped she wouldn't have to fight.

Upon entering the café, Natalia noticed Ashley and made a beeline to her. Ashley was dressed as simply as always, in jeans and plain t-shirt. Her socks, purple to match her shirt, barely showed between her jean cuffs and sensible athletic shoes. The young girl, no more than 20 years of age, seemed to be conflicted in her devotion to Slayers. Though she often stated all Hellspawn should die, she was quick to try and find ways to save them. She had also been the only one on Natalia's side when the Slayers captured her and Wayne. She was the only Slayer Natalia could still talk to.

Natalia took the seat next to Ashley and slung the backpack onto the counter. The waitress came over immediately. Natalia took note of this, as it seemed highly irregular for this café. The older woman had never been here before at this time of day. The waitress outfit was convincing, even had a badge with her name on it. The name badge was engraved, showing permanence, not a temporary name printed out on paper. Delores could be new, but Natalia would bet on Slayer with an eye for details. Natalia also knew the look in the woman's eye. She sighed and nodded to the waitress.

"Coffee please."

Delores nodded and turned to the coffee maker a few steps away. As the coffee was poured, Natalia took out the photocopies of the journals from her backpack.

"I told you I wanted to speak with you alone." Natalia spoke in a normal conversational tone.

"I am alone."

Natalia turned her back to the counter and counted the obvious Slayers in the café. "I see ten, eleven if Delores is one of yours."

"There was nothing I could have done to prevent this." She spoke so low, Natalia had to lean in to hear her.

Natalia whispered back just as softly. "All you had to do was not tell anyone we were meeting."

"Why did you contact me?" Ashley turned angrily on her stool as her voice grew loud.

"I fought something you need to know about." She looked around, then turned back to face the kitchen. "It's all in the journals, but many Slayers ignored these demons because of who talked about them. I brought photocopies as proof. I'd have brought you the creatures, but I don't know how to control them, and had to kill them instead."

Ashley took the papers and skimmed the pages. "You're kidding."

"That's what I said."

"These aren't real."

"As real as everything else."

"Let's say they're real. Why did you want to tell me?"

"Someone needs to know they exist so that they can be stopped. They'll kill humans or possibly give them diseases, if all the accounts are true. Don't you guys try and stop creatures that kill humans?" Natalia reached into her pocket, pulled out a five and placed it on the counter next to her untouched coffee. Though she had tried to keep the waitress in her sights, she had not seen Delores pour all of it and was not about to drink the coffee. "They're real, they exist. They can be killed. All the information is in the papers I gave you. Read it and be prepared. I'll see you next time."

She walked three steps before a male voice rang out.

"What makes you think we'll let you leave?"

A smile came to Natalia's lips as she turned to face the man who sat next to Ashley. He wore a black suit, but the white collar gave him away. "There are a lot of your people here. You could probably take me down, except I have friends here, too."

Fifteen humans, four of them only pretending to be human, rose from various tables in the room. All were by the main entrance and the kitchen entrance. No one would get by them. All were Vincent's men; all had been coming here for more than three weeks, establishing themselves as regulars. There were no mundanes in the café. All were either loyal to Vincent or Slayers. Natalia made sure of it.

"We leave peaceable, or you all die. Your choice."

"What can humans do against us?"

"Humans? Not much. Humans with silenced guns? Lots. Werewolves? So much more." She shrugged, a devil's smile on her lips. "It's your choice Ashley. Choose wisely."

Ashley shook noticeably. She had apparently not thought of the bloodshed a confrontation would cause. She shook her head violently. "Let her leave. We'll do this another time."

The priest stood up and forced Ashley to do the same. "You will not leave here alive."

Natalia's smile of confidence did not waver and neither did the looks on her friends' faces. The humans and werewolves were ready for bloodshed. "What's your name Father?"

"What does that matter?" He sounded righteous and angry, Natalia's favorite kind of lunatic.

"I like to know the names of the people I kill. Makes it easier to pray for their eternal souls." She mocked him.

He visibly grew more righteous. "You will beg for mercy before the end comes."

A seductive look came over her features. "That would be a great way to go."

The father took a cross out of his suit and flashed it before her. He started frothing scripture. The words ran together and became unknowable. Natalia simply yawned and watched as her people got into position. The werewolves were still human, but Rebecca grinned with anticipation, yellow eyes blazing. Charlie looked ready to launch himself at the priest, and two of the humans had stepped up behind Natalia to guard her rear. Their guns were not yet visible, but their hands were at the ready. Natalia did not want to risk a fight in such a small space, therefore turned her attention to Ashley.

"Ashley?"

She looked at Natalia, fear in her eyes.

"Who is this?"

"Father Sulta." The name was past her lips before he could slam his hand on her shoulder to silence her.

"Father Sulta?" Natalia's voice rang with confidence.

He looked at her with hate.

"There are pedestrians on the sidewalk. We're next to a major bus stop. If we start anything, humans will die. Do you really want to risk the death of humans to kill me?"

"You're a Hellspawn's whore. You have caused the death of many of my kind. You will die!"

"Yes, yes, yes. But does it have to be today?" She spoke as if adding an appointment to her busy schedule.

"There are no innocents here."

She turned, and gestured at the windows, which ran the length of the café on both sides. The shops were open, and it was a lovely day. The streets were crowded with tourists. It was why Natalia chose this café. Slayers typically tried not to kill innocents.

Father Sulta followed her gaze, outraged at the truth. He slowly stretched then cracked his neck. "Fine. Leave. Take your demons. But know this. The next time-"

"Yeahyeahyeah." She waved his threat away, bored. "The next time you see me, I kill you. Not a problem." She turned to the room at large. "File out."

Her people followed her order quickly. Charlie moved to her, faced the room, and walked backwards out of the café. He held open the door for her. Natalia stopped with one hand on the doorframe and one on the strap of her backpack. Charlie cleared his throat nervously, but something remained unfinished. She turned back to lock eyes with Ashley.

Father Sulta still had his hand on her shoulder, as if to keep her in her place. It reminded Natalia of how Zechariah had treated her.

"Come with us." The room stilled. Ashley stared at her, and Natalia saw the shock, then consideration, then blankness, steal across the girl's features. Ashley was no Slayer and both women knew it. She had never heard the angels and only ran with Slayers because her family had been killed by a demon long ago. Natalia decided to push her luck. She took a step forward, kindness in her eyes.

"Have you heard the voices yet? Or are they letting you have your own mind?" Her voice sounded motherly, and Ashley started to shake. Natalia stepped forward; her actions unclear even to herself. Charlie's hand was suddenly on her arm, tentative and cautious, and stopped her advance.

Pain gripped Ashley's features as Father Sulta clamped his hand on her shoulder. "Take her out of here or we kill her."

Cold hate surrounded Natalia's body. Though Father Sulta sounded as if he spoke to Charlie, his gaze remained locked with Natalia's until his last word. Then, his face had turned toward Ashley. Natalia didn't think Sulta had meant they would kill <u>her</u>. She had the distinct impression he meant he'd kill Ashley. Natalia made up her mind. She turned and left, hoping that one day she would be able to free Ashley from the Slayer's hold. Ashley should be free to pursue her own life and beliefs, without the undue influence of those like Father Sulta.

C3 →

Natalia sat at the desk in Vincent's library, thinking. She saw Ashley at the café yesterday morning and had a hard time getting the young woman out of her mind. She wanted to help her, but didn't know how. She tried to call her earlier, but the phone number was disconnected. For the moment, she had to let Ashley go. Natalia sighed and looked back down at the desk in front of her, where a large Slayer journal sat. In her hand was a scanner.

Most of the Slayer journals were too old to be rifled through on a regular basis. She wanted to scan each page and save the books to an external hard drive to preserve the books. Also, it was easier to skim through computer files with the "find" tool then skim the physical pages. She tried to scan one book a week, but often found herself entangled between Vincent's sheets instead. With him gone, it was easier to get this sort of work done. Vincent had been gone two nights; she went through five large books in that short time. Lost in her work she didn't hear Franklin come in until he set the tray of food on the desk. She looked up to see a grin on his face.

"Hi. Thought you might be hungry."

She stared at the bowl of stew and glass of orange juice, and sighed in contentment. She glanced at the clock on the computer. About a half an hour ago, she contemplated some crackers and cheese. It was an easy snack to pick up and eat while still working but knew this was a better idea. She lost track of when she had eaten last. Her stomach growled at her. Natalia gave Franklin a grateful smile and moved her chair over a bit to get out of the way of her delicate equipment.

"Thanks. Didn't realize how hungry I was."

"You look like you could use a break. How about moving to the couches while you eat?"

Natalia considered and nodded. Franklin took the tray and carried it over to the coffee table between the two overstuffed couches. Memories of screwing Vincent flitted through Natalia's mind as she moved to the couch. Aside from other people's bedrooms, Natalia didn't think there was a single room in the house they hadn't christened yet. She shook her head as she realized: they had never screwed in the maze room or his tower bedroom. Natalia ran her hand through her hair and wiped away her thoughts. It was only a matter of time before they did.

Natalia sat on the couch and regarded Franklin, who sat across from her. He was a quiet man and generally stayed out of her way. He talked mostly with Vincent, in private. Joseph mentioned that this was normal. Franklin was never one to reach out to people. She took it as a compliment that he chose to not only bring her dinner but to stay and chat with her as well.

Franklin was of average height with red hair and emerald, green eyes. His skin was lighter than Vincent's. The unfortunate thing was that he almost always squinted or averted his gaze, which hid his beautiful eyes and made him look untrustworthy. His lids were half closed even now, which helped to keep his thoughts secret. Natalia let her dire thoughts go and regarded the food before her.

There was a bowl of stew, a glass of orange juice and a spoon and fork. As she grabbed the spoon, she knew a fork was a good idea as well. Most times, the person who cooked the stew cut the meat and vegetables in large chucks. Stirring carefully, Natalia crushed a few of the larger vegetables then picked up the bowl. She ate a few spoonsful then looked over at Franklin, whose eyes were more revealed. He stared at her intently. She stopped shoveling stew into her mouth and stared back.

"You look like you have something to say."

"Just my curiosity kicking in. Sorry if I was staring."

"If you want to know about me, ask." She leaned back on the couch and ate the stew slowly to enjoy the flavor. Lamb stew was a staple in the house, but it tasted different each time, depending on who made it. For instance, Angie used a lot of garlic and rosemary, while her daughter usually forgot to add spices. Lucas, whose family was originally from Brazil, flavored his stew with cumin. Natalia could usually figure out in the first few spoonfuls who had made it due to the taste. She frowned into the stew as an unfamiliar flavor invaded her tastebuds.

"How long have you been with Vincent?"

"About nine years." She continued to frown at the soup, as she tried to identify its maker.

"That's a long time for a vampire to toy with a human."

She gave him a hard look, wondering where he was going with his question. "We toy with each other. And nine years is only a blink in time to a vampire."

Franklin leaned forward as she yawned. "You're the only human lover he's kept for this long. Doesn't that worry you?"

"No. Should it?"

He leaned back, trying to get comfortable. "I suppose not." He paused to watch her eat a couple more spoonfuls. "I hear you're hunting a vampire?"

"My mother's killer." She didn't like to think of Donald as a vampire. Vincent was a vampire, a far better man than Donald had ever proven to be. Donald was a bloodsucker and only used humans to feed from.

"Why sleep with a vampire? Isn't that a little...contradictory?" He shifted again, and leaned forward.

Natalia frowned at him through a mouthful of food. His attitude started to worry her. And why couldn't she identify that taste? "Vincent's a vampire. My mother's killer is a blood sucker."

"There's a difference?" He continued to watch her intently.

Natalia yawned as exhaustion gripped her. "Donald...kills," she yawned, "anyone he chooses and uses women. Vincent has built...a network of humans...he can..." she yawned again, "protect and..." Her voice was soft. She shook her head. She shut her eyes and took a deep breath, to bring her thoughts back in line. "Vincent doesn't kill anyone unless they've hurt him or someone he protects."

"Vincent has killed many in the past; used humans worse than anyone else I've ever met. He's done things that make Edwin look mild."

She gave Franklin a hard stare, which would have had more power if it hadn't been broken up by a yawn. When the yawn subsided, she gave him a quizzical look. "I've read and heard of what he's done, I know he's no saint, but he's never hurt children."

Natalia placed her spoon in the bowl, rubbed her eyes with her free hand, and wondered why she was suddenly so tired. She leaned forward, put the bowl back on the tray, and picked up the orange juice. She drank half the juice down, but nearly choked when that same unfamiliar taste exploded on her tongue. Wide-eyed, she brought her now heavy head up to stare at Franklin. The smile on his face showed the story as somewhere nearby something detonated with a muffled THOOOOM.

Natalia dropped the drugged juice and slowly stood. She had to find...someone and tell them...something. Her mind no longer actively working, she tried to go...somewhere. Natalia crashed to the ground. Her arm hit the table and tray on the way down. The soup bowl few away and spread stew all over the floor and couch. As she lay on the ground trying desperately not to fall into the blissful dark abyss of sleep, Natalia saw someone walk to Vincent's trusted friend. Her line of sight was low, as she had collapsed headfirst. She looked up with crossed eyes, but could not see who stood next to Franklin. Her mind slipped to the cold metal in her hand and her survival instinct took over. Her last unhurried action before she faded into a deep sleep was to stuff the fork into her jean pocket.

Franklin watched with a boyish grin as Natalia fell into his trap. The familiar hand on his shoulder comforted him. He turned to Edwin and gave his Captain a welcomed and friendly look. Edwin smiled magnanimously down at his servant.

"You've done me a great service Franklin. Once all this is done, you will be rewarded as promised." He turned to look at Natalia, asleep on the ground. "I think I'll have more fun with this one when she wakes. Franklin, take her to the dungeon and lock her up." He turned to three others who gathered at the entrance to the library. "Kill everyone else in the house."

His men surged about to do as ordered. Franklin locked Natalia in the dungeon, a smile on his face. He was now the only one in the household with security codes.

21

Natalia woke as a harsh scent invaded her nostrils. She pulled her head away as her eyes threatened to open. The unpleasant tang came again, and she tried to breathe through her mouth. A hand pressed against her mouth, and forced her to breathe through her nose. She inhaled deeply, and brought salty air into her lungs. Her eyes flew open wide, but her lids and head drooped back down when the smelling salts were taken away from her nose.

She was still dreadfully tired but woke up as she almost cried out in pain. Her arms sizzled with needle pricks as blood rushed back into her veins. Her stomach threatened to empty itself of the raw acid which rolled around inside. Natalia tried not to panic for herself and the others in the household as the men near her spoke.

"She's had too much sedative." The voice penetrated her mind, but she didn't recognize it.

"Get her on her feet, that'll wake her up."

Another unknown voice, but one with slightly more authority. She was unchained and hauled to her feet. Her mind cleared a little bit more, but she let her captors think she was still passed out. She even made herself a little heavier. When her dead weight didn't faze them, she understood they were vampires and probably at full blood. One of the men grabbed her under her arms and hauled her to her feet, then grabbed her around the waist. She let the man carry all her weight, and made her feet drag behind her.

They walked her down the short hall to the main dungeon, where Natalia finally heard the screams. Out of lidded eyes she perceived a human man chained to the far wall. There were six other men in the room: Edwin, who stood by the human, Franklin and four other guards. Cold hatred gripped her mind, and a plan took over her thoughts. She started to walk just a little and stopped as something poked her in her thigh through her jean pocket. She had a weapon. She would have to be in close range, but she had a weapon, and she might be able to kill the betraying bastard.

"Is she awake?" Edwin's shrill voice made her curl her lip.

"Starting to be."

"Lean her against the wall. Let's see if her presence makes this one talk. Franklin. Guard her."

She heard an odd tone in his voice but she couldn't place it and let it go. Stray thoughts wouldn't help her. She was placed on the cement floor, her back to the wall. Franklin did as told, and stood a little in front of her. The fork was in her left pocket, but she thought she would be able to reach it, as Franklin inadvertently hid her actions. She was also able to see the man chained to the wall and realized it was Charlie. It surprised her, as he was still human and the vampires in the room were still here. Edwin reached out and touched him with a cattle prod before asking him a question.

"Where are the rest of the humans?" His voice was light as if they were having a pleasant conversation.

"Is she alive?" Charlie tensed as electricity ran through his body again. Natalia watched with wonder as he once again controlled himself enough not to change. She wondered, in awe, how he was able to hold it in.

"Answer my question or you get more of the same." Edwin held the baton inches from Charlie's face.

Natalia had the fork in her right hand now, and knew she had to move. She felt good enough to move quickly but knew she might pass out if she wasn't careful. She took the time to inhale deeply twice then threw herself up and at Franklin's head. She grabbed his hair with one hand and plunged the fork into his neck with the other as if spearing a piece of meat. She then ripped out the crude weapon before Franklin could react. His jugular and carotid were ripped open, and blood spewed everywhere. He moved forward to try and get away from his attacker. She used his forward momentum to tip his head back and plunge the fork into his Adam's apple.

He finally shook her off, as blood bubbled red out of his neck and mouth. He turned around to face her and she shoulder checked him, to try and get him to the ground. She vaguely heard Edwin as he ordered his men to stay their posts. He wanted to watch the festivities. Part of her mind made a connection, but her tactical side pushed it aside for later consideration as she stepped to the downed Franklin. She brought her booted foot up to slam down on his wrist, but he grabbed her foot and tried to pull her off her feet. Gravity won, but she shifted her weight, fell on top of Franklin, grabbed the fork, and plunged it deeper into his throat. He threw her off, grabbed the fork and threw it in the opposite direction.

Natalia rolled and assessed the situation. He healed as she watched. She wanted him dead. On her way to the large room, she noticed the steel doors to the steps were closed. It would take too long to key in the code and wait for the door to open. With no exit, and no weapon, she only had one chance. Natalia just hoped he would follow. As she ran, she heard Franklin yell.

"Why aren't you getting the others to capture her? I need help Edwin!"

There was no answer but the sound of Franklin's footsteps behind her.

Natalia ran to the end of the hallway, grateful for the head start. The door at the other end of the hall was open, which made things easier. The ghul was in here. She didn't know what a ghul was but knew it would kill Franklin if she threw him into the pit. She heard Franklin behind her and smiled. As her blood pumped harder, her vision started to blur, and darken around the edges. Her determination surged forward, and a little more speed escaped her. She ran through the door, leapt across the hole, and slammed into the wall before he could reach her.

Franklin knew where she was going and grinned. He followed her into the room, leapt the across the hole, and was immediately hit in the face with her fist. He didn't think she had the strength in her to push him back, but she did. The blow pushed him back enough to make him land on the edge of the hole. His feet slipped out from under him, and he fell. His hands caught the ledge and his blood curdled with the howl from below. He stared up at the woman who grinned at the edge.

"Help me!"

"Go to Hell."

When she dressed earlier, Natalia had the urge to wear her favorite boots. They were a deep rich red, made from hard leather with a steel toe tip. She wore the boots whenever she was headed for a fight as they were almost weapons unto themselves. She was delighted she had gone with the impulse as she prodded his fingers with the inch thick, hard rubber soles. His face turned to pure terror as she very slowly and very carefully stepped on his fingers and ground his bones with her boots. He and the creature below him howled in unison as pain, then fear, echoed in the oubliette. Franklin fell when she stepped onto his other hand. Her smile was pure pleasure when she heard his bones crunch. He apparently didn't know how to fall.

A yowl of ecstasy emanated from the creature far below. Whatever the ghul was, it would feast well today. Natalia looked up as the scream stopped. Edwin stood just to the right of the doorway and stared at her. One of Edwin's men held an exhausted Charlie up. The unlikely pair moved to the left, into the room to the far wall, which allowed two more to enter the room. This left two outside the small room. She held Edwin's gaze, and wondered if she could kill him. Her epiphany of earlier came back and she voiced her opinion.

"You were planning on killing him."

He held her gaze. "Once a traitor, always a traitor."

"What happens now?" She wanted to jump across the oubliette to fight Edwin, but she couldn't jump that distance from a standing position. Though Charlie looked exhausted, Natalia was sure he was acting, but wasn't sure why.

"Vincent likes you, doesn't he?"

She stayed silent.

"I wonder how he would look at you if I changed you. Would he still love you if his greatest enemy changed you?"

She didn't even try to hold back her laughter. "Don't flatter yourself. You were nothing but an effortless distraction. A piece of lint on his fine suit, needing nothing more than a swipe to brush your existence out of his mind."

Anger contorted his face and she laughed again. When Edwin pulled a gun from under his jacket, her laughter stilled. He pointed it in Charlie's general direction. "He wasted his life to come to the house and ask for you. We captured him easily, tied him up and started interrogating him. All he did was ask for you. We finally decided to show him you were alive. Once he knew you were alive, he sagged and fell unconscious. Not much of a hero." He continued to belittle Charlie, but Natalia ignored Edwin.

She looked over at Charlie, who sat on the floor back against the wall, as she had been a few moments before. She finally caught his eye and nearly gasped. She saw the pain he had endured, the barely suppressed rage of the animal within, the love he felt for her and the caution that kept him human and understood. He needed to make sure she was okay. Now that he knew she was alive and well, he waited for the opportunity to let the rage take over so he could rescue her.

Natalia tore her eyes away and saw the hole not three feet from the edge of her toes. She knew whatever was down there was weak and hungry. It had fed, but probably not enough. Joseph warned her the ghul would kill her, but that was when she was weak and unprepared. Now, though weak and woozy, she was prepared. If she jumped down, she might die, but Edwin would not have her. If she jumped, Charlie would probably follow her. She could fight the ghul until Charlie came to get her.

Though she had her brains, her determination and steel toe boots, she didn't have any good weapons. Her eyes found the werewolf who leaned against the wall. Charlie was a weapon. Currently he was a gun without bullets, impotent with his concern for her. He could change and kill everyone in this room, then jump down to help her. Should he Blitzkrieg in the small room he would hurt her. No maybes about it. He wouldn't unleash his rage until she was safe. There was no way to escape out the door; Edwin blocked the door on this side. There were two men on the other side, who stood side by side. She didn't want to rush Edwin in case he decided to use the gun on her.

Natalia took a deep breath, stared Edwin down and silenced him. "Charlie. Do it."

It was an order and the wolf followed. Edwin tried to fire at him, but he had the safety engaged. Charlie turned Blitzkrieg and Natalia stepped forward and jumped down the oubliette.

Charlie roared his rage and was thought no more. Two of the guards were down and dust before the taste of blood penetrated his thoughts. He growled happily and went for the other one. Edwin escaped out the door, then shut and locked it behind him. Deep in the oubliette, the ghul screeched its happiness. The joyous pain reached Charlie's animal mind and an image of Natalia seared his consciousness. He had come here to help her, and she was now in the hole, possibly dying. He jumped into the abyss.

೦ଷ ଵ

Natalia landed easily in a crouched position. She looked around, tried to see the creature, and couldn't. The light from above didn't penetrate deep into the dark dank cave. She could see enough to realize there were no bones on the floor, just dust. As she assessed the situation, she took deep slow breaths, to try not to gag. The smell was awful: as if rotten meat fermented in its own juices. She breathed through her mouth, and regretted it immediately. Sweat, fear, and pain were palpable on her tongue. Natalia turned to find the ghul. Nothing peered at her from the darkness, but she knew something watched her.

Then she felt it. A cold whiff of wind swept past her ear, brushed some hair back. Or rather, pulled it back. Her eyes flew open wide; she stood, and spun around to face her attacker. There was nothing there. Natalia felt the tug in her hair again and turned again. Still nothing. This happened another time and Natalia felt panic rise. She clamped a mental door on her panic, and stopped her thoughts. If she were thinking too much, then her warrior side would not come forward. Calmed, Natalia turned in the opposite direction from the tug and saw something in the shadows.

To say the creature was gaunt was an understatement. Its skin clung to it, grey and yellow with age, dirt, and dust. There was a smear of something dark across its face. It hissed at Natalia, and showed off sharp, long teeth. It was as if the creature's teeth were all fangs instead of just two. Its arms were bent at the elbow; its hands were bent at the wrist, long claws hanging down. Natalia started to get into position, but the ghul moved. The human found herself facing a wall with the thing behind her. Natalia tried to fight and couldn't as the creature sank its teeth into her neck. Pain took over and Natalia nearly passed out.

Charlie landed on his feet, and saw nothing but Natalia, who was pressed face first against the wall. Something had its head buried in her neck, as if to suck her dry. It was naked, very dirty and grew larger as it drank from Natalia. Charlie raked the creature's back with his long claws, and caused it to pull away from Natalia. The ghul spun around as Charlie attacked. He swiped twice at the thing's neck, and took off its head. It turned to dust and Charlie roared. The joyous cry stopped short when he saw Natalia's body slumped on the ground.

Charlie changed back to human before he touched Natalia. He saw the blood on her back and hissed in sympathy. The wounds on her neck and back bled freely. He had scratched her up in his haste to kill the creature. Natalia was out cold, perhaps thankfully. Charlie ripped her shirt up more than it was and hurriedly pressed a makeshift bandage to her neck. The blood held it in place, and he turned into wolf form. Charlie did his best to lick her wounds clean, changed back to human and used the rest of her ripped shirt as a bandage for her back. It was too dark to know if he had done a good enough job, and the place reeked of death and decay. He worried about infection, but there was nothing he could do.

Charlie gathered her in his arms, and wondered how the hell he would be able to get her out of here. He looked up and knew, beyond doubt, there was no way out. He sighed, settled himself comfortably against the wall and cradled Natalia. He had to wait for help, and would keep his hand over her neck bite to staunch the bleeding. It was the worst wound. Rebecca knew where he was. It was a small hope, but it was hope. He learned long ago, that when it came to Rebecca, he could hope without worry. She would find him. He sighed again, kissed the top of Natalia's head, and started the long process of waiting.

22

Vincent pulled out his phone for the fourth time that morning, and frowned when there were still no messages. He was in one of Lorraine's limos, surrounded by comrades who spoke loudly about their victory. All he could think of was Natalia. He had a disquieting feeling that all was not well in his house. There were no calls though, therefore everything was fine. Except for the feeling that crawled into his gut and bred discontent.

It had been a successful hunt. The group of rebellious young vampires were dealt with easily. That was to be expected with himself, Joseph, Ben, Anthony, Rowland, Maxine and Julianna fighting for Lorraine's House. All were old vampires and skilled in several weapon forms. The young ones were dispatched in minutes. Now the warriors were on their way back to Lorraine's palatial estate where they would feast and spend much time in bed. Or at least he and Lorraine would. The others would have to fend for themselves. The prospect of entwining himself in Lorraine's arms didn't help quiet the worry he felt since waking.

His eyes wandered out the window, then back inside. He barely glanced at the other men until he reached Joseph, who held his gaze. Vincent scowled and fought the urge to check his cell again. He and his people had arrived two days ago. Rebecca called the first afternoon to inform him Natalia's meetings went well. She called again yesterday afternoon to ensure him all was still well. He didn't expect another call until this afternoon when Rebecca would report again. He was not in the habit of calling his home when he was away to check up: it showed distrust. Although at times he didn't trust all the men he sheltered in his house, he did trust Mierka, Rebecca, Angie, and Natalia. He knew they would call if they needed help.

Nevertheless, the disquieting feeling was almost overpowering.

It subsided as the limo drew closer to the house and he let himself relax. Perhaps it was just anxiety. He pushed it to the side and allowed himself to rely on the women who ran his house. The car finally stopped, and the back door opened to reveal Lorraine in a black silk robe. Vincent was the closest to the door and went straight for Lorraine. He kissed her on the cheek, and stepped back to admire her in her rather inappropriate outfit.

"Sire. Your warriors have returned."

"There is blood if you need it." She announced to the group at large. She linked her arm with Vincent's, started him toward the house, and almost ignored the rest. "Come. Take me to bed and tell me all about it."

The disquieting feeling a mere mouse of a whisper in the back of his thoughts, he picked Lorraine up, carried her into her house, and upstairs to her bedroom. She laughed delightedly the whole time. Behind them, a disgruntled Rowland scowled after them. Joseph, who understood Rowland's feelings leaned forward and voiced his thoughts.

"When was the last time you shared her?"

"The last time he was here." Rowland shared Lorraine's bed for many years, as long as Vincent was on the other side of the country.

"Why not take another while he sleeps within your sire's house?"

"Because currently, I don't desire another." Rowland walked into the house in search of blood. Joseph smiled to himself and followed the disgruntled vampire in as Anthony came up beside him.

"Will we be returning tomorrow night?"

"We might. Why do you ask?"

"She still makes me nervous. I don't think it was safe to leave her alone in the house."

Joseph gave a mocking grin. "Mierka is in charge. Rebecca is watching, as are the humans. Call Julia and have her check in if you desire."

Anthony shrank into himself, and felt rather like a disobedient child. "I'm sure that's not necessary."

Joseph stopped walking, placed his hand on Anthony's arm, looked around, then pulled Anthony to the side a bit. Once out of the way of the rest of the group, he gave Anthony a stern look. "Vincent might appreciate it if you did. Or did your observant eyes not notice how agitated he is acting?"

"I thought he was worried about his human."

"Yes, but with all she can do and all Mierka and the wolves are capable of, why would he be worried?"

Anthony stood in thoughtful silence for a moment. "I'll send my humans to the house."

"Send no one. Make calls first. Assess the situation, then act."

Anthony bowed slightly, then turned and left for his room. Though his sire didn't have as much security in her home as Vincent, he didn't want anyone hearing the call with Julia. It was no one's business, yet.

CS ∞

Vincent woke from his light sleep to Lorraine slowly sucking on his neck. He pushed her away, sat up, and healed the bite wound as he stood. The same feeling that had whispered quietly in his mind earlier this morning, roared. He felt strongly that something was wrong at home. Specifically, that something was wrong with Natalia.

"Vincent?" Lorraine didn't sound happy.

Vincent waved her voice away while he found his pants. His cell phone was in the front pocket. He took it out and there were no messages. It was past sunset. At the very least, Rebecca should have given him the 'all clear' call. There was nothing. He didn't even have service. With a slight frown, Vincent dialed Rebecca's number and hit the send button. He grew alarmed when his ear encountered dead air. He waited as Lorraine sat up and gave him an annoyed look.

"Vincent." It was almost an order.

He slipped on his pants and hung up his phone. "Give me your phone."

"I don't carry my phone into my bedroom." She gave him an annoyed look and sounded as if she thought he shouldn't either.

Vincent looked down at his cell phone, up at the naked Lorraine who lay seductively on the bed and back at his cell. He nodded, as he decided. His house's security was more important than his pleasure. He turned and headed out the door as Lorraine yelled at him from the bed.

Vincent found Joseph easily enough. His bodyguard was in the hallway outside Lorraine's room, a concerned look on his face. "Report."

"Anthony contacted Julia last night. She in turn spent most of today trying to call the house. None of our landlines or cell phones work. Anthony's does. Someone called our service provider and had our phones suspended as of this morning. Julia's taking care of the issue."

"Did she try reaching the farms?"

"Those lines are down as well. She's sent humans to investigate. We'll know more when she does."

"Where's Diana?" They were gathered at the head of the steps, the center of the second floor.

"Three doors down. She may not be awake. She had her tests today."

Vincent was already on the move, at her door before Joseph could finish. He knocked on the door and entered her room before anyone else reacted. Diana and another young woman were entangled in the sheets asleep. The other woman woke before Diana did, but Vincent ignored her, stormed to Diana's side of the bed, and sat her up before either could react. The other woman started to protest, but one deadly look from the vampire and she stilled, intimidated into silence.

"Diana." Her name was an order. She woke completely, sat up by

139

herself, and leaned on her arms to stay upright. Vincent held her arms anyway, squeezing her triceps lightly. "What were you doing with Natalia in my bathroom the day we left?"

"A spell. I was trying to connect our wills to make it easier to heal her. But it didn't work."

He gripped her tighter but loosened his hold when she winced. "How do you know?"

"It connects us loosely. I should be able to feel her presence. But once I left the two of you, I felt the spell release."

Vincent released her completely, closed his eyes, took a <u>large</u> breath, and let it out slowly. "We drank each other's blood when you left. Would that cause the spell to transfer to us?"

She started to shake her head and stopped. Her hand went to her mouth as she stared wide-eyed in surprise. "Only if one of you has the ability to cast spells. Lilly suspects Natalia might."

"I have a feeling she's hurt..."

"It probably means she is." Her voice was soft but panicked.

The vampire stood. "Get dressed. We leave soon, and you'll be needed."

Vincent shouted for Joseph as he left the room. Diana kissed her woman goodbye and readied herself for the early departure. Joseph, who once again anticipated Vincent's mind, was on Lorraine's phone. He informed their pilot of the early departure. Lorraine stood by him, dressed in a light summer dress, and spoke with Rowland and Maxine. Anthony had already gathered the others from House LeGris.

They were out the door, headed to Lorraine's airstrip in less than half an hour. They were in the air fifteen minutes after that. Joseph made sure Diana sat in the cockpit with the pilots to make sure she was out of the way. Vincent paced the length of the airplane, which made the others nervous. Lorraine, who had come along for support, tried several times to calm him down, but nothing worked. Rowland and Maxine also came along just in case reinforcements were necessary. Two hours into the flight, Joseph grabbed Vincent by the arm and forced him into the separate bedroom at the end of the plane.

Vincent protested and growled loudly as Joseph shut and locked the door. "What the hell do you think you're doing?"

"Vincent. We were just in a rather anticlimactic fight. We're speeding toward an unknown situation, which may prove to be deadly for our loved ones." He stared at Vincent until understanding sank into his boss' eyes. Vincent nodded. Mierka's fate was just as unknown as Natalia's. "And you have been pacing this short plane since we entered it. Do you realize how nervous you're making everyone feel with your pacing?"

The hard look came back in Vincent's eyes.

"Most of us are already on edge, <u>sir</u>. If you continue to show your impatience, a fight might erupt. And that could prove deadly for us all. If you're going to pace, at least do it out of sight."

"There isn't enough room in here." The room wasn't much bigger than the bed.

"Then bring Lorraine in here and work off your anxiety with her."

Vincent turned angrily away, walked three steps, and stopped. "Why haven't we heard anything yet?"

"Anthony called Julia a little over three hours ago. It would take about an hour to round their humans up and arm them. On a good day, it takes an hour and a half to travel from their house to yours. It's Saturday, which means traffic will be disastrous. It will take two to two and a half hours for the troops to get to your estate. Which means," he looked at his watch, "that she has not yet arrived. Julia is trustworthy and efficient. She will call as soon as she has word."

Vincent stared silently at the far wall. Joseph noticed when he relaxed, as his shoulders lowered minutely. "Send Anthony in here."

"No."

Vincent turned and glared at his friend.

"There is nothing more the man can tell you that I haven't. I'll send Lorraine in so that you can try and relax."

Joseph turned and left the small room. Vincent stewed in his own anxiety, until Lorraine came in seconds later. It didn't take long for her to get him undressed and on the bed. As the room was soundproofed, the others were spared their cries.

⋐ ⋑

By the time the plane landed in Sausalito, Vincent was no calmer. Time with Lorraine only served to remind him how much he wanted Natalia's warm, supple body pressed against his. He was distracted by news that Anthony's men along with Owen and Kim, joined the forces at Vincent's and were able to take back the house. The wolves killed ten of Edwin's vampires and found that all the humans in the house had been killed. There was no trace of Franklin, Dr. Elving, Mierka, Charlie or Natalia. And Edwin was still at large. Rebecca, Julia, and Angie met Vincent at the front door.

"Report."

"We've searched all rooms except the basement and security room, both of which have been locked out. We listened at the security room door, and something is in there, but we don't know what." She paused and looked to Joseph. "Mierka was on duty last night." She turned back to Vincent. "We couldn't hear anything from the basement, and we couldn't get into either area as you never gave me the codes to unlock those doors." Rebecca's voice rebuked him lightly, as she tried to control her own anxiety. Charlie went missing that morning against orders, and she was worried.

Vincent grabbed Rebecca, barged past the other women, and stormed to

141

the security room door. A quick search revealed the little used secret panel. The panel slid open as he grabbed Rebecca's hand. He pointed her finger, entered the code, and made sure she saw the numbers. Rebecca committed the pattern to memory and stepped back as the door slid open.

"Check the dungeon. Same code."

She left with Ben and Anthony. The door to the security room slid back completely, and he heard gasps behind him. Angie and two of her men stood with crossbows at the ready, with Joseph behind them. Mierka could still be within the destruction.

The room was in shambles. None of the equipment was whole. All the screens were blown out, the shelves were twisted metal, and the chair bled stuffing. The walls were blackened as if from an explosion. If a human or werewolf were here when the explosion occurred, they would not have survived. The onlookers could only hope Mierka was at full blood when she went on duty last night. Vincent took a moment to assess the damage, then motioned Joseph forward. His bodyguard went in without a thought, and turned quickly to grab Mierka as she attacked.

She was a mess. Her clothes were torn although she had no wounds. It was clear from her hungry attitude she had sustained massive damage and used a great deal of blood to heal herself. She was ghul.

Joseph released her slightly and allowed her to turn and sink her teeth into his flesh. He knew he could sustain the blood loss it would require to bring his woman back to sanity. Vincent beckoned to one of the humans and indicated he should remain at the ready when more blood was needed. The human nodded, handed off his weapon and bravely walked into the security room.

Vincent looked around at the others. He opened his mouth to give orders when shots were fired. His men didn't carry guns and the humans never brought theirs into the main house. Wooden arrows were more effective against vampires. Vincent turned and ran down the hall to the dungeon steps. He was there in the space of a gunshot. Rebecca was halfway up the steps, with Anthony and Ben behind her. She looked as if she wanted to rage. She turned her blazing yellow eyes to her boss.

"Edwin and two men. Guarding the dungeon. Give me leave." She talked through clenched teeth.

He stared deep into her rage and saw his own concern and hate amplified. "Kill the guards. Leave Edwin to me."

She went Blitzkrieg, tore down the steps, and bellowed her wrath. There were more shots fired, which just fueled the woman's passion. Mangled screams emanated from the dungeon, cut short by vampires dying. Less than a minute later Rebecca yelled up the stairs.

"Edwin's yours, sir. He's cowering at the top of the oubliette."

Vincent was down the steps so quickly Ben and Anthony hardly saw him. When he passed a near naked Rebecca, he was no more than wind. Edwin fired at him to no avail. The ex-Captain was pressed against the wall before he could fire more than two shots. He screamed in pain as Vincent ripped off the hand holding the gun.

"It would pleasure me greatly to kill you now, but I will follow the rules and kill you in front of an audience."

"You kill me; you'll never find your bitch."

"Vincent? VINCENT!" A familiar voice rang from the oubliette. In all the years Vincent had known the werewolf, this was the first time Charlie sounded happy to hear his boss's voice.

Rebecca ran to the edge of the hole, and leaned over as far as she dared. Relief flooded her very being. "Charlie!" Her voice turned upset. "I'm going to kick your ass when you get up here! Don't you dare to that again!"

Vincent still had Edwin pressed to the wall but was mostly ignoring him. "Anthony!"

"Sir?" Anthony was at the door to the room, with Ben right behind him.

"Take Edwin to a cell." He threw the sniveling man at them. They caught him easily, took him to a cell down the hall, and shackled him to the wall. Vincent went to the edge of the oubliette.

"Charlie? What are you doing down there?" His calm voice refused to reveal his emotions.

"Natalia jumped down so Edwin couldn't kill her or me. I followed to protect her."

Vincent stood silently immobile for a few seconds, then turned to Rebecca. "Find some rope."

Vincent jumped down the twenty-foot hole, and landed lightly on his feet. He started toward Charlie before the werewolf realized he was down. Vincent scanned the room and went to Natalia who was on her stomach, unmoving. He was by her side feeling for a pulse before Charlie could speak.

"I scratched her while killing the ghul that was down here. I tried to keep her wounds clean, but..." Charlie shrugged even though Vincent wasn't looking at him and couldn't see the gesture.

"Who took her blood?"

Vincent brushed her hair out of her face, and tried not to let his worry consume him. Her heartbeat was slow and weak, and he could smell the infection rolling off her in waves. This place was meant for death, not life. Natalia might be dying, and the healer was straight up a twenty-foot hole. He gathered her to him, and carried her into the little bit of light there was. He held her nearly lifeless body, and barely heard Charlie's answer. He had forgotten the question. She was cold. He stood with her in the low light as Charlie explained what happened. As he stared down into her trusting face, Vincent felt the urge. If he changed her, she wouldn't die.

Vincent's eyes moved from her lovely features to Charlie's frantic one. He caught the werewolf's eyes, which stilled the ramble of words. Charlie's expression went from anxious to confused to frightened understanding to acceptance. He bowed his head and fell to one knee.

"She still owns my life. If mine is necessary to save hers, I gladly give it."

"Not your life: your blood." He looked back at Natalia. "Possibly."

Charlie stood, then went to lean against the nearby wall. "When?"

"If Rebecca can't find ropes soon."

"What will she do to you?" He remembered his own attempt to change Natalia.

"I don't care. I will _not_ allow her life to end this way."

Charlie stared up at the large vampire as he stood almost in the center of the low light, and held Natalia as if she were weightless. He had the idea that Vincent would stand there contemplating her life for an eternity without thought to anything else around him. Commotion above them broke the picture.

"Vincent! We found ropes and a stretcher! Look out!"

Vincent looked up to see a now dressed Rebecca on her stomach, as she leaned over the edge. Joseph, Anthony, Ben and even Mierka stood around the edge; all with ropes in their hands. Rebecca moved out of the way and let the vampires take over. Vincent frowned as a stretcher came down the hole, lowered by ropes. He wasn't sure where it had come from but was grateful to have it. It would be the safest way to get the unconscious Natalia out of the oubliette. The strong ropes were tied around the stretcher at both ends and in the middle. Joseph, Ben, and Anthony held it in place about four feet off the ground as Vincent laid his ladylove gently on the board. He secured her with the restraints and watched as she was lifted to safety.

"Get her to Diana. Now. She's dying."

More ropes were lowered as Natalia was untied and taken upstairs. Vincent waited until Charlie was halfway up then grabbed a rope and climbed it as Joseph pulled him up. At the top he nodded thanks to Joseph and quickly left, to be by Natalia's side. The others followed; Charlie and Rebecca brought up the rear, and argued about his having run off. Vincent ignored it all, and ran up the steps four at a time. Anthony greeted him at the top of the steps and led him to the training room. He could see Diane trying to heal Natalia. Vincent went to them, and knelt by his woman.

Behind him, a crowd formed. All of Vincent's, Lorraine's and Anthony's men were gathered in the room. There were about forty people in total. Natalia was on her stomach, still unconscious. Diana had her hands on Natalia's back, over her scratches. Her bite wound was already closed. Vincent saw how deep the scratches looked and realized Diana had probably healed her partway. Charlie's claws had gone deep, and therefore, so had the infection. Her weak heartbeat suggested she had lost a great deal of blood.

Diana whispered softly, as she rocked back and forth slowly, minutely. He could barely hear her words but felt them as Natalia continued to heal. He glanced toward Diana and saw she was staring right at him. He turned his head a little and gave her his full attention. She grabbed his gaze, and held it as her words came faster and her rocking became harder. He inhaled sharply as the other presence in his being slipped away and he no longer felt Natalia. Diana closed her eyes, said some final words, shuddered and sat back. Natalia's back was healed, and her breath was regular. Vincent leaned over and felt her pulse. It was strong and steady. He looked up sharply at the healer.

"How?"

"I replenished her blood. And I cut the connection between you two." She looked and sounded exhausted.

"Why?"

"You're already connected to her enough. Anymore and the two of you would lose your individuality. Not a good thing when dealing with a vampire and human. Let her be herself until you change her." Diana leaned back and found she was close to the wall. Her eyes closed slowly. She needed a lot of rest.

Vincent wanted more information though the healer looked to be asleep. "How did you replenish her blood? I didn't think that was possible."

She looked at him, gave him a steady look. "I can do more than Lilly can."

"When will she awaken?" He watched as Diana leaned forward, brushed Natalia's hair away from her face, and gently caressed her head.

"In a moment." She sounded as if she were about to say more but didn't have a chance.

Natalia shot up, and pulled away from Diana's touch. Wide-eyed with fright, she slammed against the nearby wall, as her body shook. Concern overtook Vincent and he went to her, reached out with a careful touch, and placed his hand on her cheek. She pulled her head away violently, hesitated, then closed her eyes and nuzzled her cheek against his palm. Confusion, relief, and something else flashed across her face when she tried to pull away. That something else threatened to drive him insane, but he let it go and took her in his arms. She was safe and that was all that mattered.

Natalia grabbed him to her: a desperate, drowning woman clinging to a life raft. She gave a small cry, but no tears came. She was alive, and he was here. Natalia buried her face into Vincent's neck, and felt the strength of his being surround and encompass her. He shifted slightly, to cradle her, and carry her toward the door of the training room. Her arms were still wrapped tightly around his neck. He turned his head slightly, gave her a look of longing and kissed her. He stopped moving for a second as the kiss grew deeper. Their lips separated when a voice behind them reminded them they were not alone.

"Vincent." A feminine voice started but a male voice took over.

"We have Edwin to deal with."

Vincent turned, regarded his sire who had spoken first and Joseph, who had taken over. His guard stood by the diminutive woman, one hand on her shoulder as if to silence her. "Call my Lieutenants. Gather them here two hours after sunset tomorrow. I will deal with Edwin at that time. Until then, find rooms for those who need sleep, and humans for those who need blood."

Vincent ignored the sour look on his sire's face as he turned away. She expected to be in his bed this day, but he nearly lost Natalia, and she was the one he wanted. He left the room, and carried his prize with him.

Lorraine threw Joseph's hand off her shoulder and started after her favorite. Rowland's voice stopped her.

"Doesn't feel good to be considered second best, does it?"

She turned and gave Rowland a hard, hateful look.

"Now you know how I feel."

She stared at him, and ground her teeth as all around them people left to go to various rooms.

"Face it, my sire. You have your favorite, he has his." He stepped toward her, and caressed her cheek. His voice grew soft with desire. "And I have mine. Let's find a bed, Lorraine. Let me remind you what I'm capable of."

Lorraine's eyes closed at his touch and words. She knew what he was capable of and nodded her consent. Rowland looked at Joseph, who told him which bedroom would be theirs. They left, and Joseph made sure all the guests were taken care of before he retired to his own room. Mierka greeted him with open arms.

23

Vincent lay Natalia down on their bed, and kissed her as he started to remove what was left of her clothing. He let his fingers dance upon her skin, and relished her gasps as he tickled her. He laughed as she grasped his shirt, pulled it apart and popped the buttons. She had ruined more shirts this way than he cared to count. He obeyed when she drew him down to lie on top of her, and growled as her warmth scorched his skin. His thoughts started to leave as passion threatened to take over, but her expression from earlier replayed in his mind.

Vincent pulled back a little, to stare down into her face. "Are you well?"

Her fingers caressed his face, passed his cheeks to entwine in his silky blond hair. "Is talk really necessary?"

He traced her features with his eyes but refused to have her draw him down to her. He wanted nothing more than to delve into her, except for that look. Above all else, he wanted to know what she had been thinking. She was warm and willing though, and her blood had been replenished. He could drink if he desired. As he desired greatly, he decided to cut to the chase.

"What did you think happened when you woke in the training room and scurried to the wall in fear?"

She closed her eyes, hid the truth, and turned her head away. Her feelings engulfed her, and she sobbed in anguish. Dreams she tried desperately to ignore flooded her consciousness and she cried out in pain. She curled into a fetal position, and let it all out as Vincent shifted to wrap himself around her. He held her as she cried, and let her be vulnerable. The last time he held her like this was when Orlando died. Before that...he couldn't remember. She didn't show vulnerability often, but when she did, he comforted her, and allowed her to take his strength. After, he never spoke of it, unless she did. There was never any reason to.

When she quieted and settled more fully against him, she spoke. "I thought I died. I dreamt of my mother while I was unconscious. She came to me and told me I was nearly done. I was closer than I realized and that I knew someone who could get me the information I needed." She paused, and he knew she was leaving something out. "When I woke in the training room, I saw your face, but felt a warm touch. I thought it meant you needed to change me to save me."

He nuzzled her neck, and pressed his fangs against her tender flesh. "Would that have been such a horrible thing?"

She was silent as she considered. When she realized she had not been changed, she felt confused, relieved, and just a touch disappointed. Not much, but enough to make her realize she wanted the situation with Donald done so that she could ask Vincent to change her. She turned to him and wrapped her arms around him. "I would rather give you permission than wake to find myself changed."

"But if your life were at stake and Diana couldn't heal you?" His hand tangled in her hair, tightened, then let go to travel down her spine.

She swallowed hard, closed her eyes, and licked her dry lips. She opened her eyes and looked him in the eye. "I will forgive you."

He pulled back the smallest bit, completely surprised. It wasn't permission, but it was a definite start. Vincent, now understanding the bewildered look of earlier, grabbed his woman to him and seared himself on her skin.

 CR ❦ RO

Natalia once again lay with her back to Vincent's chest, and considered all that had transpired while her man was gone. She told him of her days without him, and informed him of Franklin's betrayal and death. He grew contemplative and finally stated that he should have known. She didn't question why, and he didn't elaborate. It wasn't his way, and she didn't feel the need to pry. There was something she did want to know about, though.

"Vincent? What was the thing in the oubliette? Joseph called it a ghul once."

He sighed heavily and his caressing hand stilled. "It's in the past, Natalia. And that's where it will stay."

"It was a vampire at one time, wasn't it?" She asked after a moment of silence.

He growled softly to indicate his unwillingness to answer, then did anyway. "We are no longer vampire when we reach that state."

"What did it do to you?"

He growled louder. "It asked too many questions."

She stopped, let him cool down and started again. "I believe I deserve to know Vincent, as it nearly killed me."

"You chose to jump into the oubliette, my love. No one from this house forced you." He started to caress her inner thigh and pressed himself against her to stop her questions to no avail.

"What would one do to deserve such punishment?"

He growled again, louder this time. "Keep pestering me, human and you will know."

"I'm not letting this drop. I want to know who it was and why it was in there."

He stared at the back of her head in annoyance. "It's called an oubliette for a reason, Natalia. Stop this questioning."

She turned to face him, as she could almost feel his hard stare. "Do the others in your house know why it was there?"

He licked his lips in agitation and his hand started to tap nervously on his thigh. Vincent did not want to speak of the ghul, but he was sure Natalia would not be dissuaded from this conversation. As memories flooded his mind, he sighed then gathered Natalia his arms. She wanted to know why the ghul existed? So be it. He would tell her.

"Her name was Laura Lynn McGarity. She was the last woman I loved before you. We met in San Francisco, the first time I lived in this area, in the 50's. She was a reporter and had heard about the wealthy businessman no one ever saw during the day. There were rumors back then that I was involved with the mob. I've always let those rumors fly, as it makes a good cover story. As long as all my paperwork is in order and everything looks legal and reported on my current identity's taxes, no one arrests me."

Vincent paused as the memories came back. They seemed to flash through his mind like an old movie reel. "Laura Lynn decided I was her big break. She found ways of integrating herself into my life, getting herself invited to my closed parties and sneaking into my clubs. Finally, after finding out who she was, and falling for her tenacious behavior, I courted her. We were together for a few months before I started showing her the real me. I bit her when I desired, and she seemed to enjoy it, but she never understood what was really happening."

"How could she not?" Natalia sounded perplexed. She enjoyed when Vincent took her blood, but the bites hurt.

"Humans have a way of hiding the truth from themselves even when it stares them in the face." He paused to press his fangs into her skin and suckle her blood. She stiffened with pain but allowed him his drink. He grew hard against her and growled as she stretched into him. He let her go. He now wanted to finish the story. Vincent grinned when she protested his pulling away. He reached behind him to the nightstand, where a small towel lay in wait. He pressed the soft fabric onto the bite wound and she settled against him when he continued the story.

"Laura Lynn refused to see the truth until the day I changed her. When she woke, she still didn't understand. I explained my world to her, and she went temporarily insane. She left my house and was picked up by the authorities, who placed her in a mental hospital for the stories she told. I found out and had her released into my custody, as I knew she would be killed out of sheer ignorance. One of the hospital's daily rituals was placing the patients in the sun to enjoy its warmth.

"Once in my home, I was able to help her find her mind again but made the mistake of trusting her completely when she turned her charms on. Eventually, she left the house and found Slayers. She brought them to one of my clubs one night and pointed me out for who I was. We took care of them easily. They had no idea how old I was and knew nothing of the strength of my house. We killed them, and I once again took her into my custody. After I judged her a traitor, we threw her in the oubliette."

They were silent as Natalia digested all he said. Then, "So I suppose you did throw her in for asking too many questions."

Vincent gave a short humorless laugh as she pulled back to look into his eyes.

"You loved her?"

Vincent wrapped his arms around Natalia again, and held her as close as he could. "Yes."

"If I betray you, will I suffer the same fate?"

He caressed her cheek with his thumb as he stared deep into her eyes. "Are your feelings for me real, Natalia? Or a ruse to blind me to a greater scheme? I believe they are real. Nine years is a long time to be with anyone, human or vampire."

She gave him a naked look and she confirmed what he already knew. There was no lie in her eyes. He leaned in and gave her a soft kiss that deepened quickly. He crushed her to him and allowed her to feel every part of his body. He rolled over, and pulled her on top of him. He urged her into a sitting position as she guided him inside her. He bared his teeth and fangs, and grunted as her heat tightened around him.

Vincent stared at the beauty above him, and marveled at his thoughts. Two nights ago, when he shared Lorraine's bed, all he could think of was feeling Natalia's warmth on every inch of his body. Now she surrounded him, seared him with her fire. All he wanted to do was grab her to him, sink his teeth into her flesh and steal her heat. He wanted to make her cold and eternal like him. He watched and felt as she rode him like the animal he was. She reared back as pleasure took over and cried out. Before the orgasm was finished, she brought her head forward, and showed him stark emotion. Their eyes locked and she started to shake. He reached up to touch her cheek and each understood how much they almost lost. Then she smiled and tightened around him. Vincent gave her a growl that turned into a bellow of pure passion.

In a movement so swift it made her lightheaded, he was on top of her. He thrust himself deep inside her as she cried out and grabbed his hair. She used the leverage to arch into him, and granted him deeper access. Her legs were wrapped around him and held on fiercely as brutal satisfaction took over them both.

A moment or so later, Vincent extracted himself from Natalia and pulled her back to the head of the bed. He enveloped her in his arms, and buried his head in her neck. A smile of absolute contentment graced her lips as he placed light kisses on her skin. They lay in each other's arms for a while, and dozed off, lost in the pleasure of being together. They remembered that there was a world outside the boundaries of their bed a few hours later when a knock sounded on the bedroom door.

Vincent, forgetting he had business to take care of, sounded angry when he answered. "WHAT?"

The door opened to reveal a smiling Joseph. "It is two hours past sunset, sir. Have you forgotten your duties?"

Vincent gave Joseph a frank look. "Yes. Yes, I have. And I plan on forgetting them for a little while longer."

"Sir, your Lieutenants are waiting downstairs."

"Let them wait." He curled his body against his lover's, wanting to sink back into her.

"Captain. Your followers await your leadership. You may entwine yourself in Natalia's charms after you kill Edwin."

Vincent extracted himself from Natalia and left the bed, but his eyes never left hers. He growled, grabbed a pair of silk pajamas from his closet, kept the pants for himself and tossed Natalia the top. She took the deep red silk shirt and slid it on over her head. She rolled up the sleeves and made sure all the buttons were buttoned. Natalia rose from the bed and stepped to her set of closets, to select a pair of panties in the same hue as the shirt. Joseph stared at the matching pair.

"It might be wiser to dress fully, sir."

Vincent took Natalia into his arms, stared down into her face, and allowed her to see his emotions. "Depends on the message I'm trying to send."

Joseph bowed and waited for his mistress and master to follow him out of their rooms and down the steps to the training room. There was quite a crowd. Present were three from Anthony's house, Lorraine and her pair, and Vincent's twelve Lieutenants: Anthony, Markus, Crystal, Morgan, Patricia, Albert, Alexandra, Dwayne, Naomi, Charita, Dominic, and Gabe. Each of his Lieutenants nodded to him in turn when Vincent regarded them. Morgan gave a curt nod, but didn't meet his gaze. Vincent had made Morgan a Lieutenant to give him enough rope to hang himself with if he were of a mind.

Vincent glanced toward Edwin, who stood in the middle of the room surrounded by the others. He was filthy. Dirt and blood coated his clothing, and he hid his missing hand. The crowd parted to allow Vincent and Natalia to enter the circle and closed in after them. Vincent let go of Natalia's arm and went to stand in front of Edwin. He looked at his Lieutenants again, then back at Edwin. Vincent crossed his arms and smirked.

"Do you remember when you came here looking to take Natalia from me?"

Edwin looked confused by the question but nodded.

"What happened that night? Answer truthfully and this will go well for you."

Edwin's confusion deepened. Was Vincent thinking of letting him go? Uncertain of his fate in his enemy's hands, the former Captain decided to play along. "I bent her over the table and screwed her while you watched and she screamed."

Vincent shook his head. "That is not what truly happened. Would you like to know why you thought that?" The humor in Vincent's voice was evident. He did not wait for an answer but leaned in closer to Edwin's ear. "You were hypnotized into believing what we wanted you to believe."

There was shock on Edwin's face. "No!"

"Would you like to know what actually transpired that day?" He turned his head slightly and smiled at Natalia. She kept her composure as Vincent spoke to Edwin again. "Your Red Tie Coronation disaster at the Red Thread was not the only time we took pleasure with each other in your presence without your consent."

Edwin stared at the couple as confusion and anger warred on his face. "What did you do to me?"

Vincent gave the vile vampire an evil grin as he spoke a phrase in Romanian. Natalia told Edwin the next time he heard that phrase, he would remember what happened that night. Edwin gripped his head, accidentally showing off his missing hand. He fell to his knees as his memories reinserted themselves. Vincent gave an evil smile then turned back to Edwin and hovered over him.

"Remember now? Remember what we did to each other as you watched oblivious? You may yet live with all those memories."

Edwin did not like the memories that surfaced in his mind, as they caused him pain and confusion. He gripped his head and tried to make sense of what was real and what was false. Within the confusion Vincent's words penetrated like no others could. 'You may yet live'. Edwin calmed his mind, stood, and faced Vincent, eyes wide with hope. Vincent had to hide his glee. He loved playing with stupid vampires almost as much as he liked playing with stupid humans. Edwin opened his mouth to speak, and Vincent let him.

"I was going to take her home, but decided she was too old and that she would be too much trouble." His eyes moved back and forth rapidly as memories flashed in front of his eyes. "I thought I was screwing her, but it was you, wasn't it? You screwed her on that damned table while I sat motionless." The look on his face was priceless and his voice was full of admiration. "You bastard."

Vincent leaned in a little closer. Those in the room who knew Vincent well waited for the inevitable. "It really was a great deal of fun having you watch and think that you had her. She knew, I knew, a few of the others in my house knew and that was enough for me. Now that everyone knows what truly transpired, including you, I feel confident that we can put this behind us and move forward. Do you wish to continue living, Edwin?"

Hope shone brightly in his voice. "Yes."

"Do you wish to continue living in this city?"

"Yes."

"Let's see what we can do about that. What are you willing to give me, Edwin?"

"Anything you ask."

Vincent closed his eyes for a moment. Edwin's hope was almost palpable. He tried not to lick his lips. The end would be too swift for this one. "I want everything you have. Can you give that to me?"

"Anything, everything. Yes." His voice trembled.

Vincent waited just a fraction of a second before he plunged ahead. "Can you bring me children?"

Those who knew Vincent gasped in surprise, which made Edwin feel very secure in his answer. His eyes shone bright with eager hope. "I knew…" He shook his head. This was not the time for that revelation. "I can bring you as many as you need."

"And if I allow you to bring me children, will you also feast on them, drain their youthful, vibrant bodies of their blood, and taste them in whatever way you wish?"

"Yes!" The word was stated in ecstasy. "Yes, whatever you wish!"

Vincent sighed heavily. "Wrong answer. Children should be left alone and kept safe from the likes of you."

It took a moment for Edwin to process what the new Captain stated, but when he understood, it blossomed on his face like a terrible, deadly flower. "No!"

The larger vampire gave a short laugh, reached out, grasped Edwin's head in his hands and snapped his neck. He then continued to twist until the former Captain's head was no longer attached to his torso. Edwin tried to protest, as he had enough blood in him to repair a snapped neck, but stopped when his head was half off. It was too long since his last meal, and he couldn't keep up with the damage. Edwin turned to dust as his head separated from his body.

24

Vincent dusted the ash off his hands and turned to Natalia, who stood stoically to the side. She had never witnessed his true strength. Even with the knowledge of what he could do, she showed no fear. A rumble began in the depth of his lungs, and rolled out slowly until all heard and turned to see what their Captain wanted. Natalia too, turned, smiled at him, and knew they would spend the next few hours reveling in each other's abilities. Her breath became hard and fast, and her expression matched his. He made a move toward her but was stopped by a feminine voice.

"Pretender!"

All heads turned to Alexandra, who had been one of Edwin's closest. She was alive only because Morgan warned her not to be at Edwin's last Red Tie Affair. Morgan vouched for her, and Vincent gave her enough room to let her prove exactly who she was loyal to. Anthony found out easily the woman's loyalty was to herself.

Vincent turned his head, and let his body move when he reached the apex of his turn. His voice dripped with sarcasm, mirth, and expectancy. "You have something to say?"

"The throne belongs to me! I was next in line!" She stepped toward him, to try to intimidate him. Edwin's sire changed her, twenty-five years ago. Vincent could take her out easily. He wasn't worried about this one.

He just stared at her, and calmly waited for an explanation. When one wasn't given, he simply turned back to Natalia. "Where were we?"

Natalia shuddered minutely and stepped closer to him. She ran her hand through his chest hair, loving the feel. She gave him a seductive smile. "I believe you were sweeping me off my feet and carrying me off to our bed."

He growled low and leaned into her neck. She was snatched from his reach and tossed across the room into the crowd before his action reached fruition. His growl turned angry and dangerous.

"Do I have your attention now?" Alexandra stepped back, seemingly to get out of his reach. He let her.

Vincent looked beyond her to Natalia, who had landed on Rowland. Her shirt rode high on her body, and exposed her underwear. Vincent watched as Lorraine helped his woman up and as both women helped Rowland up. Vincent turned his attention back to Alexandra. Vincent saw Natalia's actions. No one else did.

"No. You don't, but you do have hers." He pointed toward Natalia.

Alexandra turned to face the woman she dismissed out of hand. She had never seen her before; thought she was Vincent's toy. As she turned and saw the way the human moved, she knew she was wrong.

Natalia hadn't expected to be launched across the room into Lorraine's group, but she was. She didn't expect to feel what she had under Rowland's jacket, but she did. By the time Rowland stood and Vincent turned Alexandra's attention on her, Natalia had Rowland's gun in her hand. She didn't know why the vampire carried a gun and didn't care. It wasn't important. There were no other weapons in the room. She had to improvise and use whatever she could get her hands on.

The handgun was a semi-auto, built to hold about 15 rounds in the clip. Natalia noticed all this in the seconds it took to pull the simple black gun out of Rowland's shoulder holster, turn and point it at Alexandra. She had been trained to use guns too, years ago in Montana. It was simply better to use weapons that left less obvious traces. She sighted the vampire, aimed high on the woman's chest, and fired. Enough conventional bullets might blow the woman's head off. The bullet hit the woman's chest, and the vampire started to scream as her skin sizzled into life.

"Phosphorous rounds," thought Natalia. "The damn vampire was carrying a gun with phosphorous rounds. What an ingenious idea."

Natalia shot Alexandra in the chest again as the others in the room started to back away with fear in their eyes. Vincent, Lorraine, Rowland, and Natalia were the only ones who didn't move as the potential usurper burst into flames. Alexandra fell to her knees; all talk of taking over gone in a blaze of glorious fire. As she continued to roast, Natalia turned to slip the gun back into Rowland's holster. With the same serene movements, she walked to the door. Behind it was a fire extinguisher. She took it off the wall hanging and readied it as she walked back to the charred mess that was Alexandra. Natalia turned the extinguisher on the vampire and doused her with CO_2.

Natalia swung the small extinguisher over her shoulder, and held it with her right hand while her hand left went to her side. She leaned into her left leg, her feet shoulder width apart, ten feet from Alexandra. She stared at the kneeling mass of charred vampire, a slight smirk on her face. The room was so quiet she could hear Alexandra's skin as it crackled. She waited, and watched as more and more of the creature's skin healed. She wondered if the woman might still be capable of hurting her. Seconds later, Alexandra moved toward her. Natalia swung the extinguisher and connected with Alexandra's head when the woman was two feet from her reach. The solid "TANG!" of the extinguisher hitting her skull echoed in the high ceiling room and Alexandra went sprawling. The side of her head was sunken in, but she still healed herself.

Natalia stepped forward swiftly, swung her weapon around and brought the flat bottom down hard. The unyielding metal slammed into the vampire's head to crush bone and brain. It was finally enough. Alexandra tried once more to heal the damage, failed, and turned to dust with one final wordless sound. Natalia looked up and caught Vincent's eye, then glanced around the room. She stood tall and left the extinguisher on the ground.

"Anyone else?" Her voice was louder than it needed to be, to emphasize her agitation. Footsteps sounded as someone stepped forward from behind her. Natalia turned as Lorraine spoke.

"Me."

Vincent and his people stared at her. Vincent stepped to Natalia's side. He sounded annoyed. "You wish to challenge my right to be Captain?"

"No. I wish to challenge her." Lorraine caught Natalia's gaze and held it.

Vincent stepped in front of Natalia, to protect her and break his sire's gaze. He was infuriated. "Why?"

Lorraine approached Vincent slowly, a slight smile on her lips. Her eyes went back to Natalia when the human came out from behind her lover. "I've heard much. I want to see what she can do. There must be something special about her if you've kept her this long and haven't changed her."

"You won't learn the reason for that on the training room floor." Natalia didn't mean it to sound like an innuendo, but it did. Several others in the room snickered. Vincent gave her an incredulous look.

"Don't encourage her." He now talked through clenched teeth.

"Why not?" Natalia gave Vincent a steady look. "Diana's here if she hurts me, and if she kills me, you get what you want."

Lorraine waited for her child to realize the decision had already been made. When he shook his head and backed away, she smiled impishly. Natalia stood off center and Lorraine charged, since she had the advantage.

Natalia saw Lorraine move before Vincent was completely out of the way, but it didn't matter. When the smaller woman hit her, Natalia simply fell back and threw the vampire off her with her feet. She was up before Lorraine was, barely. Lorraine charged again but this time, Natalia grabbed her arm and used the woman's momentum to swing her into the crowd.

Lorraine crashed into Rowland and Maxine, who stopped her fall and helped her up. She turned back to Natalia, who simply waited.

Vincent watched as Lorraine walked to face off with Natalia. He gnashed his teeth, and thought about stopping the unfair fight, but Natalia was doing fine. Had she a sword, she would be winning. As it was, she held her own. When Lorraine started to circle Natalia, Vincent grew nervous. Lorraine didn't fight much, but she was deadly up close.

"You think you're too good to be a vampire?"

"Never said that." Natalia circled with Lorraine, glad for the moment to assess her target and allow for tactics. She already knew of two things she could try, one if she were quick enough, which she wasn't, and one she would do if she were desperate, which she was.

"So why not allow him to change you?" Lorraine continued to circle slowly.

"He will. When I'm ready." She readied herself for her opportunity, which would present itself shortly.

"Has anyone informed you it isn't your choice?"

Natalia frowned. "Everything in life is a choice."

Both women moved at the same instant and Vincent grew frightened. As Lorraine moved to Natalia, the human turned and lunged for the fire extinguisher she left in Alexandra's ashes. Once in her hands, she rolled to a standing position. Lorraine stumbled as she missed her target but stood quickly and continued to charge. The stumble gave Natalia enough time to swing the extinguisher up hard into the side of Lorraine's face. There was the same "TANG!" as before with a hard crunch/snap, and Lorraine flew off her feet.

Natalia waited for Lorraine to rise, but held onto the extinguisher, just in case. She heard the snap crackle as Lorraine started to stand and let the makeshift weapon go. It clattered rang to the ground as Natalia sank to her knees in front of her lover's sire. Natalia never forgot Joseph's words. As Lorraine stood tall, Natalia bowed her head to the woman who now held her life in her hands.

"What is this?" Lorraine stretched her neck a little to insure everything was in place.

"I was told once, that should I break another's neck in this room, the hurt vampire would be healing the wound with my blood."

"I wasn't made aware of this." Vincent's hand was on her shoulder, as if to protect her.

"You weren't here when it happened."

"This isn't happening." His eyes were deadly.

"I am offering my blood to her, not to you. It is her decision to take it or not as she sees fit."

"Not in my house."

Natalia brushed off her lover's hand. "You don't trust your sire?"

Lorraine raised an eyebrow, and waited for his answer with great anticipation. Vincent growled, and backed off. Lorraine stepped forward to lightly touch Natalia's neck with the back of her hand. "So, I drink your blood, then we continue to fight?"

"No."

The simple word was spoken by two male voices. Vincent looked to Joseph and waited while his bodyguard spoke.

"You take her blood, and the fight is done. If you insist on continuing the fight, Natalia will be given a proper weapon."

"Do I get a weapon?" She turned to Joseph as she spoke, a look of innocence on her face, her hand on her chest.

"You are a weapon. She gets one to even the odds. She was able to impede you three times. Would you like to see how she does when armed with a sword?" Joseph's voice indicated how much he would like to see that fight. "You take her blood, and the Captain and Master of the House takes his prize to bed, as he obviously wants to do."

Lorraine paced back and forth in front of a still kneeling Natalia as she considered Joseph's words. Vincent sent daggers at her with his look. He wished his sire would hurry and do as he knew she would. Finally, Lorraine walked to Natalia, and held her hand out. Natalia understood and held her arm out to Lorraine. When the women realized Lorraine would have to kneel to feed off her arm, Natalia stood, but bowed her head in supplication.

Lorraine stepped close to her, as she knew it would drive her child mad. She positioned herself to stare into Vincent's eyes as she sank her teeth into his human's flesh. The vampire drank four slow swallows of the human's blood. Natalia inhaled with the pain but did nothing to stop the vampire. When Lorraine pulled away Natalia used the over long shirt to stop the blood flow and watched as Lorraine walked quickly to Vincent and kissed him.

Vincent almost fell to his knees as the taste of his woman's blood on his sire's tongue nearly released the beast within him. He crushed Lorraine to him and lifted her off the ground. He kissed her deeply, as he tried to suck the taste of Natalia out of Lorraine. Not satisfied, he nearly dropped her and turned to Natalia.

A little lightheaded, Natalia opted not to watch Lorraine and her lover but knew what was going on by the stares. As she prepared herself for a lonely night, Natalia finally started to turn, only to be grabbed and kissed rather violently. Surprise made her stumble and she felt her back hit the wall. Natalia gave a wordless cry when she hit the wall. His hands pulled her underwear down, and ripped through the fragile fabric easily. Her arms wrapped around his neck, her legs wrapped around his waist, and he was inside her. He growled into her neck, as the crowd around them grew uncomfortable. He was deep inside her before she could form a thought. Her eyes locked with Lorraine's. The vampire looked shocked. Natalia laughed at the expression on her face, as she remembered Vincent's description of his sire: unadventurous. Her laugh turned into a shriek as Vincent plunged further into her.

He hadn't planned having sex with her in front of everyone. Now that he had her trapped against the wall though, he wanted nothing more than to hear her scream with pleasure as his people watched. He drew back a little to capture her eye and judge her mood. The last time he did this, she threatened violence. Her face and eyes now showed intense desire but also warned of retribution. He growled at the look, as he wanted to confront her passion. He growled again, laced his arms behind her to bind her to him and eased himself further into her. Her eyes grew wide then closed as he pulled in and out of her slowly. His pace quickened within seconds, and she howled in pleasure soon after.

When they were done, he released her, and made sure she could stand. Vincent kissed her on the lips as he pulled the waistband of his pajamas up and covered himself. He smiled his satisfaction, took her arm, and turned to face the crowd. Some met his gaze, others looked away. The people House LeGris gave him hidden looks. They had seen this spectacle before and wondered what the human planned on doing to their master. Lorraine gave him an annoyed look; Rowland stared at Natalia, a look of wonder on his face.

"Who is this?" Dominic stepped forward to ask the question. He had a lecherous look on his face as he looked Natalia up and down.

Natalia stepped away from her man, and faced the bold vampire down. He was the same height as her. Natalia stared at him coldly until he looked away and took a step back. She still scrutinized the man, and assessed him as he tried not to meet her gaze. He fidgeted in his new suit, uncomfortable with the tight cotton. It was obvious he almost never wore anything so formal. Vincent had sent his Lieutenants suits and dresses, as he knew that most did not own formal wear. The new clothing made half the assembled look uncomfortable.

As Natalia stared down Dominic, another voice echoed the question. This voice was more submissive, more admiring. "Yes, Vincent. Who is this?"

Natalia turned to the voice, smiled to Rowland, then gave him a small bow. "Natalia Mirela Liliana Dveski. Protector of House LeGris."

"How did you know?" He stepped forward, took her hand, and kissed her fingers lightly.

"Know what?" She let her voice grow seductive, to the chagrin of Lorraine and Vincent.

"That the bullets were deadly?" He shook his head. "That I had a gun?"

"I felt the gun when I was thrown into you. I didn't know it was phosphorous rounds until she caught fire."

"You took a chance it might be?" He still didn't understand why she took the gun.

She took her hand back. "I needed a weapon. I felt yours. I decided that a gun was better than nothing, as long as my aim was true. Figured I could blow her head off. The rounds were a pleasant surprise." Natalia turned to Vincent, and held out her hand to him. "Shall we go to bed?"

"Vincent!" Lorraine's voice revealed a depth of anger he had not heard before.

He sighed but turned to his sire. "My liege?"

"Next time you present this woman to me, make sure she's vampire, or I'll take care of the situation myself."

There were murmurs in the room as the implication set in. Vincent bowed to his sire with grace and dignity, then gave her a loving smile. "Thank you, my sire. I'll remember your words." He turned to the room at large. "We'll meet tomorrow to discuss business in my offices in San Francisco, two hours after sunset. Those of you who don't know where my offices are, find out. If you're late, your blood will feed the others. That is all for the evening. Joseph, see to my guests."

Vincent swept Natalia off her feet and was out of the room and up the steps before anyone else could utter a word. It had been a successful evening and he wanted to celebrate in bed with Natalia. She was more than willing to oblige.

25

Eight Months later

N atalia woke up when she was torn from her bed and thrown to the floor of her bedroom. She was on her feet in a defensive posture before her eyes were open. When she did manage to open them, she grew angry. She lowered her arms and spoke very quietly and very slowly. "What the HELL do you think you're doing?"

Anthony stood in front of her, and tried to look menacing. The look on his face wavered between hatred, triumph, and disappointment. After she told him she hypnotized him and released his memories, his attitude towards her didn't get better. If anything, he grew more nervous and wary around her. Therefore, she was used to the look of hatred, wasn't surprised to see the triumph but was slightly confused by the disappointment. She looked past him and saw Julia, who looked upset. Next to Julia were two men Natalia couldn't identify. They had deadpan looks on their faces.

"My job is to root out the traitors. I always knew the day would come when I would be able to root you out." His glanced at her nude body. "Get dressed."

Natalia folded her arms and gave him a deadly look. "Not with you watching."

"Fine. Julia will stay while you dress." He looked to Julia. "Guard yourself," he looked to Natalia again, "and don't try anything." He turned on his heel and left, and the two men followed. The door slammed behind them.

Natalia sagged and sighed heavily. She had expected this but saw that a piece of the puzzle might be missing. She regarded Julia and tried to assess the woman's opinion, gave up and simply asked. "Do you believe me a traitor?"

Julia reached up to her blue stone necklace, let her fingers wrap around the cold stone. "I await your meeting with Vincent."

Natalia shook her head as she walked past Julia to get to her closets. She opened them and slowly started to dress. "How much does Anthony know?"

"All that the spies have told him."

"How much did he tell Vincent?"

"Anthony hasn't told him about this yet."

Natalia pulled the t-shirt over her head and gave Julia a look full of disbelief. "Then how is he going to explain dragging me out of bed?"

"We know where you've been spending your days, Natalia. We know what you've been plotting. He didn't feel he had to tell Vincent anything." Her voice echoed sadness.

Natalia, in her t-shirt and underwear, walked slowly to Julia, and tried to stay calm. "He hasn't told Vincent anything?"

"We were waiting to have you present to gauge your response."

"Shit." Her hand went to her face to rub her eyebrows. She turned from Julia, paced a few steps then turned back around. Her voice showed her determination. "Is anyone else present for this revelation?"

"All in Vincent's household, and all his Lieutenants."

Natalia closed her eyes and gave her head one single shake. She opened her eyes again and looked steadily at Julia. "It is absolutely imperative that we, meaning Anthony, Vincent and I, speak privately before Anthony tells the room his news."

"Why? So you can hypnotize him again?" Her voice was inquisitive, but not mean.

She gave a harsh laugh. "Anthony knows full well…" her words stopped as she frowned. "He thinks I've hypnotized Vincent, doesn't he?"

Julia opened her mouth to speak, then closed her mouth with a snap.

Natalia gave a harsh laugh. "Vincent will laugh when I tell him that." She shook her head. "Do you believe I've hypnotized Vincent for all these years?"

Julia caught Natalia's gaze and stood stock still for a moment. Finally, her expression broke, and she shook her head. "No. No I don't. But you've been spending time with the wrong people."

Satisfied with the answer, Natalia went back to her closets and grabbed a pair of jeans. She finished dressing and turned back to Julia. "I would still like to speak with Vincent and Anthony privately. If your man won't allow that then do everything you can to convince him to speak with Vincent privately before he denounces me." She sighed, closed her eyes, and licked her lips in agitation. She opened her eyes and gave Julia a frank look. "Please."

Julia took an involuntary step back. The look on Natalia's face was too honest. Julia understood that there was something the spies didn't know about. It might cause her man problems because of it. "I'll do what I can."

Natalia bowed slightly as thanks and went to the door. Julia reached it first and opened it. The women walked to the waiting men. Julia pulled Anthony aside, and asked for a moment. Anthony gave Natalia a nasty look but let Julia lead him aside and instructed the men to take her down to Vincent.

Natalia allowed the men to escort her. One stood to each side as they walked down the steps to her waiting lover and to the people she protected. She knew how it would look and didn't care. She hoped Julia could convince Anthony to speak with Vincent privately. When they reached the training room, the men walked inside with her and led her to stand in front of Vincent. He gave Natalia an odd look before he turned his attention to Joseph, who spoke to his master quietly.

Vincent sat on his throne, the only piece of furniture in the room. He was dressed in a gray suit, with a maroon shirt and matching handkerchief in the pocket. His head was turned to the right, away from the door, and his body was closer to that side of the chair. His right elbow was planted on the armrest, his hand in front of his mouth, which hid the shape of his words.

His people were arrayed near him. Joseph stood to his right, and whispered to him as Rebecca stood to his left, and protected him. Charlie was next to her, Mierka stood by Joseph, and looked unsure of the situation. The rest of his house, werewolves included, stood against the far wall, and watched in nervous anticipation. His Lieutenants and some of their Sergeants stood by the windows, and tried not to look uncomfortable. Natalia looked around, to assess the situation. She nodded to those she knew once she caught their attention. All of House LeGris nodded back. Of the Lieutenants, only Markus returned the nod. A smile still graced her features as she turned her attention to Vincent and shuddered. The man really did look like a king.

Vincent stood when Anthony finally entered. The Captain didn't bother hiding his own smile as he sauntered over to Natalia. One hand sank into her hair as the other circled around her lower back. He crushed her against him as they kissed. Her arms snaked around him, as she deepened the kiss. Their actions made Anthony growl with anger. Vincent released her at the sound and went back to his chair. Natalia looked around again: it was clear from the faces of those gathered that no one knew exactly what was going on. Charlie suspected something, as did Mierka and Rebecca. Joseph revealed nothing.

Natalia turned her attention once more to Vincent, whose eyes roamed her body. She saw his eyes move laboriously to Anthony: as if the presence of his loyal friend displeased him. "You have something to tell me?"

"Vincent wait." Her voice was strong, not panicked. She felt all eyes on her; anticipation filled the room.

His eyes darted back to her. "You feel you need to speak first, lover?"

"Not a chance! I demand to speak my mind, before she can turn your head again!" Anthony stormed forward, pushed her aside roughly. Natalia steadied herself and gave him a pitying look.

"Sir. Please."

Vincent looked back and forth between the two trusted members of his household, and tried to determine whom he was going to listen to first. He looked to Natalia last. "Is this pertaining to where you've been spending your days, my love?"

"Yes."

Vincent sighed heavily, got up and started toward the door. "Come Anthony. We will speak privately."

Anthony hurried after his master as he ground his teeth and fumed. By the time he reached Vincent's study, the large vampire sat at his desk. Anthony shut the door as Vincent turned off the recording equipment. The men stared at each other for a moment before Anthony decided to sit down.

"Well?"

"You know where she's been spending her days?"

"She told me her plans before she started working for the mayor."

"He's sleeping with her. On top of that, she's planning things with him and Slayers."

"She tells me everything." His expression was stoic and unreadable.

Anthony was silent for a moment, then finally spoke his mind. "She isn't planning something innocent, Vincent. She means to murder other Hellspawn. We could be next. Are you under her spell? Did she hypnotize you?"

As the words penetrated, Vincent gave a harsh laugh. "She tried when we first met. I shrugged it off easily. She hasn't tried since." His expression grew soft, which surprised Anthony. "I will admit to being under a spell, of sorts."

Anthony glared at Vincent as the words sunk in. "I'm going to have to put up with her for a long time, aren't I?"

"You could leave."

Anthony nodded. "I'll think on it." The men stared at each other for a long time, then Anthony stood. "I'll still have her followed and watched, Vincent. Have her tell me what she is doing and planning and this will be easier on all of us."

Vincent nodded and stood. "Your men will protect her if needed?"

Though it was stated as a question, Anthony knew it was not a question. It was an order; one that surprised him beyond measure. A surprised look on his face, Anthony nodded and left the room.

⟡ ⟡

Once in the training room again, Anthony gave Natalia a look to chill her blood. It didn't work. He went to Julia, whispered to her, and left with Julia and his two men. Natalia looked to her left, to where Vincent stood. He placed his hand on her cheek. "It's taken care of. He knows the situation but will continue to have you watched. This time more for your protection."

She bowed. "Thank you, sire."

At her words, his hand started to tremble. She could feel the vibration in his fingertips, which caressed her jawline. She meant to say 'sir', but she didn't. The word seared his mind. He wanted to hear it again, but there was much business to take care of tonight, and she had not slept well in days. Vincent leaned in to kiss her softly on the cheek.

"I have business to attend to. I will join you in bed when I'm done."

Natalia nodded and left the room. She wanted him to sweep her in his arms and charge up the steps with her, but knew it was impossible. Her mind was too full, and he was too busy. She was in their bed before she knew it. The thick, soft mattress surrounded her and lulled her to sleep.

⟡ ⟡

Sleep did not last long. When Vincent found her, she paced in the sitting room in her robe. Without a word, he went to her, encircled her in his arms, and caressed her back softly. She rested her head on his chest and enjoyed the closeness. He picked her up, took her into the bedroom, and sat her on the bed. Vincent, concerned for his woman, knelt beside her, and gazed into her worried eyes. After a moment, he frowned softly and placed his hand on her chest near her throat.

"Why are you not wearing my necklace?"

Natalia looked to the nightstand where her necklace rested. She removed it when she started spying on the mayor. "It would mean my death Vincent. I'm trying to convince him I'm spying on you. It wouldn't do to let him see it."

"He doesn't know what it means."

She reached out to him, placed her hand on his cheek, and gave him a sad smile. "There are Slayers who do. I don't have that much time, Vincent. Let's not waste it. I've missed you."

"I've not been the one avoiding this bed, love. You've only been here to sleep in the past three weeks, Natalia. Would you mind, finally, telling me how you've made the mayor trust you?" He was speaking slowly and softly, to hide his emotions.

She looked directly into his eyes, and he saw the truth before she spoke it. "I tried to hypnotize Gary, but somehow he's still under Edwin's control."

"How? Edwin's been dead eight months." Vincent stood and sat on the bed, at the headboard. He held his hands out to Natalia and she joined him.

"He wants to be. He liked what Edwin let him do. He likes what Edwin liked. Did the things Edwin suggested because he was already thinking about it." She placed her back to Vincent's chest. He wrapped his arms around her protectively, as he waited for her to tell him what he had seen in her eyes. "I can't hypnotize him, because he already is." She paused as his arms tightened around her again. She felt his strength and relaxed against him completely. She knew he would keep her safe no matter what she would tell him. "I seduced him."

"Is it breaking Edwin's death hold?" His voice held no surprise.

"Slowly. It would probably go quicker if I were younger. But he likes to be in control, and the more I allow, the more he comes out of it."

"What does he do to you?" There was a hard edge to his tone. He was learning to control his jealousy, but it still liked to rear its ugly head.

"Nothing as interesting as what we've done."

"Were you afraid I would reprimand you or reject you for what you've done?" Vincent threw his jealousy away. It would do no good to allow it control.

She sighed. "No. I knew as long as I was doing this for the protection of House LeGris, you wouldn't disapprove of anything I did. Also, you've slept with others while we've been together."

Vincent's lip twitched in small smile as he remembered the night Mierka seduced Natalia. "As have you, but this is different." His lips brushed her hair near her ear, and he whispered his words. "I would never have you do anything to protect my people that would endanger your life, Natalia."

"You have before."

There was a long pause. "True. But don't do this unless you're comfortable with your actions."

"I'm not. But it's a means to an end."

"Having him under my control is not entirely necessary, Natalia. His second term is ending."

"He has good information on Donald."

There was another long pause. Vincent released her, turned her to face him, and looked sadly into her eyes. He caressed her cheeks with the back of his fingers and gazed intently at her. "How good?"

"Very."

She knew where he was now but couldn't get to him. She wanted to get Mayor Lawrence under Vincent's control, but couldn't if she left to find Donald. And it seemed like the mayor was trying to get Donald to San Francisco, which meant all she had to do was bide her time.

Vincent ran his fingers through her hair, and traced the lines of her face with his eyes. He loved to look at her. Her features showed her strength and determination. It was what had first attracted him to her. He knew when he first saw her what was beneath the coyness. "What will you do now?"

"Continue with the plan." Her hand reached out tentatively. Even with their bodies touching she wasn't sure she wanted to initiate contact. When her trembling fingers skated across his neck, he moved his hand to intercept hers, and placed both on his neck.

"Do you not want to touch me?"

"I'm not sure."

"Do you feel guilty?"

"I'm not sure how I feel. He enjoys touching his enemy's woman."

Vincent pulled her closer, and tried to take the pain out of her eyes. Were he human, his heart would have skipped a beat. "He remembers you from Edwin's?"

She nodded against his shoulder. "What does Anthony think of all this?"

Vincent gave a small, soft laugh. "He took it all in stride. He thought you hypnotized me."

"Julia thought you did too. I laughed when she said it."

A small laugh escaped them both, but died quickly. Vincent caressed her back as he spoke. "I'm surprised you didn't reveal the truth with an audience."

"If only House LeGris had been gathered, I would have humiliated him. They would have teased him mercilessly, but it would never have left these walls."

"That was kind of you."

"I didn't feel like being smug about this. None of this makes me feel good."

Vincent repositioned her and brought his lips to hers. He gave her a long, deep kiss, and continued the embrace until all the hesitation was gone from her touch. Certain of the look he would see on his lover's face, Vincent pulled away gently from the kiss and gazed into Natalia's eyes. "Then come back to me Natalia and let this all dissolve. Tell me what you know about Donald, and we will take care of the situation. You will no longer have to worry about revenge, only of life and blood."

Natalia's sigh turned into a slight sob. It would be so easy to lay her troubles at Vincent's feet. Someone else could go after Donald while Vincent sucked the blood out of her willing body. Vincent, sensing her thoughts, lowered his lips to her neck and growled against her skin. He knew she wouldn't allow him to change her this day, but she seemed to consider it more and more. Soon, she would say yes, and he would have what he wanted.

She sighed as his teeth scraped her skin and he pulled back. Vincent wanted to undress her, wanted to enjoy his woman, but the sigh and the look in her eyes showed how tired she truly was. If he wanted, he could easily seduce her, easily convince her she was able to take him on, but what good would that do her? She was in a dangerous situation and needed to be on her toes. Vincent gave his own sigh and brought Natalia closer to him. She leaned her head on his chest, and curled up close to him.

Vincent brushed his hand through her hair softly. He kissed the top of her head, then helped her to move to a better position.

"I thought you wanted to take advantage of my presence in your bed." Her voice was groggy.

He chuckled softly. "Sleep, my lovely Natalia. You need it more than pleasure."

She didn't respond, but he felt her pulse and breath slow. Vincent wrapped his arms around his human and stayed with her all night, to allow her to take comfort in his presence.

26

Vincent tried not to become angry as he sat and listened to his Lieutenants' ideas. No one had any good ideas on how to get Mayor Gary Lawrence under his control. Natalia managed to break Edwin's hold, finally, and now worked for him in a more official position. She was his secretary. Anthony's men still watched her, but they were doing this at the risk of their lives. The mayor was getting antsy; he watched everyone that came into his sights. He hired thugs to keep him safe. How Natalia managed to keep herself safe was beyond him. He didn't even know all the details of how she integrated herself into the mayor's life in the first place.

During all this, she became more and more withdrawn. She always came home, but she was wrapped up in her own thoughts. Even sex didn't distract her. Tonight, she looked out the window into the darkness, brow furrowed in thought. She had not contributed to the conversation in any perceivable way. Vincent brought his attention back to Morgan, who prattled on about how they could kidnap the mayor and force-feed him blood.

"That's ridiculous." Her voice surprised everyone. "Doesn't work if the target is under duress."

Morgan turned on her. "And how the hell would you know?"

Natalia continued to stare out the window, unimpressed by Morgan's anger. "Because I read Anthony's report on blood control. Perhaps you should learn how to read so you won't be as obtuse."

Snorts and short bursts of laughter erupted around the room. Vincent smiled. Morgan turned from Natalia's direction to face Vincent. "Keep your bitch on a leash, Vincent. She's insulting me."

"The truth is always insulting to the ignorant." She still stared out the window, but Vincent saw a fight glinting in her eyes and nearly purred. If she needed a fight to get out of her somber mood, he would allow it, especially with one as useless as Morgan.

"She's not my bitch, and she will always speak her mind." His usually stoic voice was rich with desire.

Morgan had been one of Edwin's favorites, of sorts. He had been on the fringes of Edwin's society, but was always treated with respect and dignity. He took it very personally that the new Captain did not afford him the same courtesies. "You give the human too many freedoms. You should drain her and throw her to your wolf slaves."

Vincent knew Morgan wouldn't have said such a thing if any of the wolves were present. It was the night of the full moon. Rebecca and Charlie were downstairs in the dungeon, locked up and sedated. Doug was out in the silver pen, tearing sheep apart. It was his turn to let loose. Vincent considered having Morgan taken out to the pen and have him repeat the words, but knew Natalia wanted a fight. And who was he to deny her what she wished?

Vincent sat back to watch the fireworks. He had never been able to watch Natalia fight from his throne. He imagined he would greatly enjoy it.

"The only slave here is you." Her words rang out clearly. Everyone knew Morgan listened to whoever was in charge and did what he had to until such a time as someone else took over. He was indeed a slave: he seemed to be the only one who didn't know it.

"What in the name of <u>Hell</u> does that mean?" Morgan turned to her, baffled by her words.

"You're a slave. No, I take that back. You're not a slave. You're a dog." Her words were ever so calm. She still faced away from Morgan. It was as if he were no more significant than the darkness beyond the glass.

"First I'm a slave; now I'm a dog? Captain, curb your bitch's tongue, or I'll cut it out."

"See that's why you're a dog. A man would have realized how foolish it was to insult a woman like me." She finally turned to him. "And a well-trained dog would never bite its master's hand, as you are clearly doing." A slight smile came to her lips. "I guess that means you're worse than a dog."

Morgan easily took the bait. He rushed Natalia, thinking to kill her, but never reached his target. Natalia used the staff that leaned against the wall next to her as a bat and used Morgan's head as a baseball. The "CRACK!" as wood hit bone echoed in the room. Morgan staggered, fell back, healed, and readied himself for the next attack.

"You owe me blood, bitch." He was hunched over slightly, as if about to charge. Natalia leveled the staff in both hands.

"I owe you nothing."

"You broke my neck. When you broke Lorraine's neck you fell to your knees and offered her your blood, so she could heal. Bow to me and give me what I deserve."

"Lorraine was worth healing." Natalia moved away from the wall, toward the center of the room where there was more space.

"It's a House LeGris rule. You said so yourself." He started to circle her. She let him.

"Yes, but you're not of House LeGris." She saw Vincent smile over Morgan's shoulder and smiled back.

"Neither was she."

"House LeGris exists because of Lorraine."

"Give me your blood!" His bellow echoed in the room.

"Come and get it."

He roared and attacked. She swung and hit him in solidly in the chest. Something cracked, she wasn't sure what. Natalia let Morgan's momentum swing the staff and her around. She pulled the weapon away before he could grab it. He was young, but even a young vampire could withstand a few hits from a staff. What she wanted was a sword. There was only one in the room, but Natalia really didn't think she would need it. She could knock him out if her hits were precise.

Precise hits would mean a quick fight though, and Natalia knew she didn't want a quick fight. She was tired of the memories which surfaced in her head and of the guilt that swam in her mind. When she fought someone worthy it helped to eliminate all thoughts. If she fought Morgan quickly, she would be frustrated instead. Consequently, she went slowly. The next few hits were not as fierce, and Morgan gained confidence. As his confidence grew, he became an easier target. Those in the room who knew her skills placed bets. Those who didn't know her wondered how soon Vincent would stop the fight.

Vincent smiled and waited for the inevitable.

After sparring carefully for a few minutes, Natalia started to feel it. Her thoughts were picked clean from her mind as Morgan learned her movements and gained confidence. Her tactical side took over as Morgan was allowed to attack her semi-successfully repeatedly. Finally, her mind clear of scattered thoughts, she began to show him what she was really made of. Because she allowed him to win for a few minutes, he didn't give up easily. The calculating warrior took over. The numerous blows she landed were harder, fiercer, and far more precise. Finally, her scattered mind completely consumed by battle adrenaline, she swept him off his feet, swung the staff to his neck and pressed hard against his throat.

"You can't choke me, human."

Her eyes narrowed as an evil grin graced her features. "I can still decapitate you. It'll take some time, but it would make me smile."

"Natalia." Vincent's voice sent shivers down her spine. It was full of the promise of pleasure.

She turned to her lover, who still simply sat in his seat. His elbows lay on the armrests and his fingers were tented in front of his face. He gazed at her with pure desire. He knew when her mind cleared and what it meant for him. He made a minute movement with his head to beckon to her. She shuddered again, dropped the staff, and sauntered over to him.

The staff clattered to the ground as Morgan gained his feet. He bellowed about something. Natalia heard his footsteps as he targeted her, but he never made it. Joseph stopped him before Morgan took five steps. Natalia continued to advance uninterrupted. When she arrived in front of Vincent she dropped to her knees.

"I am yours, sir, for the night. Use me as you see fit." She raised her eyes to his, saw what awaited her and cried out in pleasure.

Vincent tore his eyes from hers, looked around the room, then looked back to his woman. "Leave us. Now."

Natalia stood, took the two final steps to her lover, who then grabbed her and helped her straddle the throne. He waited until the room was cleared before he removed her clothing.

ᑕ ᗷ

Vincent ran his hand through her black hair and felt the warm silkiness on his cool fingers. He couldn't remember how they had ended up in the bedroom and didn't care. It had been too long since he was able to enjoy her this much. Too long since she had shown her desires and love. He missed it. But even now, with Natalia in his arms, his mind wouldn't stop.

"Tell me the information you have on Donald. Let me take care of this for you."

She shook her head as guilt consumed her. "Vincent, I have to do this myself."

"Why?"

She pulled away and sat against the headboard. "He killed my mother. I've spent most of the ensuing years gathering skills in order to be able to kill him. I've also spent many of those years ignoring clues so that I could stay with you."

He sat up next to her. "I did not know that."

"I..." she looked away. "I was afraid of confronting him, Vincent. I may now have an opportunity and I'm going to take it." She looked to him again. "I think it may also give you the opportunity to control the mayor."

He shook his head. "If that happens, it happens. I wish you safe."

She looked at him with tired, sad eyes. "I'm as safe as I can be in this situation."

"That isn't saying much."

"I know, but it has to do."

Vincent gathered her in his arms and held her close. She snuggled closer, and tried to remember when it stopped feeling strange to lay next to a seemingly dead body. The thought faded easily as he kissed her deeply. Though he wanted to convince her to allow him to find and kill Donald, he understood her desire to do it herself. He let his thoughts go and caressed her skin softly. She moaned with pleasure as thoughts faded away.

27

Joseph shook Vincent awake and called to him in an odd tone. Vincent struggled to hold onto the lovely vision of Natalia, but Joseph's voice finally penetrated.

"what…What…WHAT?" He screamed at his trusted friend.

"You're needed, sir. In the meeting room. There's…trouble."

Joseph's mock worried voice slammed away the rest of the cobwebs and Vincent was awake and angry. Whatever the trouble was, he would spill someone's blood. He hated being roused in the middle of a pleasant dream. And where was Natalia anyway? Six days ago, she slipped out before he woke and had not been home since. He sighed as he jumped out of bed and slipped on his silk pajama pants. He followed Joseph out of the room and down the steps to the double doors of his main meeting room.

The doors were closed but he could hear voices. Joseph stood in front of one door; hand on the knob waiting for his master to compose himself. Vincent stood for a moment and stared at the mirrored door. He had not yet eaten; his reflection was slightly ghostly. A smile floated to his lips as he thought of the many vampires that had been unprepared for the mirrors. Not many of his kind had them in their homes. Vincent thought mirrors a useful tool against his enemies. He could tell if they had eaten or not based on their reflection. Those who trusted him usually didn't arrive at full blood. They knew Vincent would offer them blood. Those who did not trust him almost always showed up full. Vincent felt they either didn't trust the blood or didn't trust him not to kill them. It made him smile.

Vincent stood before the mirror and made himself look more imposing as he collected his thoughts. He was almost as tall as the door and his shoulders were almost as wide as the mirror. Using his fingers, he messed up his blond hair even more than it already was, to make it look wild. His hair had been compared to a lion's mane on several occasions, even though he usually kept it short. At the moment he was rather perturbed; a wild look was probably to his advantage.

Although Vincent didn't need to, he took a deep breath. After all these years he still felt that a deep breath was the best way to calm himself. He closed his eyes and felt as his chest rose and fell unnaturally, felt the tightness around his scar as the skin stretched. He placed his right hand over the scar and smiled. He could heal the scar but didn't want to. It was a reminder of one of his greater moments. He had gained Joseph's undying loyalty and the scar in the same instant.

Fifty years after Vincent's change, Joseph had been ordered to kill him by their benefactor. According to Gautier, young Vincent was too flamboyant and public with his abilities. To weaken him they trapped Vincent in his room. After five days Joseph came to him. offered false friendship to get close, and staked him. When Joseph stumbled into him, Vincent felt the wood pierce the skin and part his muscles. Vincent did not turn to dust.

When Joseph stepped back, Vincent let the wooden stake dangle from his breast. He smiled languidly, held Joseph's stare for a full minute and slowly withdrew the stake. Joseph fell to his knees, begged for forgiveness, and pleaded for his life. Vincent smiled, forgave him, gave back the stake with instructions to use it on their benefactor. Joseph readily agreed and Gautier was dead within hours. Joseph had been by Vincent's side ever since.

Joseph never asked how Vincent fed, and Vincent never offered to tell him. It was a rather simple reason, one that his benefactor and future bodyguard overlooked. Joseph and Gautier made sure that Vincent had no access to any living beings, except for the rats in the wall. The two failed to realize Vincent would drink the blood of what they deemed lowly and disgusting creatures. The rats were ample food. Vincent smiled a hyena's smile as heat surged through him. He burst through the now open door to his meeting room.

Joseph did not follow but closed the door behind his master. He went off to watch the festivities from the security room, where he could call for help if it were needed. Mierka and Rebecca were already in the security room as Vincent's backup.

Vincent looked about the room and understood that the plan was being executed tonight. It was earlier than he and his Lieutenants had anticipated, but that was fine by him. There were about twenty people gathered in the meeting room. He recognized four of his Lieutenants, three who leaned against a wall, each with one of their own Sergeants. The rest of the group, new vampires by their attitudes and look, were gathered at his throne, which Morgan sat on. There was a reason it was the only piece of furniture in the room, and it wasn't for guests to enjoy. A low growl escaped Vincent's throat.

He bought the throne long ago in China. The armrests were dragons, the right open mouthed, the left closed. The feet were claws and the cushions were red silk. It had a high back and was made of oak. It cost him a lot of money, but it had been worth it. He enjoyed sitting in the throne so much that he had his people move it back and forth between the training room and his larger meeting room, depending on where it was needed most. Joseph and Owen moved it into the meeting room days ago. It was his throne; no one was allowed to use it.

And now Morgan was defiling it.

He composed himself and advanced toward Morgan. One of Morgan's younglings stepped into his path and tried to stop him. Vincent threw him across the room with little effort. He smiled when he heard bones break. The gasps from the rest of Morgan's entourage made Vincent grin in anticipation. His vampires would have plenty of blood tonight.

Morgan gripped the armrests. Was it fear, hatred, anger or all three that made his green eyes blaze? Vincent wasn't sure and really didn't care. He grabbed Morgan by the lapels of his off the rack suit and pulled him out of the chair. The cheap suit ripped in several places.

"Your rule is over Vincent. It's my turn now. Give up! We have you surrounded!" His voice cracked, and made him sound no older than sixteen.

"Morgan." Vincent said calmly, as he still had the upper hand. "Get out of my chair." He threw him aside like a rag doll, into his entourage, who steadied him. "Now then Morgan, do you mind telling me why you roused me out of a wonderful dream," he glanced out the large, tinted bay windows to the setting sun, "before the sun set?"

"You've been Captain a year and the mayor still hates you. It's my turn now." His whiney voice grated on Vincent's nerves.

Vincent took a step forward and Morgan stepped back. "Your turn? Do you remember how I took control? Has your hunger for power impaired your memory?"

He took three more steps forward quickly, which caused Morgan to stumble and fall. Vincent towered over the man menacingly. He leaned over carefully, bent almost in half, which brought his face within inches of Morgan's sweaty one. "I killed Edwin to gain control. Would you like to try and kill me?"

Vincent sensed movement to his right and bent his knees. When he felt the would-be assailant on his back, he stood. The youngling's momentum sent him sailing across the room. No bones crushed this time, but the thud made Vincent's lips twitch into the briefest of smiles.

"You apparently feel that one of your younglings-"

"Disciples." Morgan stated from the floor.

Vincent snorted. "Disciples?" He raised an eyebrow then shrugged. He stepped away from Morgan toward the man's younglings. "You're ridiculous, Morgan." He shook his head. "You feel that one of your younglings will be able to take me out?"

Vincent stood in front of the rest of Morgan's younglings. He presented them his back, almost as if to dare them to try something. "I'm going to give you a chance to talk with me rather than just killing you right now Morgan. Despite your lack of loyalty, you have shown yourself to be a rather valuable source of information. But you are replaceable. Therefore, you, Anthony, Kari, Markus, and I will sit down and have a nice quiet chat, while my men figure out what to do with your younglings. Agreed?"

He heard movement behind him. A voice spoke up and tried to sound tough.

"We're not going anywhere. We stay with Mor-"

The youngling's sentence cut off when Vincent's hand squeezed his throat. Vincent pulled the young vampire to his face and stared the ignorant fool down.

Vincent snorted at the ridiculous boy before him. He had white makeup all over his face and neck with black eyeliner, mascara, and black lipstick. He wore black leather…everything. He was what society called punk, goth, emo, and various other things. Vampires called these younglings an easy meal. Vincent briefly looked upon the remaining eleven boys and girls. Most seemed to finally understand what was going to happen to them. All were easy meals. He understood now how Morgan had gotten them. He hadn't looked for worthy candidates. Morgan had chosen easy targets: cannon fodder. These children were to keep him occupied while, what? Morgan tried to get the drop on him? Vincent glanced at Morgan. The man still sat on the ground. He hadn't even bothered getting up. Vincent turned back to the young one in his hand. The boy struggled and clawed at Vincent's hand, to try and pry open the vise-like grip of his long fingers. Vincent barely noticed.

"What's your name, boy?" He inquired, like a teacher asking an unruly student on the first day of class.

"damien"

It was a whisper. Vincent barely heard him. He wasn't choking him, as the boy didn't need to breathe, but he still needed air to speak. Vincent loosened his fingers and asked again.

The boy took a deep breath. In a terrified voice that tried desperately not to sound frightened stated, "DAMIEN LORD OF DARKNESS AND ALL HE SEES?"

Vincent started to laugh. He couldn't help it. The boy was pathetic. Still holding onto "The Lord of Darkness," Vincent continued to laugh. He heard Kari laugh as well. Morgan finally picked himself off the floor, stood, and tried to look dignified. Since his hair was out of place and his shirt was untucked, he failed magnificently. It made Vincent laugh even harder. He heard a few of Morgan's meals giggle nervously.

Vincent felt the heat rise in him again along with a hard heavy need. He had not eaten upon waking, and his body had started to protest. Still laughing, he looked back into the eyes of Damien, Lord of Darkness. The boy would serve as a lesson to Morgan and his 'disciples'. Lightning quick, in the middle of a laugh, he pulled Damien's neck to his mouth and pierced the soft skin with his sharp teeth. He drank deep, as he meant to drain the boy. Vincent was so absorbed by the hot liquid that ran down his throat that he didn't enjoy the screams of the other younglings.

Vincent pulled away a moment later as he licked his lips. "How old was he Morgan? Couple hours?"

The body dropped to the ground in a heap. The boy didn't have much blood in him to begin with and would not live through that much blood loss. He would be ghul soon. He would have to be dealt with before then. Vincent wiped his lips with the back of his hand and then licked the back of his hand.

"YOU BASTARD!" A girl screamed.

She came at him with a small knife. When she was within arm's length, Vincent reached out, grabbed her head in his hands and twisted hard to the right. The action broke her neck and nearly ripped her head off her body. It was rather easy. Vincent had once witnessed a just fed vampire pull off the door of a safe room. Breaking a human's neck didn't take that much pressure. Her body fell on top of Damien's, chest down, but face up with her eyes pointed toward the ceiling. Damien started to feed on the girl.

Vincent felt as battle heat coursed through his body and wondered again where Natalia was. He would want her when he was done. He frowned in frustration then turned his attention to Morgan, who grumbled under his breath.

"You didn't have to kill them."

"You killed them when you changed them without my permission." Vincent's voice was calm, but there was a sharp edge to it.

Morgan backed away from the bodies, looked down and fell to one knee. The look on his face suggested he had come to a conclusion. "I apologize, Captain. Please accept my respectful request for forgiveness. I don't know what I was thinking."

Vincent folded his arms and called out to Joseph, whom he knew watched from the security room. He waited in silence until Joseph opened the doors. Joseph, Mierka, Rebecca, Doug and Owen walked in closer to Vincent. Ben appeared, and stood in the open doorway, a staff in his hands. He guarded the doorway, and his eyes dared someone to come closer.

When the group stopped near Vincent, the vampire smiled. He waited until Morgan finally looked up at him.

"Sir? Do you accept my apology?"

There was just enough pleading in Morgan's voice to throw off most people. Vincent was not most people. He learned how to spot men like Morgan long ago and knew all their tricks. This was the bargaining stage. If Vincent were in a better mood, he would play it out, see what the man offered. He was tired of Morgan though, and had already picked out his replacement.

"Take the younglings to the dungeon. Find out who is worthy and who is not. Kill the ones who are down."

The gathered younglings gasped, and a few screamed as Rebecca and Doug changed to Blitzkrieg. Doug moved to the young vampires on the floor and killed both quickly with his long, sharp claws. Rebecca moved closer to the group of younglings and growled as the House LeGris vampires surrounded them. Three tried to flee anyway, but Rebecca jumped to one and killed him quickly. The other two stopped and moved back to the others. All the guards, save Joseph, herded the younglings out of the room and to the dungeon.

Vincent spoke again before the door closed. "Put this one in the oubliette."

Morgan's eyes grew wide. "No. No Vincent, please. Don't…"

Joseph was by Morgan's side and picked him up by the armpits. Morgan tried to fight.

"You can't do this. You said yourself: you need me. We can work something out. I'll give you anything you want. Please Vincent, JUST TELL ME WHAT YOU WANT!"

Joseph and Morgan were out in the hall now, and Morgan's shouts grew softer. Joseph would need to drink a little of Morgan's blood before he threw the young vampire into the oubliette. Vincent thought perhaps Joseph would torture Morgan instead. In the end, it wouldn't matter. Morgan would fall into the oubliette, break a few bones and before too long, would turn ghul. It made Vincent smile.

Vincent regarded Kari, Markus, and Anthony. Kari held back laughter, Markus snickered, but Anthony looked mildly annoyed.

"Kari, Markus, Anthony, please send your Sergeants out, you can bring them up to speed later."

Anthony stepped forward. "Sir, Julia has news you need to hear."

Vincent cocked his head. He liked Julia. She was the one he wanted to take Morgan's place. She could find out anything. "She may stay."

The others left of their own free will. They had been here before and knew where to go. There was always someone to drink from in the kitchen for welcomed guests. The door closed behind them, and Vincent went to his throne to sit down.

"Julia, what news?"

Julia stepped from behind Anthony's right shoulder, a startled look upon her face. Anthony noticed the difference and felt a change coming. He stood taller and waited for Julia to speak.

Julia stammered as she tried to get the words out. Vincent never spoke to her directly; she always told Anthony her news and he passed the information on to their boss. Unnerved, Julia didn't start well.

"Morgan is planning on killing you."

Vincent raised an eyebrow. "Really? Hadn't noticed."

Julia shook her head and closed her eyes as her hand stole to the blue stone pendant around her neck. She concentrated then opened her eyes to look at her Captain. Vincent watched her compose herself, and wondered what the game was.

"This was nothing. It was for his fun. He hired a Slayer."

Vincent sat up straighter. Markus and Kari looked stunned. Anthony waited for the rest.

"Do you know who he hired?"

"Name, address, phone number. Where and when he's supposed to kill you."

"Can you take care of him?"

Julia's eyes grew wide. "Y-yes. Yes, I can sir. It would be my pleasure."

Vincent stood and took two steps to bring him face to face with Julia. He placed his hands on her shoulders and leaned in to whisper into her ear. "Bring me his head and everything that was Morgan's will be yours. All his possessions, all his servants, and his title."

Vincent kissed both her cheeks then went back to his throne. A stunned Julia bowed and stepped back. She tried to step behind her sire, but Anthony wouldn't let her. Her place was now beside him as an equal, not behind him as a lesser.

"Now, then. Why didn't anyone tell me that Morgan was going to bring twelve young ones? Actually, why did no one stop him?" Vincent now sounded perturbed.

"Sir we didn't know." Kari locked her eyes with his.

He read the truth in her eyes and was satisfied, but not happy. "When did you learn?"

"When we met him here tonight."

Vincent got up and started to pace. Anthony took two steps back and pulled at Julia's elbow, to move her back to his side. Markus and Kari looked at each other but otherwise did not move. They had center stage now; it had been left up to them to watch Morgan. They performed a poor job and knew it. Vincent was extremely disappointed with Markus. He expected far more from the man, who seemed to have fallen for Kari. She taught him nothing but bad habits. Vincent would have to have her watched, to make sure his youngest member wasn't led too far astray.

"Did you have any spies on him?"

"Yes, two. One at his home and one at his favorite club."

"Did you have anyone following him or his top Sergeants?"

"We didn't think it was necessary."

This brought a hard stare from Vincent. "You didn't think it was necessary? This is a man who was planning on killing your leader, and you didn't think it was necessary?" Vincent had been halfway across the room. In less than a second, he stood menacingly in front of Kari and Markus. "I'm not happy with this news. Tell me why I shouldn't strip you of your ranks right this moment."

Kari and Markus fell to their knees. They were still alive, which only meant he still needed them, might forgive them, and give them another chance. Markus spoke first.

"Give us another chance to show you we're worthy."

"We honestly didn't know what a danger he could be. Please sir, give us another chance."

"What I find interesting," Vincent continued to pace, but slowly and more deliberately, "is that Anthony came to me five days ago with this information. I didn't do anything about it because my hope was that one of you would find out about it as well. Your spies are worthless. You should have taken care of it yourselves. Anyone else would think you deliberately performed a poor job. How are you going to prove to me it wasn't deliberate?"

"I have an idea."

Vincent turned with a smile on his face. Natalia was back and looked beautiful in a pinstripe skirt suit and black stiletto heels. He was by her side in an instant, an inscrutable expression on his face. He spoke softly, only to her. "You didn't tell me you were leaving."

She placed her hand on his chest and kept her own voice soft. "I'm sorry Vincent. I had no choice."

"There is always a choice."

Silence lay between them for a moment until he leaned in and kissed her slowly. Natalia made a noise in the back of her throat, which revealed the pain she felt in having left him. He pulled away at the sound. He gazed down into her eyes.

"There is always a choice, my love." His voice was still soft.

Pain crossed her face. "You're right. There is."

Silence descended again. It made Vincent realized that she had made a choice, and it was not to be with him. He stood a little taller and felt that in the end, she would be with him again.

"You have a plan, Natalia?"

"Don't I always?" Her expression changed to hide the pain as she walked toward the others. He followed, and wondered what she chose over him.

"What have you been up to?" His voice, thick and deep, swept over her skin.

"I found out some important information." Natalia walked past the vampires to the throne. She ran her hand over the left armrest, around the back and then down the right armrest. She gave Vincent a look as she fingered the exposed dragon teeth. "I know when we can feed him your blood."

Vincent stood by his Lieutenants, and tried not to look concerned. He wasn't comfortable with the idea of Natalia in the mayor's employment. "What have you learned?"

"He hired two Slayers and a priest to be his bodyguards. He's going in for heart surgery in two days. One Slayer and the priest will be with him at all times, the other Slayer will be outside the door, watching."

"How did you learn so much?" Kari sounded suspicious and awed.

"She has her ways." Anthony's voice held the ever-present bite as he gave Natalia a hard look. His tone of voice stilled the others; he would be the only one to question her motives.

Vincent moved to behind Natalia and paced slowly. "How do you know who these people are?"

"I called their names into the hospital. Carl Garvin, Father Sulta, and Donavon."

The room became hot and sticky with the news. Carl Garvin was more bounty hunter than Slayer. He could be bought off easily; double the bounty usually did the trick. Father Sulta was a crackpot. He didn't seem to understand that the usual tricks didn't affect all vampires. Then there was Donavon. He had been around for some years and seemed to understand too well how vampires moved, thought, and acted.

"Has Father Sulta seen you?" Vincent knew of her run-in with the Slayer.

"Yes. But he's convinced I've changed sides."

Her voice was pained. The Slayer had walked in on her and Mayor Lawrence having sex. She was bent forward over the mayor's desk; he stood behind her and grunted like a pig. Until the door opened, she had a bored expression on her face. The mayor was a poor lover, more interested in getting himself off then in pleasing his partner. When the door opened, she plastered a meek and submissive look on her face. Father Sulta closed the door and watched as the mayor climaxed. The Slayer never once let his gaze stray from her eyes, a look of triumph on his face. She shook her head, and cleared her thoughts as Vincent's voice penetrated her mind.

"So now we know where he'll be. A hospital. If not for his guards, I would be able to sneak in. We can take out Garvin and Sulta, but there's little chance of anyone killing Donavon. If I won't risk my life, I won't ask it of anyone else." He paused, looked at Markus and Kari, who looked worried. "It will be your job to take out Sulta and Garvin when Gary has been taken to the recovery room. That will help a little. But what about Donavon?"

"I have a plan in the works." She looked to Vincent and Anthony. She didn't want to continue to plan in front of the younger vampires. "Should we go someplace else and talk?"

Kari noticed the look and scowled. "You're excluding us. Why?"

Natalia stared her down, not in the least bit worried. "What I'm discussing with Vincent doesn't concern you."

It was a lie. They could continue to talk in front of Julia, Markus, and Kari, and would if Vincent demanded it. Natalia didn't trust Kari. Despite Julia's best effort, she was never able to find too much information on the woman. It didn't endear her to Natalia, and didn't want the overly ambitious woman to be present for all the planning stages.

Vincent stepped forward seemingly to protect Natalia. He didn't like the look Kari gave his lover. The daggers Kari's eyes threw at Natalia made him understand Natalia's reluctance to speak in front of Kari.

"I wish to speak with my top people first, and Natalia understands this." He looked at Julia, Kari, and Markus. "Leave us. Go feed. We'll bring you up to date if necessary."

Kari shrank back into herself but glowered at the human. She opened her mouth to speak but the room's double doors opened loudly and stopped her. Joseph strolled in to usher out the younger vampires. Vincent led the way to his study, where he could speak privately with Anthony and Natalia in relative comfort.

28

N atalia stood outside the hospital and watched from the shadows as her people went in. Mayor Lawrence was in the hospital. Donavon, or rather Donald, was inside at the mayor's door, but the others didn't know that yet. She knew she should have already pulled him away, but she was afraid. It wasn't every day one confronted her mother's killer. Still, her people would be in serious trouble if she didn't. Donald used magic to make himself more powerful than his years allowed. Natalia watched as Vincent and Joseph slipped inside the hospital. It had been a while since she had seen Vincent, and it made her heart ache. She missed her man terribly.

There was nothing she could do about that now. She had to get inside. She knew there were still a few hours before Markus, Kari, Ben, and Owen would try and lure their targets out and allow Vincent the few moments he needed to feed Mayor Lawrence his blood. They had to arrive before visiting hours were over though. They would wait in various out of the way places for midnight when there would be fewer humans.

Natalia nodded and readied herself mentally. She stepped out of the shadows and stopped cold when a familiar form turned the corner. The lone figure moved closer, and Natalia took a deep breath to stop shaking. Ashley. What was she doing here?

A cold dread worked itself into her gut. Donald had spent time with a woman while in San Francisco. Natalia had an awful feeling that the dangerous vampire was seeing Ashley. She tried to convince herself it was a coincidence; Ashley was here to visit a sick friend or relative. It was a hard lie to tell herself. Ashley had no relatives, and her Slayer friends almost never went to the hospital. Natalia learned early that coincidences didn't happen if you knew of the real terror that gripped the fragile human world. She started across the street then jogged as Ashley entered the hospital. Once inside, Natalia used the stairs to run up to the floor the mayor was on, as she knew Donald would be there. She was able to hide herself well enough to observe Donavan at the Mayor's door as she waited for the inevitable.

Natalia didn't keep an eye on most of the Slayers. Their lives were their own. Occasionally though, she searched for Ashley. She never approached her, but watched to see if the girl was headed out of the Slayer mentality. Too many times the answer was no. The girl seemed to need the Slayers and they didn't mind having her around. Natalia's thoughts parted as Ashley finally emerged from the elevator and walked quickly to Donald.

Ashley and Donald spoke for a few moments, looked around, then went to a room further down the hall. Natalia carefully walked down the hall and peered into the room, as if looking for someone she knew. She caught a glimpse of Ashley and Donald. Their lips were locked in a deep kiss and his hands roamed her body. Revulsion and hatred engulfed Natalia and she almost ran into the room. She restrained herself, left to find a hiding spot close by, and waited until Ashley emerged.

Donald went back to stand sentry and Ashley went to the elevators. Natalia made her way downstairs and waited for Ashley. Once hidden, she glanced at her watch. She still had a few hours. She needed to get Ashley away from Donald and Donald away from the hospital. She could take care of both at once, as long as she had enough time. She hoped she did.

Natalia followed Ashley home, and allowed the woman to enter her apartment in safety. When the door was almost closed, Natalia barged in and knocked Ashley to the floor.

"There's no money in the apartment and I don't have anything valuable!"

Natalia looked contemptuously at Ashley. "Get up Ashley. I'm not robbing you."

Ashley had curled up in a near fetal position, but her arms protected her head. At Natalia's words, she slowly uncurled and looked up at her attacker. "What do you want?"

"For you to get off the floor and listen to me." Her tone left no room for argument and Ashley did as instructed. "Is there anyone else in the apartment?"

"No." Ashley stood in front of Natalia. "How did you find me?"

"I was at the hospital. I saw you with Donavon."

"Why were you there?"

"I needed to speak with him."

"Why would a Slayer want to speak with a Hellspawn's bitch?"

Natalia gave her a deadpan look. "Because he's a vampire posing as a

Slayer."

Ashley's eyes grew wide. "You're lying." Her expression changed to one of total disbelief and denial. The young woman looked like a spoiled brat. "Anyway, why do you care? You've been sleeping with a vampire for years."

Cold hatred worked its way into Natalia's heart. "Don't compare them. They're nothing alike. Donavon abuses and kills the women he sleeps with. Vincent does not."

"Vincent's killed plenty of humans! I heard what type of vampire he is if he's allowed."

Natalia wanted to argue with the girl and let her know what type of man Vincent was, but knew she didn't have time. Ashley had ignored the main point, that Donald abused and killed the women he was with and therefore, Ashley's life was in danger. Natalia knew what type of man Vincent was, had seen it in person and read the accounts in the Slayer journals.

Vincent wasn't what most people would call good, but neither was he evil. She knew he killed innocents during wars. Vincent did not kill those loyal to him unless a betrayal was proven. He also did not kill indiscriminately, as Donald did. She needed to make Ashley understand the danger she was in.

"The proof of what he is, is in his apartment. Will you come with me?"

Ashley furrowed her brow in thought. "I don't know if I can trust you."

"I don't expect you to trust me. I just want you to see the truth."

"Why?"

"He killed my mother. I don't want him to kill you."

"Why do you care if he kills a Slayer?"

"Because you're about the age my kid would have been," was what Natalia was thinking. She hid the thought away quickly, denied the emotions, and gave as honest an answer as she was capable of. "You're not a Slayer. You're like me. Caught between life and reality. I don't know where I belong and neither do you."

Ashley shook her head, opened her mouth as if to speak, then closed it again. She broke away from Natalia and paced a few steps. "Why do you think he's going to kill me?"

She spoke slowly, emphasized her words, and hoped the truth would sink into Ashley's thick skull. "He killed other women before he killed my mom. I'll show you news clippings in a couple of days. Right now, all I can prove is that he's a vampire pretending to be a Slayer."

"Why would he pretend to be a Slayer?"

"He grew up in a very strict Catholic household. He grew up with a strong belief in God and killed women at a young age. He thought he was made a vampire as punishment, but then later figured out it was to be able to do as he pleased. Maybe he's acting like a Slayer to try and correct the evil he's done, maybe he wants redemption, but I don't think so. I've been in contact with someone who's been talking to him a great deal. The vampire likes being what he is because it makes it easier to attract women. Innocent women, like you."

"I'm not innocent of the world around us."

Natalia laughed slightly. "Not that type of innocent. How many men have you slept with?"

Ashley gave her an embarrassed look. "What does that have to do with anything?"

"He like virgins, or women he perceives to be virgins. Except for a couple exceptions, that's all he's been with. He kills the woman when he realizes that they're human and not perfect."

"That's ridiculous."

"Come with me to his apartment and I'll prove it."

Natalia saw the conflict on the woman's face. She was curious but didn't trust Natalia. Her brow crinkled again, and Natalia saw the glint in Ashley's eye. She felt she might be able to save the woman from Donald.

"Fine."

Natalia, overcome by emotions she didn't like to acknowledge, grabbed Ashley, and hugged her briefly. She let her go and turned for the door. "Let's go."

They left the apartment and took Ashley's little used car to Donald's apartment. He lived on the other side of the city. The car was quicker than public transportation at this time of day. They were there within twenty minutes and were glad for the public lot across the street. Natalia grabbed her small backpack as they left the car. Moments later they were at his apartment. Outside the door, Ashley started to question their brashness.

"What if he's here?"

"You know he's at the hospital watching the mayor. He'll be for the next three nights. I've been watching the man for three weeks now, I know his movements." With that she reached inside her backpack for her lock pick set. The locks were conventional and easy to pick. With the door unlocked, they went inside. Natalia closed and locked the door from the inside.

The apartment was filled with odd smells and sights. The walls were covered in archaic symbols, too old to be recognized by a non-witch. Incense and candles burned in every corner of the room and in various places throughout. Ten books were open in the center of the room and in the middle of the circle was a woman of about sixty. She had long greasy gray hair and was much too thin to be healthy. She sat on the floor naked and rocked back and forth, as she chanted.

"Who is she?"

"His witch. She's so wrapped up in the spells she's chanting that she can't perceive anything beyond the circle."

"How does that happen?"

Natalia had been in the apartment before and called Diana to find out what was going on. "She's weaving too many spells at once. It takes all her energy to weave the spells, leaving nothing to the real world."

"What are the spells she's weaving?"

"I only deciphered five. One is to make him warm; one is to make him immune to crosses and holy water; one makes him immune to the color red; one is to stop the effect of a stake and one is to make sure that if someone decapitates him, it won't kill him. He's young enough that all that still affects him. I'm not sure about the other five. They're in a language I can't identify."

"This isn't proof."

"Then let's wake her up." Natalia moved quickly and shut one of the books. The witch stuttered but kept going. It wasn't until Natalia had shut half the books that the woman started to respond better. As Natalia closed the sixth the stutter came again, more intense and the woman's eyes flew open for a brief second. Natalia felt a hand on her arm and stopped.

"Is this safe?"

"I asked a friend how to do this."

It wasn't really an answer, but it was better than the truth, which was that it might kill the woman. Natalia closed the seventh book and the woman's breath caught. It started again as tears ran down her cheeks. Natalia closed the eighth one and the woman dropped to her side. Her breath came in harsh gasps, but still she chanted. With all the books closed, she let out an anguished cry and curled up into a ball.

"Get me a blanket from the bedroom."

"Sure, yeah." Ashley turned and headed for the only hallway in the place. She was back before the woman was even aware of her surroundings. Natalia took the blanket, wrapped it around the witch, and hugged the trembling woman to her.

"You have to leave. He'll be here soon."

Natalia looked to Ashley who hunkered down and listened intently. Her face was sheer sorrow.

"It's ok. I'm here to fight him. Why are you here?"

"He kidnapped me about five years ago. Keeps me weak. He found someone else to weave a spell binding me to these books. It broke when you closed them. Thank you."

"What's your name?" Ashley's voice was more than kind.

"Gloria."

"What's his name?" Natalia ignored Ashley's odd look.

"Donavon. And he's here."

There was a smell of ozone. Natalia looked toward the smell: Donald, known as Donavon to some, stood at the door of the apartment with a furious look on his face. Natalia dropped Gloria and tried to stand. Before she was up completely, Donald retrieved a gun from behind his back. He fired the gun and Natalia knew it wasn't filled with bullets from the sound. She heard Ashley scream, and felt something prick her arm. Natalia fought against the tranquilizer, but the darkness swallowed her. His laughter followed her and caused memories of her mother's death to surface.

29
Twenty Years Earlier

Natalia looked around her hometown as she stood outside of Pastor Martin's house. She could vaguely hear Bethany and Mrs. Martin as they spoke. Though all three offered to visit Marnia with Natalia, she felt it was better if she went alone. She didn't know what state her mom would be in.

Natalia did not head for her old house right away, but went to the corner market first. She bought a water pistol, and two small empty jars with cork stoppers. She went to the Catholic Church up the street and filled the jars and water pistol with holy water. She read that holy water affected younger vampires, and hoped Donald wasn't ancient. There was a table filled with candles and wooden crosses. She took a wooden cross and stuffed some money in the donation box, not sure if a cross would work. Her research wasn't too clear on holy symbols and their effect on vampires. She placed the jars in her pocket and made sure the paring knife she took earlier had not fallen out of her jacket. If she were wrong about Donald and he was just some asshole human, a knife would be more effective than the holy items.

Natalia walked the mile to her old house, and wished she knew how to drive. The walk was not pleasant. She was too worried about being caught unawares, but it still did not take her long to reach the house. The sun had not yet set behind the mountains, and she still had two hours before it did.

The place was a mess. Donald's rig was parked in the driveway. The weeds around it were high, which proved it had been parked for a while. There was garbage strewn everywhere and the house needed to be painted. Natalia wondered if it had been this bad the last time she was here, but couldn't clearly recall.

Natalia walked up the sagging steps with the cross held out in front of her and tried the door. It was unlocked. She opened it slowly and looked around. There were dishes and dirt and dust everywhere. A kitchen chair was overturned. Natalia walked to the living room. She stepped in carefully then dropped the cross. Her mother sat in the recliner and stared at a blank TV screen.

"Mom?" She shook Marnia gently. It took a bit, but Marnia finally came to.

"Natalia, love, what time is it? I must've fallen asleep. You're going to be late for school." She tried to get up, but failed. She fell heavily back into the chair. "I'm sorry honey, I can't fix your lunch today, I don't feel too good."

"Mom! Try and focus. I'm not in school anymore. Wake up!" Natalia took her mom's hands gently in hers and took a look. There were old and new bite wounds up and down her mother's arms. Natalia had to get her mom out of here.

"Mom? We have to go now. Can you get up?"

Marnia's eyes brightened for a moment, then faded again. "Donald."

Natalia's head whipped around fast enough to see the trucker before he grabbed her. He held a cloth to her face. Before she could react, she dropped unconscious from the chloroform.

☙ ❧

When Natalia came to, she was tied to a kitchen chair. Her feet were tied to the legs and her hands were tied behind her. The chair was in the living room and had been placed to make her face her mother. Donald sat on the couch and waited for her to come around.

"Hello, Natalia. How are you?"

"Let me go."

"Do you know how long I've been waiting for you?" He had not looked at her until this point. Now, he turned his head and stared her down.

She felt unnerved. "I thought you loved my mother."

"I do. That's the problem. I loved her the moment I saw her, even though I knew she was unclean. She soiled herself with every man that came to her door."

"Mom didn't sleep with all of them. There were only three that she actually slept with." Her anger bit through her words.

"She let them think she did. They left knowing of her intimately, whether or not they had actually seen her. Isn't that just as bad? She had to tell them enough of herself to be convincing. And I fell in love with her. When she told me her trick, I fooled myself into thinking it was ok to be with her. Then I saw you, and knew the true power of temptation."

He sounded like Lucas, but Lucas had had the voices in his head. Donald was a fanatic and possibly insane. During his soliloquy Natalia moved her arms back and forth, to test her range of motion. He'd done a poor job of tying her; she could maneuver her arms to the edge of the chair. She could gather the fabric in her hands. This allowed her to reach her jacket pockets, which still contained her stash of anti-vampire weapons. She needed the knife though, and that was in the pocket on her right side, which was the side closest to Donald.

"I couldn't have you then. You were too young. That wouldn't be right. Each night, after your mother fell asleep, there you were swimming in my dreams. All I could do was chase you. You never let me catch you, not even in my dreams. It felt wrong to be with your slut mother and want her beautiful young daughter. Then, on a late-night trip, God sent me the hitchhiker, who offered me such interesting secrets. So interesting that I could not pass them up. It seemed like I was being punished for my desires. Now that I have everything I want, I must think that being made into this being is a reward for my patience."

He got up then and went to Marnia. He stood behind the recliner and caressed her dark unkempt hair. "I know now why this happened. It was so that I might have the strength to keep you within my house. Your mother loved me. You will too." He leaned into Marnia's neck, and pulled her head to one side with her hair. "But I can only have one woman."

The moment he got up from the couch Natalia grabbed the knife through the fabric of her jacket. There was no way she could pull it out, therefore she wore through the fabric with the sharp edge. The fleece ripped quickly, and she was able to pull the knife into her hands. She started on the rope as he knelt. The paring knife made short work of the rope. Once her hands were free, Natalia looked to her captor to see if he noticed her actions. He stared hard at Marnia's neck and ignored Natalia completely.

Donald's eyes closed as he bit then began to suck Marnia's life from her neck. He didn't notice when Natalia bent down to cut the rope around her feet. Once completely free, she stood, pulled out the holy water pistol and shot at Donald. She didn't really aim. Holy water probably wouldn't harm her mother. If it hurt vampires, it didn't matter where it landed on him, she hoped. It harmlessly hit her mom first, then splashed on Donald's face. He shrieked and ripped away from Marnia. Blood oozed out her wound and down her chest.

Donald stood and tried to shield himself from the repeated blasts of holy water. Natalia saw how low the pistol was and stopped firing. She had to get out while it was still sunny. All the passages she had found on vampires indicated that no matter how old, a vampire could not go out in the sun. Holy water, garlic, running water, red thread, and various holy symbols occasionally deterred vampires. When she researched, it quickly became clear that exposure to the sun was the only reliable way to kill a vampire. He couldn't follow her if she ran outside, but Natalia still wanted to save her mom. Donald stood by the recliner and watched Natalia with a livid expression on his face.

"You will be mine."

"I don't want to be."

"Then why are you here?" His lowered his arms. There were burn marks on his face.

"To save my mom." The gun stayed level with Donald's torso.

"She's mine."

"She is her own. Now back away so I can get her out of here."

He caressed her head. "She's almost gone. You can't save her."

Natalia let her eyes drop to her mom. The blood, which should have gushed out of her neck, barely trickled out. Marnia was barely breathing, and her head lolled to the side.

"I could save her life, if you agreed to stay."

Natalia watched fascinated as he took out a pocketknife and prepared to slice his palm open.

"Say yes, and your mother lives forever."

She fired her pistol. When he jumped back, she pressed forward, and continued to spray holy water. He allowed her to get close to her mom. Natalia reached down and felt for a pulse on the side of the neck that wasn't ripped open. There was nothing. Natalia sagged, her eyes closed, and he was on her.

Donald threw her to the floor, and landed on top of her. He pinned the hand that held the pistol, but she didn't let go. His other hand went to her throat and turned her head to the side. His legs were between hers, and his torso was half on her. She had no leverage.

"Do you still say no?"

"Get off me." Tears streamed down the sides of her face, and she tried to get to the vials in her pocket. A memory threatened to surface which made it hard to think. Understanding that distractions would get her killed, Natalia took the memory and locked it away to examine later.

Donald grinned at how easy it had been to overpower this young, lustful woman. He turned her head to one side, and took the time to enjoy the sight and feel of her. Natalia tried to struggle but couldn't; he was too strong. She cried out as his teeth sank into her shoulder. She whimpered as he started to suck the life out of her; she had to do something. Holding back her utter hatred of the man, she let her free hand roam along his back and side. He groaned and grew hard. She squeezed her eyes shut as she tried to get to her vials. She loosened her grip on the holy water pistol and he loosened the grip on her wrist. Her right hand went to his head to tangle in his coarse gray hair. She wrapped her legs around him as her left hand went to her pocket. She reached inside and grabbed a jar. The jars were about two inches long and an inch thick and wide. She held one vial by the neck, to make it lay on the back of her hand, then wrapped both arms around his back.

Jar uncorked, she lowered her left hand to his shirttail and pulled his shirt up a little, to expose his lower back. She rested the hand that held the vial on his belt so he wouldn't feel the cold glass. Her thumb sat at the mouth of the jar, and stopped the liquid from running out too soon. Her right hand went back to the floor, to carefully find the pistol. He pulled away from the bite finally, so she squeezed her legs together and ground her hips into his. His mouth went to hers and he gave her a bloody kiss. Natalia tried hard not to gag on the taste of her own blood. Her hand found the pistol.

With the pistol finally back in her hand, she wrapped her legs around him tightly. This ensured he didn't move before she could hurt him. She upended the vial onto his lower back, near the top of his jeans and fired the water pistol. He shrieked as the water ran down his crack and hit his eye in the same instant. He threw himself off her and fell into Marnia. The recliner and both bodies flew backward. Natalia was up in a flash, and headed toward the kitchen door. He was up before she reached the archway. He grabbed her by the arm and leg and threw her across the room. She watched her trajectory and shifted slightly to hit the window.

Natalia landed in a heap outside the window. Her back was as cut up as her clothing. Natalia didn't notice. She raced to the driveway, where there was still some fading sun. She felt weak. Donald had taken a lot of her blood, but she kept going anyway. If she stopped too soon, she might die. As she ran, she took off her jacket and ripped off a chunk to use as a bandage for her shoulder. She hoped the wound wouldn't kill her.

30
Present Day

Natalia woke to the sound of screams. She looked around through groggy vision and blurred thoughts. There was nothing familiar about the room she was in, and the place smelled dusty. Her head lolled downward as she tried to revive herself and she realized she was tied to a chair. As her perception became more acute, she realized she was tied to a plastic lawn chair. Memories surfaced, and a childlike sob escaped her throat. It was followed by a muffled scream from outside the room and Natalia came fully awake.

Although the sound was muffled, she recognized the voice. Ashley was in an adjacent room, and someone was hurting her. Natalia strained against the ropes and cursed. The knots were too strong; too tightly bound. She was trapped. A frustrated sound escaped her, but she calmed herself and looked around the room a bit more. She needed a sharp object. There was nothing handy, but there were several vases she could knock over if needed. She couldn't do it now, as Donald would hear and come running. Unable to do anything else she waited and plotted.

She had two paths she could follow; both depended on whether or not Donald remembered her. The different paths led to the same conclusion: Donald's death. Natalia started to meditate, to drown out all thoughts and sounds and smells. She needed to think clearly. Donald was probably hurting Ashley in another room. She was unsure of Gloria's whereabouts, but knew that even if she were here, the witch would be unable to help. The woman was too weak for a fight. By the time the door to her prison opened, Natalia knew what she had to do, regardless of Donald's reaction to her.

The first person she saw when the door opened was Ashley. Her cloths were ripped, and any exposed skin had cuts, blood, bruises or all three. Natalia kept her face blank; she had to play her cards right. As she wondered if her plan would work, she looked up at her captor, and almost bulked. He had lost an eye. She caused that. They stared each other down for a moment, then Donald threw Ashley into the room and closed and locked the door. Her chance had passed, but she was confident she would have more.

Ashley curled up on the floor and sobbed.

"Ashley. Ashley! ASHLEY!" The girl finally looked up at her. Natalia saw the depth of the pain in her eyes and her heart went out to her. There was no time for sorrow now. "I know you're hurt, but I need your help."

Ashley's eyes rolled, and she buried her head in her arms.

"Ashley. Listen to me. You have two choices: survive or let the abyss swallow you whole. I let it once." She paused as pain threatened to engulf her. Natalia cleared her mind and looked Ashley in the eye. "It cost me a child and the ability to have any. Get up. Push it aside. Get me loose."

Ashley sat up, a look of horror on her face. "Push it aside? He hit me! He asked me to sleep with him and hit me when I said no!"

"And he's going to do it again, unless you help me."

"Gloria tried to help me, and she's dead." Ashley pulled her knees to her chest and wrapped her arms around her legs.

Natalia's voice grew soft and kind. "What happened to Gloria?"

"Back in San Francisco, you passed out. He grabbed me and took me into his bedroom. Before he could do anything, Gloria came in and started a spell. He bit her and drank all her blood. I started to scream, and he used the gun on me. I passed out. When I woke up, we were here."

"Where's here?"

"Tahoe, I think. I'm not sure. He kept you drugged and let me wake up. Told me he wanted to make sure I was on his side. I saw a phone book for Lake Tahoe the first day he let me free. He started to court me three days ago, told me that whatever you told me was a lie. That you were trying to turn me away from him."

Natalia's heart pounded. "Does he know who I am?"

"He says you look familiar, but I didn't tell him anything about you. That's when he started to get mean." Tears came to her eyes. "He beat me for the first time yesterday. When he was done, he insisted we pray together. He... he asked God to help me see his way. Asked God to help him seduce me." More tears slid down her cheeks. "When I said I wasn't going to sleep with him again, he hit me again and told me I would give in eventually. That God would help me see the light. After he was done, he threw me in here.

"I tried to wake you, but I couldn't. He came in this morning, fed you a meal shake, cleaned you up and then took me out. He started to apologize to me, tried to win me over again, even let me shower and fixed me breakfast. When he tried to get me to bed, I refused…" she shuddered and continued. "He tried to convince me I had it wrong. That God sent me to him to be his wife." She gave Natalia a haunted look. "How can he say something like that?"

Natalia heard the anger in the girl's voice and was glad. Anger would help her recover.

"When I continued to refuse, he beat me up and then forced us to pray again. I…I don't understand. God isn't supposed to help people like him."

"Ashley. Please untie my ropes so I can help you." Her voice was kind, but it was unmistakably a command. Ashley nodded absentmindedly, got up, and did as instructed.

Once untied, Natalia rubbed blood back into her arms and started to search for anything that could be used as a weapon. There were three plastic vases in the room, the chair she had been sitting on and some larger furniture: a dresser, a nightstand, and a bed. The closet was bare, but there were some jeans and t-shirts in the dresser. She looked to Ashley, then handed her a new t-shirt. After examining all corners, Natalia knew there were no weapons. Were he human, she could have used the vases to knock him out, or possibly scratch him up with the lawn chair. Either option would just piss off a vampire. There was no real wood in the room. The furniture was plastic and unbreakable. Good idea for a young vampire.

"What are you doing?"

"First rule of thumb in a situation like this: arm yourself." Natalia stopped for a moment, then turned to Ashley. "How long have we been here?"

She was quiet for a moment, then furrowed her brow. "Four days?"

"Why don't I feel weak?"

"He's been keeping us fed. The meal shake he gave you this morning wasn't the first one." Ashley sat on the bed, still shell-shocked.

Understanding took hold of Natalia's mind and she nearly trembled. One look at Ashley and she slammed her thoughts down, to let her warrior mind take over. This wasn't a fight with weapons, but it was a fight for freedom. He was keeping them strong because he was going to keep them. They were his next victims. Natalia sat on the bed next to Ashley and held her tight.

"Ashley. Listen to me very carefully. Donavon is a monster. Even before he was changed, he would hold women captive, either by his words or by his actions. He keeps them for long periods of time, convinces them to become his 'wife', and then kills them once he's done with them." She pulled away to look directly into Ashley's eyes. "If we don't do this correctly, we'll be his next victims."

Terror took over Ashley's face and her eyes grew wide.

Natalia crushed Ashley against her chest to keep her screams from escaping the walls. She whispered into the girl's ear, to try to calm her. "Hon, you have to stop screaming. If you don't, Donavon will come in here and he may kill us. Please stop." But she continued. Natalia tried a different tactic. "If you don't stop, I'm going to knock you out." Still, she screamed. "Ashley, if you don't stop screaming, I'll throw you down on the floor, let him hear you and allow him to take you when he comes in."

Ashley pulled away in horror. Her voice was a bare whisper. "You wouldn't."

"Never. But I had to get you to calm down. Are you done screaming?"

She stared at Natalia open mouthed and wide eyed until the words penetrated. Then she blinked, closed her mouth, and nodded. "Yeah."

"Good. Are you strong enough to help me?"

"I – I don't know." There was helplessness in her voice.

"That's ok. Thanks for being honest. I'm going to tell you the plan and then you can decide, ok?"

Ashley nodded and listened as Natalia laid out the plan.

31

By the time Donald came into the room again, Natalia learned two things. One: there were no windows in this room. Two: all three vases were unbreakable. She had wrapped one up in a blanket, tried to break it in various ways, but it didn't work. They had to come up with another plan. Ashley thought she could handle it but wasn't sure. The plan was for Ashley to try and convince him she was on his side. She would tell him she wanted to be his wife, to be able to get to a phone and possibly call the police. She had seen a landline phone in the living room but didn't know if it worked. If he gave her some liberty she was going to find out.

If for some reason Donald didn't believe her, Natalia would step in and tell him who she was. Then she would do everything she could to get Ashley out of the house. Her priorities had shifted. The girl had to be kept safe. Although she didn't tell Ashley the psychology behind it, Natalia knew what it was. Ashley was roughly the same age as her own child would have been, and Ashley was way too much like her. They were kindred spirits and she wanted to keep her alive. It probably wasn't smart to use the girl as bait, but Donald had already started a relationship with her. It might be easier to get free if Donald thought the girl was his.

When Donald finally came into the room, he carried a tray with two plates of food. Natalia smelled the food and heard her stomach growl. He handed her the plate silently and watched her every move. Natalia didn't hesitate. She was starving. If the food was drugged, she didn't care. She needed nourishment. He took his eyes off her and turned to Ashley. He gave her the other plate and caressed her hair after she took it.

"Why did you free her? I told you she was telling you lies."

Ashley looked panicked, caught Natalia's calm expression as she bit into the boneless chicken breast and was able to calm down herself. "She was going to talk if she were freed or not. And although I can hear her, I don't have to listen."

Donald looked down at her with great joy. His smile brightened his face, and he held his hand out to her. "Come with me, have dinner with me in the kitchen. You'll be more comfortable."

Ashley gave him a look she hoped was close to innocent delight and took his hand. "Ok."

"No." Both of them looked at Natalia. Ashley with confusion; Donald with anger.

"This doesn't concern you."

She gave Ashley a caring look. "Yes, it does." She stood and faced Donald. She had forgotten she was taller. "You don't remember me, do you?"

He said nothing and gave her an evil eye.

"I can't look that different. Sure, my hair's a little bit gray, and I have laugh lines, but mom looked like this before you killed her."

"What's your name?" He was curious. She had his attention.

"Natalia Dveski. And yours is Donald." She gave him a hard, cold look that chilled Ashley's blood. The young woman stepped away from the pair; she wanted badly to leave.

Donald reached out a trembling hand to touch her cheek. His touch was as cold as Vincent's, but his flesh was dead. Vincent was a vampire; Donald was a bloodsucker, a parasite who wanted nothing more than to feed off living bodies. A single tear rolled down her cheek as his hand slid from her cheek to her neck, where his mark still rested on her shoulder. An odd, almost blissful smile came to his face. His voice was rough but kind.

"I knew you would return to me Natalia. I knew one day you would be mine." He leaned in and whispered in her ear. "I was upset you made me kill Gloria, but now I have you and the child. You've made me very happy Natalia. Now I have everything I want."

Natalia backed away. She stared him down, determination set on her face. "No. You want me; you can have me. I won't put up a fight. I'll do anything you want. You touch Ashley again and I <u>will</u> rip your dick off and stuff it into your mouth. Understand?"

His demeanor changed drastically. There was anger and hatred on his face now. He stepped forward and gave her a hard slap. "That's not how it works. I'm in charge. You do what I say."

The blow sent her sprawling onto the bed. She posed herself seductively on the bed, but left her face a mask of hate. She was on her side, bottom leg stretched out, and top leg bent at the knee. His eye roamed. Her voice dripped with false desire. "And I will. Everything you desire is yours. Except her."

"And if I take her?" He tried to stare her down.

Natalia stood. "I will fight you every step of the way and I <u>will</u> manage to kill you." She closed the distance between them, slipped her hand between his legs and gave his balls a pleasant squeeze. She leaned in and whispered in his ear. "Wouldn't you prefer me willing?"

He groaned, and she knew she had him. She wrapped her arms around him, and let him feel every part of her body. She turned with him slightly and locked eyes with Ashley.

"Call for help," she mouthed.

Ashley looked very confused but understood the message the second time around. She nodded frantically as Natalia pulled away and led Donald out of the room. She found the other bedroom, led him inside, closed the door and went to the bed. She stood by the bed and looked around as he approached. The furniture was plastic and there was nothing within sight that she could use as a weapon. She hoped Ashley would be able to get to the phone.

"What do you want to do to me?" She didn't try and keep the revulsion out of her voice.

"I want you to beg God for forgiveness." He grinned as he raised his tightly closed fist.

j k

Natalia lay on the bed on her stomach, not moving. Ashley sat on the bed, washed her wounds, and spoke softly. The phone didn't work, and Ashley hadn't been able to find a door or a window. Air moved through the cabin, but the vents were hidden. There were no spots for doors or windows. There had to be a way in and out, but as of yet, Ashley hadn't been able to find it. It was probably why Donald no longer locked the bedroom door.

Donald took Natalia into his room twice. Each time, he followed the same pattern as with Ashley. He beat her, prayed with her, asked her to be his wife, then beat her when she said no. Though he didn't use his full strength as that would break bones, he did a lot of damage. After the second time, Ashley had pleaded with him. She begged him to allow her to clean Natalia's wounds. If the wounds weren't kept clean, she might get an infection and die. Donald agreed and had shown Ashley where the first aid kit was. When he brought food, Ashley fed her like a child. Natalia had been in too much pain to consider moving.

Terrified, Ashley started to understand the situation. There were no weapons in the house, or anything that could be used as a weapon. They never had any utensils, and their plates were paper. The tray was nowhere to be found unless in his hands. Natalia knew the girl was missing something but hadn't had a chance to search the house herself. She would at the first opportunity.

☙ ❧

Natalia had her opportunity after the third time Donald tortured her. He had to go to town for groceries; told them he would be back soon. Natalia lay on his bed in a haze, and tried not to pass out. She tried her necklace on him, but it didn't work. Her own mind was too frazzled. When he beat her, she fought back and bit and scratched him. She couldn't create enough damage at once to do any good. He was well fed and healed his wounds quickly. As he didn't take her blood or Ashley's, Natalia figured he had another source; she just didn't know what or where.

Ashley ran in after Donald left, and shook her gently. "He's gone! Natalia, please! He's gone! You need to get up."

"Are you sure he's gone?" She sounded defeated.

"Yes. I looked in all the rooms." A terrified yet stubborn look graced her features.

Determination gripped Natalia and Ashley sighed in relief. Natalia rolled over, sat up, scooted to the end of the bed, and stood up. She was in a lot of pain, but they were on limited time. She breathed carefully, and concentrated on searching to forget the pain. She assigned Ashley to search for weapons in Donald's bedroom, the only room that hadn't been searched. Meanwhile, Natalia searched the living room for a way out. She searched so hard she almost missed the minor fix she performed on the landline phone.

Natalia was searching the walls at floor level for cracks that would signify a secret door. As she passed the phone jack, she plugged in the phone and kept moving. She passed the jack by her body length before she stopped dead and realized what she had done. She shook as she turned and followed the cord to the phone. She sat on her knees for a full minute before she picked up the phone. A sob of relief escaped her lips when she heard the dial tone. The low buzz was her salvation.

"Ashley!"

The girl came running. There was hope in Natalia's voice and it was hard to ignore.

"The phone wasn't plugged in. Keep watch."

Ashley did as instructed, and kept silent as Natalia stared at the phone. She wanted desperately to call Vincent to hear his voice. As she stared at the keypad, she nearly fell to the floor; horror shook the foundation of her mind. She had no idea what Vincent's number was. It was programmed into her cell phone for when she needed it. It was so rare for her to call him anyway. The abyss yawned open before her, but Natalia pulled her mind back together. All she needed was one number, and it wasn't 911.

She had no idea where she was and knew the human authorities couldn't handle this situation. Natalia pulled herself together and dialed the one number from Vincent's house that she knew. In all the years she'd known him, he had never once changed his number. And he picked up even if he didn't know the number.

"Charlie speaking."

"Charlie!" It was as frantic as she would ever allow her voice to be.

"Nat?" He sounded extremely worried. "Where in Hell are you? Let me get Vincent."

"There's no time! Charlie, listen to me! I've been kidnapped. I don't know where I am. You need to trace the call-"

The phone was ripped from her hand, and she was knocked to the floor. Donald placed the phone back on the table and glowered at her. She cried out as her hope was torn asunder and thrown to the wind. The bellow that issued from her throat made Donald stagger back. She flew up from the floor and attacked him, her hands going for his throat. Her nails dug in and found his jugular. He pulled at her hands, but she held on and ripped his skin off. He healed quickly, let her hands go and punched her in the face. She went staggering back into the phone. She had time to spot Ashley, who lay motionless on the floor. They hadn't even heard him come in. Where was the door? She hoped Charlie would be able to find it quicker than she and Ashley had.

"You bitch. You lied to me." He stayed in his place, as anger gripped his features.

Shock grabbed her features as his words penetrated. She didn't know what he referred to but decided to go with it. "What did you expect? You killed my mother and trapped Ashley and me. Did you really think I ever wanted you to touch me, you filthy bastard?"

She had her hands on the phone. She never wanted to use it as a weapon before in the hopes that she might use it, but the only call she'd be able to make was made. The phone was a holdover from the 70's. Heavy, made from mostly metal, thick plastic, and lots of wires. It looked old fashioned too. The keypad was square with plastic buttons, utilitarian rather than fashionable. A good weapon. She positioned her hands on the phone, ready to use it.

Donald wasn't charging. He just stood there, as anger and confusion twisted his already ugly face. The phone rang and they both jumped. Donald moved, but so did Natalia. She pulled the receiver off the hook as she grabbed the phone and back peddled. Donald tried to grab her, but she tripped, and he flew over her.

"Natalia!" A distorted voice screamed.

"Get here now!"

It was an order. She had no idea if the caller heard. The jack was pulled from the wall as she stood and faced Donald. She unplugged the receiver at the phone, to keep the freed piece out of her way. He advanced in the blink of an eye. She swung as she held on hard to the phone. Her makeshift weapon landed, but on his arm, not his head. The bell inside protested. He swung and punched her in the stomach. Her breath left her, and she doubled over. She had never trained in hand-to-hand combat with the vampires. There was no point to training in hand-to-hand combat when she knew she was at a disadvantage. As she sank to the floor, she understood her mistake.

Donald breezed over and picked her up by her hair and neck. He held her off the floor, which was a feat, as she was taller than he by a few inches. She held herself very still, as she knew one wrong move could end her life. She could still hurt him; she just had to get loose.

"When the other one wakes up, I'm going to make you watch as I rip her apart." He brought her a little closer to his face, and set her on the ground. She let her hands fall to her side and waited to get closer. "And then I'm going to keep you here until you see things my way. And then, then, I'll make you mine."

Natalia summoned all the love for the man who waited for her in San Francisco and gave Donald the smile she loved to give Vincent. Donald let her go. She stepped closer and ran her hands up his thighs and to his waistband. Still smiling her most seductive smile, she knelt in front of him and unzipped his zipper. Donald trembled, and she tried not to gag. She pulled down his pants and underwear.

"But that's what I want. To be like you." She tried to devour him, but Donald backhanded her before she could touch him.

"Did you really think I was going to fall for that?" He stood there and laughed at her.

Natalia grimaced, grabbed the phone, rammed into his knees, and knocked him to the ground. She gripped the phone in her hands and slammed it down between his legs. The bell inside protested loudly as he howled in utter pain and kicked her away. Natalia dropped the phone as she hit the ground.

Donald grabbed his crotch, doubled over in torturous pain.

"I told you, you'd never touch her again."

She spat in his face, rolled over quickly, and went for the phone again. She reached it just as his hand grabbed her ankle. She swung the phone, missed but used the momentum to flip onto her back. He was on her before she could think and sank his teeth deep into her neck. Every part of her wanted to scream. She took that voice and fed it down her arm to the hand that held the phone. She used her anger to hit him hard in the side of his face. It caused his head to rip away from her neck, and gave her a nasty wound. She barely noticed. He attacked the same side of her neck, to try to draw out more blood. She let him. It gave her a good target.

When his mouth was once more attached to her neck, she used her anger to smash the phone into the side of his head for the second time. He grunted but held on. She hit him again. And again. And again. Blood and gray matter splattered her face, but she kept hitting. He just kept sucking; probably thought he could heal himself with her blood. He did try, but she hit him over and over. He finally let go with a bellow and threw himself off her. He hissed at her, and staggered back as his brain oozed out of his head. She could see him try to heal; it was an impressive sight. She gathered her feet under her and realized how much blood he had taken. She still managed to get to her feet.

Natalia locked eyes with her hated bloodsucker. Her face set in an inscrutable expression, she hid how weak she felt and advanced. He saw her coming and hissed as he decided to fight. They met halfway; she swung, he tried to grab at her arms. He did manage to get a hold of her, but only because she let him. She slammed the phone down into the open wound on his head, directly into his brain. He staggered back again, and tried to get away. She chased him. He was headed for Ashley, who was an easy meal. Natalia felt her vision blur and knew she didn't have much left in her. She had to end it. She jumped him, knocked him to the ground. She straddled him as he turned, and held onto him with her legs.

Natalia took a good look at him, then slammed the phone down on his face. She brought the phone up, changed her grip and used the wedge shape as a blunt axe on his throat. The first blow crushed his windpipe. The third broke through skin and bone. With the tenth, she was halfway through his throat. He scratched her arms and punched her, in an effort to move her. But he had lost too much blood. She lost count of the blows by the time he turned to dust.

Natalia swayed off balance for a few seconds then keeled over from blood loss. Her neck still bled. He hadn't hit her jugular dead on, but he had grazed it. There was no stopping the blood. The world spun away, and Natalia passed out.

32

Charlie stood at the bottom of the steps, and wondered where the hell the door was. He and the other werewolves were in a cabin near Lake Tahoe, high in the mountains. There had been five women in the cabin, who attacked when they say the intruders. As they had no weapons, the Blitzkriegs won easily. It was not a pleasant victory.

The wolves searched the house but found no trace of Natalia. This is where she called from two days ago though, and had to be here. It had been a hard place to find. No one owned it; it didn't exist on any map. Though there was a phone here, the phone number belonged to a closed-up house in a nearby town. The phone and cable lines that led from it to here looked spliced together by an amateur. None of the wolves were sure how the phone lines worked.

Charlie was frantic the entire time they searched, but they found the place. Now, with no trace of Natalia in the two-room cabin, Charlie was faced with an impassable door. He growled, turned Blitzkrieg and attacked the wall. The plywood gave away easily to his large form, and he slammed through the other side, into a shelf full of canned goods. Full of mindless rage, he attacked the cans, and nearly broke teeth on the heavy aluminum. He changed back when he understood that all was well, and the French cut green beans weren't trying to keep him from Natalia.

Charlie stumbled into the kitchen, and nearly tripped over downed cans. He heard the others coming down the steps after him and looked around. At the entryway to the living room stood a girl. There was dried blood and bruises all over her and she looked frightened beyond reckoning. She shook like the last leaf on an otherwise barren tree. She sank to her knees as Charlie approached her.

"Please don't hurt me." Her voice was too quiet to hear. Charlie watched as she shaped the words.

"Where's Natalia?" He said it slowly. She looked beyond him as the other people filed in. Keeping the rage out of his voice was proving hard. "We're not going to hurt you. Where's Natalia?"

The girl simply pointed. Charlie was through the door before she finished pointing and by Natalia's side before anyone else could move. There were bandages over most of her arms, and around her neck. He felt for her pulse, and nearly died when he couldn't find one. Her skin was still warm; therefore, he placed his hand on her chest under her left breast and heaved a sigh of relief. He could feel a faint heartbeat.

Rebecca knelt next to him. "Alive?"

He nodded; his eyes closed. He didn't remove his hand from her reassuring heartbeat. It was slow and weak, and he was very worried. "We should've brought a vampire. Mierka, Ben, someone."

"We couldn't. The inauguration is tonight, and Vincent needs them all there." Her voice was kind and Charlie loved her for it.

"Why did he let Diana leave?"

"He didn't know, and Diana didn't have a choice. Pick Natalia up, we're leaving."

He spoke softly. "What do we do with the girl?"

"She's the Slayer Natalia was trying to protect. We protect her."

"How are we supposed to do that?" He slipped his hands under Natalia's back, picked her up, and cradled her carefully to him.

"We take her with us. Let's go."

Rebecca led the way out. They tried to hurry past the dead bodies, but Ashley saw the woman and nearly fell apart. Doug led her outside and spoke softly to her. She seemed better after their talk. It was a long ride back to San Francisco. Ashley clung to Doug, who had no problem with the attention. The others thought it in bad taste that he allowed it. Charlie held Natalia in his arms the whole way, and said nothing to the others. His face set in a dead expression, he stared out the front window of the minivan and silently repeated to himself, "She's not going to die she's not going to die she's not going to die." He hoped he spoke the truth.

Getting home took a lot less time as they knew the way. They pulled up to the mansion about four hours later. Doug went with Ashley to the werewolf house. Rebecca helped Charlie out of the van and watched as he walked to the front door and inside. There had still been daylight when they left Natalia's prison. It was now completely dark, and the party was in full swing. Rebecca had no idea what Charlie planned on doing, but Natalia was his charge. He would do what was best for her, not for Vincent. Rebecca shook her head, walked around the side of the house, and entered by the back door. She snuck up to her bedroom, and hoped Charlie would be there shortly.

CB ᙠᎠ

Vincent smoothed out the deep purple shirt, and tucked it into his waistband. He strapped on the cummerbund, slipped on the fine Italian suit jacket, and buttoned two buttons. He took a calming breath, and felt his scar tighten and the cummerbund squeeze his mid-section. He stared at the dress that hung on the closet door. It was deep purple and went well with her red stone necklace that also hung from the wooden hanger. Natalia was not here. He had not seen her since the night he placed Morgan in the oubliette. She left while he and Anthony talked, and said she needed to retrieve something from the bedroom. She took some of her clothes and left with no word.

Two days ago, she tried to contact Charlie. Why him, he wasn't sure and didn't really care. Charlie reported her frantic voice and her short words, and the near scream at the end. He called the number back and nearly ran out of the house after hearing her command. Joseph stopped him, and informed him it was still daylight. By sunset, Charlie and the others were well on their way. Joseph convinced him of his duty. Vincent stayed but cursed himself for letting Diana go. The healer was in North Carolina, on a mission for her house. His woman was dying or dead, and he was stuck here.

They had spent most of the past ten years in each other's sight. With a few exceptions, he always ended the night with her in his arms. The times they spent apart left him wanting. Those times were short, quick, compared to the past month without her.

But it was the night of his inauguration ball, and everything had fallen into place. Natalia's plan to control the mayor worked like a charm. When they arrived at the mayor's hospital room a week and a half ago, Donavon was gone. They waited a good long time to be sure, but he never returned. Markus waited until Father Sulta emerged to grab a smoke on the roof; the only place an addict could safely sneak a puff on a nearly outlawed cigarette.

Markus lured Father Sulta away from the hospital with the promise of bringing him to the traitorous Natalia. The man followed like a hungry puppy to The Red Thread, where Kari and two others ambushed him. He fought hard and killed Markus before Kari was able to kill the priest. The loss was not small. Vincent had seen great potential in Markus. He knew he had to find a replacement for the man's office, but he had trouble with it.

Garvin had been easier. Once Sulta left the room, Ben entered with Vincent in tow and offered the bounty hunter triple what the mayor paid him. The greedy man followed Ben out to the car in a secluded part of the parking lot, where Owen captured him quickly and quietly. Garvin now hung in one of Vincent's dungeons, skinned alive. More torture awaited him.

The mayor slept through the whole thing and was now in his control.

After he waltzed into Mayor Lawrence's hospital room, Vincent fed the sleeping man his blood. He whispered instructions into his ear. The next night, Mayor Lawrence invited him into the room and begged for blood. Vincent caressed the man's head as the mayor gratefully drank from his wrist. Once he left the hospital, Mayor Lawrence came each night to Vincent's home and begged for his porridge. Vincent fed the mayor his blood faithfully for the past week and a half, but none of it mattered. Everything had fallen into place, and yet he still wanted Natalia. He clipped on his cufflinks and walked out the door. His guests waited for his appearance.

Vincent could hear the voices from the top of the stairs. Everything had been opened at sunset. There were over one hundred people gathered, including his Lieutenants. Except of course, for Markus. Vincent stopped in the middle of the stairs, cleared his head, and pushed aside the dire thoughts. He would think of it later, after the party. Joseph was at the bottom of the steps to announce him. Vincent gave him a sharp nod and walked confidently down the steps.

He entered a quiet room. The mayor was the first to approach him. The human bowed to him as Vincent walked toward the throne, which had been placed on a stage for the occasion. Except for a long table with food for the non-vampires, the throne was once again the only piece of furniture in the room. Vincent approached the throne, as the mayor clung to his side like a shadow. Vincent climbed the steps to his throne, and the mayor waited patiently at the foot of the stage. Once Vincent was seated, Mayor Lawrence fell to one knee.

"You have something to say to me."

"Yes, sir. I look forward to working with you in turning this city around. We will need to talk about the situation in the days to come and work out a plan that will benefit the citizens of this great city. When you have time, please contact me and I will make sure to see you at your convenience."

Vincent smiled. "Thank you, Mayor. When I have my schedule with me, I will call you."

The man bowed again, then turned and left. Though it appeared that the mayor was under his own control, he was not. Vincent spent many hours grooming the mayor to make sure the broken human knew exactly what to say. Vincent smiled a hyena's smile. Those close enough to see it shivered, just a little bit afraid.

"With that unpleasantness done, we have a few things to celebrate. Anthony, Julia, front and center." Anthony and Julia came forward, dressed in the same colors, blood red. Vincent sent them the matching suit and dress. He liked his people to dress with style, especially when being promoted. Vincent stood and took a small dagger from his side. He jumped down from the stage and walked to the duo.

"Julia, you have proven yourself worthy of being one of my Lieutenants. Finding out all you did about Morgan and then taking out his Slayer has earned you a place by my side, in my circle. Step forward. You will take Morgan's place as Reconnaissance Lieutenant. All his holdings, all his possessions are now yours. Drink and accept my offer."

Vincent sliced open his skin with the dagger and held his wrist out to Julia who placed her lips to his wrist. He brought her closer to his body, to feel her chill. He hadn't been with Natalia in so long that he let Julia drink a little bit longer than necessary. It felt good to have a woman in his arms. He pulled his hand away and closed the wound. He drank extra before dressing, but it still left him a little lightheaded. Julia licked her lips, and took her place beside Anthony. She concentrated to make sure she wasn't under Vincent's control, then stood tall and nodded. Vincent then looked to Anthony.

Anthony stepped forward when he was bid and bowed. "Anthony, apart from Joseph you have been by my side longer than anyone else in my protection. You have also proven yourself beyond question. You will be my First Lieutenant. You will be the one everyone else reports to. Stand and accept my offer."

Anthony's head bowed lower as his whole body sagged. "I cannot accept, sir, as I have not told you my greatest fear." He raised his eyes to his leader. A lot passed between them in the moment before Anthony spoke again. "I still do not trust the human that shares your bed."

"Vincent!" A strangled voice broke the quiet and then made it even denser. Heads turned as Charlie carried Natalia into the room. The wolf looked frantic, and his shirt and jeans were ripped. Natalia was wrapped in a blanket. Her arms and neck were bandaged, and every inch of exposed skin was bruised.

Vincent pocketed his knife and walked toward them. "Charlie?"

"She's bad. I think she's dying."

Vincent stood before Charlie and lifted Natalia into his arms. He gave the werewolf a grateful look. Charlie bowed and left. Natalia stirred slightly, and her eyes fluttered open. A ghost of a smile floated across her lips when she saw Vincent. "Hello, lover."

"Natalia. What happened?" He sank to his knees, worried.

"Donavon...Donald's dead. Killed him."

He brushed her greasy hair out of her face. "They're both dead? What did they do to you, love?"

Her eyes rolled, and she moved her head a little. "Same...dead..."

Vincent stared into her face, tried to make sense of her words, and slowly remembered. When she had killed the Slayer in the dungeon, she mentioned that Donald was posing as a Slayer. Were Donald and Donavon the same person? He would have to wait for an answer. There was something far more important to find out about. Vincent caressed her cheek, and let his hand linger at her neck. She inhaled sharply at his cold touch but did not pull away. Her pulse was slow and very weak. Diana was not here.

A set expression slowly drifted over his features. "Natalia? Natalia let me change you."

Her eyes opened slowly and found his. "…please…"

He shuddered, and brought her a little closer to his chest. He kissed the top of her head, then her cooling lips, and repositioned her to better reach her tender neck. He closed his eyes and prepared himself for the bite. His lips touched her throat when he remembered his rule. His Lieutenants and his people could not change a human without his approval and the approval of one Lieutenant. He could not change anyone without the approval of all his Lieutenants. He had learned that keeping the numbers small kept his people safe. It also stopped his people from changing anyone on a whim.

Vincent pulled back and noticed his Lieutenants all stood in a large circle around him. He caught Joseph's eye and motioned the man to take Natalia. Joseph knelt and took the lady. Vincent made sure she was comfortable, then stood. Natalia had passed out. He hoped this would be quick.

"I told you once before of my intentions of changing Natalia. I now ask outright for your approval. Any objections?"

One by one his Lieutenants gave their consent. When they were done, Vincent turned to Anthony, and awaited the man's words.

"Anthony, speak your mind."

Anthony stood silently, and looked at Natalia with unmasked distrust. He looked up at his Captain. "You don't need my consent to change her."

The men stared each other down for a long, silent moment. Vincent balled his hands into fists and hid them behind his back. "Order must be maintained."

They stared at each other for another moment. Anthony was right, his consent wasn't necessary, except that it was. There were those in the room who wanted chaos in the Bay Area. Some were currently in the room. If Vincent did as he wanted, he would face another war. He wanted to leave this area to the humans and return to Montana with Natalia.

The large vampire looked around the room at the people gathered as Anthony continued to stay silent. Once he captured Anthony's gaze again, Vincent stated the same line again. "Order must be maintained. You know what is at stake."

Anthony shook his head almost violently. "I do not trust her. I do not wish for you to give her more power."

Vincent's eyes narrowed and his voice became soft. "You know more about her than most here and yet you still do not trust her."

"It is because I know so much that I do not trust her." Anthony did not hide his words. Many in the room heard him.

Vincent nodded. "This is why I am making you my First Lieutenant. I trust your judgment, even when I do not agree." He sighed deeply, and startled some of those present. "Since I don't have your consent, I won't change her. Order must be maintained. Now if you'll excuse me, I wish to be with Natalia. This may be our last night together."

He was quiet for a moment then turned toward Natalia and Joseph.

"Sir, let me change her."

The quiet voice crept up his skin and pierced Vincent's eardrums. His voice and body trembled, tight with anticipation. "Joseph? What did you say?"

Joseph stood, and cradled Natalia like a child. "I ask my Captain to give me leave to change this woman into a vampire. To make her my child, so that she will live. I believe she would be an asset to my family. I ask further that one Lieutenant step forward and give their consent as well."

The room was quiet for a moment, then Julia took a step forward, away from Anthony. "I give my consent." She turned to Anthony and gave a little shrug as her hand went to her ever-present blue stone pendant. She spoke quietly. "I trust her."

Anthony scowled but said nothing.

A fire burned within Vincent. Hope blossomed. "You have my consent. Go quickly before it's too late."

Joseph nodded and walked out of the room. He took his precious cargo with him out the door and up the steps to Vincent's room.

Anthony started to turn away, perhaps to leave, but Vincent's hand on his shoulder stopped him. "We're not done."

Anthony turned and locked eyes with Vincent. "I didn't think the ritual was going to continue."

"I decided three weeks ago to make you my First Lieutenant." He paused, then decided to be truthful of his own feelings. "Your attitude and thoughts on the woman I love changes nothing." The men stared at each other for a moment as Vincent's words sank in. The room stayed quiet, as most did not know how rare it was for Vincent to state his feelings. The moment passed and Vincent used his fingernail to rip open his wrist. It hurt like hell, but it proved a point. He held his bleeping wrist out to Anthony. "Drink and accept what I offer."

Anthony looked at his Captain and watched the blood drip from the open wound. He realized, for the first time, what the position meant. Vincent expected him to be his successor.

Anthony fell to his knees and licked the blood off the floor. There were only a few drops, but he did it anyway. When the floor was clean, Vincent leaned down and offered him his wrist. Anthony took three swallows then pulled back. Vincent willed the wound closed and held out that arm to help Anthony to his feet. He pulled his friend to him, kissed both cheeks and pulled back smiling. This night was getting better and better.

Julia started to applaud and reminded Vincent that he did have guests. He turned, bowed, and started to mingle. His inauguration was a success, and soon Joseph would bring down his changed woman. Vincent grinned with anticipation.

33

The party was going well, but Joseph left half an hour ago and there was still no sign of Natalia. Vincent tried not to check the time, but couldn't help it. At the one-hour point, he started to look for a reason to go upstairs and seek them out. At an hour and a half, he stopped looking, excused himself and left the grand ballroom. He managed to keep his pace steady until his foot hit the steps and then he was a blur in the eyes of onlookers.

He ran through his sitting room to his bedroom. He paused for a second before he moved to the bathroom to enter the code into the secret keypad. Vincent went through the maze on autopilot. He was up the steps and through the entryway in the span of a normal man's single step. He glowered at Joseph, who still sat on the bed with Natalia.

"I thought you would have brought her downstairs by now." He was always grateful that he didn't have to hide what he felt around Joseph.

Joseph sat with his back to the headboard, Natalia between his legs, her back to his chest. Fresh bandages covered her wounds and her hair looked soft and clean. She was wrapped in a terry cloth robe. "I would have, had I changed her."

Vincent stopped at the foot of the bed as various emotions exploded on his face. Joseph smiled as pain, joy, confusion, and ten years of desire flashed across his master's features.

"You waited?"

"After bringing her upstairs, I cleaned her wounds and her hair and body. Since then, I have been waiting for one of two things to occur: her to fade further and require my help, or for you to get antsy enough to come up and change her yourself. She has been deep asleep since she collapsed."

"You said you would change her."

"And you have waited ten long years to have the opportunity. She should be yours."

Vincent stood immobile; rock solid in his determination not to touch the still human Natalia. "I wasn't given permission."

Joseph gathered Natalia a little more fully in his arms, stood and brought her to Vincent. "He didn't give you permission because you were too pig headed to allow him to know why he didn't trust her. Had you told him sooner, he would have had a longer chance to get to know her and trust her. It's your fault he said no."

He held the woman out to his master who involuntarily took her. Vincent held his beloved close, felt her warmth, and shook with the desire to change her.

"I was denied."

Joseph caught his master's eye. "She is your child. Has been since the moment she waltzed into your life."

Vincent looked down at Natalia's unconscious form. "Order must be-"

"Don't insult me. Only three will know. You will never tell, she will listen to you on this, and you know how well I keep your secrets."

Vincent raised his eyes to Joseph. "What do you gain from this?"

"Perhaps a little freedom? Jacqueline wishes to leave for a while. And for the first time, she wishes for me to come along. I refuse to leave for any length of time if I am still bound to you by my promise of long ago."

"So, I lose you, but I gain her." Vincent leaned down and softly kissed her lips. He could take her warmth; he could have her as his child. All it would cost him was his most loyal servant and if anyone found out, he could lose control over his people.

But who would know? And how long would it really matter? San Francisco was only one of his homes and he wanted to leave it. The realization stole into his mind, grew, exploded, and made him shudder. Eyes closed, he walked the five steps to the head of the bed. He turned, sat down while Natalia was cradled in his arms. "You have your freedom, friend. You may travel with Mierka, as she desires. Now leave us. Tell my guests…whatever you wish. We may be back down, we may not."

Joseph bowed, but Vincent didn't notice. He was too busy arranging himself and Natalia on the bed. He loosened his clothes, kicked off his shoes and untied her robe. He leaned against the headboard and placed Natalia between his legs with her back to his chest, much as Joseph had. Vincent gently brushed her gray and black hair out of the way, leaned into her neck and bit her tender flesh.

Her blood ran over his tongue and down his throat: sweet, salty, life giving. He listened for her heartbeat as the flow slowed. When all was gone, he pulled away, brought his arms out in front of her, slit his wrist and brought his wounded arm to her lips. He tilted her head back, to help his blood run down her throat. Vincent growled deeply as he thought of the carnage they would be able to create with their bodies.

Natalia's body relaxed completely against him, and he felt her temperature drop. Vincent pulled his wrist away from her mouth, held her body, and waited for her to wake. He should have known she would come out fighting.

Natalia launched herself across the room, and slammed into the closets. She turned and regarded the room. Her arms were held in front of her close to her torso, ready to strike. She looked frantically around the room a few times before she found Vincent's eyes.

"Did you change me or did he?"

Vincent stood slowly, and held her gaze as he walked the few steps to her. He placed his hand on her cheek, leaned in, and whispered the words he wished to say for many years. "I am your sire."

She sagged against him in great relief, and grabbed his lapels in her fists. His arms went around her, and held her to him tightly.

"How did you know?"

"It didn't hurt when I slammed into the closets."

Vincent gave a small chuckle and squeezed her tighter to him. She felt so good in his arms. He did not want to let go, but he pulled back a little and looked into her eyes before he placed a loving kiss on her lips.

When the kiss ended, Natalia laid her head on his chest and sighed deeply. "I thought he killed me."

"He almost did, but we found you in time." He frowned as he led her back to the bed. "Why did you call Charlie?"

"I couldn't remember any other number. I never memorized yours."

He nodded as he sat on the bed. Natalia waited until he was situated on the bed before she joined him. She sat between his legs, and leaned her back against his chest. He allowed the silence for a moment then started to carefully caress her arms. He didn't touch her bruises but nevertheless brought her attention to them. "What did he do to you, Natalia?"

She shook her head, and made a noise in the back of her throat. "It's in the past Vincent. Leave it there."

Vincent lifted her face back up to peer into her eyes. "Natalia, love. I've just drank an enormous amount of your blood and made you able to take my animal desires. I strongly suggest, dear love, that if you don't have the mental capacity to take me on, you tell me now, and I will control my desires until you are more prepared."

She shrank away from him, a look of revulsion trying not to cling to her features. She backed away until she no longer touched him. "Donald hit me over and over. Then prayed that God would help me understand he would be a good husband. Then he beat me again. What is it you plan on doing?"

"I would never hit you in anger. I have used whips, flails, and other implements to entice pain during pleasure. You know this."

She looked away and closed her eyes. "It's hard…"

Vincent moved to her slowly, carefully, and sat close to her, but did not touch her. He held out his hand and waited until she placed her hand in his. "I'll never touch you unless you want me to, Natalia. But you can't let what he did to you kill you. He's gone. You're not." He gazed into her eyes as he raised his free hand and caressed her cheek softly. "Try healing your body. Learn of your new abilities, the rest will come with time."

Despite his gentle touch and voice, her voice was rough and angry. "I don't want to heal. I want to forget."

"You know better than that, love. Traumatic events will change you irrevocably, and if you remember, you will put yourself through a great deal of emotional pain. If you remember, you learn from the experience and are better able to deal with the next traumatic event. In other words, you grow stronger. If you forget, you tear yourself apart, mind and body, until you have nothing left inside you except a frightened child screaming for acceptance and help. You die, Natalia. You die."

The glare she gave him showed Vincent that the timid mouse was fading. He moved his hands away from her as tears ran down her cheeks.

"Heal your bruises, love." His voice was kind.

She swallowed hard as she nodded. Learning how to be a vampire would help distract her from her memories for a while. "How?"

"Concentrate. It's like flexing a muscle."

Natalia stared at her arms, and with her eyes, traced each bruise, each scratch as Vincent removed the bandages. Her limbs bare, she concentrated, willed each wound away. She started with a small one, watched wide-eyed as it disappeared. She inhaled sharply, then tried another. By the time her arms were clear, she trembled for a different reason. She sat up straight, flexed her fingers and rotated her arms to see all sides. She raised and lowered them, turned them all about, amazed at her wound free skin. She performed the new miracle on the rest of her body, and removed the bruises, scratches, and bites. She saved her neck for last.

Natalia removed the bandage on her neck and with her fingers felt as her bite wound faded to nothing. She looked at Vincent when her body was once again the temple he worshipped. Her eyes were sharp and alert, free of fear. It lasted a mere moment, then shifted into a confused quizzical expression. There was a new sensation working its way from deep within her. She tilted her head to the side and regarded Vincent with a crinkled brow.

"I think I'm hungry. But it feels different."

Vincent purred. He took her arm and pulled them both to the headboard, which he once more leaned against. He pulled himself away from her long enough to remove his jacket and shirt then guided her onto his lap. She took his lead, straddled him carefully, and lay her hands on his shoulders. She frowned in concentration. "You're not cold."

"Yes, I am, but so are you. There's no longer a difference in how we feel."

Natalia ran her hands down his chest, and marveled at the change. Sex with him would be a new experience. She smiled at him, and nearly snickered at her thoughts. Vincent saw the look and caressed her cheek as if he knew her thoughts. He ran one hand up her back and urged her closer. His hand tangled in her hair to cradle her head as he directed her lips to his throat. He turned his head to sigh in her ear. His voice thick with desire, he could only manage a whisper. "I have much blood. Take what you need if you're hungry."

He felt her hesitate but held her in place. She whispered to him, her cool words tickled his ear and his mind. "I wonder if I'll still be susceptible to your blood control?"

His voice was thick. "I'll not take advantage of you if you are. Not tonight."

Her nails dug into his arms, as hunger took over her thoughts. She concentrated and willed her teeth to elongate. Soon, her pointed teeth scratched her questing tongue. She started toward his neck, hesitated then leaned in and scraped the sharp points on Vincent's neck. Then she stopped. She pulled back, a look of uncertainty on her face.

"I'm not – I don't –"

He placed a quieting finger on her lips. "I wish to feel your teeth in my neck, Natalia. If you miss, I can heal."

Something suddenly occurred to her. "You never fed off my neck. Why?"

"Never feed from a human's neck. It may very well kill them." He moved her head back to his neck. "I'm a vampire and can heal myself. Bite me, Natalia. Allow me this one fantasy tonight."

Natalia closed her eyes and thought for a moment. Then she positioned her lips over his jugular, opened her mouth and bit down into his neck. Blood poured from his wound and spilled down his shoulder. Natalia retracted her teeth as her lips made a seal on his skin. She started to suck the blood into her mouth and Vincent tightened his hold. He grunted as she continued to suck. She pulled away when he grew hard, unsure if she were ready to confront his abilities.

Vincent made a disappointed noise and healed Natalia's first bite. He removed the desire from his eyes, and allowed Natalia to shy away. She shook her head and crossed her arms in front of her breasts. "I'm not ready."

"There's a celebration downstairs. Do you wish to join it?"

An almost sly expression graced her features. "Yes. Yes, I do."

He purred when he saw his warrior in the expression. He envisioned them as they entered ballroom. She would be on his arm, dressed in the purple silk that hung on his closet door downstairs. He smiled, pulled himself off the bed and bowed. "I'll retrieve your dress, madam. Wait here."

He left and was back before Natalia could move. Vincent returned with a dress and shoes that matched his suit. "I don't think I'm under your control."

Vincent gave her a sly smile. "Good. I prefer when you're your own woman Natalia."

Natalia frowned as a name floated into her mind. "What happened to Ashley?"

He furrowed his brow as he laid her clothing out on the bed. "Ashley? The Slayer you believe is like you?"

"She was with me. Donald kidnapped us both."

"I must plead ignorance, Natalia." He reached into his pocket and pulled his cell out and tossed it to her. "Call Charlie. He brought you in."

She caught the phone deftly and quickly opened it. She dialed without thinking. "It's me. Where's Ashley?" There was a pause and Vincent swore he heard Charlie's relieved and excited voice. Natalia smile. "Yes, I'm fine. I'll tell you more tomorrow. Where's Ashley?" She was quiet for a moment. "Thank you." Natalia hung up and looked through Vincent's contact list until she found the right number. She started to speak as soon as she heard Doug's voice.

"Charlie said Ashley was with you." She paused to listen. "Do yourself a favor. Don't leave her alone. She may try something stupid." She paused again. "Just stay on your guard. She's not a fighter, but she's still, well; she still thinks she's a Slayer." Pause. "Ok. Thanks." She hung up.

"They brought a Slayer into this house?" Vincent took his slightly wrinkled shirt, jacket and cummerbund off the bed and started to dress.

She handed the phone back. "She can't fight. Doug said she was deep asleep. I don't think there's anything to worry about."

"Then why warn him?" He slipped the phone into his pocket and tucked in his shirt. He paused to watch as Natalia took the dress off the hanger and slipped it over her head.

"Because she's a scared woman who's just been through a hellish experience." She smoothed the dress out over her curves and presented him her back. Vincent grasped the dress at the bottom of the zipper and slowly zipped her up. She turned, smiled, and handed him her necklace. "If you would?"

He stared at the stone in his hand and closed his eyes. He briefly made a fist around the precious pendant then grasped the ends of the chain in both hands. Natalia turned around as Vincent slipped the necklace over her head and around her neck. With pleasure he secured the clasp then let his hands trail down the back of her dress then to her front at her stomach. He brought her closer, nuzzling her neck.

"This should never have left your neck, Natalia."

"Agreed." She reached up to feel the stone, then stretched her fingers to the other that still hung around her neck. Natalia pulled away, slipped on her heels, turned, and presented herself to her man. "How do I look?"

His hand caressed her cheek. "Lovely, Natalia. Do you really need to ask?"

"I like hearing your opinion."

He licked his lips at the look in her eyes, then shook his head. She wasn't ready for his desires. "Shall we adjourn to the party?"

Natalia nodded and took his offered arm. She smiled at him out of the corner of her eye as he led the way downstairs. Once inside the bathroom, she paused. "It's strange. I always thought Joseph would be my sire."

"Because of the dream?"

"Yes."

"In the dream, he gives you a goblet of blood, correct?" He started them toward the bedroom.

"Yes."

"We gain no substance from a goblet of blood, though it does taste good. We must take from a living creature."

"So, my dream was a lie?"

Vincent stopped walking when they were in the bedroom. How could he have forgotten? He took out his remote and turned off the security cameras. Mierka was in the security room. If she heard any of this conversation, she would say nothing, Joseph would make sure of that. He still didn't want to risk it. As he placed the remote back into his pocket, he turned back to Natalia and stared deep into her eyes. "Not entirely. No one can know I'm your sire. You must act as if Joseph is your sire."

She took a step back. "Why?"

"When I asked for permission to change you, Anthony refused. Joseph asked for permission, and it was granted. He brought you up here and waited for me to come for you."

She frowned, and thought of her dream. Having Joseph hand her a useless goblet could indicate that he was her false sire. She shook her head. Did it really matter what she had dreamt? Looking back, she realized she wanted Vincent to change her from the moment she first saw him. Natalia stepped closer to him and wrapped her arms around his neck. "Why do you look disgruntled? It was your right."

He took a deep breath and exhaled slowly, then slipped his hands around his newly created child. "If one of my Lieutenants were to find out that their Captain changed someone without their permission, it could create chaos. It would give some of them a reason to try and take over or to change as many humans as they wanted. My control in this city is still too new to be tested."

Natalia's eyes showed her acquiescence. "I will do as you ask, my sire."

Vincent shuddered and gripped her closer. They were in their old bedroom, not two feet from the bed. His eyes slid toward the bed. He bared his teeth and growled. "Show me your teeth and say that child."

Uncertainty gripped her as she realized that her lover could do to her what Donald had done. Part of her wanted to push away, to run away, but she closed her eyes took a deep slow breath and let it out in a rush through clenched teeth. Vincent started to pull away, but she held on. She could trust this one. Ten years with him proved that. She didn't want her past few days with Donald to ruin the trust they had built. Natalia opened her eyes, found Vincent's gaze, and held it. A twinkle came into her eye and her smile grew seductive. She pushed away from him and teased him with her attitude.

"You'll not see my fangs until I sink them into your flesh." She turned her back on him and waltzed out of the room.

Vincent stood immobile as her words echoed in his mind. He stopped himself from rushing her and slamming her into the far wall. His hands clenched into fists; he took a deep ragged breath and let it out in a huge whoosh. He muttered to himself as he followed her out of the room. He cursed her nature but loved it at the same time. It seemed as if she were trying to find her way back to herself. He was so involved with his thoughts he ran into Natalia, who had stopped halfway into the sitting room. Vincent apologized and looked in the direction she stared. Angie stood by one of the couches, her hand on the shoulder of a young man who sat on the couch.

"Angie. You weren't invited." His voice indicated he was slightly upset.

"Joseph let us know we might be needed." She glanced at the young man, who stood. "This is my youngest, Nick. He turned 18 last month. He's old enough to take the oath and give your woman her first meal."

"Joseph let you in here. Instructed you to wait?" Angie nodded, and Vincent turned to Natalia. "Are you hungry, love?"

"Yes." Natalia stared at the human. He was smaller than Vincent, with brown hair and eyes. He wore tight jeans and a red t-shirt. He walked to Vincent and Natalia and bowed low before his masters. He straightened and spoke the oath for the first time in his life. None of the humans on the farms were allowed to take the oath or give their blood until they were legally adults. Vincent had his people abide by human laws whenever possible.

"The blood that runs through my veins keeps me alive, as does the protection of House LeGris. By my words and my actions may those who protect me find within me what they need to live. The blood that runs through my veins keeps me alive. May it keep you alive as well."

He held his hand out to Natalia. Her hand trembled as she reached out and took his. The boy led her to the couch, sat down and pulled her into his lap. He presented her his arm and waited. Natalia looked to Vincent for guidance. He walked over, knelt, and took the boy's arm. Vincent positioned the vulnerable limb in front of Natalia's face and tapped halfway up the boy's arm. "Bite gently. Count the swallows. Take between four and six."

Natalia took Nick's arm and brought his warm flesh to her lips. She saw where the veins were close to his skin, and positioned the arm under her chin. She then found Vincent's gaze, opened her mouth, bared her teeth, and sank her fangs into Nick's arm. The human grunted in sheer pain and fought against the urge to pull away. Natalia retracted her fangs and very carefully drank five swallows down. She deliberately pulled her mouth away from the life-giving elixir. Angie swooped in and placed gauze on her son's arm. Vincent reached out, helped Natalia to stand, and stepped away to allow the human to stand.

Nick scooted to the edge of the couch, stood carefully, and allowed his mother to help him. Angie made sure Nick's bandage was in place, then turned to Vincent. He took a drink from her quickly then watched as both left the room. He then turned to his own child, who still had blood on her lips. Vincent moved closer and kissed her mouth clean of blood. It reminded him of how hungry he was. Angie's treat had not been enough. There were more humans downstairs. He smoothed out Natalia's dress, kissed her again and once more presented her his arm.

"How was it?"

They started toward the door before Natalia spoke. "There was a part of me that wanted to unleash the anger I feel upon him."

"Natalia, love. As the years pass, you will learn your limitations. I will most likely be there to help you find them and surpass them, but should you harm the humans I protect, I will count it as betrayal. And you know what I do to betrayers." His voice was light, conversational, but she heard the warning.

"I will do as my sire wishes." She whispered the words. They were halfway down the grand staircase and guests were close by. Vincent turned to her, growled low, and looked at her through half closed eyes. She smiled mischievously.

"Don't test me on this, Natalia."

She stopped at the bottom of the steps, turned, placed her hand on her beloved's cheek and dropped the act. "I won't love. Not on this. Too much is at stake."

Vincent nodded as he saw in her eyes that she spoke the truth. He turned and led her into the ballroom. The room quieted as they stepped through the doors. Natalia raised her head; she felt like a queen. She let go of Vincent and walked across the room to Joseph, who stood with Anthony and Julia. Her heels clicked on the floor and helped to draw all the attention to her. Once in front of Joseph, she bowed, to paid him his dues. Joseph took her hand when she offered and pulled her to him. He embraced her and gave her a deep soft kiss. His hands roamed her body and explored that which he had already discovered.

Joseph pulled away slightly and whispered to her as he smiled. "This is my perk."

"You're an evil man."

"Did you ever doubt?"

"Vincent will have your head."

The smile turned nefarious. "He can't."

Natalia tried to pull away but found she couldn't. His arms were still wrapped around her. Her eyes reflected her near panic. The look dropped when he didn't release her, and turned colder than her now dead heart. "Remember, sire. I can still best you with a sword."

Joseph laughed and released her to Vincent, who pretended to wait patiently nearby. She gave her 'sire' another bow and turned to her sire. Joseph was going to take advantage of the situation, perhaps as much as he could. Vincent caught her to him and kissed her passionately, which wiped away Joseph's touch. Natalia suddenly didn't care what Joseph expected of her. In her lover's arms, nothing mattered. Now, she was like him, vampire, and would be by his side for as long as they wanted it.

The kiss ended, and Natalia had a hard time coming back to reality. He gave her time, then took her around the room and introduced her to his guests, the ones that mattered, anyway. By the end of the evening, her head was spun from the brown nosing. Even Kari acted subservient. Natalia took it all in stride.

Vincent wondered how she could act nonchalant when she was only rescued and changed hours prior. But the look on her face said it all; her determination won out. She would act as if everything were fine in front of his guests. Later, she would reveal her pain to him. He would be there to comfort her, as he had been for the past ten years.

It was nearly morning when Vincent finally carried Natalia to their tower bedroom. He lay her on the bed and slowly kissed away all the pain of Donald. After the evening's festivities, he wanted to rip her apart and tear into her very body. He wanted to lap up her blood while she returned the action, but it would have to wait. She still did not have the mental capacity to be able to take the stress of it. Since he knew this, he let her lead. He waited ten years to change her; he could wait ten more to enjoy her body the way he wanted. Vincent could afford to wait. He had time, and now, she did as well.

34

Vincent and Natalia were less pleased when they were woken before the sun went down. Natalia, not used to her new body and its limitations, barely opened her eyes when someone knocked on the door. She had no energy. Vincent looked over at Natalia, ignored the knock and reached for his lover. Before he could wrap his arms around her, the door opened to reveal Joseph.

Vincent glared at the man.

"There is a disturbance that requires your attention and hers."

"The sun isn't down."

"There are humans waiting in the sitting room. It's regarding Ashley. She's terrified and screaming for Natalia."

Vincent rubbed his eyes as he sighed. "She'll need blood to wake. I'm low."

Joseph nodded and moved into the room. Vincent slipped his arms around Natalia and sat her up. He spoke to her softly to wake her as Joseph slit his arm and brought the bleeding wound to her lips. She took from him hungrily and woke fully. With her eyes open, Natalia pulled away from Joseph's arm.

"What's going on?" She leaned back and found she was in Vincent's lap. She smiled and closed her eyes again.

"Unfortunately, we are needed elsewhere." Vincent did not sound pleased.

She pulled away and looked into his eyes. "I thought we would spend a lot more time in bed."

He smiled but shook his head. "As did I. Ashley is asking for you."

The name made Natalia close her eyes. She nodded then pulled herself out of bed. Joseph handed her a dress. She took it and slipped into it. The red silk fell smoothly over her body. Vincent found his clothing and dressed partially. When they were ready, the couple followed Joseph down the steps, through the maze room, bathroom, and bedroom. At the door, he turned to his master and mistress.

"There are humans if you need more blood."

Vincent nodded and Joseph opened the door. The trio walked into the sitting room and saw several humans. Vincent instructed Natalia to take blood from more than one human, as she needed the sustenance. He looked to Joseph.

"After this interruption is done, make sure to bring more humans. I want to make sure Natalia is well fed."

Joseph smirked and nodded. Once filled, the three left the room. They could hear Ashley calling for Natalia as soon as they were at the top of the steps. The woman sounded hoarse. Natalia paused halfway down, her hand over her heart. Ashley sounded terrified. She let go of Vincent's arm and hurried down the stairs to the training room. Werewolves in human form, and actual humans surrounded her. As soon as Ashley saw Natalia, she cried out.

"Natalia! Thank God!"

The people moved to allow Natalia through. Natalia went to Ashley and slipped her arms around the woman.

"It's ok, Ashley. I'm here."

Ashley let Natalia hold her for a moment, then pushed away roughly. There was fear in her eyes. "Are they going to change me too?"

Confusion exploded on Natalia's features, then she calmed and shook her head. "No, Ashley. No vampire here changes a human without their permission. I've been with Vincent ten years as a human. I told him I wanted to be turned, but on my terms. Last night," she paused to stop herself from saying who was her real sire, "I was changed because I wanted to be."

No one seemed to notice the pause, for which Natalia was grateful. Ashley still looked terrified.

"Ashley?" She waited until the young woman looked her way. "What do you want?"

"Wh - what?" It was as if she had never thought of that before.

Natalia took a step closer. The question had been simple, the confusion on Ashley's face made Natalia rethink her strategy. She had always wanted to help the woman find her place in the world. Maybe now, with no Slayer to interfere, she had the chance. "What do you want out of life? Have you ever really thought of that before?"

Ashley blinked for a moment before she shook her head.

"Do you want time to think about it?"

She gave a terrified look at the people around her. "Here?"

Natalia took another step. "Ashley, no one is going to hurt you unless you try to hurt them."

The young woman looked around again then burst into tears and fell to the ground. She sat there and allowed Natalia to come close enough to hold her. Natalia's heart broke as she took Ashley in her arms. She didn't know what to do for the woman. She looked to Vincent and saw no emotions in his eyes. This was her call. She looked to the others in the room and almost frowned when she saw Anthony and Julia. She didn't really want Anthony here, but she couldn't tell him to leave. Vincent invited the pair to stay the day. They were a part of the LeGris family. They had every right to be here, but Natalia didn't want Anthony here. He would probably disagree with anything she said or did.

The new vampire sighed and knew no one's opinion of her actions mattered. Ashley was her problem and she had to take care of her. Natalia pulled away from her and looked into the young woman's eyes.

"Ashley, have you ever heard the voices of the angels?"

Ashley shook minutely but stayed silent as she looked away from Natalia.

"Ashley. Look at me and tell me the truth. Please." Her voice was kind.

Tears streamed down Ashley's face. "Father Sulta said I would if I prayed enough."

Natalia tried not to react badly to the name. "Father Sulta isn't here. There are no Slayers here, Ashley. Look at me." When she finally did, Natalia continued. "The angels don't talk to anyone they don't want to talk to. From what I've learned a human is either chosen to be a Slayer by the angels, or they aren't. There is no amount of praying that can change that. You are your own woman, Ashley, free to live your own life. What do you want to do with it?"

Ashley looked to Natalia silently for a few minutes as she thought about it. Slowly, her expression changed to complete and utter defeat. "I don't know. Something killed my family long ago. All of them died except me." She looked to Natalia, then toward the werewolves, then back to Natalia. "All the men I've encountered, even the ones who seemed nice have used me."

A cold chill worked its way into Natalia's heart. "All of them?"

Ashley looked to the werewolves again, caught someone's eye and looked down at the ground. "Yeah."

Natalia lifted Ashley's head and looked into her eyes. "One moment."

Natalia stood, but Ashley tried to stop her. "It doesn't matter, Natalia."

Ashley sounded scared. Natalia knelt back down. "Yes, it does." She placed a gentle hand on the human's cheek. "No one deserves to be hurt like that. Let me take care of this."

Ashley frowned for a moment, opened her mouth to speak then simply hung her head and nodded as if ashamed. Natalia looked at Julia.

"Can you watch her?"

Julia nodded and came over. She knelt, slipped her arms around Ashley, and talked to her quietly to distract her from Natalia's actions. Natalia nodded, stood, and looked around. The others in the room had heard most of the conversation, but not all. She looked to the werewolves and in particular to Doug. He had a grin on his face. Natalia stood taller. "Did you take advantage of her, Doug?"

The grin dropped as Natalia moved slowly toward him. Mierka and Rebecca suddenly flanked Natalia. He looked confused. "I didn't take advantage of her. She didn't say no."

Natalia felt herself move before she finished thinking about it. She found herself with her hand around Doug's throat; Doug's back was against the wall. The look in her eye was anything but kind.

"When I was fourteen, I slept with a man, a human, I didn't want to sleep with. I never said no. It was even my idea. Doesn't mean he should have said yes." The look on her face changed to one of utter hatred. "You took advantage of a woman in a bad situation. I'm willing to bet she looked like hell when you found us. You did not sleep with a willing woman. You slept with a confused, depressed one."

"Natalia!"

More than one voice called her name. She wasn't sure who called to her, but when Rebecca stepped to her side, Natalia pulled herself away from Doug. Her hand stayed around his throat. Rebecca and Natalia looked each other in the eyes for a moment before Rebecca spoke.

"This one's mine. Go take care of yours."

Natalia let Doug go, then bowed to the Alpha wolf. She went back to Ashley and stood behind her as Rebecca glared at Doug. Behind Rebecca, Mierka cracked her knuckles.

Doug looked to the three rather powerful women in the room, who stared him down and his eyes grew wide. "It wasn't like that! She wanted to!"

"When we found her, she was in no shape to make any kind of decision. She was terrified. What did you say to her at the cabin, Doug?" Rebecca spoke calmly, but all heard the hard edge to her tone.

Doug grew angry. "What does it matter anyway? She isn't one of us! You need to deal with her, not me!"

Rebecca could see his anger start to rise. She could sense he wanted to change and fight. She placed a gentle hand on his shoulder. "I remind you Doug, I'm your alpha. Don't change and fight or you will deal with worse than you've ever dealt with before."

Her voice was deadly calm. Those around her who had heard it before stepped away. Rebecca as a human was often jovial, and almost always friendly. When she had to fight, her seriousness came out. She was a force unto herself, a warrior who knew how to control all her aspects. Charlie stepped behind his wife to show solidarity. Before anyone else could move, a voice rang out.

"Enough!"

The room stilled and all looked to Vincent.

"Natalia, take Ashley into the library. Rebecca, Doug, Joseph, go to my study. Mierka, security room. The rest of you, go find something to do." He turned to Anthony as the others started to move. He spoke quietly to Anthony. "Stay outside my study until I'm done."

Anthony nodded and turned to Julia. "I'll be fine. Go back to bed if you desire. It's still light out. We can't leave yet."

Julia nodded and headed out the door. Anthony looked for Natalia, but she and the young woman were already gone. He frowned but followed Vincent out of the room.

35

Vincent slammed his office door behind him and glared at Doug. He didn't let the man explain. His voice was deadly calm. "Did you sleep with the woman?"

Doug started to snarl, thought better of it, and stopped. He was by the end of the study, near the couch. Vincent was on the other side of the small room, almost guarding the door. Rebecca leaned against the wall near the only window and Joseph stood to the other side of the window. There was nowhere he could go and the creatures in this room looked ready to tear him apart. Doug took a deep breath and decided to stay calm.

"I don't think what I did was wrong. When we rescued her, I told her we would take care of her, that I would make sure nothing happened to her. She snuggled up and seemed to be enjoying my company. When we got back here, I took her to my room."

Vincent crossed his arms. "Why?"

"I didn't know where else to take her."

"There are several rooms that lock from the outside in the guest house. You had plenty of places to take her, you chose to take her to your room." Vincent was not pleased. He looked to Rebecca and saw his alpha was not pleased either. "Rebecca? Your wolf; your call."

Rebecca looked at Doug, her expression blank. Finally, she shook her head. "If this were your only infraction, I would be tempted to discipline you and allow you to stay. But it isn't."

"Hey! You said…" started Doug.

Vincent looked sharply at Rebecca and interrupted Doug. "What else is there?"

She stood tall and looked to her master. "You call me the Alpha of your werewolves. You always stated that if something happened and I thought it beneath you, that I need not bring it to your attention. Does that hold true?"

Vincent gave her a steady look, then nodded once. "It does."

"Then it doesn't matter what he did. It just matters that something happened, and I find I no longer want Doug on my team. I want him gone."

The Alpha werewolf looked her master steadily in the eye as she said this. Her gaze did not falter, and she did not look away.

"Are you certain?" Vincent's voice was steady.

When Rebecca nodded again, Vincent nodded as well. He turned to Doug and moved out of the way of the door. "Gather your things and get out. Quickly."

Doug did not hesitate and nearly ran out the door. Joseph started for the door, but Vincent placed a hand on Joseph's chest to stop him. Vincent looked again toward Rebecca. "Are you certain?"

She looked Vincent dead in the eye. "I know what it means when we let them go like this, Vincent. I listen to your word. I follow your rules."

He nodded and turned to Joseph. "Make sure no one finds the remains."

Joseph smirked. "You should know me better than that, sir."

Vincent glared and allowed Joseph to leave. Rebecca looked him in the eye one last time, nodded and left as well. Vincent took a moment to compose himself and left the study. Outside the door stood Anthony.

"When he joined, did you remove traces of his life?"

"Don't I always?"

Vincent raised an eyebrow.

Anthony gave him a steady look, then added, "We know where more are, if needed."

Vincent shook his head. "Not yet. We may not stay in the area long enough to need more. Rebecca and Charlie are enough, for the moment."

Anthony nodded and the men moved toward the library. A human stood outside the closed doors. Vincent frowned. "Yes?"

"Sir, one of your guests from last night stayed up all day and drank from as many of us as possible. He took more than he should have from all of us."

"Where is he now?"

"In his room."

Vincent nodded. "Were his actions recorded?"

"Yes, sir."

"Tell Mierka to kill him."

The human nodded and walked away. Vincent turned to Anthony and raised an eyebrow at the look on the younger vampire's face.

"You didn't ask the vampire's name."

Vincent turned his head, walked to the double doors, and placed his hands on the knobs. "If that were important, the human would have said his name."

"You trust them."

"Implicitly. They know what happens when they lie." He opened the doors then and walked into the library, surprised to see Angie, Natalia and Ashely sitting on the floor.

೧ ೮

Natalia led Ashley to the library, but stopped in the doorway. Two people stood by the desk. Natalia recognized Angie, but wasn't sure who the other person was. She frowned at Angie. "We're interrupting. I need the room."

Angie locked eyes with Natalia and gave a minute shake of her head. "I'm sure you'll need to feed."

The other person, a man, still looked at Angie. Natalia's eyes slid to the man, then back to Angie. "Yes, you're right. Your friend will leave now though."

The man turned, glared at Natalia but left. Natalia looked at Angie. "Who was he?"

She shook her head. "I don't know. He was here last night for the party and stayed with one of the other guests. Several other humans told me he was trying to feed off all of them. And he wasn't being kind about it. He's taking more than he needs."

Natalia frowned. "Is there anything that can be done about him?"

"I alerted those in the security room."

She nodded. "Good."

"But what was he going to do to you?" Ashley's terrified voice ripped through the room. Natalia and Angie looked at her, but Angie spoke.

"I was biding my time until someone came." She sounded confident.

"But what if no one came?" She sounded hysterical. "No one ever comes! No one ever helps!"

Natalia reached out to Ashley. "That's not true. It may feel true a lot, but people do help."

"No! They don't! They never do!" Tears streamed down her face as she started to back away from Natalia. "You don't get it! Everywhere I turned, no one helped! Not even you."

Natalia's heart broke. "I tried before and I'm trying now. Ashley, tell me what you want from me, and I'll give it to you. No matter what it is, I'll do it."

Ashley stood stock still, a dire look on her face. "I want to die. Kill me."

Shock tore through Natalia. "No."

"See! You won't even give me peace!" She collapsed to the ground in a heap of tears. "I want to die. There's nothing here for me."

232

Natalia sank to her knees as if she could feel Ashley's pain. In a way, with all that she had been through in her life, she did understand. She looked at the young woman and saw herself, saw her younger self, all she had been through and hung her head. If the woman wanted death, who was she to deny her. "Alright."

"What?" Ashley's voice held relief.

"No." Angie's voice was strong, confident but held more kindness than anything else.

Ashley and Natalia looked at Angie in surprise. They had forgotten momentarily they were not alone. Ashley looked at her in disbelief, but Angie moved toward her and knelt beside her.

"This world is ugly, yes, and often full of pain, but death doesn't have to be the answer."

"You don't know what I've been through." The pain in her voice sliced through the two others in the room.

Angie held her hands out to Ashley. "You could tell me. You could let me try and help you."

Ashley seemed to shrink back into herself. "I don't want a Hellspawn to help me."

Angie gave a soft smile. "Well then it's a good thing I'm human."

Confusion flooded Ashley's face. She turned to look at Natalia. "There are humans here?"

"Yes. They feed Vincent and the other vampires in this house, but it's their choice."

Ashley shook her head. "I don't want vampires feeding off me."

"They won't. It's our choice to have them feed off us. No means no. Every time."

"But that guy in here before…"

"He was not of Vincent's household." Angie reached out to Ashley. "What's your name? I'm Angie."

"Ash…Ashley." She seemed rather hesitant, but Natalia could hear hope and started to feel it as well.

"Ashley, Vincent has a lot of land. We humans live on the land, farm it for food and circulate through this house to feed the vampires. We're not allowed to do so until we're eighteen. But there are also humans on the land who are over the age of eighteen who don't allow the vampires to feed off them for various reasons. If you want a place to heal, we can take you in and help you. In whatever way you need. You won't be fed off, you'll never come to this house, but you will be asked to help on the farms."

Ashley looked at Angie in disbelief. Natalia held her tongue. This sounded too good to be true, but was probably exactly what the young woman needed.

"Men… I don't want to be around men."

"There are several farms on these lands and many houses. Most are family houses, but there are a couple that are men only and a couple that are women only, for various reasons. You can live on one that has women only."

"She needs therapy." Natalia said quietly.

"She does." Angie nodded and looked at Natalia. "We'll find a therapist for her, a woman." She looked back to Ashley. "How does that sound?"

"I…I…" She looked at Natalia. "I don't know." She hung her head. "I've been thinking of suicide for so long. I thought death was my only option."

Natalia placed her hand on Ashley's arm. "It doesn't have to be."

The three women turned to the doors as they opened loudly. Vincent filled the doorway. Ashley gasped in surprise and fear. Natalia and Angie stood to regard the imposing vampire.

"What is this?" Vincent looked to Angie as he and Anthony moved into the library and close to the women.

Angie looked at Ashley and held her hands out to the young woman. "I will protect you."

Ashley looked at the woman for a long time, then finally reached out and took Angie's hands. She stood with Angie's help and looked toward the men. Vincent raised an eyebrow and Angie met his gaze.

"This woman needs help to heal from the horrors of this world. I have chosen to give her sanctuary on my farms."

Vincent looked at Natalia and waited.

Natalia turned to look at Angie then Ashley. Her voice was kind when she spoke. "Is this what you want?"

Ashley looked at Angie and felt as the woman slipped her arm around her waist. She waited for the inevitable. Whenever a man slipped his hand around her waist, the hand always went to her ass and squeezed. She took a few breaths and when it didn't happen, relief flooded her. She looked at Natalia with hope in her heart and nodded.

Natalia smiled, nodded, and turned back to Vincent. "She wishes to live with the humans and heal."

"She isn't hurt." Anthony's harsh voice made Ashley shrink back.

"Not all pain is visible." Natalia bit back.

Vincent looked to Angie. "She follows our rules."

"She will learn them."

He looked at Natalia. "I will hold you responsible if something goes awry."

"Wait… really? It's that easy?" Ashley sounded terrified, as if she felt all this was a ruse.

Vincent looked at the terrified woman and she shrank against Angie. "Why wouldn't it be?"

The color drained from her face, and she looked away. "It never has been."

"It won't be easy, Ashley. Farm work is hard, as is dealing with trauma." Angie spoke gently.

"I…but…I just want to be safe."

Angie turned herself and Ashley to look her in the eyes. "You are."

"But he's a vampire." She sounded confused.

Angie gave a kind smile. "Not all men are evil. Not even vampires."

"She's right." Natalia said with confidence.

Ashley looked into Angie's eyes for a long moment, and thought about things greatly. Angie was older, probably older than Natalia. "How long have you been here?"

"I was born on these lands fifty-six years ago. I'll die here of old age."

Tears streamed down Ashley's face. "Ok. Yes. Ok."

Angie smiled, and looked over the young woman's shoulder to Vincent. "May we leave?"

Vincent nodded. Angie slipped her arm around Ashley's waist and led the woman out of the library as Anthony glared. Once they were gone, he turned to Vincent.

"I don't trust her."

"It's a good thing you don't live here then." Natalia's voice held nothing but contempt.

He bared his teeth at Natalia and glared at her, but spoke to Vincent. "She may try to kill you all. We don't know her true motivation."

"Natalia? Do you believe she will kill us?"

Natalia thought about it for a long time. "She might be thinking about it, but she won't have an opportunity. By the time she has the mental capacity and the knowledge to kill us, I doubt she'll want to."

"I don't like that answer." Anthony's voice held contempt.

Vincent looked between his two trusted people and wondered who would be right in the end. He shook his head and looked at Anthony. "Again, you don't live here."

"She has no right." He sounded perplexed.

Vincent waited for more, then looked at Natalia as she spoke.

"She wanted to die. Angie stepped in to offer her sanctuary. I backed up her idea as I felt it was better to help the woman than to kill her. If I'm still Protector of House LeGris, and my rank still stands, then I should be able to do my job without waiting for permission. If things changed when I did, the Master of this House would have informed me."

"She's right." Vincent's voice was calm.

"She has a right to allow a Slayer into your house?" Anthony didn't sound pleased.

"She's not a Slayer, just a traumatized human." Natalia sounded annoyed with the conversation.

Vincent placed a hand on her shoulder to calm her. "Her rank is her permission. Natalia knows well what will happen if her actions cause the death of one of mine."

"Thank you, sir."

A look passed between them, and Vincent understood that she was using that word instead of 'sire'. He inhaled sharply. "This is done."

"Sir!" Anthony's surprised voice sounded loud in the room.

Vincent turned to Anthony and sighed. "I trust that Natalia did the right thing. She is our protector and knows what happens when one betrays me."

Anthony pursed his lips, turned on his heel and left the room. He almost ran into Mierka, as she headed to the security room. She smirked and continued on her way. He followed her.

"She gave a Slayer sanctuary."

Mierka smiled. "He let her stay? Good."

"You think this is good?"

She shrugged. "Some people deserve help."

"This entire house has gone insane. She is capable of a lot more than we know."

They were in the security room. Mierka took her seat. "Doubt it. Doug had several guns in his room, and swords. She didn't bother taking anything before trying to find Natalia. Look, if you're really worried about it, just keep an eye on her. But you know, maybe do a better job of it than you ever did with Natalia."

Anthony glared at her but left and stormed away. As he passed the library, he realized that Vincent and Natalia were still in the room. Instead of saying anything, he regarded them as they held each other. It was obvious in their tenderness with one another what they felt for each other. Anthony stood quietly and stared back and forth at Vincent and Natalia. He marveled at the interaction between them.

As he continued to stare, he slowly understood that Natalia would never hurt Vincent. If she did, Vincent would undoubtedly torture her slowly over a long period of time. He had seen it before; he just refused to believe it. Anthony nodded once and left the library. He would have Ashley watched until he was satisfied she wasn't a threat. He would still have Natalia watched as well, but would no longer oppose her without true reason. She was a vampire now and would be bound by the same rules as all under Vincent's protection.

ॐ ॐ

Vincent broke away from Natalia. "You seemed surprised I accepted Ashley as well."

"A little, but you don't kill without reason. She didn't do anything."

He nodded. "Do you wish to return to our bedroom?"

Natalia sighed and gave a weary smile. "Yes."

He nodded and picked Natalia up as he smiled. In no time, they were in the sitting room. Vincent set her on her feet, took out his remotes and turned off the audio and video recorders. Done, he put the remote away and took her in his arms. The kiss he gave her helped to wipe away some of the confusion of the day.

"Come. We need not think of this anymore today. Our bed awaits. We can keep each other company for as long as we want."

She frowned slightly. "Don't you have duties to attend to when the sun goes down?"

He sighed. "I took over as Captain to get rid of Edwin. Now that he is gone and the mayor is under my control, I will return control of the city over to its citizens. Those that know nothing of us. That may take a while, but with your help, the nastier of Edwin's lot will be dispatched easily."

"You're planning on killing most of them, aren't you?"

"That has always been the plan. I wanted to kill them and return to Montana quickly, but after Christopher left, we had to bide our time. Now, it's our turn to take care of things." He turned and held out his arm. She took it and they continued to the tower bedroom. "I'm glad things worked out the way they did, Natalia. If this had all been done quickly, we would not have met."

She squeezed his arm. "There were a lot of deaths."

"Death is inevitable."

"True."

They were in the tower bedroom now, the bed before them. He turned to her and lifted her head to look into her eyes. "We have time to be together. Do you wish to spend an eternity with me, Natalia?"

She moved closer. "I do."

He caressed her cheek then picked her up and carried her the short distance to the bed. "As do I, my dear. As do I."

Vincent placed Natalia on the bed and gave her a deep kiss. Natalia helped him undress and returned the kisses and caresses he lavished on her body. Vincent's movements became rougher, but Natalia hesitated. When she almost pulled away, Vincent looked down into her eyes.

"You're safe here."

"I know but..." She looked away from him.

Vincent gave her a tender kiss that took her breath away. His lips moved to her ear. "Lead my love. Tell me what you wish for as long as you need. Tell me what you want, and I will do everything in my power to grant your desires."

She shuddered as she understood he meant much more than tonight. She embraced him roughly and buried her head in his neck. Natalia, determination taking over, opened her mouth and sank her new vampire teeth into her lover's neck.

Vincent gripped the bed tightly as he felt Natalia's fangs in his neck. His growl was nearly a roar. He shuddered when she drank his blood and pulled away when she finished to look into her eyes.

Natalia licked the last of his blood from her lips and smiled seductively. "Your move, vampire."

Vincent grinned viciously. For a moment they stared at each other, each daring the other to continue. When Vincent understood Natalia was ready for him, his grin widened. He kissed her hard and shuddered at the taste of his own blood on her tongue. After that, there was no turning back. Vincent taught Natalia more about himself than he could previously. She learned a great deal about her own limitations, and found she wanted to learn more, but only if Vincent was her teacher.

Fin

ABOUT THE AUTHOR

Cat Stark was raised in California and now lives in Illinois with her fiancé. She hopes to continue writing and publishing for years to come.
Find her here:
Website: catstark.com
Twitter: @catstarkwriter
Facebook: facebook.com/catstarkwriter/

www.ingramcontent.com/pod-product-compliance
Lightning Source LLC
Chambersburg PA
CBHW060546260626
47161CB00003B/1071